WILLOW

VIRGINIA ANDREWS®

WILLOW

POCKET BOOKS
New York   London   Toronto   Sydney

First published in the US by Pocket Books, 2002
a division of Simon and Schuster Inc.
First published in Great Britain by Simon & Schuster UK Ltd, 2003
This edition published by Pocket Books, 2003
An imprint of Simon & Schuster UK Ltd
A CBS COMPANY

5 7 9 10 8 6 4

Simon & Schuster UK Ltd
Africa House
64–78 Kingsway
London WC2B 6AH

Simon & Schuster Australia
Sydney

A CIP catalogue record for this book is available
from the British Library

ISBN 0-7434-6139-8

Printed and bound in Great Britain by
Cox & Wyman Ltd, Reading, Berkshire

Prologue

I walked hesitantly down the corridor to my sophomore English class at the University of North Carolina as if I already knew the trouble that awaited me. I could actually feel the increasing trembling in my body, the quickening of my heartbeat, and the spreading of the small patch of ice at the base of my spine. The moment I had awakened this morning, I sensed something was seriously wrong back home. It was as if a dark storm cloud had floated by earlier and had paused overhead long enough to rain a chill down into my heart. Almost as soon as I opened my eyes, I wanted to call Daddy, but I didn't. My boyfriend, Allan Simpson, a prelaw student, was fond of teasing me whenever I had what my Portuguese nanny, Isabella Martino, used to call the *dreads*—dark, ominous feelings that moved up your spine like mercury in a thermometer.

"I can't believe you let a superstitious old woman affect you like that," he said. "The dreads? The ability to feel trouble coming? Really, Willow, you're almost nineteen. You're not a child."

I knew I wasn't a child, but how could I not have been influenced more by her than by anyone else and carried that influence into my adulthood? Up until I was nearly seventeen, when she finally left us to return to her family in Brazil, Isabella, whom I fondly called Amou, had more to do with my upbringing than my own mother, who had leaped upon the opportunity to let me know I was adopted as soon as I could understand what the word meant. Afterward, she didn't hesitate to put the word in front of *mother* whenever she used it in reference to me. Other children my age had mothers; I had an adoptive mother.

My father never did that, and so I never thought of him as anyone other than my father, Daddy.

I began to call Isabella Amou just about the time I began to speak. In fact, I feel quite certain that I pronounced that word way before I said any other understandable word. Amou's eyes were always full of laughter when I said it, full of sparkling lights.

"Amou, Amou," she would cry, and began to refer to herself the same way. "Do it for Amou, Willow. One more spoonful," she would urge, and I would eat one more spoonful.

She had been referring to me as *amou um* from the moment she had begun to care for me, to hold me in her arms and rock me to sleep as she sang one of her favorite Portuguese children's songs. In Portuguese, *amou um* means "loved one," and I simply echoed it back at her, only choosing to shorten it because it was so much easier for a two-year-old to do so. I insisted on calling her Amou despite my adoptive mother's always correcting me and lecturing me, sometimes quite emphatically, to call her Isabella and not Amou, especially if I did it in front of my adoptive mother's friends, who would grimace and ask, "What did she say?" It was practically impossible for any of them to understand, which made my adoptive mother angrier and angrier.

I can recall her seizing me by the shoulders when I was no more than three, three and a half, and shaking me roughly as she chastised me, screaming, "Are you an absolute idiot already, Willow De Beers?"

When my adoptive mother was angry at me, she always used my whole name. It was as if she were reminding me that the entire family would suffer for any mistakes I had made, reminding me that I carried the family name and I should consider it a greater gift than life itself, for, after all, wasn't it true that I had been born without a name, without an identity, almost without blood?

"Don't you understand what I am telling you? Her name is Isabella, Isabella. Say it. Say it!" she demanded, and I cried and pressed my lips together because I was terrified that somehow the word *Isabella* would escape my mouth and bring a stab of pain to Amou, who stood by, holding her breath and feeling guilty but too frightened to come to my defense, I'm sure.

"Willow De Beers, you say Isabella. Say it. I want to hear that you can say it. Say it!" she insisted. She had her face so close to mine, I could see the tiny blood vessels in her temples. I remember thinking her blood was blue. Mine was red, but hers was blue. Why were we different? Did this mean something really was wrong with me, just as she often claimed?

She shook me again, and I stared with frightened eyes at a woman I hardly recognized as my mother, adoptive or otherwise. It took my breath away to see that she could speak and look so out of control. How could I help but cringe and swallow back any words, much less say the one she wanted me to say?

"Say it, or I'll stuff you into one of my luggage trunks and send you away to one of those countries where other little adopted girls have nothing to eat and have to sleep on beds of hay. Isabella can tell you about that. Would you like that? Well? Would you?"

I started to cry softly, my body shaking almost as hard as it had when she had seized my shoulders.

Fortunately, my father was nearby, which wasn't often enough for me, because whenever he was home, he always came to my defense. He interceded in his calm doctor's voice.

"I'm afraid you won't get anywhere with her that way, Alberta. You are frightening her, and when an infant is frightened, she cannot accept information, much less imprint it," he told her.

"Please, Claude, spare me your psychiatric jargon. We are not all patients under your tender loving care in your mental hospital," she threw at him as if she were tossing a gift back in his face.

I can vividly recall the look on his face. I remember all of his expressions, but those he reserved for my adoptive mother were truly special. Now that I'm older and can put it into words and ideas, I realize he looked back at her that day and on many similar occasions afterward as if he really were looking at one of his patients. She either ignored it or didn't realize it.

She turned from him and glared at me. I thought she still might lash out and slap me, but she turned away and slapped at her own ankle-length flowing skirt, snapping the material as she rushed off, the heavy scent of her perfume lingering like a constant reminder of her fury.

I often looked back on those early days and thought that married to a woman like my adoptive mother, my father couldn't have been a happy man, despite her physical beauty and despite his great success and his national reputation as a psychiatrist with his own clinic, which he called the Willows and after which I had been named. My adoptive mother claimed she had nothing to do with naming me. She made that clear to anyone and everyone who remarked about it. I remember thinking there was something wrong with my name. It was probably why I was too shy to reply when anyone asked me who I was. That embarrassed my adoptive mother, who, ironically, was really the cause of it. However, she was not about to take the blame for that.

"Who would name a child after a nuthouse," she ranted at me one day, "even if it was where you were conceived and where you were born?"

Where I was conceived and born?

I didn't know this until I was nearly eight. Daddy tried to keep her from ever telling me, but my dea sweet A.M., as I often referred to her years later in m', thoughts and when I spoke about her to Amou, had been permitting it to slip out in various innuendos and suggestions for years, until she simply sat me down in the living room one afternoon and told me.

"Pay attention!" she ordered. These were nearly always her first words to me, as if she were afraid I would fix my gaze on something else and ignore her completely, just the way Daddy often did. She wouldn't start until she was satisfied my eyes were directed at her.

"You should know how you came to be living here with us," she began. "Maybe then you'll be a little more appreciative and be more obedient and listen to me when I speak, for I am trying to help you," she added in a much sweeter, softer tone of voice. Even then, I knew enough to brace myself for some terrible aftermath whenever she was too nice to me.

She pulled herself up, staring at me a long moment, the displeasure suddenly so clear in her face, in the cold glint in her otherwise beautiful blue eyes, that I couldn't deny it even if I wanted, even if I could pretend she cared about me. She was the only one permitted to have illusions and fantasies in our house. My dolls weren't permitted to speak back to me; my toy teacups were forever empty.

After a short moment of hesitation, confirming her decision to do it, to tell me what my father had forbidden her to tell me, she brought her face close to mine and asked in a dark, throaty voice, "Do you know how you were made? Do you have any idea at all?"

Of course, I shook my head. How would I know such a thing? My little body tightened with anticipation. It felt as if I had lightning inside my stomach and thunder in my bones.

"One of the assistants at your father's precious clinic apparently raped a patient. So much for his so-called exceptional professional staff," she said, her lips hinged at the corners with disgust. "Do you understand what I am telling you, Willow De Beers? You were born as a result of a rape!"

I didn't know what rape meant, but she was determined that I would understand.

"You're only in the third grade, but I know how street smart kids are nowadays. I know you know babies don't get brought here by storks or any other fairy tale, right?"

"Babies come from the hospital," I said.

"Normal women have their babies delivered in a hospital, yes, but first they are made at home or somewhere else convenient. Half the country was probably conceived in the back of an automobile," she muttered. She always tilted her head down toward her right shoulder when she said something that disgusted her. It was as if she were going to spit the period at the end of her sentence.

I was really confused now. Why was she telling me all this? At first, I hoped she was just being a good mother, trying to get me to understand something important, but I soon realized she had a different purpose.

"The man through his pee-pee puts his part into the woman through her pee-pee, and there's an egg in the woman that grows into a baby. You don't need to understand much more than that to understand what I'm saying."

I know I grimaced. It all sounded awful. Why would a woman permit a man to pee into her? Surely, my adoptive mother was trying to frighten me again.

"When a woman doesn't want a man to do it and he does it anyway, forcing her to have a baby, that's called rape. Understand? Well?" she asked quickly.

I nodded, afraid to say no even though it wasn't all that clear to me yet, especially why a man would want to make a baby with a woman if the woman didn't want him to do it.

"This patient, this mentally disturbed young woman, according to your father, never knew what was happening inside her until she was quite far along in her pregnancy. How everyone could be so oblivious to it, even including that mental case, is beyond me, but what do I know about the inner workings of Dr. De Beers's looney farm?" she muttered.

How strange it was to me to hear her refer to her husband and my daddy as Dr. De Beers, as though he were a complete stranger, but she did that often, including right to his face, especially at the dinner table. Why she would ridicule the clinic Daddy was so proud he had created was another mystery and surprise to me.

"Our Dr. De Beers is not permitted to talk about what goes on there. Everything has to be kept so secret. All that stuff about doctor-patient confidentiality.

If you ask me, it's because either the doctor is ashamed he is taking money for what he is doing, or the patient is ashamed of what she or he has been saying and doing. That's all there really is to that," she lectured as if there were a number of other people besides me in the living room. I didn't know it, but Amou was just outside the door, listening and trembling for me.

"I don't know how I was so weak as to agree to permit him to adopt you and bring you here in the first place, but I did. Anyway, this is why I have to be so stern with you, Willow," she said, turning calmly reasonable again. Then she leaned toward me, her eyes widening. "You might have inherited some madness," she whispered, which left me so terrified that I couldn't speak or sleep for days. I might have inherited madness! Even then, I understood what that could mean.

On the few occasions I had been at Daddy's clinic up to that time, I had seen patients who looked so disturbed and terrifying to me even from a safe distance that I had nightmares about it. Was she right? Could I be like one of them? Would I end up in Daddy's clinic, too?

For days, I moped about, afraid to look at myself in the mirror and terrified of what everyone else saw when he or she looked at me. I felt myself shrinking more and more into that small hiding place in my brain where I could feel safe and unafraid, even if that place felt like a cage. The more introverted I became, the more mentally ill I appeared, especially to my A.M.

Daddy finally noticed and asked Amou why I was looking so unhappy those days. When Amou told Daddy what my adoptive mother had done and said, he was very upset with her and tried to reassure me that there was absolutely nothing wrong with me. He called me to his office and spoke softly, reassuringly, to me, wiping away an errant tear or two with his soft thumb.

"Who should know better than I do, Willow?" he asked with a smile. "Evaluating people, judging whether or not they are sick, is my profession."

That seemed reasonable, but he wasn't with me that often. Maybe he didn't know enough or see enough. That seemed just as reasonable.

And then he told me a startling thing. "That doll you love so much—remember I told you someone had made it for me to give to you? Well, your mother made it for you, Willow, and it's very pretty, isn't it? Someone who's so sick couldn't have done that."

That did make me feel a little better, but unfortunately, his being upset about what my A.M. had done didn't stop her from complaining about me whenever she saw something she considered wrong. She was determined to paint everything as evidence that I had indeed inherited a mental sickness. I didn't like listening to her, so I ignored her, and she complained that I had an attention deficit disorder, even though there was no evidence of that at school. She claimed the teachers were simply too burdened to notice or, worse, not qualified.

She heard me talking to myself, so I must be a schizophrenic. Once, she even tried to stop me by making me wear tape over my mouth when I played in my room, especially when she had guests visiting and feared they would overhear me. She mistook my mixture of Portuguese words with English words as a sort of insane gibberish.

When Daddy learned about what she had done with the tape, he put an end to it, too, but that didn't stop her effort to establish that I had mental problems. Because I cried at the drop of a pin, or dropped my eyes when she looked at me, I was a paranoid. How could I help but be afraid of her? Even when she spoke nicely to me or stroked my hair and complimented Amou on how well she kept me, I was waiting for some ugly or terrible comment to be tagged on at the end, even if it was just a wagging of her head and a sigh to indicate that I was somehow beyond hope and all that was done for me would be wasted. She was that convinced I carried the seed of some mental aberration inside me.

One morning, she even scooped up my drawings and my coloring books to show Daddy how I was revealing some deep-seated mental disturbance through my distorted faces and figures. I think she suspected some of them were depictions of her, and she couldn't imagine how anyone, especially me, could see her as anything but beautiful.

"You're supposed to be such a great expert," she told my father, rushing into his office and waving the childish artwork in his face. "I don't know how you can't see this, see what you have brought home. She's an embarrassment. I see the way my friends look at her. I was a fool to agree to it, even with Isabella here to do most of the dirty work.

"You should put her someplace where she can get

the proper treatment and not leave her here to be a burden on me."

"She doesn't have to go anyplace, Alberta. There is nothing abnormal about those pictures or her behavior," Daddy insisted in his typically even tone of voice. "You simply don't have experience with children, Alberta, or you would know."

"Go on, throw that in my face. Throw it in my face that I have been unable to have children!" she screamed at him, and marched out of his office, slamming the door behind her hard enough to shake even our big house.

Amou and I would have had to be deaf not to have heard it all. She would embrace me and whisper, "Don't cry, *pequeninho,* little one. Amou always be here. No one is going to give you away."

Knowing that my mother, even my adoptive mother, didn't really want me was like living in a house made of cards, a cardboard home that would fall apart in a heavy rain or blow apart in a strong wind and leave me naked and alone or falling forever down a deep, dark tunnel. My nightmares were an ongoing series of such horrid events.

I wasn't the only thing that my A.M. complained about, however. In fact, she seemed never to be without some grievance, whether it be about me, Amou, the other servants, or the people who worked on our grounds—anyone and everything. She often paraded her complaints through our home, stringing them behind her like rattling cans tied to the rear bumper of a just-married couple's car. Maybe that was why Daddy

spent so much of his time away from home and, quently, away from me.

How many times had I glanced in at him sacrosanct home office in the evening without izing I was there and seen him just staring out window that looked west on our South Caroli erty just outside the small community of Spri From the corner of the doorway, I would c wistful expression playing on his lips and in h he gazed up at the moon. It shone through thin they looked like smoke and captured sha shadow in its golden net of light.

When I was older and I caught him sittin that office, I could almost see the will-o'-th grets of all the things he should have done Of course, I worried that I was included, he thought my adoptive mother was ri shouldn't have brought me home. Later, much as suggested it, he would reassure n never had the slightest doubt or hesitatio

There were other regrets playing o opportunities, moments not seized, to just let pass him in the night. I had n and troubling those regrets were for have none until I went home this t horrible time that justified my *drea*

1

Saying Goodbye

I recognized the dean of students' secretary, Mrs. Schwartz, standing in my classroom doorway. She was shifting her weight nervously from one foot to the other and rubbing one palm against the other as if she were sanding down a block of wood. She gave each of my classmates a flashbulb smile as they entered, then quickly turned back to the hallway. I didn't know for certain yet, but I had a hunch she was waiting there for me. As usual, she was dressed in her navy-blue suit with her lace-trimmed white blouse and stiletto shoes—practically her work uniform.

"Oh, dear," she said, reaching out for me as I approached. She seized my hand and drew me closer. "We have received a rather frantic call from your aunt Agnes Delroy. Apparently, she was unable to reach you at your apartment last night or this morning and has been burning up the telephone lines between here and Charleston," she ran on, obviously infected by my aunt's histrionics. Aunt Agnes often had that effect on people.

I could not tell her why I hadn't been able to receive Aunt Agnes's call. I had spent the night at Allan's apartment, and that wasn't anyone's business but mine. I was positive, however, that Aunt Agnes had been suspicious, especially if she had tried late in the evening, and had overdone her exasperation over failing to reach me. My father's fifty-one-year-old sister was the sort of person who expected that anyone she called or beckoned was just waiting to serve and fulfill her requests. She and I never got along, anyway. She never came out and said it in so many words, but she considered an adopted child somehow inferior, despite my achievements, especially a child whose mother was a patient in a mental clinic.

But even if my adoptive mother had given birth to me, Aunt Agnes would have been critical. I always knew she believed my father had married beneath the family. My adoptive mother came from one of those old Southern families that had lost most of its wealth but desperately clung to its heritage. That was not good enough for Aunt Agnes. Money, heritage, position in society, and certainly power were the pillars upon which she built her church, and if one was weak, the church would collapse.

My father tolerated Aunt Agnes rather than loved her as a sister and once told me that her husband, Uncle Darwood, probably had welcomed the Grim Reaper with open arms, seeing death as an avenue of escape, even though it wasn't any sort of pleasant

ture of Portuguese words with English words as a sort of insane gibberish.

When Daddy learned about what she had done with the tape, he put an end to it, too, but that didn't stop her effort to establish that I had mental problems. Because I cried at the drop of a pin, or dropped my eyes when she looked at me, I was a paranoid. How could I help but be afraid of her? Even when she spoke nicely to me or stroked my hair and complimented Amou on how well she kept me, I was waiting for some ugly or terrible comment to be tagged on at the end, even if it was just a wagging of her head and a sigh to indicate that I was somehow beyond hope and all that was done for me would be wasted. She was that convinced I carried the seed of some mental aberration inside me.

One morning, she even scooped up my drawings and my coloring books to show Daddy how I was revealing some deep-seated mental disturbance through my distorted faces and figures. I think she suspected some of them were depictions of her, and she couldn't imagine how anyone, especially me, could see her as anything but beautiful.

"You're supposed to be such a great expert," she told my father, rushing into his office and waving the childish artwork in his face. "I don't know how you can't see this, see what you have brought home. She's an embarrassment. I see the way my friends look at her. I was a fool to agree to it, even with Isabella here to do most of the dirty work.

"You should put her someplace where she can get

the proper treatment and not leave her here to be a burden on me."

"She doesn't have to go anyplace, Alberta. There is nothing abnormal about those pictures or her behavior," Daddy insisted in his typically even tone of voice. "You simply don't have experience with children, Alberta, or you would know."

"Go on, throw that in my face. Throw it in my face that I have been unable to have children!" she screamed at him, and marched out of his office, slamming the door behind her hard enough to shake even our big house.

Amou and I would have had to be deaf not to have heard it all. She would embrace me and whisper, "Don't cry, *pequeninho*, little one. Amou always be here. No one is going to give you away."

Knowing that my mother, even my adoptive mother, didn't really want me was like living in a house made of cards, a cardboard home that would fall apart in a heavy rain or blow apart in a strong wind and leave me naked and alone or falling forever down a deep, dark tunnel. My nightmares were an ongoing series of such horrid events.

I wasn't the only thing that my A.M. complained about, however. In fact, she seemed never to be without some grievance, whether it be about me, Amou, the other servants, or the people who worked on our grounds—anyone and everything. She often paraded her complaints through our home, stringing them behind her like rattling cans tied to the rear bumper of a just-married couple's car. Maybe that was why Daddy

spent so much of his time away from home and, conse-
quently, away from me.

How many times had I glanced in at him in his
sacrosanct home office in the evening without his realizing I was there and seen him just staring out the bay
window that looked west on our South Carolina property just outside the small community of Spring City?
From the corner of the doorway, I would catch that
wistful expression playing on his lips and in his eyes as
he gazed up at the moon. It shone through clouds so
thin they looked like smoke and captured shadow after
shadow in its golden net of light.

When I was older and I caught him sitting alone in
that office, I could almost see the will-o'-the-wisp regrets of all the things he should have done differently.
Of course, I worried that I was included, that maybe
he thought my adoptive mother was right, that he
shouldn't have brought me home. Later, if I even so
much as suggested it, he would reassure me that he had
never had the slightest doubt or hesitation.

There were other regrets playing on his face: lost
opportunities, moments not seized, too many ships he
just let pass him in the night. I had no idea how deep
and troubling those regrets were for him, and I would
have none until I went home this time, this dark and
horrible time that justified my *dreads*.

1

Saying Goodbye

I recognized the dean of students' secretary, Mrs. Schwartz, standing in my classroom doorway. She was shifting her weight nervously from one foot to the other and rubbing one palm against the other as if she were sanding down a block of wood. She gave each of my classmates a flashbulb smile as they entered, then quickly turned back to the hallway. I didn't know for certain yet, but I had a hunch she was waiting there for me. As usual, she was dressed in her navy-blue suit with her lace-trimmed white blouse and stiletto shoes—practically her work uniform.

"Oh, dear," she said, reaching out for me as I approached. She seized my hand and drew me closer. "We have received a rather frantic call from your aunt Agnes Delroy. Apparently, she was unable to reach you at your apartment last night or this morning and has been burning up the telephone lines between here and Charleston," she ran on, obviously infected by my aunt's histrionics. Aunt Agnes often had that effect on people.

I could not tell her why I hadn't been able to receive Aunt Agnes's call. I had spent the night at Allan's apartment, and that wasn't anyone's business but mine. I was positive, however, that Aunt Agnes had been suspicious, especially if she had tried late in the evening, and had overdone her exasperation over failing to reach me. My father's fifty-one-year-old sister was the sort of person who expected that anyone she called or beckoned was just waiting to serve and fulfill her requests. She and I never got along, anyway. She never came out and said it in so many words, but she considered an adopted child somehow inferior, despite my achievements, especially a child whose mother was a patient in a mental clinic.

But even if my adoptive mother had given birth to me, Aunt Agnes would have been critical. I always knew she believed my father had married beneath the family. My adoptive mother came from one of those old Southern families that had lost most of its wealth but desperately clung to its heritage. That was not good enough for Aunt Agnes. Money, heritage, position in society, and certainly power were the pillars upon which she built her church, and if one was weak, the church would collapse.

My father tolerated Aunt Agnes rather than loved her as a sister and once told me that her husband, Uncle Darwood, probably had welcomed the Grim Reaper with open arms, seeing death as an avenue of escape, even though it wasn't any sort of pleasant death. He was a very serious closet alcoholic and had drowned his liver with all his unhappiness.

Talking about Aunt Agnes and Uncle Darwood was one of the few things Daddy and I could have a warm, loving time doing together, basking in each other's laughter, soaking in the warm intimacy of a private hour when we were just father and daughter, alone, almost discovering each other for the very first time. This was some months after my adoptive mother's death, which ironically was the catalyst that finally drew us closer. It was almost as if she had cast a long, deep shadow over Daddy and me, keeping us both hidden from each other most of the time.

"What's wrong, Mrs. Schwartz?" I asked, sucking back my breath and swallowing it down into my lungs, already burning with anxiety.

A few of my classmates lingered just behind her in the room, waiting to hear.

"Your aunt says your father's been rushed to the Spring City General Hospital and you should come as quickly as you can." She pressed her right palm against her chest. It was as if those words had been burning inside her and now she was relieved.

"Why? Has my father been in an accident?" I asked.

It was how my adoptive mother had died less than two years ago, rushing home in the midst of a winter storm that dropped tiny icicles as sharp and as deadly as tiny knives out of the grumbling sky. She was hurrying home to get ready for a charity event. The police said she misjudged a turn and spun in circles in her small Mercedes before she hit the guardrail and went over and over, down into oblivion. I was sure she died upset that she wasn't properly dressed for it.

I remember thinking how horrible it all was, but I also remember I didn't cry as any other daughter would have done. I didn't feel that wrenching in my gut that comes when someone close to you is ripped away, and I felt guilty about that afterward. I even considered that my lack of emotion was indeed evidence of some mental problem, that maybe she had been right about me all along.

"No. It's heart trouble, I'm afraid," Mrs. Schwartz replied, her face so dark with sorrow she looked as if she were already at his funeral. "She said you should get right there. I'm sorry, dear. I'll see that all of your teachers know why you're not attending classes."

There is a moment after you hear bad news when your body goes into rebellion. You've heard shocking words. Everything is processed in your mind, but your brain becomes like those change machines that keep sending your dollar bill back out at you because it's creased or torn or put in upside down. The bad news has to be reprocessed and reprocessed until, finally, it takes hold and sinks down through your spine, ordering your defiant shoulders and hips and legs to obey the commands and turn you around so you can leave.

My lungs seemed to fill completely with hot air, threatening to explode. I was sure I would be blown to pieces right in front of everyone. All I could do was hold my breath and bite down on my lower lip to keep myself from bursting into tears.

As I walked away, I heard Mrs. Schwartz's stilettos

clicking over the floor behind me, building in rhythm
like a drumroll, chasing me out the door and to my
car in the student parking lot. Daddy had made me a
present of the car a week before I was to leave for my
second year of college. My intention was to go into
psychology myself and perhaps become a school psychologist. I wanted to work with young people because, based on my own experience growing up, I
thought I could have the best effect on someone's life
if I could get to him or her early enough.

When I arrived at my apartment, I played back my
answering machine and heard Aunt Agnes's annoyed
voice crying, "Where are you? Why aren't you home
at this hour, especially when I need to talk with you?
Call me immediately, no matter how late." Her voice
trailed off with "I wouldn't think a college student
could stay out this late."

I phoned Allan and told him the news. I knew he
would still be at home. He had a late-morning class
and then a full afternoon, including an important exam
for which he had to study.

"I've already called for a cab to take me to the airport," I told him.

I hadn't, but I knew how he hated distractions whenever he had an exam. Still, I wished he would volunteer
to come by and take me to the airport. It wasn't only
because I didn't want to leave my car there. I wanted to
be hugged and reassured before I boarded the plane.

Allan and I had been going together for nearly
a year. We had met at a college mixer when I was a
freshman. Barely eighteen at the time, I was hardly a

worldly woman and, unlike most of my girlfriends, could easily count on one hand how many boys I had even cared to consider as boyfriends. I used to worry that I was incapable of a serious relationship, but the truth was most of the boys I had known always seemed immature to me. Maybe I was too demanding, expecting somehow to find a younger version of my father: serious but not solemn, confident but not arrogant.

Allan seemed that way to me the first time I met him. Besides being a very good-looking man with a strong, masculine mouth, a perfect nose in size and shape, and strikingly dark blue eyes, Allan had a sureness about him, a steady focus that caused him to stand head and shoulders above the young college men around me who were still very obvious and insecure. Their laughter gushed like broken water pipes. Their courage came from beer and whiskey and shattered in the morning with the light of reality. Like vampires, they avoided mirrors. If they were so disappointing to themselves, I thought, what would they be to me?

"Good," Allan said. "Call me as soon as you find out what's happening," he added, hurrying me off the phone, which was a great disappointment to me, even though I knew he was doing it to get back to those books and notes and pursuit of his career. Sometimes, I wished I were competing with another woman. At least then I'd have a fighting chance.

"Okay." My voice cracked even over one simple word. I was already in a tight ball. Still, I managed to throw together a carry-on bag and call for the taxi.

I had to fly to Columbia, South Carolina. It wasn't a

long trip, but the next scheduled flight wasn't for another hour and a half, and I found that nothing I did, read, or looked at on television in the airport calmed me down very much. If I glanced at my watch once, I glanced at it twenty times. I was still far too numb to take note of any of the people around me, the activity and noise. Finally, I heard the call for my flight and went to the gate. My heart was thumping.

Daddy's heart had given him trouble? How could this be? He was only fifty-nine. I knew of no warnings, but I also knew my father was capable of hiding something like that from me. I had no idea yet how much he did hide, how much of a man of secrets he had been.

As childish and unrealistic as it was, I simply saw my father as invulnerable, someone so strong and so powerful that he was beyond the reach of ordinary tragedy and illness. It would take the act of some supernatural being, some wicked mythological god, to bring him down into the real world where mere mortals lived. I couldn't recall him ever being seriously ill. Except for an occasional cold, he seemed above it all. Even with a cough and a cold, he managed to go to work.

Everything he did in his life was always well organized, methodical, measured. For as long as I could remember, he ate the same things for breakfast: half a grapefruit, a mixture of oat and wheat bran cereals with strawberries, a cup of coffee, and, occasionally, a slice of four-grain bread. On weekends, he substituted the homemade date and nut bread Amou prepared, and on special occasions, he had her cheese and mushroom omelet with pieces of fruit cut perfectly to frame it on his plate.

Everything that was his in our house was kept in its proper place. I doubted that I would ever meet or get to know a neater man. He used to joke about himself and say he was obviously an obsessive compulsive. If the pen and pencil holder on his desk was moved an inch to the right or the left, he would notice. Amou was terrified whenever she went in there to clean, afraid she would move something and disturb him.

For exercise, Daddy took long walks on our property, for we had one hundred fifty acres with wooded paths, two rather large ponds, and a stream that twisted itself over rocks and hills to empty into a larger stream that fed into the Congaree River. He walked twice a week, and the walks lasted exactly two hours. I could adjust my watch around his walks, in fact.

As far as I knew, my adoptive mother never walked with him. He liked walking alone and told me once that he did a great deal of his creative thinking on those walks. I would have thought the wildlife and the scenery would have conspired to keep him from doing much of that, but my father seemed to have the power to turn off the world around him at will and fix his mind on whatever he wanted to focus on at the time.

Certainly, no one was better at ignoring my A.M. She would rant and rave about something, and most of the time he would stare at her, nodding at the proper moment, never changing his expression much more than occasionally lifting one of his dark brown eyebrows as a sort of exclamation point. He always promised to do whatever he could about the problem. Sometimes he did do something, but most of the time the problems either solved themselves or simply wilted and dropped from the branches of my A.M.'s tree of complaints.

Physically, Daddy wasn't intimidating. He was only about five-foot-ten, and he was always slim. He looked like a tennis player, and that was indeed the only actual sport he had played in college. His power lay in his eyes; when he fixed them on you, you would swear he was taller, bigger. I imagined that, especially for his patients, it was like being caught like a fugitive in a spotlight, unable to break out of it no matter how you twisted and turned in hopes of escape.

His eyes weren't set too deeply, nor were they extraordinarily large, yet they were always what my friends and other people who met him recalled most vividly. I used to laugh at my girlfriends, who were actually more than intimidated; they were afraid of him. They believed he could see into their thoughts since he was a famous psychiatrist.

I was always very proud of my father, but having the chief psychiatrist of a world-famous mental clinic as my father did put pressures on me that other girls my age could never even begin to understand.

Daddy was a handler. He rarely raised his voice or chastised me as would the parents of my friends. Now that I intended to become a student of psychology myself, I understood his techniques. My childhood relationship with him was built on questions, questions he wanted me to answer immediately or search inside myself to find the answers to, even at the ripe old age of four.

"Why is your mother angry at you, Willow?"

"Why do you think we're displeased with what you've done, Willow?"

"Why am I upset with what you've said to your mother, Willow?"

I could paper the walls of my memory with his questions.

My girlfriends worried about my father's psychological expertise from another point of view.

"How can you get away with anything?" they complained to me. "Your father would know immediately if you lie to him or cook up some phony excuse."

"I don't lie to him," I said, and they shook their heads at me with pity drooling from their eyes and lips, as well as some worry that I could get them into trouble. "However," I added, "I can fool my mother and often do."

That they not only understood but appreciated. It was as if getting past your parents was the initiation we all had to undergo to become full-fledged teenagers.

Somehow, lying to my adoptive mother on occasion didn't weigh too heavily on my conscience. Either the lies were too light or my conscience was too thick, whereas lying to Daddy would have been like stepping on a paper-thin sheet of ice.

Often, I thought my A.M. welcomed lies as long as the lies helped her to avoid some conflict or some disappointment. She was terrified of unhappiness because someone sometime in her life had convinced her that sadness was what aged people the fastest and the most. Her belief was reinforced by the faces of some of Daddy's patients, especially the women. Depression, she was persuaded, aged them twenty to thirty years, especially around their eyes—red, sunken and sad.

Anger was second on the list of youth killers, even though she succumbed to it more often than she would have liked. Scowling not only created wrinkles where there were none, but it deepened any that were naturally there. Thus, when offered the choice of following a deception or facing an ugly or unpleasant truth, my adoptive mother lunged for the lie the way some drowning person would stretch and jump for a life preserver.

She was truly a very beautiful woman, elegant and always in style. She often traveled to Paris, without Daddy, to shop for the newest fashions. Nearly as tall as Daddy, she had the figure of a runway model; to her way of thinking, being overweight was just as much an agent of age as anything. Women who gained and lost weight on a regular basis, she once told me, stretch their skin and create wrinkles, not only in their faces but also on their legs and even on and around their breasts.

"What's uglier than a woman in a V-neck gown with ripples of skin around her cleavage? Why, even a drop of perspiration flowing down from the base of her throat would get discouraged and evaporate," she told me once while she turned each and every way in front of her full-length mirror, scrutinizing her figure for any signs of imperfection.

All of my girlfriends were in awe of my adoptive mother, but that was because they didn't live with her.

They saw her only from afar, looked at her the way they would look at some beautiful celebrity. From the things they said, I understood that their mothers were quite envious of mine, too.

I worried that I could never have her sort of figure. I was five-foot-six. I had hair the color of a tarnished penny, whereas my A.M. had hair a shade lighter than fool's gold which actually glittered in the light. She kept it quite short, but she had a shelf of wigs in her closet so she could change styles at a whim.

One feature I had that neither she nor Daddy had were tiny freckles along the crests of my cheeks. I have a much lighter complexion than either of them as well. None of that was remarkable considering I was adopted, of course, but my adoptive mother was always jealous of my nose, claiming it was perfect and in proportion with my mouth and my eyes, speaking about it as if it were all a waste on me.

When I was a little girl, she warned me about my weight and predicted that I would always be chunky since I didn't have her genes. She pointed out my bloated cheeks and told me that was a good indication of what was to be.

"Your real mother must have been a chunky woman with a double chin," she declared. "Probably with oversized, sagging breasts and a waist you could tie an ocean liner to when it was in port. She was probably short and squatty with ballooned cheeks and tiny eyes. Medicine, especially the medicine they give mentally ill people, can do that to a person, you know, and then their offspring inherit it."

She drew so many ugly visions of my real mother for me that I was sure I had been born to some sort of circus freak. I hated thinking about her and secretly harbored the hope that I had been created in a laboratory. Someday my father would reveal it, and it would shut my mother's mouth.

Amou said my adoptive mother was wrong about my baby fat, anyway, and was quick to cheer me up whenever my A.M. said things like that to me.

"Your mama is so worried about being *infeliz,* unhappy, and the wrinkles that would come, you'd think she would make sure you never be sad," she muttered.

Amou said many things under her breath, things I wasn't supposed to hear, much less understand. Sometimes she would use as many Portuguese words as she could, but I got so I understood those words, even the curse words, because I sat by observing and listening when she and her sister Marisa met for lunch at our house every other Sunday.

Actually, even as a child, I understood a great deal more than anyone thought, especially about myself.

But not quite as much as I needed to understand. Not yet.

That was coming.

It waited for me on a shelf in Daddy's office like a secret whispered in a dead man's ear.

When I arrived at the airport in Columbia, I was very surprised to see my cousin Margaret Selby Delroy waiting for me at the arrival gate. It had been at least three years since we had seen and spoken to each other, the last time being at Uncle Darwood's funeral. The family had given out the story that he had died of heart failure. His alcoholism was an embarrassment that Aunt Agnes simply would not acknowledge. Like so many friends and relatives of my parents, the Delroys traveled on a bus without windows from one fantasy to another, shifting their eyes quickly away from anyone who would dare actually to look at them when they wove one of their illusions.

Margaret was only six months younger than I was, and comparisons were inevitable, I guess. She was two inches taller, but, contrary to my adoptive mother's predictions, I was the one who lost all her baby fat. The roundness evaporated from my face as if some magical sculptor molded my visage a little every night, bringing my high cheekbones out, thinning my lips, shaping my jaw and the lines of my neck and shoulders, firming and curving my breasts and narrowing my waist, until one day I looked at myself in my ivory oval vanity mirror and felt my heart go skipping with the real possibility that I was going to be attractive after all.

Amou was the only one I dared tell. I did it in the form of a question, of course.

"Do you think I'm getting pretty, Amou?" I asked her one afternoon in the kitchen. I liked helping her prepare dinner.

She stopped what she was doing and looked at me with that soft smile on her lips that I had grown to think of as my true sunlight.

"It's like you've been wearing a child's mask and slowly, slowly, it's disappearing and you be coming out. But don't be staring at yourself all day," she warned. "Worst thing a woman can do is fall in love with herself before a good man do. You know what happens then?" she added, leaving the answer floating around us like the whispers of ghosts. I knew she was talking about my A.M., of course.

And about young women like Margaret Selby Delroy, despite the roundness in her face that betrayed her self-indulgence and kept her from being attractive. Her softness came from being spoiled and waited upon hand and foot. Her hips were a little too wide, and she had these puffy little fingers, swollen under the glitter of her expensive rings. Her lips always looked swollen and uneven, and her eyes, although an attractive hazel, seemed in retreat because of her plump cheeks.

But there was no limit to what she and her mother would spend on her coiffure, her wardrobe, and her cosmetics. From her early teen years until now, everything she did and everything her mother had done to and for her was designed for one purpose: to find her a suitable husband, even to the extent of sending her to charm school. Their planning and conniving had apparently worked, for she was now engaged to marry Ashley Standard Roberts, the son of the publisher of the *Charleston Times*. I had not met him, but I had seen their picture in the social pages of the newspaper.

They looked more like brother and sister to me, both at least ten to fifteen pounds overweight, he with that born-with-a-silver-spoon-in-his-mouth look that suggested the most difficult thing he had to do every day was get himself out of his king-size bed and go to the bathroom. There was surely someone around to help him choose his clothes, clean up after him, and chauffeur him through the world as if he were here simply to visit and taste hors d'oeuvres.

"Willow!" Margaret Selby called and waved to me emphatically even though she was directly in my sight. Maybe she was afraid I wouldn't recognize her in her Fendi quilted black skirt suit and velvet hat in winter white. It had taupe satin trim and a swooping brim and would make her stand out in any crowd. As I drew closer, I saw she had gained a few more pounds. In fact, the outfit fit her shoulders too tightly and looked as if it would take Superman to pull her arms out of the suit jacket.

Couldn't she see how foolish she looked? I wondered. Margaret worshiped expensive clothing but really had no sense of style, I thought.

We hugged.

"I didn't expect to find you here," I said. I didn't mean it in any mean way. I simply never anticipated she would be concerned.

"You know how my mother is. She hates facing any unpleasantness alone and simply insisted I go along— not that I can do much of anything but sit and twist my hands. And I do have so much to do for my upcoming wedding," she concluded with a pout designed to draw out my sympathy.

"How's my father?" I asked dryly.

"Oh. Nothing's new that I know about since I left the hospital to meet you."

"What *do* you know?"

She shrugged. "Let's see," she said as we started

out. "He was at home, not actually in the house, but returning from one of those famous constitutionals of his. Mother calls them that, although I don't have any idea why a walk resembles a government document," she inserted. "Do you have any luggage to get?" she asked before I could explain.

"No, no," I said. "This is all I brought. I left in a terrible hurry, obviously."

"Oh, right. Of course. You have things at home to wear, I'm sure."

"I'm not worried about what I'll wear, Margaret. What else do you know about my father's condition?"

"What else? Oh. So he was walking toward the house when he apparently collapsed. Fortunately, Miles . . . is that his name, your father's housekeeper?"

"Yes, yes."

How many years would it take for her to remember his name? People like my cousin selected their memories with snobbery, conveniently forgetting anyone or anything they considered beneath them.

"So funny having a man for a housekeeper. Mama says he does your father's laundry, cleans and cooks for him now, too."

"Miles has been with my father for nearly twenty years," I said. "He's not really just his housekeeper. He's been his driver and cared for the property all that time, looking after the grounds, doing maintenance. I think by now it would no longer be a novelty."

"Right," she said. "But wasn't he a former patient of his?" she whispered.

"Margaret, please. What else happened to my father?"

"Oh, Miles looked out a window and saw him lying on the ground and rushed out to him. He called for paramedics, who claimed they revived your father, and then they got him to the hospital. Miles called my mother, and we just put everything down and came rushing here. We had to cancel at least a half dozen appointments—caterers, flower people, you know."

She laughed, a very loud cackle for someone who was supposed to be so ladylike, I thought.

"Whenever I complain about all the work I have to do planning my own wedding, Ashley says we should just elope. Can you imagine if we did? How many people would be disappointed? Hundreds. He's not serious, of course. He just likes to tease me.

"Mother says that shows he really cares about me. Men like to tease the women they love. It's a form of genuine affection," she declared with a single nod to serve as punctuation to mark the absolute, irrefutable truth.

I stopped and turned to face her.

"What were my father's diagnosis and prognosis, Margaret?"

"All I know is he had a heart attack. What does prognosis mean?" she asked, and grimaced quickly, anticipating criticism. "I know you're going to get into all that medical stuff and become like some sort of mental doctor, Willow, but not everyone studies the dictionary."

"You don't have to study the dictionary to know the meaning of prognosis," I said with forced patience. "It just means what they think his chances for recovery will be."

"Oh. Well, I don't know any of that," she said. "I haven't been here that long, Willow. We absolutely flew from your house to the hospital, and it's been very difficult just sitting around the waiting room. They hardly have any magazines to read, and as far as I know, Mother has had only one conversation with any sort of doctor. She didn't tell me anything except to go get you, and here I am. I have a car just outside, but the driver is not a very nice man. He kept saying he can't wait at the curb. They won't let him. Everyone thinks a bomb is going to go off at the airports these days. It really makes it difficult for those of us who are used to comforts and convenience. You would think they would make some sort of accommodation."

"Let's go," I said, already exhausted with my effort to squeeze even a tidbit of real information out of her.

"How is college life? Have you met anyone?"

I didn't answer. I kept walking, but that didn't discourage my cousin Margaret. People like her can easily have a conversation with themselves, I thought.

"I bet it's hard for you to meet someone. I don't know why you want to be a psychological doctor. People, men especially, can't feel too comfortable in the company of a psychiatrist. They're always suspicious of them, expecting them to analyze and judge them upon every word and gesture they make. You'll never have any real friends, Willow, much less a real love relationship. People simply won't trust you."

"Is that your mother's dogma?" I quipped as we stepped out of the airport.

"My mother's dog what?"

"Forget it, Margaret," I said, bursting out onto the sidewalk. I could feel the urgency coming to a head inside me. "Where's the car?"

"Oh. I think it was that one," she said, nodding at a black Lincoln Town Car. She waved emphatically, but the driver just stared at us. "I guess that isn't him. I can't tell one of those cars from another. Where is he? I told you he was not a pleasant driver."

I charged forward toward the taxi stand.

"Where are you going?"

"To the hospital," I called back.

"But . . . our car. You can't just take an ordinary taxi, Willow."

I stepped into the next taxi. Margaret stood there on the sidewalk staring in at me.

"Are you coming or not?" I demanded, holding the door open.

She looked up and down.

"Maybe he misunderstood," she said, "and thought I didn't need him to take us back."

"Get in!"

She grimaced and got into the cab as if she were about to sit in the electric chair. I reached past her and pulled the door shut.

"Spring City General, and as quickly as you can," I urged the driver.

"Right," he said, and we shot away from the curb.

"Well, my goodness," Margaret said. "Now I know what it must feel like to be kidnapped."

Who in his right mind would want to kidnap you? I thought, and mentally urged the traffic to move along faster.

"Mother says it's good to occupy your mind with other things when you're in a situation like this," Margaret rattled on as our taxi wove in and out of traffic.

I could hear her droning in the background, but I really didn't hear a word she was saying. Her voice took on the monotony of bees gathering nectar in our garden. I pushed it away. *I'm more like my father than I believed I was,* I thought, and smiled to myself. *I'm learning how to focus and turn off people.*

"It's not funny," I finally heard Margaret say. She practically shouted in my ear.

"What?"

"The shape of the wedding cake is very significant. Just think of the picture of it with Ashley and me."

I shook my head. "Who said it was funny?"

"You were smiling like you thought it was," she accused with a pout, drawing up her puckered little prune mouth like a drawstring purse.

"I was thinking of something else, Margaret. I didn't hear anything about your cake."

"What? Why were you thinking of something else?"

"I was doing just what you advised me to do, Margaret. I was occupying my mind," I said as we pulled up to the front of the hospital.

I paid the driver quickly and practically jogged into

the lobby, Margaret moaning and groaning about having to keep up with my pace.

"Where?" I said, spinning on her and nearly knocking her over with my carry-on bag. For a moment, she looked absolutely confused. "Where do they have my father?"

"Oh. Something called CCU, I think."

"Well, lead the way, Margaret."

She sauntered to the elevator, smiled at a young intern emerging, and then got in and pushed the button for the second floor.

"I've always been afraid of your father," she confessed. "He always looks so disapproving."

"It might be because he disapproves," I muttered, and stepped out to follow the signs indicating the direction of the CCU.

I pulled up short at the doorway of the waiting room. Aunt Agnes was sitting on the sofa and looking up at a nurse. She was nodding gently and dabbing her eyes with the end of her silk handkerchief. I had rarely seen her cry, but on the few occasions I had, she seemed capable of controlling the flow of her tears, permitting them to emerge only one at a time, alternately from eye to eye, and only after each had fully appeared. She pressed the corner of the handkerchief with her right forefinger and touched each tear cautiously, absorbing it and then moving over in anticipation of the next.

She had my father's eyes and mouth, but her chin was nearly nonexistent, sweeping up sharply under her lower lip and into the flow of her jawbone, and very tight, pale skin, a shade lighter than the sepia tones in old photographs. Her forehead looked infected with age spots she tried to keep as hidden as possible under long bangs of gray hair the color of a wet mop.

Unlike my adoptive mother, Aunt Agnes refused to wear a wig. She thought it was vain and undignified to battle too hard against aging. Aside from a little lipstick and some rouge, her store of cosmetics was anemic compared to the arsenal of skin creams, eye shadow, brushes, pencils, and makeup kits my adoptive mother had kept ready for her wars against wicked time.

Aunt Agnes had been a thin woman for as long as I could remember. Amou used to refer to her as *Senhora do Passaro*, "Bird Lady," because of her fragile bone structure and the way her nose had turned downward with age and become beaklike. I also thought she fluttered when she entered a room, always doing a little shiver as if she were throwing off some chill she had anticipated in coming to our home to speak with my father.

When she saw me, she reached up and put her hand on the nurse's wrist, and the nurse turned.

"Oh, it's my niece, his daughter," I heard her say. "Finally."

The look on the nurse's face was as good as a sword through my heart. I barely felt myself walk up to them. Aunt Agnes shook her head.

"We lost him," she said. "Just twenty minutes ago."

I stared down at her and smiled with incredulity as if she had said the most ridiculous thing. *Lost him? How can we lose Daddy?* Because of my silence and my expression, the nurse felt obligated to add to it.

"There was just too much heart damage. I'm sorry," she said.

Margaret, who finally caught up with me, just went right into a tirade about greeting me at the airport and our trip back to the hospital.

"You've got to speak to whoever got you that car service, Mother. The driver wasn't around, and we had to take an ordinary taxicab. Willow wanted to get right over here. I told him to wait at the curb, but he was an unpleasant man, and . . ."

"Shut up!" I screamed at her.

She looked as if I had slapped her. She brought her hand to her cheek and stepped back.

"Willow's father has passed away, Margaret Selby," my aunt explained.

"Oh," she said, her eyes widening with the realization. "Oh, dear."

I turned to the nurse. "I want to see my father," I said sharply. I don't know how I managed that many words. My throat had already begun to close and felt as dry as soil in a drought.

"Of course," she said, reaching out to touch my arm. "I'll take you to him."

I set my bag down to follow her.

"I'll start seeing to arrangements, dear," Aunt Agnes called after me.

"Oh, Mother," Margaret moaned, "a funeral."

I felt as if I were sleepwalking. Everything around me seemed vague, foggy. I kept swallowing down the urge to scream. So often people feel that they can scream away their troubles like some giant blowing unpleasant and ugly things out of his way. My heart-beat was so tiny, I imagined my heart itself was wither-ing, closing up like a clam somewhere deep in my chest. In fact, I thought I was shrinking, growing smaller and smaller until I was just a little girl again, a little girl being brought to see her daddy.

I stood in the doorway as if I were waiting for him to sit up on the gurney and beckon to me. The nurse stood at my side, wondering why I was so hesitant, I'm sure.

"I'm sorry," she said. "It's never easy losing a par-ent, no matter how old they are. My mother was eighty-six when she died last year, but I still felt as if the world had dropped out from under me."

I looked at her and nodded. "I'd like to be alone with him for a while," I said.

"Of course. Just call for me if you need anything," she said.

If I need anything? I need a second chance. I need to have gotten here before he died. Could you please arrange for that? I thought.

I looked at Daddy lying there so peacefully. His red-dish-brown beard was as trim and neat as ever. He hadn't been gone that long, so his skin wasn't the pale of the dead yet. They had closed his eyes. I wished they hadn't. I needed to look into those eyes one more time, even though they would be empty. At least I could remember what had been there.

It took a few more moments for me to draw close enough to take his hand. Funny, I thought as I held his hand in mine, my father had never once raised his hand to me, not even to pat me on the rear end. His anger, his chastising, lived in his voice, in those eyes, in his whole demeanor, and for as long as I could remember, that was sufficient.

My adoptive mother didn't hesitate to take a swipe at me now and again, even if it was always more like waving away a fly. She was very protective of her hands. Too many women her age showed their age in their hands, and she was determined that wouldn't happen to her. With Amou in our home, my A.M. never washed a dish or wiped a piece of furniture. The only thing she cleaned was her own body, and as gently as she would clean a piece of fine china.

"I'm sorry I didn't get here fast enough, Daddy," I began. I took a deep breath. Tears were trapped beneath my lids. I thought I was looking at him through a fishbowl. "But we were never really people who made much of goodbyes, anyway, were we? You accompanied me when I first went off to college, but, unlike the other parents we saw, there were no tears, no desperate hugs, no efforts to cling to the little girl who once was. We were so mature about it, weren't we?" I said, smiling down at him. "We knew how to deal with what for other people were very traumatic experiences.

"Focus, focus, remember?" I laughed. "I don't think you realized how much you lectured me on the trip. I bet you were like that because you were afraid of saying goodbye. I know I was, Daddy. Even though I never shed a tear in front of you or said anything to make you unhappy, I was afraid to say goodbye to you.

"Mother was already gone, but she had missed so

many special occasions in my life, anyway. One more didn't seem to matter all that much.

" 'Well,' you kept saying. 'Well, well, well, I suppose I should be going,' you said. 'You'll call me should you need anything, of course,' you told me, assuring yourself more than me, I think.

"Of course, I would call you. So much of our lives was built around *of course,* Daddy."

I stared at him. He was starting to look more like a statue, a monument of himself, a body already lying in state. It occurred to me that I had rarely seen my father asleep. Neither he nor my adoptive mother welcomed me into their bedroom that often, even if I had a bad dream. He would always come to me and talk the dream out of my head. He reassured me but left me to sleep in my own bed.

"I'm sorry I didn't get here in time, Daddy," I repeated. "There were so many things to say. We had just begun saying them to each other. We had many years of silence to make up for. What do I do now?"

I smiled because, even though his lips were sealed forever and ever, I could hear his response. Naturally, it was in the form of a question.

"What do you do now, Willow? What do you think you should do now?"

"I guess I should finish college and marry Allan or someone like him and eventually have a family of my own. I don't know all the details of our finances, but I will very soon, and I hope I can keep our home. Is that a good answer, Daddy?"

"Is it?"

"I think so."

"Then it is," he would say.

And it occurred to me that I was all right, that it didn't matter that I didn't get back in time to see him take his last breath on this earth, because he was with me forever and ever, his voice always there. I would always hear his questions, be guided by his wisdom. It was not something that died with his body. He had planted them in me like seeds, and they had blossomed and taken root. They would always keep me steady and guide me and help me to see the way.

I leaned over and kissed his cold forehead. Kisses were as rare as birds in winter at our house. My adoptive mother was always afraid of smudging her lipstick. She greeted people with an air kiss, a smack of the lips near their ears, and if she ever kissed me, which was something she was more or less forced to do in front of others, it was still as if she were using her lips to push me away.

Daddy kissed me, but it was always a quick kiss, almost like someone afraid of being caught doing it, which I thought quite funny considering he was a psychiatrist. *Do psychiatrists analyze themselves all the time?* I wondered. Did Daddy worry about why he was so afraid of being affectionate?

I brushed aside some strands of his hair, which was something I had never done when he was alive. Sometimes, we would look at each other across a room, and I would see the desire to hold me. I would catch him staring at me with a warm smile on his lips. I could sense the struggle going on within him, the battle between the urge to embrace me, to kiss me, to be my father completely, and this iron restraint that snapped his head around or darkened his eyes or made him sigh and walk away.

Why?

Why was that inhibition there? What had I done to cause it—or what had he done?

It occurred to me that he had fears, too; my strong and powerful father was afraid of something. Even with all his psychological techniques, his proven methodology, he was like one of his own patients, haunted by something too powerful to ignore or escape.

What?

What could possibly do that to him?

I missed my chance to ask him the questions the way he would ask them of me. That I did regret.

But I was about to discover that I didn't need to rush back here to ask the questions.

The answers were waiting for me. I had merely to look in the right places, behind the shadows that for so many years had kept them securely hidden.

2

A Letter from My Father

"Why is it," Daddy once asked at dinner, "that people are more adept at deceiving themselves than they are at deceiving other people?"

My adoptive mother raised her eyes to the ceiling so often in our house, I used to wonder if she actually saw something up there, or maybe someone, some compassionate invisible friend who sympathized with her daily turmoil.

"I absolutely hate it, Claude, when you bring home your work, when you use us as your sounding board and treat us as if we were your patients. I'm sure in your mind everyone but you is crazy," she said.

I shifted my eyes from him to her and to him as if watching a tennis match, but I dared not say anything or even look too hard at my A.M. I was a teenager by then but still under the rule she had laid down as gospel: children speak only when they are spoken to at the dinner table, especially at *her* dinner table.

"You know I hate that term, Alberta. People are not crazy. They suffer from a variety of maladies, psychoses, and neuroses. It's difficult enough to get the public not to use the term, but the wife of a psychiatrist should be the last one to be heard uttering it," he said in his measured, soft tone. I often thought that no one, not even a Buddhist monk, had more self-control than my father.

My adoptive mother pursed her lips. "Yes, doctor," she quipped. "All right," she said, returning to her food with a deep sigh, "tell us what you're talking about now. Who's deceiving herself?"

She lifted her head quickly and glared at him with fire in her eyes, just daring him to accuse her of having that fault.

"I didn't mean anyone in particular, Alberta. It's simply an observation about the human condition, a rhetorical question. I am just trying to make intelligent conversation."

She raised her eyebrows. "Oh, you're just making intelligent conversation. Yesterday, when I wanted to talk about redoing the pool decking, you barely grunted," she reminded him.

"That's not exactly the sort of conversation I was re-ferring to, Alberta."

"It's conversation, isn't it? What? It's not intelligent enough for you?"

"Okay, okay," he said. "I'm sorry. I didn't mean to upset you," he told her, and returned to his food.

Silence dropped over us like a lead curtain.

I remembered that question he posed, however, and it came back to me, flashing like a movie marquee when Aunt Agnes, Margaret Selby, and I returned to my house from the hospital. Surely, I thought the moment I set eyes on the stone pillars at the driveway entrance, I had been deceiving myself thinking I could live in this house without Daddy. Despite my adoptive mother's continual decorating and redecorating, it was his personality that loomed over every important room.

His chair at the head of the table would be terribly empty, and I could never get myself to sit in that seat. His favorite overstuffed armchair in the living room would still bear the imprint and wear from his body, and I could never look at it without seeing him in it, his feet up, reading one of his journals or his books. Certainly, his office was like the heart of the house. Rarely did he treat patients in our home, but important people still came to see him and went directly to it. From it, he would issue his orders to Miles and, when Amou was still with us, to her. All of his plaques, awards, and cherished photographs were on those walls. How could it ever be anything else but my father's office?

Upstairs, his and my adoptive mother's bedroom remained the central suite. I couldn't see myself moving into it. What would it become, a shrine? Perhaps I could give away his clothing the way we gave away my A.M.'s, but there were too many personal things of his that I would never relinquish, and as for the bed itself with its oversize headboard and canopy, why would I sell it?

And what about the walking paths? Could I look

down any and not anticipate his lanky form trudging slowly back from one of his famous strolls? Or look at one of the benches along the way and not think of him resting, thinking, composing one of his scientific papers in his mind?

Regardless of how my adoptive mother tinkered with our property and the house, Daddy loved it so. Of course, she never believed that he cared. If he questioned something she wanted to do to a room or on the property, she would stop and shake her head and ask, "Why do you even ask about it, Claude? You spend most of your time at your precious clinic. That has become more your home than this. It's a wonder you remember where your socks are."

She didn't understand him, I thought. Although he wasn't there as much as he would have liked, his house was truly a meditative place for him, a sanctuary. At least, that was what I believed. With him gone, it would all be so hollow to me, a shell of what was once a home and a family.

"You've got to think about what you will do with this property," Aunt Agnes said as soon as we drove through the entrance at the driveway. It was as if she could read my mind. "It's far too much of a responsibility for a young woman of your age. You're in college, anyway. Who would look after it?"

"Who does now?" I responded. "Who has looked after it all these years?"

"That man of your father's? Really, Willow, I could never understand how he put so much trust in someone like that," she snapped.

"Did he or didn't he kill his own child?" Margaret Selby demanded of me.

"He didn't kill his daughter, no. She was killed in a car accident."

"But he was driving, and he was drunk, wasn't he?"

"He didn't mean for her to be hurt. Alcoholism is a disease," I said.

"How can alcoholism be a disease? You can't catch it, can you, Mother?"

"People who can't control their bad habits classify them as diseases. It's convenient," she replied.

"That's not true," I said. "There is scientific evidence . . ."

"I never understood why your father went into psychiatry," she said. It was something I had heard her say on other occasions. "Our father wanted and expected he would become a successful heart specialist and perform those bypass operations. At least with that, you have something concrete to show for your efforts."

I bristled. I couldn't ignore everything, I thought. *Forgive me, Daddy.*

"Your brother, my father, was one of this country's most respected psychiatrists, Aunt Agnes. This is hardly the time to try to tear down his achievements," I said when the car came to a stop.

I couldn't wait to get out. I felt as if I had been locked in a jail cell and could hardly breathe.

Miles was at the door, standing there with his head slightly bowed. The mere sight of him freed the tears lodged beneath my eyelids. They streamed freely

down my cheeks when I saw from his face that he had
been crying awhile.

He was nearly sixty-five now, but if my adoptive
mother were alive, she could point him out as evidence
to support her theory that mental disturbances aged a
person. He looked more like seventy-five, eighty.
Despite his six feet, two inches, he actually appeared
shorter than average, slumping and squeezing his
shoulders inward, dropping his neck down into his
chest cavity. Daddy was always working with him to
help him build his self-confidence.

My cousin wasn't entirely wrong in her accusation.
Miles believed he was responsible for his daughter's
death, and that was what drove him to attempt suicide
and then to Daddy's clinic. His wife had left him. His
family had disowned him. It was Daddy who helped
him live with the tragedy and go on, helping to convince him that his poor departed child would certainly
want him to continue.

"Willow," he managed through those pale, trembling lips.

We hugged. I could feel Aunt Agnes and Margaret
Selby shaking their heads behind me. How could I be
so intimate with a servant?

"I got to him as quickly as I could," he said. "The
moment I saw he had fallen."

"I know you did, Miles," I said, and offered him my
best smile of reassurance. He welcomed it with a tiny
smile of his own.

"I'll brew some tea for you," he said as we entered
the house. "We'll have to order in some food now that

we have some overnight guests." He looked at Aunt
Agnes and Margaret Selby. "Your father and I didn't
require much these days."

"I'll take care of all that," Aunt Agnes said, coming
up behind us. "See that we have clean linen in our bedrooms and enough towels and washcloths," she ordered, marching past him with her shoulders back in a
military posture.

"How long are we going to stay here, Mother?"
Margaret Selby asked.

"Until we are no longer required," she replied.
"Now, go to your room and rest and then freshen up.
People will be coming to offer their condolences, I'm
sure. I'll see to the proper refreshments," she told me.
"First, I'll evaluate what is in this house."

She marched down the hallway toward the kitchen
and pantry. Miles and I simply stood there, almost like
disinterested observers. Margaret Selby released a
small groan of frustration and then pressed my arm.

"I'll just take a little rest and then be with you as
much as you like, Willow. I remember what a trying
time it was when my father died, but Mother"—she
looked after Aunt Agnes—"is so good at things like
this. You can depend on her just like I always do."

She leaned in to kiss me on the cheek and then hurried up the stairway.

Miles and I looked at each other, both fighting off
an urge to break into laughter at her anemic attempt to
be sincere and concerned.

"I'll be in Daddy's office, Miles."

"Very good, Willow. I'll bring you in a cup of tea

and some biscuits. You know, the ones your father is so fond of," he said, and then realized instantly that we would both have to change our verb tenses forever in relation to Daddy. "The ones he was fond of."

"Thank you, Miles," I said.

I walked on, past the entrance to the kitchen where I could hear Aunt Agnes opening and closing cabinets, taking her instant inventory. Some people invite the opportunity to take charge of other people's lives, I thought. They are like firemen who can't help but welcome the challenge, the battle, the surge of adrenaline, forgetting for the moment that the theater in which they are performing their necessary roles is a theater featuring pure misery for someone else.

"My goodness," I heard Aunt Agnes declare to Miles when he went into the kitchen. "You would think my brother was living off his Social Security. I haven't seen pantries as bare as this since I worked with Meals on Wheels for the house-bound elderly."

"Dr. De Beers had all he required," Miles remarked firmly. "He lacked nothing he wanted."

She grunted her displeasure, but I was positive Miles wasn't going to kowtow.

I smiled to myself and walked on toward the office, well in the rear of the house.

Our house was a large Gothic revival and too grim for my adoptive mother, who was fond of saying, "It always looks like it's scowling at me when I drive up, no matter how I dress the windows."

If she could have, she would have ripped it down and started over, but the house had been in my father's family for nearly one hundred fifty years. It at least gave my adoptive mother reason to feel some superiority over her acquaintances who lived in more modern structures or whose homes didn't have the history ours did.

We had two stories with a large attic that ran nearly the entire length of the home. The house had one prominent gable and one on each side. Most of the windows had drip-mold crowns and were arched to protect them from water running down the face of the building. We had a one-story porch with flattened arch supports.

My adoptive mother was always trying to find a way to replace the pointed-arch front door because she thought it looked too devilish—the entrance to hell, she called it. But it was too much a part of the architecture, and despite her desire to change the feel of the house, she was afraid of looking foolish or losing its historical uniqueness.

We had five bedrooms, maid's quarters Amou had used and which Miles now used, a separate living room and den, a very large dining room with a table that could seat twelve comfortably, and, of course, Daddy's office.

I paused in the doorway. Although it was never set in stone or voiced with regal authority, it was understood that I was not to go playing or exploring in Daddy's office when he wasn't there. Even my A.M. rarely went in there when he wasn't occupying his desk. She never put it in so many words, but she gave the distinct impression that she felt the mental illnesses Daddy treated, the patients he occasionally saw in that office, could be infectious, as if paranoia or compulsive obsessions were spread through germs. I knew for a fact that she had never sat in any chair a patient had sat in and had never sat on the couch in that office.

If Daddy sensed her feelings, he didn't do anything to change them. I think he enjoyed having a place to go in his home where he could feel insulated. As I stood in the doorway and looked in at his large, dark cherry wood desk and his high-backed leather chair, I smiled, recalling my adoptive mother standing in this doorway and making some demand or another on him without crossing her imaginary line. I knew he deliberately spoke more softly than usual because she would keep asking him to repeat something and she would raise her voice. Frustrated, she would stomp away. Once, I was there quickly enough to see a tiny smile on his lips. He winked at me, and I felt as though he had passed a secret note for me to bury at the bottom of one of my dresser drawers.

About ten years ago, Daddy had a cabinetmaker construct new shelving over the left wall. Besides shelves, it had a row of small cabinets at the very top. He kept his books, papers, and reports on the shelves, in the middle of which stood a miniature grandfather clock, which was a gift from a very appreciative Englishman whose daughter Daddy had treated successfully at his clinic. On it the man had inscribed "To be ill is human, to heal divine," a play on Alexander Pope's famous line "To err is human, to forgive divine." The clock was gilded with precious jewels at each of the Roman numerals. Daddy used to say it had a distinctly English accent to its *tick-tock* and went *tick-talk* instead. Listening to it now brought a smile to my lips and helped me feel his presence in the room.

There was so much that would do that, however. The closet door was slightly open, and I could see one of his tweed sports jackets with the leather elbow patches. Daddy liked this very manly scented cologne, which, although he never smoked, had the aroma of some fine tobacco. When I walked in, I realized it still hung vividly in the air.

I moved slowly around the office, gazing as if for the first time at his plaques, his awards, and the pictures he had chosen to hang prominently. There were a number of framed photographs of him with important political people, even the governor of the state and a senator, but in a central location were two pictures of me, one when I was about five, all dressed up for a party my adoptive mother had arranged to celebrate their anniversary, and another of me at my middle-school graduation with both him and my A.M. at my side. She looked as if she were trying to get someone's attention. Her gaze was off left, distracted. Daddy was looking at me, his face caught in one of the most affectionate gazes I had ever seen. I had forgotten this picture.

I paused at his desk chair. The very thought of sitting in it was inhibiting. I never had. Glancing over his desk, I saw a yellow pad with most of the first page completed. A quick perusal told me he was putting down thoughts for a new paper on bipolar disorder. It appeared he was going to discuss the benefits of being in nature. The meditative power of his famous walks was to find a place in his therapy again and again. How disappointing that he would never finish this, I thought. He had so much yet to give.

The ringing of the phone jolted me out of my reverie. For a moment, I just stared at the receiver. I never answered the phone in here, of course, but it rang on. Finally, I picked it up and said hello. It was our family attorney, Mr. Bassinger.

"Willow, my deepest regrets and condolences," he began.

I had met him only a few times, usually at social occasions. He was a man pushing seventy, nearly ten years older than Daddy, but he and Daddy had been friends for as long as I could remember.

"Thank you, Mr. Bassinger. It's still all too fresh and raw to be real to me," I added.

"I understand. I'm calling because your aunt just phoned my office with the news and asked that I get right on the legal matters that become necessary."

"No grass grows under Aunt Agnes's feet," I said.

"Yes," he said in a noncommittal tone. She had obviously forced him to put on his lawyer's face first and then his family friend face. "I just want you to be reassured that I'll be right on it and will review it all with you at the proper time. I can tell you quickly, however, that except for what your father left to his clinic, you are the sole beneficiary, which, of course, includes the house and the property."

"Thank you, Mr. Bassinger."

"One more thing," he continued. "I have an envelope with papers in it in my vault that I was instructed not to give to you until your father's passing. I will bring them by later today, if that's all right with you."

"Yes, of course. What does it involve?"

"Willow, I am not lying to you when I tell you it was handed to me sealed and I never opened it, nor did your father give me any further information or instructions about it."

"I see," I said. It made my heart pound, although I had no idea why it should.

"Once again, I am very sorry. I always told him I would go before he did. You are far too young to have lost both your parents, and he was far too young as well."

"Yes," I said. "I wasn't aware that he had any heart trouble at all."

"The shoemaker without shoes, caring more for other people than he did for himself, a truly great man. I'll be by later."

I thanked him again and hung up.

Aunt Agnes appeared in the office doorway, standing just at the threshold, precisely the way my adoptive mother would have.

"The funeral is arranged for the day after tomorrow, Willow. I expect you will have many callers, so I have hired a service to provide maids and take care of the food we will need. It would be far beyond Miles's abilities to do anything significant. When I phoned the funeral parlor, I learned your father had left explicit instructions for nearly everything. You don't have to pick out a casket, do any of that. He was very thoughtful that way. Even as a young boy, he was the most organized person in our family. My mother never had to criticize him for the way he kept his things, unlike most boys his age."

She paused as Miles brought in my tea and biscuits on a tray.

"Why are you having that in here?" she asked when he set it down on the table in front of the leather sofa.

"Thank you, Miles," I said instead of responding to her immediately.

He left the office. I stirred the cup and, without looking at her, said, "I'd like to be alone for a while, Aunt Agnes."

She blew some air out through her tight lips and left the doorway.

I glanced at my father's chair as if he were still there. I could see him give me that wink. It brought a smile to my face and then a flow of tears.

Bad news travels with the wind. It's as if everyone who hears it feels an obligation to pass it along, or maybe a need to get rid of it before it affects them and their lives as well. I like to compare it to a hot potato. You move it to another's hand before it burns your own.

The phone began ringing incessantly. Aunt Agnes took it on herself to answer all the calls. I didn't mind that and for a while was actually grateful she was there to sponge up the flow of sympathy that was threatening to become a tidal wave. Daddy not only had many, many professional friends in all fields of medicine, but there were so many people at the clinic who were thunderstruck.

I remembered how full of mourners the house had

become after my adoptive mother's accident. From the way the phone was ringing off the hook, it threatened to be even fuller. Aunt Agnes was scurrying every which way, shouting orders at Miles, insisting we get in a maid service immediately to clean up a house she considered quite neglected.

"I don't know what your father was thinking when he dismissed all of his servants except for Miles shortly after your mother's death. I suppose with you off to college and her gone, he thought he didn't have the same requirements. As if the women in this house made the most dirt and dust and mess of it," she muttered. "Did you see the layers of dust in the living room? I don't imagine either your father or that Miles ever set foot in it after your mother's death, and I can't tell you what's going on in the guest bedrooms, Willow."

"I don't think the people coming to pay their respects are going to inspect the furniture, Aunt Agnes."

"Why, of course they will," she snapped back. "People are always snooping in everyone else's business. Don't worry about it. I'll handle it," she declared. "Where is that Margaret Selby? I have things for her to do," she added, and went rushing off to find my cousin, who was most likely chatting away with her girlfriends back in Charleston, complaining about being trapped in the house of death.

I finally felt up to calling Allan and went to my bedroom to do so. I got his answering machine and left the sad message. Then I tried to get some rest, for I knew Aunt Agnes, for all her blustering about, was correct: people would start coming to our home as soon as they could, and I would have an obligation to Daddy's memory to greet them properly.

A little more than an hour and a half later, my phone woke me. I had my own number, so Aunt Agnes couldn't pick up this call first. It was Allan.

"Hey," he said. "Sorry to hear about your father. I guess he was a lot worse than you were first told."

"I wasn't told anything really, Allan."

"Um," he said. "That's too bad. He was a relatively young man, right?"

"Just about sixty."

"Right, right. So when is the funeral?"

"Day after tomorrow."

"Right, right," he said. He sounded so distracted to me. "Well, you know I would be there if I could, Willow, but I have that constitutional law exam, and Heller is a tyrant. You'd have to be dead yourself to get excused from the test, and he would insist you take it the first minute after you were resurrected in either heaven or hell," he added with a small laugh. "I really respect him, though. I want to do well in his class."

He continued to talk about his work as if my father's death were just another event in the course of a day. I imagined he was simply trying to help me get my mind off it for a while. That was the purpose of visitors at a time like this, wasn't it? Allan was simply trying to ease my pain.

"Will you come right back afterward?" he asked finally.

"As soon as I can straighten out all that has to be done, I will."

"Well, is there anything you want me to do for you at school, Willow?"

"No."

"Keep your chin up. I'll miss you, but I'll keep myself busy until you return. Call me if you need anything, okay?"

"Okay," I said. I was waiting to hear more, to hear how much he cherished me, how much he wished he could be at my side to comfort me and hold me. I was waiting to hear him say "I love you."

"Oh," he said as if he had forgotten to tell me one more important detail. "Love you."

"Love you, too," I said.

I felt so empty inside after I hung up. His call should have filled me with more warmth, helped me face the next moment. I lay there staring up at the ceiling until I heard a knock at my bedroom door.

"Willow?" Margaret Selby called. "Are you awake?"

"Yes," I said, sitting up. "Come in."

She opened the door and peered in first.

"It's all right, Margaret. Come in."

"Oh, good," she said as if she were escaping from someone in the hallway.

She was now wearing a black crepe bolero jacket over a fit and flared slip dress. Ordinarily, I would have thought it a very pretty outfit, but once again, she looked as if she had bought it before she gained an additional dozen or so pounds.

"Mother thought this would be appropriate," she said, turning. "What do you think?"

"Anyone who's worried about clothes at a time like

this is a candidate for my father's clinic," I muttered, then rose and went into the bathroom.

"Well, it just shows respect if you look good, Willow. If I wore a pair of jeans, even designer jeans, it wouldn't be very nice, now, would it?"

She heard the tinkle. "Are you peeing?" she cried.

"Voiding urine," I replied.

"Ugh. Close the door. My goodness, you'd never know we're from the same family," she complained.

I flushed the toilet and stripped to jump into the shower.

"Mother sent me up here to tell you your father's accountant and his wife have arrived," she called. "She thinks you should come downstairs. Oh, and your mother's brothers and their wives are coming to the funeral, as well as your cousins Lucille Ann, Merrilou, Branson, and Lance. Isn't Lance the good-looking one?"

I didn't reply. I stepped into the shower, which drowned her out, but she didn't stop talking. When I shut off the water and stepped out of the stall, she was in the middle of a sentence, apparently describing some time in the past when she had a crush on my cousin Lance. I wrapped the towel around myself and came out of the bathroom.

"Weddings and funerals bring families together," she concluded. "They will all be coming to my wedding in three months, I'm sure. We've invited them all, even your mother's relatives.

"Was there someone you wanted me to invite for you?" she asked, still trying to find out if I had a boyfriend at college.

"Margaret Selby," I said, turning to her, "I appreciate how much your wedding means to you and how excited you are about it, but believe me when I tell you, I can't think about anything but the fact that the day after tomorrow, I'll be burying my father beside my mother in the cold ground of the cemetery."

She stared at me a moment and then burst into tears. "I was only trying to keep you from thinking about it. I didn't mean my wedding was more important than your father. I'm sorry. I—"

"Margaret."

She turned and rushed out of my bedroom. I stared after her a moment and then turned to my closet to find something appropriate to wear, too. Daddy would tell me I was being too harsh on her, I'm sure. He had the amazing ability to look at everything from the other person's perspective. If I hoped to be anywhere nearly as successful as he was, I thought, I'd better learn how to do that better than I could at the moment.

I dressed and went downstairs. Aunt Agnes was holding court in the living room, sitting in the highback Victorian chair and looking like the queen she thought she was. Daddy's accountant, Lester McRoe, who also handled the clinic's books, was, as Margaret Selby had told me, there with his wife. From the way he looked, however, I had the sense he had been summoned. When I entered, the conversation abruptly halted. His wife greeted me first with a hug, and then he took my hand and offered his condolences.

"It was such a shock to hear it," he said. "I want you to know I'll be available to help you through anything as soon as you require it. I have all the information you need about the estate, the trusts . . ."

"Thank you," I said quickly.

"Your father was a very organized man."

"I know," I said. "I appreciate what you're saying, but I'm not ready to talk about those things."

I looked at Aunt Agnes, who obviously was. For the moment, pragmatism, even my father's, seemed like the enemy of love, of caring. Everyone deserved to be mourned properly, at least by the people who cherished him or her, I thought.

"These are very serious matters, Willow," Aunt Agnes declared.

"I know that, but a funeral for my father is pretty serious business, too, Aunt Agnes."

"No one is saying it isn't, but—"

"Thank you. And thank you for your concerns, Mr. McRoe," I said sharply and decisively, closing the door on any further discussion.

Mr. McRoe glanced at his wife, who looked as if she had advised him against coming to the house with this purpose in mind and now was nodding her "I told you so." He stepped back, a little embarrassed at his eagerness to do his fiscal duty. Fortunately, the ungraceful silence was quickly filled by the arrival of other people who wanted to offer their condolences, people who were closer to my father, dear friends and associates.

Aunt Agnes's arrangements did seem appropriate, however. I was happy that everything was organized. Margaret Selby reappeared, her eyes bloodshot from crying over my outburst. Everyone mistook that for her sorrow over my father's death, and she quickly accepted it and talked about how sad she was. I shook my head, smiling to myself and thinking that Daddy would remind me how much of a child she still was and how that was really all Aunt Agnes's fault.

About an hour later, Mr. Bassinger appeared with his wife, Thelma. After greeting my aunt and Margaret Selby, he hugged me and asked if he and I could excuse ourselves and speak privately for a few moments. Under Aunt Agnes's suspicious eyes, we left the gathering and went to my father's office. He carried the large manila envelope he had described on the phone.

For a moment, we both stood there, staring at his desk.

"I am having trouble believing he is gone, Willow. He had such a presence, such a powerful presence. When I came in just now, I really expected he would be sitting here, smiling at us, wondering what all the fuss was about, and demanding to know who all those people were out there."

"I know," I said, smiling.

He stared a moment more and then took a deep breath and turned to me. "I wouldn't burden you with any sort of legal information so soon if it wasn't for his forceful insistence that I get this to you as quickly as possible after his death. He wasn't often so emphatic about any of his instructions. You know how even-tempered a man he was.

"Anyway, here it is," he said, handing me the envelope. "I was told to give it to you and add only the following instructions: read it when you have a quiet moment, and be sure to read it in strict privacy. He underscored the privacy part."

I looked at the envelope. It was very thick.

"How long have you had this in your vault, Mr. Bassinger?"

"He gave it to me about six months or so after he had brought you home to live with him and your mother," he replied.

"You've had this for nearly nineteen years?"

He nodded. "I left a note on it myself instructing my partner to return it to your father in the event of my death, which I really expected would predate his. We joked about it often, but he was far more clairvoyant than I knew, apparently," he said, tears coming to his eyes.

We hugged, and I put the envelope in Daddy's desk drawer before I accompanied Mr. Bassinger back to the living room and all the people who had arrived. I would have to wait a while longer to see what was in the envelope, I thought, but it was never far from my thoughts over the next few hours. All that time, I saw how my aunt was studying me, craning her neck in a birdlike way at times to watch for any communication between me and Mr. Bassinger.

When Mr. and Mrs. Bassinger left, he whispered, "Call me if there is anything you need to know as a result of you-know-what," he said.

I thanked him. After another hour, the last guest departed. Aunt Agnes, still very curious, pounced.

"What is it Mr. Bassinger wanted that couldn't wait another day or so?" she demanded.

"We're arranging to do what has to be done," I answered cryptically.

"I thought you were still too raw with sorrow for any of that. Isn't that what you told Mr. McRoe?" she pointed out, stabbing me with her hard, penetrating gaze.

"Thank you for all you've done, Aunt Agnes," I said with a smile. "We all had better get some rest," I added as if I hadn't heard her comment.

Margaret Selby was already closing her eyes.

I turned and left them both in the living room. When I entered Daddy's office, I closed the door behind me and snapped the lock. Then I went to his desk and, for the first time, sat in his chair. I opened the drawer and put the envelope on the desk. For a long moment, I just stared at it. All the preparations, the instructions, had frightened me a bit. What did this envelope contain?

Slowly, I worked it open using Daddy's ivory letter opener, and then I pulled out a packet of paper filled with his writing.

I took another deep breath and began to read the first page. It was a letter to me.

Dear Willow,

Let me begin by first begging for your forgiveness. What you are about to learn should have been something you have known all your life. Just about every other child does, or certainly should. It has been the heaviest burden of my life carrying this secret inside me. The truth of it is that your mother did not know this, either. There were times I feared she would come to suspect it, but ironically, her devotion to herself, her interest in herself, blinded her. Actually, I think of the saying "There are none so blind as those who will not see." She wouldn't look for these revelations. She wouldn't see them if they were right in front of her. Perhaps she was better off. Sometimes, it is better to be in some ignorance.

I can't deny I was tempted to leave you in some ignorance, but I knew in my heart that would be unfair. What I did not have the courage to do was to reveal the enclosed while I was still alive. There are so many reasons for my cowardice, I suppose, but none of them justifies it.

Even so, I beg for your forgiveness. Believe me when I tell you I have suffered more than you will, and believe me when I tell you my most important reason was always to be sure you would be a happy person. I hope and pray you still will be.

I know I never said it enough, and it can never be said too much, but I want you to begin with this knowledge:

I love you, Willow.

I love you.

Daddy

The tears rolling down my face were falling onto the paper. I pushed it aside and flicked them off my cheeks as fast as they were coming. For a long moment, I sat there, fighting to catch my breath, fighting to ease the ache in my chest. It finally subsided. I swallowed the lump in my throat and sat forward again, my fingers trembling as I peeled away the top sheet and began to read the next page.

It began:

> *If someone had told me that someday I would fall in love with one of my patients, I would have recommended that he or she become one of my patients.*
>
> *Now I have to admit that this most improbable event has occurred.*

3

The Truth Revealed

I don't know how many times my father's miniature grandfather clock bonged the hour. I never heard it after I began to read his diary. I was mesmerized, fascinated to the point of forgetting time, forgetting fatigue. I was glued to his chair and read through most of the night, pausing occasionally to take a breath, to cry, to laugh. Often, I lifted my eyes from the pages to ask myself again and again, were these my father's words? Were these the words, the descriptions, the utterances of the man I knew?

The author of these words did not seem like a man who saw the world through a doctor's clinical eyes. This wasn't the organized, at times unemotional man I knew, the man who was afraid to hug me, to hold my hand, to kiss my cheek, the man I never saw cry, not even at my adoptive mother's funeral.

The man in these pages was a man who could feel things deeply, whose emotional roller coaster went from deep melancholy to utter ecstasy, whose pronouncements of love brought a blush to my cheeks, whose words rivaled the pages of the best romance novel.

He moved quickly into a warm, detailed description of how he fell in love with his patient Grace Montgomery, and even how he began to make love to her. The clinic, which to me had seemed a cold, bare world, suddenly took on the ambience of a romantic escape. He actually wrote: *I couldn't wait to get there every morning. It was as if I had found the doorway to paradise.*

Daddy's descriptions of the views of the river running behind the clinic, even the halls and the rooms in the evening, the music he used to calm patients—all of it took on a beauty and warmth I never knew existed for him.

When you're with someone you love, he wrote, *the most mundane things suddenly become wonderful.*

I found myself falling in love with my father through his wonderful expressions of love, through his obvious joy and his renewal of youth and excitement.

Daddy explained how he kept Grace Montgomery at his clinic far beyond what was necessary and how happy she was, because not only was she just as much in love with him as he was with her, but she had reasons to avoid hurrying home to Palm Beach, Florida. He never got into those reasons.

It surprised me at first that Daddy would have permitted her to become pregnant, that he wouldn't have taken the proper precautions, but the love affair he described and their times together rang with spontaneity, with the sort of impulsive action more often associated with much younger people. It was truly as if their love affair had rejuvenated them both, brought them both back to a time when they were hardly more than teenagers.

They discussed abortion, but Grace Montgomery fervently wished to give birth to the child she believed embodied their great love. At first, he was opposed, but soon he gave in to the idea, and then he made plans to adopt the child—who, of course, was me.

He elaborated on the deception and then revealed that he had made an agreement with my adoptive mother. In exchange for allowing him to take in this foundling, he gave her money and autonomy. She could go anywhere she wanted, do anything she wanted, and have anything she wanted. All those discussions they used to have over changes in the house or their lives were more show than substance because the outcome was determined at the start. She would get her way no matter what. He was permitted only to attempt to give her some reasons to change her mind, but she rarely did.

Her aloofness from me and her criticism of me made far more sense now. She did not know that my father was my real father, but that did not change her resentment of me and of his determination to keep me and make me a member of the family. In the beginning, she offered to try to mold me into what she considered an acceptable child and young woman. It was, according to my father, something of an interim peace agreement.

No matter how much he reassured her that there was no terrible madness gestating in me, she clung to the belief that I would someday prove to be unbalanced. It was why he was so instrumental in acquiring Amou. He knew from the beginning that she would be more of a mother to me than my adoptive mother would want to be or could be.

He then went into a long explanation of how and why he married my adoptive mother in the first place. Despite what I saw of her in our home at times, I would have to agree with him that she could be a very charming woman. They apparently had some good years in the beginning.

Not long after my birth and subsequent adoption, my real mother left the clinic. His description of their parting brought a flood of tears to my eyes. They both knew that his career, all his good work, all he had built up during his life, was in jeopardy, otherwise.

By the time I finished reading, I was truly physically and emotionally exhausted. I put all the pages back into the envelope and then hid it well under a pile of folders in one of my father's file cabinets. It terrified me just to imagine Aunt Agnes getting her hands on it.

I went up to my room, my heart tossing and turning in a sea of emotions. When my head finally rested on my pillow, I felt as if I were sinking in that sea, all of the sadness, the joy, the fears, and the pleasures I'd read of and felt washing over me. I tossed and turned as if my bed were a small boat being rocked in a storm and actually woke up more exhausted than I was when I had gone to sleep.

Aunt Agnes didn't temper her voice in consideration of my still being asleep. I heard the house echoing with the orders she was shouting at the temporary hired help. It sounded as if she were rearranging the furniture below. Doors were slammed, and there were heavy footsteps up and down the stairway. The weight of what was to come kept me from rising, but I had to find the strength to face the day.

People began arriving soon after breakfast, and the steady flow never stopped until close to nine that night. The one visitor who interested me more than anyone at the moment was Dr. Renaldo Price, the chief administrator at my father's clinic. He was a man of about fifty but with a completely gray head of hair. He had been with my father from the beginning and surely knew the secrets that were buried in the envelope I had hidden under the files in Daddy's office.

I didn't see him very often. My adoptive mother was never fond of socializing with Daddy's colleagues, especially the ones at the clinic.

"What could be worse than sitting at a dinner table with a group of psychiatrists?" she flippantly told him. "Everyone will be analyzing everyone else. I'd be afraid to utter a sound, and I'd be so self-conscious of every gesture, I'd be on pins and needles. I'd rather go to dinner with some of your patients," she said.

At first, he thought it was funny, but as time went by, I was sure he regretted the limitations she imposed. He was fond of his staff and enjoyed being with them.

Slowly, piece by piece, she took apart the house of pleasure he had constructed, I thought. Maybe that was why he was so vulnerable to Cupid's arrow, even in his own clinic and with his own patient.

The few times I was able to meet and speak to Dr. Price, I found him to be a very kind, gentle man, with a fatherly demeanor about him. When he looked at me with his soft, hazel eyes, I felt he was really looking at me, listening to me, and wasn't like so many adults I knew, being polite, half distracted, not believing I, a child, was worth the investment of attention. One other thing made me feel comfortable with him: he never talked down to me. He spoke to me just the way he would speak to any adult and made me feel the things I told him were important and significant.

Now, here we were years later, neither of us feeling particularly talkative. Nevertheless, we spoke for a while in the living room. The chatter of the visitors had grown quite loud, overwhelming, in fact. Just like so many of these sad affairs I had attended with my father in the past, people were renewing old friendships, moving the conversation away from the tragedy to more comfortable zones. They were like horses with blinders, afraid to turn right or left for fear of catching someone wiping away a tear or speaking through trembling lips.

Margaret Selby was certainly helping the younger people feel at ease. She was rattling on and on about her impending wedding, reviewing the details as if she were embarking on a military campaign instead of a social event. She pounced on my cousin Lance the moment he entered the room, hardly giving him time to greet me or Aunt Agnes. I laughed to myself as I watched him searching for some avenue of escape, but she was relentless—and whatever she was saying brought blush after blush to his face.

I had to admit, Aunt Agnes's arrangements were well suited to all this. Despite the darkness of the occasion, it soon took on a festive air. It disturbed me, but at the same time, I understood everyone's need to get their hands out of the coffin, so to speak, as quickly as they could, especially the relatives.

Most of my relatives were little more than strangers to me, names, voices, faces I passed quickly when I thumbed through family albums. They could have been faces in a mail-order catalogue, for all I cared or knew, and they were as insignificant to me now.

"You're holding up well, Willow," Dr. Price told me. "Your father would be very proud of you." He looked out the window so I wouldn't see the tears filling his eyes.

"Take a walk with me, Dr. Price?" I asked. He looked surprised but pleased by my request.

Once again, Aunt Agnes's eyes followed me like a searchlight until I was out of the room. I led Dr. Price out the rear door and walked with him toward one of my father's famous paths. It was an unusually warm fall day with a few clouds looking like small dabs of whipped cream on blue icing. The breeze was gentle, barely lifting the leaves or stirring the grass. This was hardly a day for bereavement, I thought. It was more of a day to celebrate life.

"Your father was very proud of your college work the first year, Willow," Dr. Price said. He smiled. "I remember him telling me, 'I wasn't on the dean's list the first semester of college. I guess I can't call her a chip off the old block.' "

"How could he, anyway, Dr. Price? I am an adopted child, aren't I?" I asked pointedly, my eyes fixed on his.

He shifted his gaze guiltily away, pretending interest in the flight of a sparrow.

"Right?" I pursued.

"Your father wouldn't have treated you any differently had you not been," he said. "Believe me."

"Oh, I believe you, Dr. Price, but perhaps that was because I really wasn't some orphan, some stranger, someone not of his blood," I said.

He looked at me, his face freezing, his eyelids holding wide.

"Let's sit for a while," I suggested, pausing at one of the stone benches.

He looked back at the house and then sat beside me. We were both quiet for a long moment. The sparrow he had been watching perched itself on the fountain in front of us, strutted about, and then looked at us curiously. Something else caught its interest, and it was off again.

"How did you find out?" Dr. Price asked finally.

"He told me," I said.

He turned sharply. "He told you? But he vowed to me he never would."

"While he was alive, perhaps, but he told me after he died," I said.

"I don't understand," Dr. Price said, shaking his head.

"He left me his diary."

"Diary? Claude kept a personal diary? How extraordinary," he said.

"You've known from the beginning, haven't you?" I asked him.

"Well, maybe not from the very beginning. I don't know what he wrote, but from what he described, it wasn't exactly an instantaneous thing. Of course, no one knew anything, although we had a nurse back then, Mrs. Gordon, Nadine Gordon, who had deep enough suspicions to question some of the therapy. Actually, I think she had a crush on your father herself. She left about five months before you were born. She gave no reason, just her notice, and as far as I knew, neither your father nor anyone else at the clinic has ever heard from her.

"Look," he continued, "I'm not going to say it didn't border on unethical and certainly unprofessional. If it had involved anyone else but your father, I wouldn't say 'border.' I would say flatly that's what it was, and if the physician was under me, he would have been fired on the spot, but . . ."

"But what, Dr. Price?"

"But I do believe your father made every effort for it not to happen the way it did. He even tried moving her to my patient load, but she began to regress badly, and we made the medical decision to shift her back to him. I might add they were both equally unhappy, anyway. The doctor was taking on the symptoms of the patient."

"What were her symptoms, Dr. Price?"

He raised his eyebrows. "Now, Willow, you know what patient-doctor confidentiality means."

"But this is different. We're talking about the woman who was my real mother," I pointed out.

"Only biologically. You had no relationship with her, and it was a long time ago. She has a new life. It wouldn't be right to dig up her past, now, would it?"

I stared at him and then turned away. "I don't know if you knew much about my childhood here, Dr. Price," I said, looking out at the sprawling lawn and woods in the distance. "My adoptive mother didn't know I was really my father's child, but she knew I was born in the clinic and that my biological mother, as you call her, was a patient in that clinic. I grew up with her waiting for me to act out, have a breakdown, dance naked in the streets, whatever. Every child has imaginary friends, but she interpreted it as the beginning of schizophrenia. If I cried, I was paranoid; if I was shy, I was depressed; on and on until . . ."

"Until what?"

"Until I began to wonder about myself. I know that there are some forms of mental illness that can be inherited. I have a right to know why my biological mother was in the clinic. What was her diagnosis, her prognosis? How is she doing now? Is she in a clinic somewhere else, for example?"

He leaned forward and stared at the ground. "I haven't looked at her file for years," he said.

"Is the day after tomorrow too soon for you to look again?" I asked. Tomorrow was Daddy's funeral.

He looked up sharply. "Are you returning to college immediately?"

"I expect to, yes," I said.

"Good. Perhaps we should go back inside," he suggested, rising.

I stood up, and he held out his arm. We started toward the house.

"Well?" I asked before we stepped back inside.

He nodded. "I'll look at her file the day after tomorrow."

"I'll stop by the clinic then," I said.

He shook his head and looked at me with a small smile playing on his lips. "There's no doubt in my mind you are the daughter of Claude De Beers. You have his grit and determination, that's for sure," he said.

"I think deep in my heart I knew. All these years, I knew. He told me in the way he gazed at me from time to time, the way he watched me at work and at play. I think he was afraid to tell me while my adoptive mother was alive, and afterward, I think he was afraid for exactly the reasons I'm asking you to look into my mother's files. He was afraid that once I found out what her problems were, I would live my whole life waiting for the second shoe to drop, expecting something similar to be wrong with myself and, perhaps because of that, never having a real relationship with anyone."

"Then maybe you are better off leaving well enough alone, Willow," he said.

"It's not well enough, Doctor," I said.

He nodded and then smiled. "Okay," he said. "Okay."

It was another exhausting day for me. Margaret Selby, on the other hand, seemed energized. According to her, everyone was excited about her upcoming wedding and grateful they had been invited. It was all she could talk about after everyone had left. Even Aunt Agnes looked embarrassed and finally told her to go to bed.

"Tomorrow will be a terrible day for us all, Margaret Selby. It will take strength."

"Yes," she said, and then brightened with the thought of calling Ashley and telling him about all the relatives who would attend their wedding.

I excused myself and headed back toward Daddy's office. Aunt Agnes followed.

"Just a minute, Willow," she called after me. I turned and waited for her to approach.

"Yes, Aunt Agnes?"

"I had a brief conversation with Mr. Bassinger and, of course, a long conversation with Mr. McRoe. Your father set up some intricate financial programs, trusts and corporate pensions and insurance policies. It's all very complicated. I want you to know I'll remain here for a few days and review it all with you," she said.

"I'm not remaining here for a few days, Aunt Agnes."

"What?"

"The morning after the funeral, I'm seeing Mr. Bassinger for a few hours, and then I'm heading back to college," I said, avoiding any mention of visiting the clinic.

"That's absolutely out of the question," she declared. "There is simply too much left to do."

"Miles will look after the house, and all the paperwork that is required will be completed. I have full faith in Mr. Bassinger to have it all laid out for me.

There is no need for you to bother. Whatever my father left to you, you'll get," I said dryly.

She pulled her shoulders back sharply. "I am certainly not in any way dependent upon anything he might have left me, nor am I some parasitic relative hovering over the bones. I can assure you that I am well off on my own. However, there are a number of things that were dear to my father and mother, and I would like to lay claim to some of that, if you don't object. They belong with me now. They should go with the relative who is truly tied to them," she added, which was her way of reminding me that I was adopted.

"Feel free to shop," I said, waving at the walls. "Just don't touch anything that was my father's."

I heard her suck in her breath as I turned and left her standing like a statue of ice in the hallway. Right after I entered Daddy's office, I locked the door again. I then proceeded to make a thorough search of his files and papers, hoping to find more references to Grace Montgomery.

Sifting through fat files filled with charts, evaluations of psychological studies, notes Daddy used for his own papers, and piles of articles and clippings he had hoarded over the years took hours, but I had the hope that there would be something well hidden, something sandwiched between documents.

After nearly two hours, I was about to give up when I separated an article on paranoid-schizophrenia from an article about the side effects of some new mood-enhancing drug and saw an envelope yellowed by time. It had no return address and had been sent to

Daddy at the clinic. On the bottom of the envelope, however, was the word *Personal*.

I sat on the floor in front of the file cabinet and stared at the envelope, my heart suddenly tripping. Footsteps outside the office door made me hesitate a moment. Then there was a knock.

"Yes?"

"I'm going to sleep now," Aunt Agnes said. "Is there anything you would like to know about tomorrow?"

"No," I said sharply, probably too sharply. She was silent.

"If you think of something, you can ask me in the morning. I'll be up early."

"Thank you," I said.

Once again, there was a pause, and then I heard her footsteps trail away down the corridor.

How I hated to have to be so secretive in my own home, but I had painfully discovered that this was a house in which shadows hovered in corners like small creatures embracing those secrets and keeping them in the dark for as long as they could. The walls were like sponges, soaking up the whispers, burying the sadness as deep down in the very foundation as possible. I felt as if I were peeling away one deception after another and drawing closer and closer to the truth. Would it free me, or would it chain me to an identity that was so heavy with trouble that I would be dragged under as well?

My trembling fingers opened the envelope and pulled out the tissue-thin letter within it. I opened it gently, afraid it would suddenly, through some magical curse, crumble into dust in my palms. The writing was nearly faded and gone. I had to move closer to the light to read.

Dear Claude,

I know we agreed I would not write or call you, but I had to thank you for the pictures of Willow and the letter you wrote describing her.

You were right. She is so beautiful.

Of course, I was worried about her, about what she would be like. You know my fears better than anyone, but from what you tell me about her, I feel confident I can put those fears aside. And this woman you described, this Isabella (or, as Willow calls her, Amou), sounds wonderful. I'm so happy you have her.

Of course, I have the pictures hidden where only I can see them.

How insane it sounds for me to tell you how much I miss the Willows. I suppose you and I turned it into a fantasyland, and I know how you feel about not facing reality.

I want to assure you I am doing fine.

I have my ocean to comfort and inspire me.

And I have our memories.

I am truly a wealthy woman again.

Love always,
Grace

I read and reread the letter four times. When you read things written by people you know, you can hear their voices. It's as if they are speaking to you. However, I had no idea what my real mother sounded like. I thought if I kept reading, if I studied each and every word, I might get some hint, some indication, some inflection. I was that desperate to know every detail about her.

Frustrated but fascinated, I put the letter in with my father's diary, taking great care to keep it as hidden as it was before, and then I went up to bed, growing increasingly anxious with every step I took that would bring me closer to morning and the funeral.

The funeral was even bigger than I had anticipated. Daddy's large obituary in the newspapers alerted not only his associates and businesspeople who had known him for years but also many of the families of his patients. I don't think I truly appreciated just how loved and respected he had been. It was quite overwhelming to see the seemingly endless line of cars, the crowd of mourners that spilled out of the church. Arrangements had to be made to put speakers on the doors so the mourners who couldn't get in could listen to the minister and to the eulogy delivered by Dr. Price.

After Daddy was laid to rest next to my adoptive mother, members of our family returned to the house for what would be their final expressions of sympathy and their goodbyes. The way my adoptive mother's brothers, sisters, nieces, and nephews talked about the funeral, someone would have thought it had been a theatrical event. It was as if they had to offer their reviews, from the flowers to the church service—even to how well the cars were organized along the funeral procession.

Later in the afternoon, after I had said goodbye to people I really didn't know, despite their relationship to us, Mr. Bassinger, Aunt Agnes, Margaret Selby, and I gathered in the living room, and he went through the main provisions of the will. He explained how Daddy had wisely set up trusts and protected the estate. I had inherited more money and property than I had anticipated, every added number widening Aunt Agnes's eyes until she looked as if her eyeballs would pop out and roll into her lap. Margaret Selby, on the other hand, was so bored she actually excused herself to make a phone call.

I was happy to see that the clinic would continue, that Daddy had carefully provided for a smooth transition. Dr. Price explained to me how there would be someone to fill Daddy's place, although, he emphasized, no one would ever do it as well as he had.

Not completely to my surprise, Aunt Agnes drew out a list of items she felt my father would have wanted her to have.

"Since they really were hand-me-downs from our parents," she emphasized.

It was quite an extensive list, even including some furniture. When she was finished reciting it, she looked up at Mr. Bassinger, who calmly said it was completely up to me. None of it legally belonged to her. She spun around, prepared to make a vigorous argument, when I smiled at her and said, "It's fine. Take it all, and enjoy it."

She was left speechless.

Mr. Bassinger bid me goodbye and promised to have all the paperwork prepared. We hugged, and he left. Not more than a half hour later, Margaret Selby and Aunt Agnes were at the front door as well. Their car had come to take them to the airport.

"I'll see to a van to take the items I have listed," she told me.

Almost for the fun of it and just to show her I was capable of being as cold and impersonal as she could be, I made her wait while I made a copy of her precious list.

"Miles will have this," I told her when I returned to the entryway. "He'll be sure it's all taken care of for you."

She took back the list and folded it into her purse. "My advice to you is to put the house on the market," she snapped.

"Thank you, Aunt Agnes. Actually, thank you for being here and doing all that you did," I added sincerely.

It warmed her eyes.

"Mama, can't we get going?" Margaret Selby begged. "We have so much more to do."

"Yes, yes, go on," she said, waving at the door.

Margaret Selby started out.

"You could say goodbye to your cousin, Margaret Selby. I know I've taught you proper manners."

"Oh. Sorry. I'm so occupied," Margaret Selby told me. She gave me a perfunctory kiss and hug and flew out the door.

"Do call me if you have any problems whatsoever, Willow," Aunt Agnes said.

"I will. Thank you."

She looked back at the house, and for a moment, I felt sorry for her. There were real tears in her eyes.

"It's very difficult to be the last one alive in your family. All the memories are painful."

"Weren't there good memories, precious memories, Aunt Agnes?"

"Yes, but they just make you realize how lonely you really are," she added prophetically. "Goodbye." She hugged me tighter than she ever had and then turned and hurried out after Margaret Selby. I stood in the doorway and watched their limousine go down the driveway.

Now that I was alone, I was able to retrieve Daddy's diary and my real mother's letter from the hiding place in Daddy's office. I brought them up to my room to pack with my other things for my return to school. Early in the evening, Allan called, and I described the day, the funeral, the way it all had ended. He listened patiently and assured me that when I returned tomorrow night, he would be there for me.

I mentioned nothing yet of my father's secret love and my real mother. I wanted to see Dr. Price first and learn whatever else I could from what was at the clinic. I hadn't decided what I would do with the information, anyway.

Before I went to sleep, Miles and I had some leftovers to eat. Over the last dozen or so years especially, he had become my father's most trusted companion. He talked about him with such affection I wondered if he were capable of staying there without him.

"Oh, don't worry none about that," he said. "Far as

I'm concerned, Dr. De Beers is just away and expecting me to have everything in tiptop shape when he comes home as usual," he declared, bringing a smile to my face. "But don't you worry about me and my future, either. When you want this house sold, you sell it. I'm fine. The doctor took good care of my future for me."

"I can't imagine this house without you in it, Miles, no matter who gets to own it."

"Well, I can't abide the idea of strangers in it, someone else in his office. I couldn't stay on, no matter what they offered me."

"I know." I gazed around the dining room. "Aunt Agnes might not be all wrong about it. Coming home and knowing he won't be here when I arrive is going to be hard."

Miles nodded. "I understand," he said. "He did a great deal for me and the memory of my poor baby."

"I know you did a lot for him as well, Miles."

"I'd like to think that," he said.

He was surprised and happy with the intensity of the hug and the kiss I gave him before I went up to sleep. Somehow, I felt I could touch my father through the people he had touched.

As I was preparing for bed, my phone rang. I expected it was probably Allan calling back to see if I was all right, but it wasn't. It was a greater and even more welcome surprise.

It was Amou, calling me from Rio de Janeiro.

"Willow," she said, "my cousin Tina called me a little while ago because she saw the story in the newspaper. I'm so sorry. He was a great man."

"Amou, how are you?"

"*Eu sou bem,* I am well for a *velha senhora,*" she said.

I laughed. "You'll never be an old lady to me, Amou."

"I wish you could tell my bones that," she said. "How are you now, Willow?"

"I'll be all right, Amou."

"You go back to college?"

"Yes."

"I'm sorry I wasn't there for you," she said.

"You were here, Amou. *Você está sempre em meu coração,*" I told her. It was something she always said to me. It meant "You are always in my heart."

She laughed. "Maybe someday when you are graduated, you come to Brazil," she said. "You almost speak the language."

"I will, Amou. I will."

"That will be a happy day for me. I know how hard it must be for you without a mama and a papa now."

I hesitated, and then I said it. "I am not without a mama, Amou."

She was quiet.

"You always knew that, didn't you, Amou?"

"Who told you this thing?" she asked.

"My father left me letters, his diary. He wanted me to know. He must have trusted you very much."

"He was afraid for you. You must be careful, Willow. A truth buried so long will not be the flower you wish or expect it would be. Some seeds are better left buried," she warned.

"Maybe, Amou. Maybe not."

"I worry for you," she said.

"And I worry for you," I replied.

She laughed. *"Vá com deus,"* she said.

"You go with God, too," I told her.

After I hung up, all the tears I had kept inside broke out. I thought I could soak the bed.

Somehow, I managed to get myself settled down and in bed under the blanket. And then, just as my Aunt Agnes had predicted, I shut off the lights and began to face the loneliest night of my life in my house of memories.

4

A Fateful Decision

The Willows was Daddy's baby from the beginning. He had been a practicing psychiatrist for nearly five years before he learned of a rather sophisticated rest home that was going out of business not more than fifteen miles from our estate in Spring City. He brought the investors together, and they visited the facility.

What attracted Daddy immediately was the location. The home had been constructed on a hill overlooking the Congaree River. The structure was surrounded with open field but also at least eight hundred acres of open pine woods composed of longleaf, loblolly, and pond pine. The woods contained a wide variety of ferns, legumes, and wildflowers.

It had always been a linchpin of Daddy's philosophy concerning therapy that nature and the immediate environment had a dramatic effect on the mental well-being of his patients. There was a peacefulness, calm and tranquility about the Willows that made it so attractive to him.

What gave it its name and what was so unique about it were the six wonderful weeping willow trees in the front that rose to heights of close to forty feet. The original owners considered them to be the most romantic trees because of how gracefully they bowed and stirred with the breeze. The branches were full of olive-green leaves that hung in pendulous curtains to the ground.

Behind them, the building loomed. It was eclectic in style, with a number of Italian Renaissance features and a unique recessed porch that always made me feel as if I were entering a tunnel or some dark, mysterious world. It was a three-story building that had been expanded over the years.

Mainly because of the way my adoptive mother characterized Daddy's clinic as a building full of insanity, I had always been afraid to go there. My heart would pound just approaching the property. Daddy was very careful to keep me away from any direct contact with patients who had severe problems. And despite what my A.M. said, the people I saw enjoying the lounge, watching television, playing board games, or just reading generally didn't look any stranger to me than the people I saw on the outside. Still, I was afraid to look directly at them for long. Once, I caught sight of a young girl, probably no more than fifteen, marching through the hallway angrily, her long black hair stringy and knotted, her hands clenched into fists, and her arms extended and locked at the elbows. She turned her head toward me as if she could feel my eyes on her, and I gasped because her eyes were wide and furious. The attendant moved her along, and as she disappeared around a corner, I could see her shoulders lifting as if her whole upper body were going to break away and float to the ceiling.

I had a nightmare about it and woke up crying. My adoptive mother bawled out Daddy, warning him that he would only nurture the disturbances within me if he brought me back to that world. She loved to say that, "back to that world," as if I could actually recall my birth in the clinic.

Even now, even after all these years, I could feel the trembling in my body as I drove into the parking area. I actually had trouble breathing and had to sit in the car for a moment after I had turned off the engine. I took as deep a breath as I could and stepped out. With my head down, just like when I was a little girl walking toward that entrance, I started for the building.

For as long as I could remember, Edith Hamilton had been the receptionist. She sat behind a horseshoe-shaped desk, now covered with computer equipment. The sixty-year-old woman smiled at the sight of me. She had dark brown eyes and hair that was becoming completely Confederate gray. She kept it styled short and neat, almost like a helmet. At the funeral yesterday, she was crying harder than most. I recalled how my adoptive mother had accused Daddy of encouraging Edith to have a crush on him.

"No woman dotes on a man as much as she does without fantasizing about him in bed," she declared.

Of course, Daddy denied it all. Now, I thought to myself how ironic it was that my adoptive mother had accused Daddy of harboring romances in his clinic. If only she had known how close to the truth she was, I thought.

"How are you, dear?" Miss Hamilton asked as I approached. She came around her desk to embrace me. Just the sight of me brought tears to her eyes, and that brought tears to mine.

"I'm all right, Edith."

She always insisted I call her Edith. She was a divorced woman who had returned to her maiden name but insisted I call her Edith, even when I was only six or seven years old. Her marriage hadn't lasted a year, and she had never found anyone after that. I wondered if perhaps she had gone to Daddy for some sort of counseling—and maybe my adoptive mother was right, regardless of what Daddy thought; maybe Edith had dreamed of being with him and let that fantasy take control of her life. Here I was being an amateur psychoanalyst already, I thought, and laughed at myself.

"Dr. Price is waiting for you," she told me. "You know where his office is now?"

"Yes," I said. He had moved to the office adjacent to Daddy's a few years ago.

I started for it. It was just a habit of mine now to walk through the corridors without moving my head very much. I had never wanted to look to the right or left, into the recreational rooms or the small cafeteria, to see the patients. But today I couldn't help thinking my mother was here once, sitting at that card table or working on her arts and crafts. Maybe she was like that woman seated in front of the window, looking at it as if it were a television set. In her mind, she could be seeing some of her favorite programs. How odd all this was to me in light of what I now knew.

I knocked on Dr. Price's office door and entered. He was standing by the window with his hands behind his back and turned to smile at me.

"When you drove up in your father's car just now, I had the wild fantasy that everything that has happened was just a nightmare and he would be stepping out of the automobile."

"How I wish that were true," I said.

He nodded. "Going back to college today?"

"I expect to, yes."

"That's good. Get right back into the ebb and flow of things, occupy your mind, stay busy. That's what I'm doing, whether I like it or not," he said, nodding at a pile of folders on the corner of his desk. "We're at full capacity, you know."

"I don't know whether to say that's good or bad."

He laughed. "You're right, a doctor with no patients would starve. Police need crooks; mechanics need broken-down cars; doctors need sick people. I suppose you could divide the world between people who make a living off someone else's trouble and misery and those who make a living off people's extravagances. I should sell jewelry," he quipped, and I laughed again.

We were both obviously very nervous.

"I'll let you read this," he said, putting his hands on a folder at the center of his desk. "I have to see a few patients, and that will take a while. When I return, I'll

try to answer any questions you might have, and then I
sincerely hope you put it all behind you, Willow.
Devote yourself to yourself now. That's my best advice, and I feel certain it would have been your father's
as well."

"Thank you, Dr. Price."

He stared at me a moment and then handed me my
mother's file. Under my breast, my heart sounded like
heavy rain against a window. I sat on the leather settee.
Dr. Price took one more glance at me and left the office. I was alone with the truth.

I remember when I was in my early teens, I found one
of Daddy's patient folders on a table in the den. I knew it
was supposed to be very private. It was like looking into
someone's head, as if you had Superman's X-ray vision
but could see more than just a brain; you could see that
person's very thoughts, dreams, memories, and fantasies. What was more private than your thoughts? What
trust or what great and desperate need it took to be honest about them! To tell another person, a stranger, who
was supposedly trained not to react as any other person
would, not to laugh at you or look at you strangely and
make you feel foolish. You couldn't be more naked.

I was terrified I'd be discovered if I looked into that
folder, but the temptation was too great. My adoptive
mother was always telling me I was on the verge of becoming one of Daddy's patients. Here was one. How
alike were we?

Taking care to be sure no one would see me do it, I
had opened the folder and begun to read. It was very
disappointing. The writing was so technical, I didn't

understand much at all. I knew it was about a seven-teen-year-old boy who had a schizophrenic disorder. He believed his parents had conspired with television producers, radio producers, and music producers to control him and as a result suffered a psychosomatic hearing disorder. In other words, he was deaf.

Reading that had put such terror and fear in my heart, I felt as if my fingers were burned by the pages and shut the folder as quickly as I could. Would such a horrible thing happen to me? Was my adoptive mother right? What had I inherited? What horrible mental illness waited outside my door looking for an opportunity to take hold of me and turn me into a name on a folder like this?

I was afraid to ask Daddy about any of it, afraid to let him know I had snuck a peek at one of his very private folders, and yet I longed to be reassured. Surely, he sensed it in my questions. Years later, on one of our walks together after my adoptive mother's death, I confessed about the folder. He laughed and said, "I had a suspicion you were into that one, worrying about your hearing, your sight, afraid you might wake up one morning and be unable to speak."

"Whatever happened to that boy, Daddy?" I asked.

"I'm happy to say we were able to move him on to a residence house where he continued to make slow progress toward a normal life. He was very intelligent and quite a challenge. There were some medications that helped and medications he has to remain on for the rest of his life, I'm afraid; but it's good to have drugs that can help people like him."

I had wanted to ask him about my real mother then, but I was actually afraid of the answers. I didn't know he was my real father, of course. It might have been different for me if I had known. I might have asked. But back then, I didn't want to know what was possible in my future, and I knew if I learned about her, I would be forever expecting some terrible thing to happen to me. It was better to remain in the dark about it—which was really Amou's advice the night before, I thought as I contemplated the folder now in my hands.

However, I had come too far, and Daddy's romance gave me a sense of some security. He couldn't fall in love with someone who was as sick as that young man, could he? She had left the clinic. She had been cured, hadn't she? She was certainly capable of a great love affair. I was no longer afraid.

I opened the folder and read about Grace Montgomery's history of depression, which brought her to Daddy's clinic when she was just twenty-five. She had been referred by a Dr. Donald Anderson, who had a psychiatric practice in Palm Beach, Florida. After some psychoanalysis, she revealed her stepfather often behaved inappropriately. This grew to the point where he forced himself on her, and she became pregnant.

She apparently kept her pregnancy hidden because of her own embarrassment and feelings of failure. Toward the end of her pregnancy, she was practically kept under house arrest by her mother; then she delivered and went into a deeper depression. She had been treated with various drugs for some time before finally being referred to Daddy.

She was suffering all the symptoms of acute melancholia: low self-esteem, inability to find pleasure in anything, insomnia, and a tendency toward being suicidal. I read how Daddy adjusted her medications and soon began to make progress with her in therapy. The date of her release from the clinic was shortly after my own birthdate. With that was the simple notation that she had returned to her family in Palm Beach for follow-up as needed with Dr. Anderson.

Much of the folder contained technical medical data, lists of medications and dosages. Aside from the brief account of her history, there was little to give me a sense of who she was. There were no pictures and, other than the paraphrasing of some of the information she gave in the therapy sessions, no statements by her. I could have been reading any other dysfunctional person's psychological history.

I was sitting and thinking about all this when Dr. Price returned.

"What else can you tell me about her, Dr. Price?" I asked him immediately.

"Not much," he said. "Remember, she wasn't my patient really. She was your father's."

"Have you ever heard from her or about her since? I mean from her doctor in Palm Beach?"

"No. My guess is that was a decision your father and she had made," he added. He took the folder from me and sat behind his desk. "You have to remember, this was all quite a long time ago, Willow."

"I know. I'm nearly nineteen," I said.

He smiled.

"At least, from reading that, you can be reassured that you're not in the line of fire of some mental malady. Her problems were related to the behavior of the people around her. You've had quite a different upbringing."

I raised my eyebrows. "My adoptive mother could easily have filled every available room in this place, Dr. Price."

He laughed. "Yes, but your father was there and that wonderful housekeeper who was much more of a mother to you, anyway. What was her name?"

"Amou," I said.

He smiled. "That was your name for her. In other words, you had love in your home, the sort of love she"—he put his hand on my mother's folder—"apparently never had. Go on back to college, Willow. Make a life for yourself, and please, please keep in close touch with me."

I rose. "Thank you, Dr. Price."

We hugged, and he escorted me to the door.

"The day she left," he began.

"Yes?"

"Your father watched from under the willow trees. He stood out there and saw the car come for her. I was standing by my window looking out at him. I could feel the pain in his heart. It was that palpable, even from some distance. Her car left the grounds, and he turned and walked off and didn't return to his office for hours."

"That was Daddy . . . his precious walks."

"Yes, but I always admired him for his ability to lose so much and yet to rebound, to continue his great work, and to find purpose in life. You've got to do the same, Willow."

"I will," I promised.

"Good."

He kissed me goodbye, and I left the clinic after saying goodbye to Edith as well. I got into Daddy's car and drove away, imagining Daddy standing under the willow trees the day my mother left him forever and ever. She had left me, too, of course.

But I wasn't trapped the way Daddy was trapped. I wouldn't be left behind forever. I was suddenly very determined about that. The decision was made back in the clinic the moment I opened that folder.

I drove on.

I arrived back in Chapel Hill, North Carolina, early in the evening and went directly to my apartment. After I settled in, I called Allan.

"I'll be right over," he said the moment he heard my voice.

That filled my heart with joy. I needed him more than ever. He really did rush over, and in less than a quarter of an hour, he was at my door. The moment I opened it, he took me into his arms, and we kissed. He held me tightly, stroking my hair and telling me how much I had been in his thoughts. How I wished he had rushed over and held me like this before I had left.

"You poor kid," he said, leading me back into my small living room.

After my first year, I wanted to be on my own. Life in the dormitory was not terrible, but I wanted to be more serious about my studies than most of the girls around me. In so many ways, I felt older. I did think about finding a roommate to share the expenses, but I went ahead and found a decent two-bedroom apartment first, turning the second bedroom into a study for the time being. Maybe I was being too cautious, but I wanted a roommate who had the same strong focus that I had on a career for herself.

My seriousness about my career and education was one of the things Allan said drew me to him. He said we were so alike in our determination to make profitable use of our time and fulfill our ambitions. Other girls were fluff to him. He said their heads were full of cotton candy and they were as forgettable as a glass of club soda.

He pressed his forehead to mine and held my shoulders, something that always made me laugh.

"Are you all right?"

"Yes," I said, but in a small voice, the voice I had when I was five or six.

We went to the sofa.

"Losing both your parents before you're twenty." He sighed. "That's got to be terrible, even for someone who was adopted." He sat beside me, holding my hand.

We hadn't been dating very long before I told him I was an adopted child. I didn't tell him my mother was a patient in my father's clinic and that I was born there. Up until now, I was afraid to face that myself and was afraid of what Allan would think of me if he knew.

I didn't even have to tell him I was an adopted child. Maybe it wasn't politically smart, but I have always tried to be as honest with people as I could be, avoiding half-truths and little white lies that when strung together usually created enough falsity to hang yourself. I blamed all that on Daddy or his nearly obsessive determination to face reality and to avoid illusions. He had an effective way of getting me to be like him in that respect. Usually, he would ask a simple question in a very calm voice.

"That's not what you saw, now, was it, Willow?" Or "That's not what really happened, was it?"

Who else but someone so steeped in reality he couldn't live with the smallest of fantasies would send the love of his life away, refusing to fool himself and her about their future prospects together, even if it would mean a little more time to be with each other?

"A great deal happened while I was home for this terribly sad event, Allan," I began.

"I bet," he said. "You have anything cold to drink?" he asked, half listening to me. "My throat feels like ten-day-old bread." He jumped up, went into the kitchen, and opened the refrigerator. "I'm having a beer," he shouted back to me. "You want anything, Willow?"

"No."

He poured himself a glass and returned, smiling.

"I aced Heller's exam," he said. "He posted the grades this morning . . . one of his A++'s, and you know how hard it is to get that out of Heller. I don't think he gives out more than two or three a semester," he said proudly.

He brushed back some wild strands of his flaxen

blond hair and sprawled on the sofa, putting his legs over my lap. He sipped his beer and then laughed.

"What?"

"I half expected you would greet me with how right that Portuguese nanny of yours was about the dreads," he replied smiling.

"Well, she was, wasn't she?"

He shrugged. "Coincidence. I believe just about everything we ascribe to spiritual powers is basically just that. Anyway, it's over. You're here, and I'm going to do all I can to help you get back on track and stay on the dean's list," he continued. He drank more of his beer.

"I'm not going to do that just yet, Allan," I said. I moved his legs off my lap. They were getting heavy.

He sat up, annoyed. "Sure you are," he said firmly. "You'll get back into it. I'll see to it. I'll study with you, help you with any papers that are due, any research. There's no reason for you not to get right on track again. You know, when the going gets tough, the tough get going."

He downed the remainder of his beer.

"What you need is a little cuddling and loving, honey. Just listen to the love doctor himself." He reached around my shoulders to embrace me and pull me closer to him. He started to nudge my neck with his lips and let his hand drop down over my breast.

I put my hands on his chest and pushed back. "You don't understand what I'm telling you, Allan."

"Well, then, what are you telling me?" he asked with ribbons of anger trailing his words.

"I'm taking a leave from college. I decided on the way home."

"Huh?" He smiled, confused. "Just because your father died? Hey, let me tell you something, Willow. I didn't meet him but that one time, but I'm sure he wouldn't want you to do that. Besides, you can grieve only so long, and then you run out of tears and look around and realize you've got nothing intelligent to do with yourself. No, no, you'll stay in school, hear? Your father's gone, so I'll have to take over and give you the guidance he would have given you."

"I don't need a father figure, Allan. I'm capable of making my own decisions."

"Sure you are, but just not at the moment." He leaned toward me again, his smile widening with lust.

I kept my hand out to hold him away. "I'm not taking a leave to mourn my father's passing, Allan."

"I don't understand." He shook his head. "Why would you leave college now, in the middle of a semester? Why would you leave me?" he followed, raising his voice.

"I told you, a great deal happened back home," I began. I sat back and looked at the floor as I spoke. "My father had left instructions with the family lawyer to give me a diary he had written years ago."

"A diary?"

"Yes, a diary, a love story, actually. In it, he revealed who my real mother was."

"You're kidding, right?"

"No."

He dropped his smile so fast I thought I saw it fall to

the floor. "That doesn't sound very professional of him. Doesn't sound like good psychological practice."

"It had nothing to do with that in the end."

"How did he know who your mother was? Did he get the information from the agency?"

"No. My mother was one of his patients."

"Patients?" He sat back and grimaced. "You're kidding. One of his patients?"

"Yes. I always knew that my mother was one of his patients," I said.

"I don't remember you telling me that."

"I was always sensitive about it. I didn't lie to you. I just wasn't able to speak about it. My adoptive mother never let me forget it and always had me thinking something would be wrong with me."

He nodded. "I see," he said, and then realized what I had said. "But why did your father write a whole diary about it?"

"He wrote it because he wanted me to know and appreciate that he was really my father," I said quickly.

Once again, Allan stared for a long moment as the information settled in slowly. "What are you saying— your father had sex with one of his patients?"

"It wasn't just sex. It was a real love affair," I said.

He grimaced. "I never would have thought that about him. He was pretty well known and respected."

"It wasn't what you're making it sound like, Allan. He didn't take advantage of a patient. They fell in love. It was not a one-time thing."

He looked skeptical.

"I'm telling you the truth."

"His truth," he muttered.

"The truth!" I cried. "My father couldn't stomach a lie. He was incapable of it."

"He lied to your adoptive mother, didn't he? Or did he tell her what he had done, too?" he asked.

I felt the heat rising into my face. "That was different. That wasn't a lie, exactly."

"Well, what do you call it? Did he have some fancy psychological term for it?"

"You don't understand," I said. "They had a different sort of relationship after a few years."

He shrugged. "I'm not judging anyone. I'm just surprised to hear it, that's all." He thought a moment and then looked at me strangely.

"What?"

"What was wrong with your real mother? Was she a schizophrenic or something?"

"No. She suffered from acute depression," I said, "but she was cured enough to leave and return to her family, and that's why I'm taking a leave from my studies."

"I don't understand."

"I've decided to go to her, to find her, to get to know her," I explained.

"Well, why can't you do that later, after the school year ends?" he asked.

"I would just think about it all the time. It would be hard to concentrate on my work," I told him.

"So take a weekend or something and go introduce yourself to her."

"You don't get to know your real mother and her family over a weekend, Allan."

"It's a start."

"I feel it's something I've got to do. I was hoping you would be understanding and even supportive," I said.

His eyes grew small, dark. "Maybe you shouldn't give in to these impulses, Willow. Maybe it's not healthy."

"What do you mean?"

"Mental illness can be inherited, right? You could have inclinations, chemical imbalances like your real mother has. Maybe you should go see a psychiatrist now yourself."

I stared at him. Was he serious?

"Who else would decide on the spur of the moment to stop pursuing her career and go searching for a disturbed woman?" he continued.

"I'm not searching for a disturbed woman. I'm searching for my mother, the woman my father loved with all his heart. The man who wrote that diary was almost another man. I wish I could have known him that way, and I want to spend time with my mother because, through her, I think I can."

"He's dead, gone. What difference can it make now?"

"All the difference in the world to me," I said, the tears now burning under my lids.

"This is sick." He shook his head. "What am I supposed to do, wait around here while you go playing psychological detective all over the country? I thought we had a relationship," he moaned. How small he suddenly sounded to me, the man I once thought resembled my father, the man of strength and confidence and intelligence.

"I can't believe you don't understand," I said. I ground away the tears with my small fist. "I'm disappointed in you."

"You're disappointed in me? That's a laugh." He stood up and paced for a moment, glanced at me, and then stopped. "You'll feel differently in the morning," he decided. "It's all too traumatic at the moment."

"I don't think so, Allan."

"We'll see." I recognized the little smirk that invaded his face whenever he was becoming sexy. He stepped closer and reached out for me.

"I'm really very tired, Allan."

"So? Let me help you revive yourself."

"I just need a good night's sleep, I think."

"You always sleep better after we make love, Willow," he reminded me.

I started to shake my head when he seized my hand and pulled me up and into his arms.

"Allan, please," I said. He gagged my next words with a kiss and kept his lips hard against mine to drive down any resistance.

"C'mon," he urged, tugging me toward my bedroom. "Let the doctor take over, Dr. Love Machine."

That was his nickname for himself.

He pulled me along.

"I don't feel right doing this now, Allan. It's too soon."

"Nonsense. The only way to get back with the living is to live."

"My heart won't be in it, Allan."

"That's all right. There are other parts of you that will," he said smugly.

"Stop it, Allan. I don't like you when you act like this."

"Like what? Loving you? Wanting you? What is wrong with you?"

He paused, and I pulled my hand from his.

"Nothing is wrong with me except I just lost my father and I'm feeling terrible about it. It takes time to get over a great sorrow. Fortunately for you, you haven't experienced anything like this yet. Your family is intact."

"Practicing your amateur psychology on me already, huh?" he said with a cold grin. "Just practice it on yourself. Tell yourself how much you need this, need me, want me, and let go," he urged.

He embraced me again, kissing me on the neck and lifting my sweater at the same time until his hands were over my breasts. He moaned and then dropped his arm under me and lifted me, holding me like a child.

"Allan, don't . . ."

He placed me on my bed, and before I could turn away, he was beside me, kissing me and fumbling with the zipper of my skirt. I seized his wrist.

"I don't want to do this now, Allan," I insisted.

He ignored me and tried to kiss me, but I turned away, and he froze.

"All right," he said suddenly, and backed away. He stood up and brushed down his shirt and his pants. "Fine. Soak in your misery and your sadness if you like, and don't let me try to help you."

"I appreciate your helping me, Allan, but let's just sit with each other and talk and—"

"Right. Sit and talk about adoptive mothers and real mothers and mentally ill mothers."

"Allan!"

"You know, Willow, it just might be that you really have inherited some of your mother's problems, that your terrible fears are justified. Maybe you even like being like this. I would certainly worry about having children with you," he added.

It was as if he had slashed me with a razor. I felt the blood rise to the surface all over my body and especially up my neck and into my face. I sat up and stared at him hard.

"Don't worry about it, Allan. You'll never have that concern. You and I will never have a child together."

He nodded. "Right," he said. "Okay. Go on. Quit school, and chase your madness all over the country."

He turned and stormed out of my bedroom. A moment later, I heard the door to my apartment open and slam closed behind him. Then there was a deep, heavy silence.

How many other doors would be slammed on me in the days, months, and years to come? I wondered.

I fell back onto my pillow and stared up at the ceiling. Allan had made me feel terrible, but I was doing what I had to do, I thought, and besides, what I feared would happen once he had learned the truth about me had happened. Maybe it was for the best. Maybe I was lucky to learn what he was really like now before it was too late.

That seemed reasonable, but it didn't help me to feel better. I cried as if another person I loved in my life had died, and then I got myself ready for bed.

I was up most of the night, tossing and turning over my decision and then planning how I would go about this search for my real mother. I looked wild and exhausted in the morning. Even a shower didn't help. Nevertheless, I had made up my mind and drove to school to see the dean of students, Anthony Thorne. Mrs. Schwartz made sure he made time for me.

Dean Thorne was a tall, dark-haired man with a great deal of charm and personality, the sort of man who seemed created for his position: smooth, politically astute, and as comfortable in his suit and tie behind his desk as he would be in a warm bath. I remembered thinking no one smiled with his eyes as well as he did—nor flirted with the coeds, either.

"Willow," he said, rising and extending his hand to me. "Please accept my sincere condolences. I read your father's obituary in the paper the other day. What an impressive man he must have been. I'm sure a great many people will be missing him."

"Thank you."

"How can I help you, Willow?" he said, and indicated I should take the seat in front of his desk.

"I want to take a leave of absence, Dean Thorne."

He nodded as he went back to his chair. He confronted so many student problems and complaints that he looked as if he wore the desk between him and the student like a suit of armor.

"At the end of the semester?"

"No, right now. I need to get excused from my classes without any penalty," I said.

"I see. You're not quite halfway through with the semester, but I suppose if you have a great deal of family business, family affairs to look after . . ."

"Yes," I said quickly.

"Well, I'm sorry about this. You're doing so well. I hate to see that interrupted for any reason. Isn't there any other way?"

"No," I said firmly.

He held his gaze on me a long moment and then leaned back in his chair, flashing that soft smile that showed a set of perfect white teeth, a mouth made for television toothpaste commercials.

"If it's a matter of some counseling, Willow, I can arrange for something."

"I don't think I'd have trouble finding psychological counseling if I needed it, Dean Thorne," I said, perhaps too bluntly. He actually winced.

"Of course. That's logical. Well, then, if it's a firm decision on your part, I'll write it up for your teachers and expect to see you here at the beginning of the next semester."

"Thank you," I said, rising.

He stood up and reached over the desk for my hand. He held it tightly. "Is it truly a firm decision? I have to be a little persistent," he explained with that famous smile, "or I'm not doing the job I was hired to do."

"It is."

I looked at his hand over mine, and he released it and stepped back, his head nodding and bobbing like those puppets people sometimes keep in the rear window of their automobiles. He held the smile until I walked out and closed the door softly behind me.

It was over and done.

I was on my way to meet my mother for the first time in my life. Even thinking it seemed weird.

And frightening.

I wondered if it would be just as frightening for her.

5

Welcome to Palm Beach

All I knew was that she had lived in Palm Beach, Florida. I didn't know if she was still there. If she was, I didn't think I could just knock on her door and announce, "Here I am, your long-lost daughter." This was something I had to do slowly, gradually, sensibly. It would be too much of a shock for both of us to do it any other way.

I didn't know anyone in Palm Beach and certainly no one I could trust to help me. I did know the name of the psychiatrist who had recommended my mother to Daddy, Dr. Anderson, whom I intended to see as soon as I arrived. I had concocted a cover story, and now I wondered if I was capable of carrying it off. I was going to pretend that I was on a work-research project for my studies. That way, I thought I might get him to help me without my having to tell him the truth and

Daddy's secret. I would soon discover how good an actress I could be, I supposed, how much I had learned from my adoptive mother.

Despite not living all that far away, I had never been to Palm Beach. My adoptive mother had visited with some friends. She often took vacations by herself, complaining that Daddy worked too hard and wouldn't take the time off, and she wasn't going to suffer because of him. Aside from the occasional shopping spree, I never traveled with her anywhere. The few times we took vacations when I was younger, we usually went to one of the Caribbean islands and once all the way to Hawaii, but Amou always came along to look after me. It was almost as if we were on a separate holiday, eating our meals apart from my parents and visiting sites children would appreciate.

To book my plane tickets and a hotel, I called my father's travel agent back in South Carolina. Every time I spoke with people who had known my father and, of course, knew what had happened to him, I heard the underlying tone of surprise in their voices at hearing mine and the underlying curiosity about what I was doing. My father had just passed away, and here I was asking his travel agent to make arrangements for me to visit one of the world's most famous luxury playgrounds. All of the travel agent's questions were attempts to solve the puzzle and satisfy her curiosity.

"How long will you be staying? It's expensive. Do you have to be in Palm Beach itself? I can find you very nice lodging in West Palm Beach," she suggested, "unless you have to be close to people you're meeting or something."

"No, I want to be in Palm Beach."

I thought it was important to dive right into what was, or had been, my mother's world. Daddy always said you can learn about people by learning about their environment first. What were the forces that shaped and influenced them? He was a strong believer in the effects of the social and physical world on the character and personality of his patients; that was why he had spent so much time learning about the families and, if possible, actually visiting their homes. Many of his colleagues were moving toward an emphasis on genetic and chemical influences while he remained firm in his beliefs.

"Well, I can find you a hotel that has apartment facilities, your own kitchen, if you like, and if you don't mind being a little distance from the beach and from Worth Avenue, I can save you a lot of money.

"If you want to be right in the Palm Beach world, I would probably look for a room at The Breakers or the Four Seasons, the Palm Beach Hilton. See what I mean? Upscale resorts like that. They're expensive," she warned. "That's why you have to tell me how long you intend on staying, what you want to do, et cetera."

Her questions did set me back for a moment. Really, what was I doing? Was I falling under the hypnotic power of my fantasy, a dream in which I saw this beautiful woman who was so overwhelmed and excited by my appearance that she insisted I move in with her immediately and live in a plush Palm Beach estate? We would spend every day together, learning about each other. We would breakfast, lunch, and go to dinner at fine restaurants. In the afternoons, we would sit around her magnificent pool and talk and talk until we were both exhausted.

In the evening, we would take long walks on the beach together. With the ocean, silvery and calm, in the background, she would knit one story about my father into another, creating a tapestry of their history. She would make me laugh and cry. We would drink wine and listen to music and reminisce about him in ways I never dreamed, and in the end, we would love each other just the way a mother and daughter should love each other. Miraculously, I would make up for all the lost time without her and compensate for the hard life my adoptive mother had inflicted upon me. My real mother would feel just terrible about all that and declare firmly that she and my father had made a mistake.

"We should have taken them all on," she would say. "We should have defied everyone and remained together. He would have gotten a divorce and maybe moved down here to start his career all over. We would have been a family, a real family."

"We will be," I would tell her, and quickly plug up the leak in our dam of newfound happiness that kept out all the sorrow of the past. She would smile, and we would walk on, hand in hand, both of us wrapped in contentment, protected, saved. This was truly Daddy's greatest legacy to me, his gift of a new life and a new family.

"No," I told the travel agent. "I'm not interested in any small apartment. Book me a room in The Breakers for a week," I said decisively. I remembered my adoptive mother had stayed there every time she had gone to Palm Beach. I wasn't going to treat myself any

worse than she had treated herself. "I'll see what I
need after that."

"I'll try, Willow, but you have to remember it's the
season down there. Even the three- and four-star hotels
get filled up quickly."

"You always managed to get what my father or my
mother needed," I reminded her. "I'm sure if you try
hard, you'll do it for me as well."

She was quiet a moment. "Of course," she said. "I
thought you were in college," she finally had the courage
to blurt. "Is there some sort of mid-semester break?"

"This is my telephone number," I replied instead of
answering her question. "Please call me back within
the hour."

Was everyone's life so dull that they just had to
poke their noses into mine, or anyone else's for that
matter? People like her resembled pigs to me, pigs dip-
ping their snouts in the trough of gossip.

"I'll get right on it," she said, her voice smarting
from the rebuff.

She called back in twenty minutes, sounding surprised herself that she had been able to get me into the
hotel at such a late hour.

"Someone must have canceled at the last moment.
You're lucky."

"Yes, I'm lucky," I said dryly. "Please arrange for a
car for me as well."

"Do you want a convertible?"

She was offering me luxury now almost as a punish-
ment for daring to be happy so quickly.

"It's not important," I said.

Right after I made my travel arrangements, I called and made an appointment with Dr. Anderson. He knew who I was, of course and, according to his secretary, had moved his schedule around to accommodate me.

It occurred to me after I hung up that he probably thought I wanted to see him for sorrow counseling. He surely knew by now that my father had died. He was adjusting his workload as a professional courtesy. *Who knows,* I thought, *maybe I do need counseling.* Maybe Allan wasn't all wrong. I certainly had a right to question my own sanity after learning all the secrets buried in my home and my father's past. I was like someone in a boat rocked so hard I was still spinning even in calm waters.

Not knowing how long I would actually be staying in Palm Beach, I didn't know how much to pack, but I ended up with two suitcases. It was only when I turned to leave my small college apartment that the enormity of what I was attempting to do weighed on me. Would I make a total fool of myself and come running back, too late to be reinstated in my classes? How could I ask for that, anyway? I'm in; I'm out; I'm in. Would everyone think I had gone mad? Dean Thorne looked as if he had thought so. Allan certainly did.

I was still smarting from that disappointment, but it was like getting a scratch after you had suffered a far more serious wound. I was too numb from what had happened to really feel the pain he had inflicted, even though I had hoped for and even expected his support. Instead, he had given me threats and ultimatums. He did leave me feeling I was a high-strung, emotionally unstable young woman, and that took from my vault of self-confidence, leaving me vulnerable and insecure just when I had to be the complete opposite.

It was a short flight to the West Palm Beach airport. My father's travel agent was right: it was the season and very busy. The airport was jammed with tourists from all over western Europe as well as the northern and midwestern United States. It took me nearly a half hour to get my luggage and then more than that to get my rental car. By the time I headed for Palm Beach itself, it was close to seven P.M.

I followed the directions the rental car agent had given me. They weren't difficult at all, but even so, when I crossed over the Flagler Bridge, named for one of the founders of this ritzy community, I looked for a sign and couldn't find one. I pulled over to the side and called to a woman who was walking what resembled a miniature hippopotamus. It had loose skin in thick, wrinkled folds, especially on its forehead. I later learned it was a very popular dog here, a Chinese shar-pei. The dog's leash as well as its collar seemed to be made of mink; the collar was also studded with jewels.

The woman stopped and turned to me. It was what I would consider a warm, humid evening, but she wore a chic designer knit pantsuit with a shawl over her shoulders and strutted in a pair of high-heeled shoes that looked rather formal for taking a dog for a walk. She pulled her head back as if my automobile smelled bad and said, "What is it?"

"I wanted to be sure I'm in Palm Beach," I said.

"Of course you're in Palm Beach. If you do not

know that, you certainly do not belong here," she replied through a mouth so tight she looked as if she had lockjaw. She turned and continued walking without offering any more assistance.

I smiled in astonishment, shook my head, and drove on, following the directions to the Breakers that I had been given at the rental car desk. I was soon driving the wide streets lined with tall coconut palm trees. If wealth had an aroma, it would undulate through the air around you in Palm Beach and make it impossible to breathe any other scent, I thought. I couldn't count how many chauffeur-driven limousines were parked along the streets or moving around me. I suddenly felt self-conscious driving a midsize, inexpensive rental. It was like going to a party in a pair of jeans and a blouse and finding out everyone else was formally dressed. Some pedestrians who looked my way appeared absolutely indignant. *It's just my imagination,* I told myself, *my imagination and my nervousness.*

Finally, The Breakers hotel came into view. The palms along the entrance were lit with colored spotlights, and the illuminated twin towers with pennants snapping in the breeze made it look more like a castle than a resort. Maybe I was entering a fantasy after all, I thought, falling through some tunnel like Alice in Wonderland.

The valet parking attendants and the porters swarmed over me when I pulled in. Moments later, I was at the desk, gazing around the lobby and wondering how I had gotten myself here, how I had left my tiny apartment heavy with sorrow and sadness and come so quickly to this glamorous place. The hand-painted ceilings, Venetian chandeliers, and fifteenth-century tapestries showed that the hotel's builders had clearly been heavily influenced by the Italian Renaissance.

What opulence, I thought. The Breakers was as luxurious a resort as any in the world. There were many women in fancy, expensive dresses and men in tuxedos and designer suits moving through the lobby, their laughter like music building the excitement around me. No wonder my father's travel agent was so interested in why I wanted to come here so soon after my father's passing. This was no stopover and no place for someone in mourning to use as a quiet retreat.

My room had an ocean view. For a few moments after the porter showed me my room and brought in my luggage, I stood by the window gazing. I was mesmerized by the sea. The sight of some vacationers walking on the beach and the sounds of the music I could hear below made me feel strangely invisible. I couldn't be part of all that I saw and heard—and yet, I was here.

I was hungry but decided to remain in my room and just order room service. I tried distracting myself with television, but my mind was determined to keep all my fears and questions streaking across the marquee of my attention. Had I made a terrible mistake? Was I foolish to leave school on an impulse? Was I wrong to ignore Amou and Dr. Price and Allan? What was I doing here?

I felt as twisted and knotted inside as a ball of rubber bands. Later, it seemed they were all stretching and snapping in my stomach. I was sorry I had eaten anything. Pretty soon, I vomited; then I curled up in the bed and cried until I welcomed the exhaustion that would carry me off into a few hours of sleep.

My eyes snapped open many times during the night, and when the sunlight penetrated the curtains, they opened again, but I was so groggy I forced myself to remain in bed. I fell back to sleep, a deeper sleep this time, and when I woke, I glanced at the clock and realized I had only a little more than a half hour to get over to Dr. Anderson's office.

Thrown into a panic, I rose, showered, and tried to dress and brush my hair all in less than fifteen minutes. Having any breakfast was out of the question. I barely had time to swallow a glass of water. I rushed out of my room and into the lobby. It took longer than I had anticipated getting my car, too. Mercedes, BMWs, and Rolls-Royces were all brought up before mine as if they had to get the well-to-do guests away before they were contaminated.

Finally, my car came, and I asked directions, trying desperately to absorb what I was being told. Nevertheless, I did get lost. Fortunately, I spotted a police car parked near a curb, and the officers directed me well enough to get me to Dr. Anderson's office only five minutes late.

When I shut off the engine, I took some deep breaths and glanced at myself in the visor mirror. I looked like a wild madwoman, just the sort of person who would be coming here, perhaps. I closed my eyes and swallowed back a lump. It was really like someone experiencing stagefright. For a moment, I couldn't move. Then I opened the car door and stepped out.

If ever there was an attempt to hide the real purpose of an office, this was it. The building looked like a residence, and there were no signs announcing whose offices were in there, nothing but simple nameplates near the front door. Apparently, a dentist and an accountant were in the same building. I went inside and found the door to Dr. Anderson's offices on my right.

Dr. Anderson's receptionist looked like someone who was on her way to a formal dinner party. She was at a computer, but she was wearing an elegant knit skirt suit and a pair of what looked like flawless diamond teardrop earrings. She was a very attractive woman, maybe in her mid-thirties, with soft blue eyes and straight, light brown hair.

"Willow De Beers?" she asked before I approached the desk.

"Yes. I'm sorry I'm a little late, but I got lost," I explained.

"Late?" She widened her smile. "Most of Dr. Anderson's patients consider twenty minutes to a half hour late to be on time. We build it into our schedule," she said. "Let me tell him you are here. He'll probably be surprised you're so close to your appointment," she added, and rose to knock on the inner office door. She opened it, leaned in, and announced my arrival.

My heart was thumping so hard I thought I wouldn't be able to take the next step. Would he be like Daddy and see right through my contrived story? But I couldn't very well tell him what my father had told only his closest associate and me in his diary. Who knew how he would react, what he would think? If my mother was still in some form of treatment, he might very well blame it on my father's actions, actions any other psychiatrist would certainly consider unprofessional.

I would be devastated if all I accomplished was to embarrass my father, even though he was gone. In fact, it would be even worse because he was no longer here to defend himself.

"Please show her in," I heard Dr. Anderson say. He had a deep baritone voice.

His receptionist nodded at me and stepped aside as I entered.

Dr. Anderson started around his light oak desk. Amou would call him *uma bebida longa de água,* "a long drink of water," I thought. He was well over six feet tall, probably six-foot-six or -seven, very slim with a prominent Adam's apple and a sharply jutting chin. His brown eyes were set deeply under a wide forehead, creased with small ripples that reached into his temples. He had a long thin nose but thick lips under a neatly trimmed mustache that had more red in it than brown—quite similar to my father's, actually. He extended his long hand to me.

"How do you do," he said. "Please," he added, practically tugging me to the soft leather chair in front of his desk. "I heard about your father only a few hours before you phoned my office," he explained, standing there for a moment and nodding at me. "I'm so sorry. He was actually somewhat of a mentor to me. I think

I've read everything he's written. What a loss to the world of psychiatric medicine."

"Thank you," I said.

He had a way of folding his arms over his chest and pressing back on his upper torso as if that were the only way he could keep his shoulders straight. Very tall people had a tendency to slouch and diminish the distance between themselves and everyone else, but his posture made him look like an old statue of a cigar-store Indian.

"How can I help you?" he asked, still not moving back to his chair.

Here I go, I thought, like some drama student about to step onto the stage for her first performance before a real audience.

"My father taught me that the only way to deal successfully with disappointments, sadness, tragedy, and defeats in life was to immerse yourself immediately in some productive activity. One thing he would definitely not want is for me to sit at home and mourn him for days and days and drop out of social and educational activities. He would say I was fanning the flames," I added. "Stoking the hot coals of my own misery."

"Yes," Dr. Anderson said, smiling as if he fondly recalled my father saying something similar to him, and then he started around his desk, which looked as if everything on it were arranged in some sort of geometric pattern.

I glanced around. Unlike Daddy's office, this looked like someone's sitting room at home. The curtains coordinated with the carpet and furniture, as well as the carefully chosen artwork, the vases, and even the artificial flowers that were in those vases. Everything was in harmony.

I told myself this was actually a place to treat patients, and therefore helping them feel comfortable was important. Daddy's was a work office; all that was in it was arranged for his needs and his pleasure.

"So how are you keeping yourself busy?" Dr. Anderson asked.

"I attend the University of North Carolina. I was in the middle of a project at school when he passed away."

Dr. Anderson nodded. His eyes seemed to move forward in his skull as he studied me. His staring without speaking began to make me even more nervous. As far as I knew, Daddy never made his patients feel like specimens caught under a microscope's lens. I remember one of his patients' fathers remarking that his daughter thought she was simply having an informal conversation with him. "You don't even realize you're telling him the most intimate things," she'd remarked.

"It was a work-study research project. I mean, it is, and it's very important to me," I told Dr. Anderson.

"What is your major?" he asked.

"Oh. Sorry. I am going into psychology."

"I should have guessed," he said, smiling. He put his elbows on his desk and pressed his palms against his chest, as if he were once again doing something to keep his shoulders back. "What's your project?"

"Well, it's a study of the wealthy and how they distinguish between the real and the unreal, the important and the unimportant events in their lives," I said, and held my breath in anticipation of his thinking it stupid or contrived.

Instead, he nodded and continued to smile, but I felt the need to elaborate.

"My question is whether money, so much money, creates bigger illusions and makes it more difficult to function down in the reality of everyday life."

"The old ivory tower, huh?"

"Yes, exactly," I said.

"Well, you're right to come to Palm Beach for that research. I can't think of a more representative capital of wealth, but if you're here to learn whether money corrupts or not, my dear Willow, I can assure you, it does."

"I'm sure you can, but that won't do for a thesis conclusion my teacher will accept, even if it comes directly from a prominent psychiatrist," I said, and he laughed.

"Well, I'm a bit relieved to know you're not here for sorrow therapy," he said, sitting back. "Not that I wouldn't have been more than happy to have helped you, but I'm not quite sure what I can do for your project."

"Well, considering my topic and my major, I thought there would be no one better to recommend me, give me a letter of introduction, perhaps, than one of the more prominent psychiatrists in Palm Beach. People are naturally very reticent to speak with strangers and give them the kinds of answers, sincere and truthful answers, I'll need."

He nodded. I noticed he liked little pauses in the conversation. He was a man who obviously measured his words carefully, who knew the importance they often carried even in what some would call small talk.

"Okay," he said. "I'd be happy to do that for you—depending on whom you want to meet, of course. In some cases, it might actually be disadvantageous to have my name associated with your project. There are people who still believe psychiatry is a voodoo art form."

"Yes, and for that reason, I would like to remain incognito."

"Incognito?"

"My father had a national reputation, published a great deal, was honored by governors, even a president. People would just naturally associate my name with his and might be very unwilling to talk because of the fear of being analyzed."

"Interesting. Yes," he said, nodding. "That's possible, I suppose, but I'm not sure most of the people you might meet here would know who he was."

"Still," I insisted, "it would be prudent to have a pseudonym, don't you think?"

"Maybe," he said thoughtfully. "Okay. What's your pseudonym?" he asked.

"Isabel Amou," I said. I thought it would be good luck to call myself that.

"Isabel Amou? Unusual name. Well, then, did your father help you design this project?"

"Yes. We talked about it, and he indicated he had some patients from Palm Beach from time to time and thought it would be a good place for the study."

Dr. Anderson nodded, still smiling, but his smile was a little less full.

"He recalled one family in particular, and I remember him saying you had referred this woman to his clinic."

I said it all quickly because I was afraid I might stutter and stumble.

"Oh?"

"And I wondered if she were still living here and if she were still in therapy with you and if she would be a good subject for my study."

"Well," he said, shaking his head, "that is quite an unusual request. I don't really know how to react to that. I thought you simply meant letters of introduction to prominent Palm Beach residents, but actual patients or families of patients, well . . ."

"I wouldn't ask you to tell me anything about her. My father didn't, of course. He just mentioned the family name, Montgomery. I think he called them one of 'the core,' is that right?" I asked quickly.

"Yes," Dr. Anderson said, laughing. "It's almost like the families who came over on the *Mayflower*. They are some of the original residents, the A-list, so to speak. He was correct about that."

I nodded, encouraged. "I believe he was going to call you for me right before he died."

"I see. Very unfortunate. He was still a young man," he added.

"Yes. Anyway, I wondered if that family is still living in Palm Beach."

"Well, yes, but the individual in question is not in therapy—at least not with me, that is. However, it probably wouldn't look right for me to go sending students to my patients' homes," he said, scrunching up his nose, "even ones with pseudonyms. I hope you understand."

"Oh, yes. I'm sorry. I didn't mean to put you in any uncomfortable position because of my project."

"Oh, no, it was perfectly correct for your father to think of sending you to speak to me about your topic." He thought a moment.

"What I could do," he continued, "is introduce you simply as what you are . . . someone writing a paper on Palm Beach society. You'll find a number of people who will want to talk to you about that. I'm sure you'll find your own leads after speaking to one or two individuals."

"Yes, I suppose so," I said, not hiding my disappointment.

"However, I can see why your father suggested her family to you," he added.

"You can?"

My heart began to pound. He didn't know anything. He couldn't know anything, could he? Of course, he could. He could have had sessions with her after she had left my father's clinic, and she might have told him everything.

"Yes, especially in light of the topic you are researching. That's a family that has lost its wealth and social standing but has managed to remain living here."

"Oh. How?"

"They have rented out their residence to another family." He thought and smiled. "A family," he continued, "who would be perfect subjects for your study."

"Really?"

"Yes. I guess there's no problem about your speaking to them," he said. "I will make a phone call for you."

"But . . ."

"I'm not sending you off on a wild goose chase. I'm sure they will be helpful. And I'd be happy to contribute myself, in a more general way, of course."

"Thank you."

"Is there anything I can answer for you right now in that regard? I've been here for most of my professional life," he added. "I've had some interesting situations I could speak about: patients who were so devastated by the deaths of their French poodles that they actually attempted suicide, for example. I had a woman, the wife of a prominent billionaire, who was convinced she could never buy and wear anything original. She had such an obsession about it, she wouldn't leave her home and lived like a mad recluse, dressing only in one of her mother's old ball gowns. That was a challenge. I made house calls. Where else but in Palm Beach can you find a therapist making house calls?" he added with a laugh. "By all rights, she should have been institutionalized, but they would sooner have kept her locked up in a room.

"So," he concluded, "please feel free to ask me anything you want."

He sat back, waiting for my brilliant inquiries. I could feel the panic swirling around within me, building into a tornado of hysteria.

"I think I'd like to see something of the world here first, get a sense of it so that I don't waste your time with generalities," I said.

He nodded but looked disappointed.

"I'd like permission to return as soon as I've begun my study," I quickly added.

"Absolutely. I'll find the time for you. I'd want to do it for your father," he said. "He did a great deal for me and was always available whenever I needed his expertise."

"Thank you."

I stood up, and he rose and came around the desk.

"I'll have my receptionist write out the address you need, and as I said, I'll make a call and alert these people that you are coming to see them. I'll try to think of one or two other people who would be of some value to your project. The rest will depend on your own talents and abilities."

"As it should," I said.

He smiled. "I see Dr. De Beers had a good influence on his own child. You are very fortunate to have grown up with him as a father, I'm sure."

"Yes, yes, I was," I said.

He opened the door and told the receptionist to write out the address for what he called Joya del Mar.

"Excuse me, but is that a hotel?" I asked the receptionist as she wrote on a slip of paper.

She looked up at Dr. Anderson, who laughed.

"No. You know you're in a core home in Palm Beach when the house and the grounds have a name. This one simply means "Jewel of the Sea." It has its own beach front. I suppose to most people in this country, it would look like a resort. But don't let me give any of this away," he said, winking. "You're about to discover another country, another world, which, as you might imagine, and as you just heard through some small examples, provides me with plenty of work."

His receptionist laughed.

I thanked them both and left.

Outside, I released all the hot, pent-up air in my lungs. I clutched the note with the address in my hand.

I had found out what I had come to find out.

My mother was still here. She was not in therapy. She was out there somewhere, waiting for something to fill the empty spot in her life and never imagining, perhaps, what it was she was waiting for. Would she be disappointed when I appeared on her doorstep? Would she be angry because I was threatening her new life, her very sanity, perhaps? Would I bring too much pain along with me?

Aside from that one letter in which she had remarked about the pictures of me my father had sent, there was no other evidence that she had tried to find out about me. Perhaps she had come to terms with it all. She had traveled past her regret and her sadness. What right did I have to bring her back to it?

6

Joya del Mar

I decided to return to The Breakers for some breakfast. My nerves kept me from having much of an appetite, but I knew I should eat something before attempting to do any more. For a while I sat sipping my coffee, nibbling on a danish, and staring at the slip of paper on which Dr. Anderson's secretary had written the address that had been my mother's. What would the people who lived there now tell me that would matter to me? Why bother with them at all?

Wasn't I wasting my time pretending to be a student doing a study of Palm Beach life? Shouldn't I just find out where my mother was and go directly to her, shock or no shock? Was I just procrastinating? Now that I was actually here and I had gone forward with my first steps, the tension had my fingers trembling so much that I almost spilled my coffee twice.

I sat there fighting with myself, truly a split personality.

One part of me was urging me to check out of the hotel immediately and just return to college.

Go home, the voice told me. *The dean will fix everything again. Your teachers, your friends, maybe even Allan would attribute your impulsive actions to the terrible grief following your father's death. After all, the woman you're attempting to see and get to know is really a stranger. What you're doing to her is unfair. Do you dare simply appear and explode in her face like some sort of bomb? What if you were responsible for driving her to another breakdown? Wouldn't the rest of her family blame you and hate you and rightly so? What good would you have accomplished? Could you accomplish more than simply satisfying your curiosity, anyway?*

The other side of me snapped back with just as much passion: *Your cowardice is making you selfish. Of course you should go. Why shouldn't she see you, get to know you and to know what happened during all these years? A real relationship is not a one-sided affair. You will give to her as much as, if not more than, she will give to you. Maybe not having you, not having a family, has left her a broken, lonely person. You have the power to repair that, to restore some meaning to her life, too. Couldn't it be that your father intended for you to do this someday? Why else would he have left you his diary?*

Who do you think you are? my counter self asked. *You can't do that, restore meaning to someone's life. You have enough trouble doing it for yourself, much less for someone else. You're carrying too much psy-*

chological baggage. You're like a handicapped person diving into the water to save a drowning victim.

Nonsense. Don't listen to that. You are your father's daughter. You have his backbone. You can do it.

"Excuse me," I heard a soft voice say. For a moment, I thought that was in my mind, too. "I know it's not any of my business, but are you all right, miss?"

I looked up and into the deepest, dark blue eyes I had ever seen. There was a brightness to them, a distinct glint of intelligence, but the way the young man lifted his eyebrows and curled his strong, straight lips at the corners indicated an underlying current of amusement in this handsome, well-tanned face. That complexion, his beautiful eyes, and his perfectly straight white teeth made the face seem positively electric, cinematic. His styled dark brown hair was just on the border between being distinguished and businesslike and a little wild, young, carefree.

He wasn't quite six feet tall, but he filled out his gray pinstriped suit jacket with athletic broad shoulders. It was a custom-made suit, fitted to his slim waist. I caught sight of a gold cufflink with a tiny diamond in the center. It glittered in the sunlight that seemed like a spotlight capturing both of us on some stage for the moment.

I saw him glance at another man at the table across from mine and wink. He, too, was in a suit and tie and looked about the same age, which I estimated to be thirty at the most.

"What?"

He widened his smile. "My associate and I couldn't help but notice how troubled you looked," he explained. "I should add that I am a trial attorney and make it my business to read people's faces, especially when they are on the witness stand or they are sitting in a jury. I'm very good at it. Can I help you in any way?"

"No," I said sharply.

That he was right about me suddenly annoyed me. I didn't like the fact that I was under observation, especially without my being aware of it. It was embarrassing. Had I been talking to myself? Were my lips moving? Did they think I was some sort of crackpot? The way my adoptive mother used to pounce on me if I spoke to my imaginary friends or my dolls came storming back.

I looked at this man and then at his friend again. What audacity!

"I'm usually not mistaken," he insisted when I didn't reply quickly enough for him.

"Well, you're not in a courtroom now," I said as sharply as I could. "And you are mistaken."

The humor and warmth in his eyes popped like a bubble, and those blues took on the steely, cold glint of someone who had been reprimanded. The speed with which he changed expression actually quickened my heartbeat.

"I didn't mean to be intrusive," he said, pulling back. "I'm sorry."

He turned quickly and returned to his table. His associate asked him something, but he shook his head and put his credit card on the bill. I tried not to look at them, but I was so self-conscious now. I signaled the waiter for my bill, signed it, and actually left before they paid theirs.

I was outside waiting for my car moments later. Out of the corner of my eye, I saw them approaching, but they didn't have to wait for their vehicle. They got into the gold Rolls-Royce Corniche convertible that had been parked nearby, glittering like a jeweled chariot in the sun. That, plus the self-satisfied grin on their faces, infuriated me as they drove off.

Minutes later, I got into my rental car and started for my mother's family property, hoping that whatever turmoil that arrogant young man had discerned in my face would not be as visible to anyone else I was about to meet.

Dr. Anderson's receptionist had scribbled some quick directions for me on the same slip of paper. Perusing the map the car rental agency had given me, I was able to find my way easily to South Ocean Boulevard. The majestic properties, walled estates well hidden by the sixty-foot-high hedges, reinforced what I had read in the Palm Beach magazine in my hotel room. These were homes built to be monuments to pleasure and privacy.

When I reached Joya del Mar, I was no less impressed. I pulled up to the walled gates which looked as if they locked away their inhabitants from the outside world forever. For a moment, I puzzled over how anyone announced his or her arrival. I saw a television camera in the top corner of the gate, but what was I supposed to do, wait here until someone looked at a monitor and saw I had pulled into the drive? Finally, I spotted what looked like a call box almost completely obscured by a pink bougainvillea bush. I had to get out to press the button. After a moment, I heard a man in a very irritable voice say, "Yes?"

"My name is Isabel Amou," I said. "Dr. Anderson was supposed to call to . . ."

"Yes, yes," I heard, in the same tone of impatience.

The entry groaned and started to part. I hurried back to my vehicle and watched the gates slowly open as if they were doing so reluctantly, against their better judgment. When they had parted and I was able to look into the estate, I truly thought I was entering the closest to heaven on earth man could create.

The mauve driveway looked as though it were swept and scrubbed after each and every car drove over it. It continued for what looked like a good third of a mile toward the Mediterranean-style pearl-white mansion that loomed against an azure sky. Against the walls of the grounds to my right and left, oleander bushes close to twenty feet high bloomed in salmon pink, red, and white blossoms, a startling sea of color. The grass over the grounds was more like fine green carpet, trimmed and cut so perfectly that one would think it was maintained by a small army of gardeners on their knees, each armed with a pair of scissors.

On my right was a very large pond with a fountain jetting over some smooth boulders. An egret was perched to the side of one of the boulders, standing on one leg, so still I thought at first it was a statue. Then it moved, and I smiled to myself.

Closer to the house, the royal coconut palm trees stood like sentinels lining the circular entry drive. In addition to the main building, the house spread over four pavilion-like structures punctuated by graceful arches. The entrance was under a loggia or arcade made of cast stone. I could see the ocean behind the house and another building down toward the beach.

My heart was thumping so hard, I had to sit quietly for a few moments before attempting to turn off the engine and get out of the car. I was here under false pretenses. What if these people saw right through me and asked me to leave? What if they made a big scene? Not only wouldn't I have met my real mother, but I would have embarrassed her without having met her and without her knowing I was here. I felt as if I were caught in some hurricane of my own making, spinning from one mistake to another. Once again, I thought I should turn right around and go home before it was too late and I was swimming in a pool of dark regret.

A knock on the passenger-side window caused me to jump and cry out in surprise because I was so deep in my own thoughts. A plump, short man with hair like Harpo Marx peered in at me, his chubby-fingered right hand shading his eyes. His nose widened with the lifting of his lips, so pink I thought he might be wearing lipstick.

He wore a tuxedo jacket and a bow tie. He gestured for me to roll down the window. I turned on the key and pressed the button for it.

"Thank you," he said, and wiped his forehead with the back of his right hand. "I'm sorry, but you must come in now if you're coming in. Mr. and Mrs. Eaton want to go to bed."

"Pardon me?"

"You are this Isabel Amou, are you not?"

"Yes," I said.

"Well, either get out and come in, or please drive away," he said in a voice wrapped in intolerance. He turned and started back toward the front entrance. He had a squat body and waddled like a duck, his wide hips swinging the tails of his tuxedo jacket as he moved along.

I got out and followed him. At the door, he turned, pressed his lips tightly, and nodded to indicate I should continue into the house. I paused in the large entryway. On the right was hung a tremendous tapestry depicting lords and ladies adoring Bacchus, the Greek-Roman god of wine. It looked like an authentic piece of fifteenth-century art, faded and distressed with time.

"This way," he said, gesturing to his right to direct me over the marble floors. Along the hallway were hung gold-leaf family crests. I wondered if they belonged to my mother's family or the tenant's.

Just ahead of us, I heard a loud female peal of laughter and then a man's voice saying, "She said that? How ticky-tacky."

My eyes were everywhere, nibbling at the grand art, the statuary, the frescoes, the marble-topped tables holding large Lladro and Lalique figurines, the Bristol crystal chandeliers, and the wall sconces with cherubs seemingly growing out of them. We passed two lavish Dresden urns and entered a sitting room with a coffered ceiling and more tapestries, frescoes, and paintings. Every bit of available floor and wall space was occupied with some valuable work of art.

Before me stood a large convex fireplace covered with a mosaic of colorful shards of tile. For a moment, I was so taken with everything in the house I didn't notice the couple sprawled on the circular sofa. At their feet was an oversized marble table holding two bottles of champagne in ice buckets and what looked like a silver tray of beluga caviar on crackers.

The man sat up. He wore an elegantly styled light gray tuxedo with dark gray pinstripes, gray satin lapels, and a round diamond where a bow tie ordinarily would be. He was a handsome man of about fifty, I thought, with streaks of gray at his temples, but none running through his wavy, thick sable hair. His lightly tanned face was still dark enough to contrast with and highlight his hazel eyes. Despite his narrow, lean face, there was a hint of an oncoming, not to be denied, double chin. He was not stout, but he was a good ten to fifteen pounds overweight. A smile of curiosity and some impishness formed first around his eyes and then softened his lips.

"Well, hello there," he said. "Welcome to Joya del Mar."

The woman beside him cackled. She was still somewhat slouched. She wore a light mauve silk crepe gown with spaghetti straps and a slit to her thigh that revealed a trim, attractive left leg. Off-white iridescent sequins and pearl flowers were sewn on the bodice of her dress. She had her shoes kicked off and stared at me with a silly grin on her face.

I thought she was a woman in her mid- to late forties who had held onto a youthful look, perhaps with the help of a cosmetic surgeon's magic wand. She had her long brown hair streaked vermilion and swept back from her face, a face with kitten features: small button nose, soft, pretty mouth, and cerulean eyes. A small dimple flashed in her left cheek.

"I'm sorry," I said. "I didn't know you were on your way someplace. Perhaps I could come back at another time and . . ."

They both laughed.

"On our way? Hardly," he said. "We've just come home."

"Oh."

"We were at the charity ball at Mar-a-Lago. You must have just arrived in Palm Beach if you didn't know that was being held last night."

"And this morning," his wife added.

They both laughed again.

"Yes, it did go well into the morning. As you see, we're having a little breakfast," he added, nodding at the tray of caviar and the champagne.

"Asher, perhaps you should introduce us," his wife suggested, "and offer the young lady a glass of shampoo."

"Champagne," Asher said. "I'm Asher Eaton, and this foolish woman beside me is my wife, Hope."

"Oh, please call me Bunny," she said, finally sitting up.

I smiled. "I'm Isabel Amou."

"Yes, we know. We received Dr. Anderson's call just as you walked in."

"Oh, I'm sorry," I said. "I didn't mean to burst in on you like this."

"It's all right. For ten minutes or so," Asher Eaton said. "After that, we must, like vampires, go to bed, I'm afraid. A bit too much of everything last night."

"And this morning," Bunny reminded him.

"And this morning. So, how about some champagne?" he asked, tipping the bottle toward a glass.

"No, thank you. It's still early for me," I said.

"Have a seat, please," he offered, holding his hand toward the settee across from them. "Are you a reporter or a writer?" he asked as soon as I sat.

"Oh, no, no, I'm still a college student," I said.

They stared a moment and then glanced at each other.

"Oh, we thought Dr. Anderson had said you were writing about Palm Beach society."

"I am, but it's a college project, a sociological study," I explained.

Mrs. Eaton's excitement deflated from her face like air out of a balloon. She sank back into her slouch. "I was wondering why you didn't bring a camera," she said. "Last Friday, we were featured in the *Shiny Sheet*," she added with pride.

I shook my head. "I'm afraid I'm not familiar with it."

"Of course you are. It's the *Palm Beach Daily News*. We just call it that because of the paper it's printed on," she said, almost snapping at me.

"Oh. Yes. Why were you featured?"

"We had an affair here," she said, shaking her head. "The event to raise funds for battered women. We raised two hundred and seventy-five thousand dollars. Really, I'm not quite sure why you've chosen us for your . . . what did you call it, study of Palm Beach society?"

"Why don't you give her a chance to explain it all, Bunny?"

"Fine," she said with a bit of a pout. Then her eyebrows rose, and her eyes widened. "It wasn't Dr. Anderson who recommended us, was it? I've never been in therapy, and neither has Asher, nor has either of our children. I mean, just because we've rented the property from Grace Montgomery . . . it would be like guilt by association, wouldn't it, Asher?"

"You're not giving the girl a chance," he repeated, and ate some caviar on a cracker.

"Who's Grace Montgomery?" I asked as casually as I could.

"Our landlord," Asher Eaton replied, and smiled at his wife. She widened her smile. "It's a mutually beneficial arrangement," he continued.

"I'll say," Bunny said. "If it weren't for us, she'd be living in Boca or, worse yet, Delray Beach in one of those retirement communities. You know," she continued, sitting up with some energy, "Florida is not, contrary to what everyone thinks, God's waiting room. There are people living here who are still very young and vigorous, and our social life compares with the social life anywhere, including Monte Carlo. Why, half my friends spend their summers in Monte Carlo."

"You're doing it again, Bunny," Asher said after sipping from his glass of champagne. "You're not giving the girl a chance to say anything, to explain."

"I'm tired," she moaned. "I didn't realize how tired I was."

"Perhaps I could speak with Mrs. Montgomery," I suggested. "Do you know where she is living?"

The two of them seemed to freeze for a moment. Then Bunny burst into laughter. "Where she's living? Why, dear, she's living in what was once the help's quarters down by the beach. Where else could she be living? We should be charging her rent," she told Asher.

"We've got a pretty good arrangement here, Bunny. You know that."

"I know, but it's still a bit of an embarrassment from time to time, especially when I have an outdoor party and worry that either she or that depressing son of hers will somehow come in contact with my guests," she said.

"Son?"

I remembered reading in the folder that she had been pregnant by her stepfather, but I wanted them to think I knew absolutely nothing about the Montgomery family.

"Yes," Bunny said. "She had a son with her stepfather, Kirby Scott. That's the truth, no matter what fiction she might tell you or anyone else, for that matter."

"What sort of fiction?" I asked.

"That Linden, that's her son, was really her mother's, Jackie Lee Houston Montgomery's, child," Asher said.

"Yes, poor dear Jackie Lee. She was childless with Winston, of course. The man was twenty-five years her senior, but a woman with a sixteen-year-old daughter from a previous marriage didn't have all that much choice, and besides, he was old money, one of the core families. Her first husband was a naval officer, Roland

Houston. When he was killed in a helicopter accident, she came to Palm Beach with her daughter to start over, and even though Winston was twenty-five years older, he . . ."

"Twenty-seven," Asher interrupted.

"What?"

"Winston Montgomery was twenty-seven years older than Jackie Lee Houston," Asher corrected.

"Twenty-seven, twenty-eight, what's the difference? He died five or six years into their marriage, and she took up with Kirby, who seduced Grace, who was a dark, depressing girl to begin with. She actually ended up in a mental clinic for years, you know."

"Leaving Jackie Lee Houston Montgomery Scott to bring up Linden as if he were her own child and not her grandchild, by the way," Asher added. "Kirby ran her money out and deserted her and his child." Asher followed this with a very big and long yawn. "Got to get to bed. We have the Alzheimer Ball tonight, remember?"

He laughed. "Get it? Remember?"

"I got it, I got it," Bunny said, sitting up again.

"Then this Grace Montgomery and her son live in the beach house on this property?" I asked.

"Yes. Linden can be found down at the beach most of the time, painting. He fancies himself something of an artist, but you'd have to be in a deep depression to want to buy one of his pictures. They all look like nightmares, the ones you get after eating too much spicy food," Bunny said.

"So let me understand this," Asher said. "You're here to study Palm Beach society the same way a sociologist might study some primitive tribe or something?"

"Something like that," I said, smiling.

"Interesting."

"Yes, very," we heard, and all turned toward the entryway, where stood the arrogant but handsome man I had told off back at the Breakers. I couldn't imagine what he was doing here. Had he followed me?

"Thatcher, you're just in time to rescue us from being put under a sociological microscope," Asher Eaton said.

"Really? Well, rescuing people is my business," he said, still holding his smile on me like a flashlight.

All I could do was stare back.

"Good," Asher said. "Let me introduce you, then. Isabel, this is our son, Thatcher Eaton."

"We've met," Thatcher Eaton said before I could. "Sort of, that is."

"Really? How?" Bunny Eaton asked, now perking up again. "You must have been visiting the courthouse first, then. He practically lives there," she said.

"Mother, really."

"A more dedicated, determined workaholic you won't find anywhere, even in New York," she continued.

"Mother," he warned.

"I have been after him for years now to slow down, relax, and have some fun. One would think he came from one of those puritanical families, an entirely different world with different values and religious principles. He'll have to marry a librarian, and one who works in the law library at that," she continued. She looked very serious and very angry about it.

Thatcher sighed deeply and shook his head. "Look at the two of you. Did you just come home?" he asked. "I stopped by expressly to see if you two behaved, and, as I feared, you haven't. Again," he added, his eyes wide.

Asher stood up. "It's your mother. She doesn't know when to say 'uncle.' "

"Right, go on and blame it all on me. I have the wide shoulders. I can bear it," she said with great drama. Then she yawned so wide and long I thought it would last a full minute. "Let's go to bed, Asher. Miss . . . I'm sorry. What was your name?"

"Isabel Amou."

"Amou. Amou? What is that?"

"Portuguese," I said.

She raised her eyebrows. "Do we know anyone in Palm Beach who is Portuguese, Asher?"

"Only the Brazilian ambassador, Bunny."

"Oh, is he Portuguese?"

"That's what they speak, and that's where his family harks from, Portugal."

"Well, how am I supposed to remember that? If you're from Brazil, it seems to me you should speak Brazilian. Why else do they call it the Brazilian Court Hotel, for instance? Why don't they call it the Portuguese Court Hotel?"

Asher stared at her a moment. "I'm tired," he said. "Bunny."

"Good night, Thatcher," she said, and stopped to kiss him on the cheek. Then she turned back to me. "I do hope I'll see you when I'm more awake, Isabel," she said.

"Me, too," Asher said. "Come back tomorrow, say about brunch time, all right?"

"I'm not sure," I said.

"Of course you will," Thatcher volunteered for me. "I'll see to it, Dad."

"We'll have lobster, grilled," Asher promised. "And we can talk all about the social ills of Palm Beach society. I'll try to invite some criminals."

Bunny Eaton laughed and put her arm through his, leaning her head against his shoulder.

I watched the two of them leave. Thatcher and I confronted each other for a moment, and then he smiled.

"Look," he began, "if we weren't fated to meet like this, we wouldn't have met. I'm sorry I was showing off for my associate this morning."

"What did you do, bet that you could pick me up?"

"Something like that."

"Sorry to disappoint you and cause you to lose," I said.

"Oh, but I haven't. At least, not yet," he said, stepping closer.

"That's what you think," I said, and started out.

"Wait. Don't leave yet. Tell me more about your work. Really. Maybe I can help you. I know a lot about the people here. I represent many of them. I heard some of what Dad told you. I even represent our landlord, Mrs. Montgomery," he added.

That gave me enough pause to give him encouragement.

"Come on, sit for a while. You want something more sensible to drink, a soft drink, ice water?"

"Ice water would be nice," I said.

"Me, too. Jennings," he called, and the house servant who had come out to fetch me appeared as if he had been waiting in the wings. "Would you be so kind as to bring us both tumblers of ice water?"

"Very good, sir," Jennings said.

Thatcher sat where his father had been sitting, and I took my place on the settee again.

"So what is it you're up to, exactly?" Thatcher asked.

I hesitated. Somehow, I sensed that it would be far more difficult to fool him than it was to fool Dr. Anderson or Mr. and Mrs. Eaton. He seemed skeptical before he had heard even a word.

"I'm doing a research project for my sociology class, a study of different segments of our society. I decided to concentrate on the Palm Beach world because, from what I have read, it seems very different from the rest of America."

He laughed. "That, my dear Isabel, is the biggest understatement I have ever heard. Seems very different?"

I felt myself turn crimson. "I just meant it as a figure of speech," I said sharply.

"No, no, you're right. You just don't know how right you are. This is . . . more than another world. It's another planet. I concluded a lawsuit last week in which I represented a Palm Beach hotel that was being sued by a guest who had to keep her shar-pei in a recreational vehicle in the hotel parking lot. She ran the engine all night to keep up the air conditioner, and the engine stalled. The dog suffered in the heat for a few hours, and she brought it to a vet who said it was dehydrated. So she sued the hotel."

"And?"

"What do you think?" he asked. "The hotel offered to pay the vet bill and some ridiculous number to compensate her for her anxiety. Before that, I had to take the deposition of the vet, the parking lot attendants, and an expert on the recreational vehicle's engine and air conditioner."

He laughed. "It wasn't exactly what I envisioned I would be doing when I passed the bar exam."

"Then why did you do it?" I shot back.

Jennings brought us our tumblers of ice water, and I thanked him. He nodded and started to remove the champagne buckets and the tray of caviar. Thatcher sipped his water and waited until Jennings left.

"Money, I guess," he finally replied.

"You're a gun for hire?"

He laughed again. "Don't tell me you're one of those people who believes the responsibility for most of our social ills lies at the feet of the country's lawyers," he said.

I sipped my water. "Maybe not most. Only seventy to eighty percent."

That brought a loud, deep laugh. "How old are you?" he followed.

"Why?"

"You seem a little too self-assured for a co-ed. What year of college did you say you were in?"

"I didn't say."

"Well?"

"I'm in graduate studies," I said, trying to pull the words back into my mouth almost as soon as they left my lips. How many lies would my big lie beget?

"Graduate studies?" He shook his head. "The sort of project you're doing sounds like graduate level, all right. What are you aiming to become?"

"Psychologist," I said.

"Then you have come to the right place," he said. His eyes twinkled a bit, and then he put down his tumbler of water and stood up. "Would you like to see the grounds?"

I hesitated.

"You could ask me questions about Palm Beach society, and I'll give you truthful and full responses. Tape me, if you like," he said. "You do have a tape recorder, don't you?"

"No."

"I don't see a notebook, either. Committing everything to memory?"

"It was supposed to be an introductory meeting," I said quickly.

"Good idea," he said. "Establish rapport first. That's very smart, Miss Amou. Amou? Has to do with love, doesn't it? What an unusual name, or is it a name that fits your personality?"

"Maybe I shouldn't take up any more of your time."

"No, it's fine. I'm between things, and I need a break after the tiring case I just described," he said, smiling. "Come on. We'll go out through the loggia at the rear of the house."

I rose and walked with him.

"Most of the estate homes here were built in Mediterranean Revival, British Colonial, Georgian, Monterey, and Bermudan styles. As you can see from this home—mansion, I should say—they're all designed to take advantage of the weather, catching the breezes and the sunlight. That's why you usually have so many windows. This house with its rambling effect, the wings with varied roof heights, seems more like a small village, doesn't it?" he asked.

"Yes. You seem to know a great deal about Palm Beach."

"Born and bred, along with my older sister, Whitney. She's married to Hans Shugar, a trust baby who inherited the Shugar detergent fortune. It's a German company, but the products are sold throughout Europe and the Far East. They live on El Vedado, one of the Three Ells, three streets that run parallel from South Ocean Boulevard to Lake Worth . . . the neighborhood for the bluest of the blue bloods. Hans bought a mansion for four million and ripped it down to build their Georgian estate," he said with a bit of a smirk.

"You sound disapproving."

"My sister is beyond spoiled. She's in a class by herself. She wanted to live there, but there was no house she liked. You will soon discover that people here have a different view of money. It's almost an annoyance to have to go through a bank or exchange to get what you want. You get the feeling they believe they should be able to wave their hands, much less a wand, at whatever they want, and it should just come to them."

"I take it back. You're not disapproving. You're bitter. Why?"

He looked as if he were going to tell me something dreadful for a moment and then quickly smiled.

"No, not really. I'm amused. Well, there it is," he said, holding up his arm and sweeping it about as we stood on the patio. "The ocean. We have nearly two hundred feet of private beach, but the beach to the right is rarely used by anyone, so it's as good as having a thousand or more."

I gazed at the water and then looked over at the pool which had its own loggia that included a sitting area and a dining table. There were probably kings and queens in the world who didn't have as much as this or a home as beautiful, I thought.

As if he could read my thoughts, Thatcher added, "Before the Montgomery family came to own this, it was owned by a French count who modeled it after a home of his on the Côte d'Azur. Winston Montgomery added to the house and built that oversized beach house as a residence for servants."

I looked to my left at the building in which my real mother now resided with her son. Anywhere else in America, it would be a fine-looking home, but in the shadow of this exquisite and magnificent estate, it looked almost drab.

"What does she do?"

"Who?"

"Grace Montgomery," I said.

"Keeps house for her son and herself is all, I guess. She's a nice lady, quiet, keeps to herself. She's had a hard life."

"You said you represented the family. What did you do for them?"

"Oh, it had to do with the estate, other relatives who tried to get control of it, claiming she wasn't capable of making decisions . . . typical wealthy family infighting. I kept the wolves at bay," he concluded with some pride.

"I'd like to meet her," I said almost under my breath.

"That's not going to be easy. She's too shy a person to be the subject of any sort of study. I do have a number of people I could recommend, however. I think they would be perfect subjects for you, the type who are so eager to talk about themselves they'll reveal what would otherwise be the most embarrassing details of one's life and family."

I stared at the beach house.

He followed my gaze. "She rarely wanders off the property. Linden does their shopping."

"She sounds perfect for what I want," I said.

He pulled his head back and curled his lips. "What exactly is the title of your study?"

"The Psychological and Moral Implications of Extreme Wealth," I said.

"She doesn't fit the description anymore. She's what we call land rich, and it's heavily mortgaged at that. She doesn't attend the galas. She's been dropped from the A-list and doesn't get invited to any parties, except the ones my parents have here. She doesn't summer in Europe, and she doesn't feed off Worth Avenue boutiques and restaurants. She's not really a Palm Beach person anymore. She's actually a hermit," he declared. "Our sort of bag lady. She doesn't own any expensive jewelry. Her wardrobe, if she still has any, is practically antique. She walks around here in a housecoat and sandals whenever I do see her out during the day, which is a pity because she was once a very attractive lady. To the residents of high society, she's as good as dead—and that's not just because she was once in a mental clinic. Many people here are into one form of therapy or another. It's almost essential. She's persona non grata because she's poor now."

"You're making her sound more and more perfect to me," I told him.

"She won't talk to you," he insisted.

"Maybe if I just met her . . ."

"Boy, are you persistent. Okay," he said before I could respond. "I'll tell you what I'll do. I'll negotiate."

"Pardon me?"

"I'll introduce you to her if you'll agree to go to dinner with me tonight," he said.

"That's not negotiating. That's a form of blackmail," I snapped at him.

"All's fair in love and war," he quipped with that winning smile of his.

"You'd do this just to win a bet with your associate?"

"No. To win a bet with myself," he replied. "Besides, after meeting you, I've decided it's something I really want to do. Well?"

"Okay," I said after taking a deep breath. "Introduce me."

He smiled and nodded at the beach house. "Shall we?"

I suddenly felt so weak I wasn't sure I could walk

the distance. A moan escaped my lips, and he turned to see that my face was white.

"Hey, are you all right? Here, sit down a moment." He guided me to one of the chairs.

"I'm okay," I said.

"You look a little peaked. I saw you didn't eat much breakfast today. Aren't you well?"

"I'm fine, really. It's just travel and everything, especially not getting enough sleep."

"Let me get you something, some orange juice. That's what you need to do . . . raise your blood sugar level. No arguments. I'm a quasi-doctor after all the medical malpractice cases I've handled, and not only ones involving dogs," he added with a smile. "Just sit. I'll be right back," he insisted, and hurried into the house.

I closed my eyes and fought to get hold of myself. What a moment to show weakness, I thought. I took another deep breath, and when I opened my eyes again and looked out at the beach, I saw a young man in a white shirt and jeans trekking along, his head down. He carried an easel under his arm and a black leather case in his left hand. He was barefoot.

His blond hair was so bright in the sunshine it looked frosted. It was long, nearly to his shoulders, and hung limply over his ears and down the sides of his face. I couldn't see much of his face because he never lifted his head as he walked. He kept close enough to the sea to step into the trail of the waves as they spread over the sand and retreated.

"Ah," Thatcher said as he returned and saw the direction of my gaze. "Linden is returning home already.

Usually, he finds a spot out there and stays most of the day. Maybe he's hungry for lunch. Here." He placed the glass of orange juice in front of me. "Freshly squeezed. I saw to it myself."

"Thank you." I drank it. It was good.

"Linden!" he shouted. "Hey, Linden!"

The young man didn't lift his head.

"He hears me," Thatcher said, "but he couldn't care less. Sure you still want me to introduce you to that mad family?"

"Yes," I said after drinking the juice. "Please."

I stood up.

"All right. Right this way," he said, leading me down the steps from the loggia.

We crossed behind the pool. The water ran over a shelf of slate and looked absolutely delicious and inviting. It was practically the color of the ocean, too. Once again, Thatcher seemed to read my mind.

"It's a saltwater pool," he said. "Better for your skin. Anytime you want to take a dip . . ."

"Thank you."

"No problem. The rich are generous when it comes to showing off their wealth and property, you'll find. If you qualify as someone who will show her appreciation, that is."

"Why do you remain here if you find the people so superficial?" I asked him.

He stopped and looked at me and then at the sea. "I'm not sure I belong anywhere else," he said. "Maybe I'm a coward after all. That's what attracted me to you this morning," he added.

"What?"

"You looked like someone who belonged out there."
He nodded at the horizon.

"Out where?"

"There. The real world," he said. And then he added
something that practically rang bells in my heart.
"Grace Montgomery is like you that way. She's no
longer part of this place.

"Maybe she will talk to you," he concluded, and we
walked on toward the beach house, the bells still
sounding in my heart and in my bones.

7

Thatcher

The walkway between two rows of hedges led up to the much smaller loggia and the front entrance of the beach house. The building looked as if it had once been painted the same rich pearl white. Now the walls looked faded from the sea air. There were two second-floor balconies that faced the ocean, each with a set of potted palm trees, and vines ran along the sides of the building, reaching the tiled roof.

"Servants do well here," Thatcher said. "There are twenty rooms in the building, not including the dining room and two sitting rooms. My parents' servants live here as well, of course. That also makes the Montgomerys untouchables," he concluded with a tone of bitterness. "Living with servants.

"Okay, here we go," he said, and rang the door buzzer. No one came, so he rang it again. "They just might not respond at all," Thatcher said. "But it still counts as far as our bargain," he insisted.

That brought a smile to my face just as the door did open. Linden stood there gazing out at us. He was a fragile-looking young man with an immediately angry face. His straggly hair, which I had thought looked frosted, out of the sunlight looked pale yellow. The expression in his dark eyes, the turn of his lips, the way he held his body so stiffly with his hands tightened into fists, made him appear downright belligerent.

"What is it?" he demanded instead of any sort of civil greeting.

"We have an interesting guest who would love the opportunity to speak with your mother, if she is available," Thatcher said calmly.

"Why?" Linden demanded. He took a step toward us, trying to keep his eyes on Thatcher but dropping them to me. I thought I caught a note of some interest that overcame his suspicion. I was encouraged by it and smiled.

"This is Miss Isabel Amou. She is in graduate school, and she thinks speaking with your mother would be interesting and might help her with a project she has undertaken, Linden. It's nothing to be concerned about. I think you know by now that I wouldn't do anything that would cause your mother worry, but just the opposite, right?"

Thatcher was talking to him in a tone of voice that he might use to speak with a young contentious boy, trying to handle him the way Daddy might, I thought. Linden, however, continued to stand there like an immovable object, his features hardened, cold, full of distrust.

"I called to you before when we saw you walking home on the beach," Thatcher continued to fill the pregnant pause, "but I guess you couldn't hear me over the sound of the sea."

Linden looked at him with an expression that clearly indicated he had heard but didn't care to speak with Thatcher.

"What brings you in so early today?" Thatcher continued, determined not to permit any silences among us. "Didn't you catch anything artistic out there?"

He turned to me to explain. "Linden once told me he was a sort of fisherman, casting his artistic eyes at the sea like a rod to pull in his inspiration. Wasn't that how you put it, Linden?"

"It wasn't told so you could use it as something with which to amuse people," he replied.

"Oh, no, that's not what I'm doing. I'm truly impressed with what you said, and from the look on Miss Amou's face, I would conclude she is as well. Isn't that right, Miss Amou?"

"Yes," I said, looking from him to Linden. He studied me with a pair of eyes that looked capable of probing my very soul. What he saw didn't displease him. His narrow shoulders relaxed, and his lips softened.

"What is this project he speaks about?" Linden asked me.

"As he said, I'm a student doing a sociological project, a work-study assignment involving Palm Beach society," I began.

"We're not in Palm Beach society," Linden said sharply, his lips tight and bitter.

"Oh, but you are, Linden. One can't live here and not be part of that," Thatcher said.

"We can," Linden challenged. "It would be a waste of time to speak with my mother. She doesn't attend any functions or socialize with any of the royals," he added, his words so dry they drew the corners of his lips down.

"She has a history here, doesn't she?" Thatcher pursued. "Why don't you let her decide for herself, Linden? Miss Amou is not here to do anyone any harm. She's not writing for the *Shiny* or any other paper. This isn't an exposé. It's a legitimate study project. Your mother might actually enjoy speaking with her, Linden."

"I doubt it," Linden insisted.

"Well, why don't we at least let her make that decision?" Thatcher pursued.

I wasn't sure if Thatcher was not used to being denied anything or if he was trying to ingratiate himself with me, but whatever his motive, Linden was moved by his determination.

"You're just wasting your time," he said, relenting. "Wait here."

He turned and went into the house. Thatcher smiled at me. "Difficult young man. He scares most people, and not only with his art, which sells from time to time but not enough to command any real numbers for him. I can show you some pieces at a gallery on Worth Avenue, if you like."

"Yes, I would like that," I said quickly.

"I thought so. The dark, the disturbed, the dangerous are far more enticing than what we would call normal and level-headed, aren't they? It's why Iago is a far more interesting character in Shakespeare's *Othello* than Othello is himself. Don't you agree?" he asked with that impish little smile on his lips.

Despite my resistance, he was charming me. I could feel it through my body—this warm, titillating sensation sparking little fires of passion inside me where I had never imagined they would start. For a moment or two, it took my attention away from the dramatic meeting I was about to experience. *Talk about your kaleidoscope of emotions,* I thought. *I'm frightened, excited, and aroused all simultaneously.*

"He's right, though. Just as I told you, they really are out of it when it comes to Palm Beach social life. I'm afraid this isn't going to be very valuable for you."

If you only knew how valuable it was, I thought.

The sound of footsteps in the hallway seized my heart like a strong hand and squeezed the pounding down to a barely felt tap in my chest. She appeared from around the corner of the hallway. Her hair, the same color as mine, only streaked with some gray, was tied behind in a thick ponytail. She had a light complexion, and as she drew closer, I could see I had inherited my freckles from her. We had the same nose, the same turquoise eyes, but the shape of my face was closer to my father's.

Despite the simple way she wore her hair, the absence of any makeup, and the plain faded blue housecoat she wore, she had a quiet, truly angelic beauty. Her neck was slim, and all of her features had an almost childlike look; I was especially struck by the innocence and vulnerability in those eyes.

My adoptive mother would have been so disappointed, I thought. Regardless of the turmoil and difficulties in her life, my real mother looked relatively unscathed by age. With just some thin crow's-feet at the corners of her eyes, her complexion was milky smooth. She had a nice figure with a small waist and graceful hands. She wore no jewelry, no earrings, not even a wristwatch.

"Hello, Grace," Thatcher said quickly. "How are you?"

Her smile consisted solely of pulling in the corners of her lips slightly and a flash of brightness in her eyes. It was as if she were afraid of holding cheerfulness in her face too long, as if she distrusted it or the disappointments that often followed. Linden came up behind her, still glaring with some hostility at us.

"I'm fine, Thatcher," she said. Her voice was soft, nearly inaudible. "How can I help you?"

"I have someone who would like to meet you," he said, turning to me.

She then looked at me, and for a moment, her eyes widened with more than just curiosity. Her gaze was intense, deep, searching my face as if she had been looking for me for years and years, as if she knew. It drew the breath from my lungs. I almost expected her to ask if I was who she thought I was. I actually hoped she would so I could let the truth burst out and end this pathetic attempt to hide my true purpose from her and Linden.

"This is Isabel Amou," Thatcher continued. "She's doing a study of Palm Beach society as a class assignment."

"Amou?" she asked, her eyebrows lifting. She was still looking at me. I would finally have to speak.

"Yes," I said, nearly as breathless as she had been.

Her eyes narrowed with more suspicion, putting my heart into a quicker pitter-patter. "What is it you want from me?" she followed.

Thatcher smiled as if to say, *Well, I did my part. Now it's up to you.*

"I would just like to talk to you about your experiences living here," I said quickly. "Growing up so wealthy and . . ."

"Experiences?"

"You have a unique sort of history, and I thought your views about the Palm Beach world would be very informative and add to my work," I struggled to say. "It's not easy to find people with a distinctly different perspective and opinions."

She looked at me harder. My heart began to thump now. I could feel her closing in, the way her eyes perused my face, the way her lips began to open and pull back into that gentle smile. I held my breath. Was she just going to burst out and ask if I was Claude De Beers's daughter? Her daughter?

But before she could respond, Linden surged forward.

"This is ridiculous!" he cried, and came up beside her, practically nudging her out of the way. "What are we now, some sort of new species to be dissected? Are we being singled out because of our financial situation? Who put you up to this?" he demanded of me.

"No one! I just thought . . . I mean, when I learned about you, I . . ."

"So, there it is. You learned about us? People were talking about us, is that it? We were the subject of some gossip, and you thought you'd come here and exploit us."

"Linden," Thatcher said softly, "relax."

"No! How many times are we to be ridiculed in someone's column or living room, huh? How often are we supposed to be made to feel inferior because we are not invited to some ball or charity tea, huh?"

"I don't know anything about any of that," I said quickly. "I came here to speak to Mr. and Mrs. Eaton, and I learned about you, and—"

"There, you see!" Linden cried, shaking his right forefinger in the air between him and Thatcher. "Your parents turned her onto us, Thatcher. Pointed us out as some sort of freakish curiosity caged on the property."

"Take it easy, Linden," Thatcher said softly. "You know my parents don't do that, and besides, no one wants to upset either you or your mother here."

"Then get out," he said. "Leave us alone."

His face was crimson now, his eyes bulging and the veins in his neck straining.

"Please, don't upset yourself so, Linden," my mother begged him.

"Then tell them to go!" he shouted.

"Okay, Linden, okay," Thatcher said, reaching to

take my arm. "We're sorry we disturbed you, Grace. As you heard her say, the young lady was simply looking for a variety of views and approaches to Palm Beach society. No harm intended, believe me. I remember when I was a college student and I had to do some work-study. It's never easy to depend on the kindness of strangers," he concluded.

"I'm surprised we weren't offered some sort of fee," Linden muttered.

"Is that what you're looking for, Linden?" Thatcher fired back at him.

Linden's face seemed to drain instantly of blood, except for around his lips. "What do you think I am, a lawyer, charging people by the minute for every breath I take?" he shot back.

Thatcher laughed. "Okay. Sorry, Grace," he repeated, and urged me back and out of the house.

My mother had kept her eyes on me the whole time. My eyes never left her, either. An expression of pain crossed her face, and she almost stepped forward to stop us from leaving, but instantly Linden was between us and slammed the door sharply the moment we stepped out, shutting me off from my mother without my saying another word to her or her to me.

"I kind of warned you about that," Thatcher said, his face now free to reflect the anger he felt. "He's the one who should have been sent to a mental institution, not her. I feel sorry for her with that burden to carry."

He fired his words at the closed door and then turned to me.

"Hey, you all right?" he asked. "You look like you're trembling."

"Yes," I said, embracing myself and hurrying off the loggia and down the sidewalk. He caught up quickly.

"Hey, take it easy," he said, grabbing my arm. "Don't let that bother you. I'll set you up with some great subjects. You won't be able to stop them talking, and they'll talk about the most intimate details of their lives, too. Around here, some people wear their dysfunctional family life as if it were a badge of achievement or something."

I kept my head down as we continued to walk back to the main house.

"Take Helen Krescan, for example," he rattled on. "She knows her husband keeps his mistress on his yacht right here in the Palm Beach harbor. She complains about it in the beauty salon all the time, but does she move for a divorce? No. She'd rather bask in self-pity or use it for some notoriety. You'll love talking with her. She'll tell you about more than just her own husband. She knows dirt on all the husbands. You can meet with her tomorrow, if you'd like.

"Hey," he said when I didn't respond. "Are you all right?"

"Yes. I don't know. Maybe this project is a bad idea," I said.

"I don't think so. I think it would be great. Don't give up just because of that," he said, nodding back at the beach house.

"I should just leave," I muttered, more to myself than to him. I looked out at the ocean. There were sailboats now and someone's magnificent yacht, all so still against the horizon they looked unreal. It was more like a movie set, something painted.

It was too easy to slip into illusion and fantasy here, I thought. This place was too dangerous for me, especially now, when I was more vulnerable than ever.

"Out of the question," Thatcher said. "You can't leave. You have an agreement to fulfill, and don't forget, I'm an attorney. I'll come by for you at seven," he said. "Give it a day or two. You'll get back on track after you have one good interview. Believe me," he promised. "Besides, tomorrow you're due at my parents' brunch. A more authentic Palm Beach couple you won't find anywhere," he assured me. "They're spoiled, self-indulgent, vain, full of prejudices, but essentially harmless," he added.

I tilted my head and gazed at him curiously.

"What?" he asked.

"You don't respect your parents at all, do you?"

He thought a moment. "I guess I never took them seriously enough to do that." He gazed at the grand estate. "When you live in all this, when you're brought up here, you can lose sight of meaningful relationships rather easily. Let me put it to you this way," he said, looking more thoughtful than ever, "in most other places, love is something you can assume because it's already there for you. Here, it's something you have to find, discover under a pile of riches and luxury. Sometimes it's there, sometimes it's not, and when it's not, you just buy another Rolls or jet to Paris."

I stared at him, surprised at his frankness and sincerity. He looked uncomfortable under my scrutiny.

"Sorry I got so heavy," he said.

"No, it's all right. Maybe you're the best subject of all for my study," I blurted. It brought a smile to his face.

"I was hoping you would think that," he said. "Consider me at your disposal."

"A busy lawyer like you?" I teased. "What about your caseload?"

"Let's see," he said, squeezing his chin with his right hand as he thought. "The most pressing case I have right now is defending Harry Stevens, the flooring company billionaire whose yacht damaged the dock. The city wants him to rebuild the entire thing, and Harry is threatening to sue them. I think I might have a little spare time."

I laughed and continued on with him through the house and to my car.

"Just get some rest," he said. "I intend to show you a good time tonight and some of the real Palm Beach nightlife as well."

He closed the door for me and stood there watching me drive off. The gates opened like magical gates in an Arabian fairy tale. I drove out and watched them close behind me. I was back in the real world again, I thought, and my mother was behind those walls but, more significantly, behind the walls of her own sadness and disappointment as well.

What a mistake I've made, I concluded. *I should have been honest from the beginning. I should have confronted her with the truth instead of this con-*

trivance which just exploded in my face in front of her.
She looked as if she would have welcomed me. I could
feel it in her gaze.

And now there was Linden to contend with, whose
confidence and trust would be that much more impossible to win. If and when I told the truth, he might believe that was a lie as well, or at least that my motives
were false. Would he ever, could he ever, welcome me
as his half-sister? I had never seen such trouble and
pain in a young man's eyes, not even at Daddy's clinic.
Why was he in such mental anguish? Was it something
he had inherited from our mother? Would I ever know?
Were there secrets even darker and deeper than the
ones I already knew?

Despite what Thatcher had ridiculed as the eagerness of people to reveal their social embarrassments,
perhaps the walls were really so high here not to keep
things from outside coming in but to keep certain
truths hidden inside. After all, the richer they were, the
tighter the doors, the stronger the locks, the thicker the
safes, and the darker and deeper the shadows looming
like cobwebs in the corners of their mansions.

Hunger and the need to relieve the intensity of my
quest led me back to the hotel, where I changed and
went down to the poolside to get some lunch. Afterward, I decided to buy a bathing suit, since I hadn't
brought one along, and found a quiet corner to lounge
in the shade and get some rest and think. For a while, I
was able to turn off the sounds of other guests, the
laughter of children, the music, and all that was around

me. I fell asleep and then woke abruptly, sensing someone nearby. When I opened my eyes, I saw a man, well into his sixties, if not seventy, standing next to my lounge chair and gazing at me. He held a tall glass with a small yellow paper umbrella sticking out of the top of it. When I opened my eyes, he rained a smile down on me as if he were some long-lost relative who had just found me.

"Yes?" I asked. "Can I help you?"

"I was hoping I could help you," he said. "I was sitting just over there." He nodded at the lounge chair across from mine. "I saw how you fell asleep." He glanced at his Rolex. "You slept for nearly an hour and a half, and with all this noise, too. Must've been tired, huh?"

"Yes," I said, sitting up and brushing back my hair.

"Hard night last night?"

"No," I said firmly, not liking the tone behind his question.

He laughed as if I were not telling the truth. "As soon as I saw your eyelids flickering, I ordered one of these for you . . . piña colada. Here," he said, extending it toward me.

"No, thank you," I said.

"Aw, you should. It's happiness in a glass, believe me," he urged, keeping his arm extended.

Who was this man, and what did he want? He was about my height and easily twenty pounds overweight. His gray hair was thinned to the point of revealing a scalp peppered with age spots, and the line of gray hair on his chest curled down over his bulging belly like piano wire and made a small circle around his belly button. There were small moles over his sagging chest. In the waistband of his boxer-style bathing shorts were two rather thick cigars. His spindly legs were ribbed with embossed veins. He wore a pair of leather slippers, and there were patches of purple around his ankles. Around his neck was draped an ostentatious gold chain.

"I'm not fond of rich, sweet drinks," I said, and he finally drew his arm back.

"No wonder you have the figure you have," he commented. Then he looked at the drink, considered it, and sipped it himself, shaking his head. "Can't resist these things."

I nodded. I was sure he was telling the truth about that.

"I guess you're here by yourself," he said. "Am I right?"

"Yes," I said.

"What's a pretty young woman like you doing all alone?" he followed, but smiled with his head tilted to the right as if he already knew the answer and was just waiting for confirmation.

I really wasn't in any mood to have a conversation with someone's grandfather, but I couldn't be impolite.

"I'm just here for a short stay, doing some research," I said.

"Research? Uh-huh. That's a new one, but it's a good one," he added quickly.

"Excuse me?"

"Hey," he said, sitting on the lounge beside mine. "I never demand a woman be honest with me, whether it's about her age, her weight, or her previous love affairs," he said, laughing. He sipped some more of the piña colada.

I just stared at him. Was this old man flirting with me? Just the thought of it nauseated me.

"Excuse me," I said, gathering my towel and slipping my feet into my sandals, "but I've got to go in."

"Hey, take it easy. Are you busy tonight?"

"Pardon me?"

"If you haven't any plans, I was wondering if you would like to go to dinner. There's a party on a friend of mine's yacht later, too. Maybe you've heard of him, Michael Thomas?"

"No," I said. I was smiling with incredulity, but he thought I was amused, I guess.

"He's the grandson of Thomas door springs, that family," he said. "You'll meet a lot of people there, interesting rich people," he added, "not that I'm not interesting and rich enough." He laughed and sipped his drink again. "My name's Gordon Lauer," he said, and waited for my reaction. "Breston-Lauer, the fragrance company?" he said.

"Oh."

"Yes," he said, smiling. "I'll get you a lifetime supply of our best products."

"Thank you, but I think you've made a mistake," I said, smiling. "I'm not really here to have a good time. Thank you for your invitation," I told him, and rose.

He sat there with a very surprised look of disbelief as I started away. Why would a man that age think I would want to be his date, no matter how rich he was? I didn't know whether to be amused or upset, but I knew I wanted to get back upstairs and away from this as soon as I could.

In my room, there was a message waiting for me from Dr. Anderson. He had made arrangements for me to see two other families if I wished. He had left their names and telephone numbers. It brought back my feelings of guilt and my anger at myself for contriving this whole scheme in the first place. I had to find a way to tell the truth, I thought, especially to my mother, and as quickly as I could.

For now, I had to get myself ready to go out to dinner with Thatcher Eaton. A part of me was laden with heavy guilt over having even an iota of excitement about it and making any effort at all to make myself attractive. Daddy's death was far too fresh. What right did I have to experience even the smallest pleasure, and besides, what did this have to do with my real purpose for coming here?

Once again, I was thrown into an argument within myself, a part of me rationalizing my actions, justifying them with, *He's helping you approach your mother. Look at how difficult Linden was. You should be grateful Thatcher is here and interested in you.*

Don't lie to yourself, Willow De Beers, said an inner voice that sounded very much like my adoptive mother's. *Be honest, at least. You're attracted to this man. You've been beguiled, and now you're taking that titillation to another level. Meeting and getting to know your mother has been put on the back burner.*

"No, that's not so," I practically shouted at my image in the mirror.

I could hear my adoptive mother's thin, deriding laugh, and I turned from the mirror and sat down hard on the bed. *I should call Thatcher and cancel,* I thought.

And then what? Go back and throw yourself at the beach house door? Just think of Linden's reaction to that. You could ruin it all forever and ever, and then what would you go home to with Allan angry at you, with your schoolwork damaged? You could fall into that maelstrom of madness you have feared your whole life, Willow De Beers.

"Oh, this is ridiculous," I cried, and jumped up to shower and wash my hair. Afterward, I brushed it so hard I nearly ripped out some strands at the roots. I just put on some lipstick and threw on the nicest dress I had brought. No one had ever gotten dressed in as much of a rage, I thought, still conflicted and angry at myself for accepting the bargain with Thatcher.

While I was still pondering whether or not I was making too much of this dinner date, the phone rang.

"I can come up to get you," Thatcher said. "I wasn't sure and thought it was better to call to see how close you are to being ready. Most of the women in Palm Beach have little respect for time, at least the women I know."

"You should get out of town more," I countered, and he laughed, obviously amused and not put off by my hard, cold tone. "I'm ready. I'll be right there."

"Terrific," he said.

Why was I so angry at him? Was it because I was afraid this bright young man would eventually see through my cover story and be upset, or was I angry at myself for feeling like a high school girl on her first real date?

Try not to talk too much, I told myself. *The less said, the better.* But maybe that was easier thought than done, especially with a man like Thatcher Eaton.

When I stepped into the lobby, he turned from the reception desk where he had been conversing with one of the female employees, who looked absolutely dazzled by him. It was difficult not to be. He wore a solid olive suit with a pearl-white mock-turtleneck shirt. The suit was fitted and brought out the richness of his tan and the sparkle in his blue eyes. He smiled and started toward me.

"I'm sorry," I said immediately, referring to my rather plain black dress. I had no pretty jewelry, either, not even earrings. "I didn't bring anything special to wear because I didn't come here to party."

"Don't apologize. You look terrific," he said. "It's actually refreshing to see a woman who is understated these days, especially here."

"Understated? You are a good lawyer, very diplomatic," I said, and he laughed.

He held up his arm for me to take. It seemed to me that everyone was looking our way. As we walked toward the door, the elderly man who had tried to pick me up at the pool came in, still in a pair of shorts and a polo shirt. He nodded at me.

"Caught your fish, I see," he said as he continued by.

Thatcher paused, a curious smile on his face. "What did he say?"

"I don't know. He's a terrible old man. He actually asked me out when I was down at the pool, tried to get me to go to some yacht party. Whatever gave him the idea is beyond me," I muttered.

Thatcher's eyes twinkled with amusement. He nodded at the valet attendant, who jumped to bring up Thatcher's Rolls.

"Why do you think that business with the elderly man was so funny?" I asked him.

"He just assumed that, being an unescorted young lady, you were here to play the Palm Beach game," Thatcher explained. He moved before the valet attendant to open the door for me. I got in quickly, and he went around and slipped in as well.

"What game?" I asked.

He started us away and smiled. "You'd be surprised at the number of young, attractive women who come here with the express purpose of becoming some wealthy old man's mistress or, hopefully, wife. Many stay at this very hotel because it's good hunting grounds."

"Well, you can be sure I'm not one of those," I said sharply.

He started to laugh, looked at me, and then shook his head.

"What?"

"I don't know. I'll have to reserve judgment for a while. You fit the first half of the definition."

"And what is that?" I said, not hiding my annoyance.

"You're certainly young and attractive."

"Just like a rich, arrogant man to think that every young and attractive woman is after his money."

That released a bigger laugh from him.

"Well? Aren't I right about that?" I demanded.

"Maybe," he said, nodding. "I don't know what your theories are about one of the wealthiest communities in America, but it's just possible you might be in for a surprise or two," he said. It sounded almost like a warning.

I've had enough surprises in my lifetime, I thought. *Thank you very much.*

"This is Worth Avenue," Thatcher said when we turned onto it. "One of the world's richest shopping malls," he added with a grin. "Like Rodeo Drive in Beverly Hills or El Paseo in Palm Desert, California."

"Hardly a mall," I said, gazing at the upscale shops, department stores, boutiques, and restaurants. Everything did look fresh and new, glittering like the diamonds and gold that were truly costume jewelry to the wealthy inhabitants.

"I don't know how much you know about Palm Beach. It always amazes people to learn it's only a fourteen-mile-long strip. Henry Morrison Flagler created it in a sense when he opened the Royal Poinciana Hotel in 1894. His home is now the Flagler Museum off Cocoanut Row. You should take a look if you have time."

"Maybe I will," I said without much commitment.

"There was once an army base at the northern end of the island in charge of coastal defense, making sure the German subs weren't coming ashore. Now there's an army of elite who make sure no riffraff come ashore," he jested.

"The season used to be only ten weeks long, but these days it goes until the end of April," he continued, sounding more like a tourist guide.

"Many of these structures, shops, and apartment buildings were created by the island's most famous architect, Addison Mizner. He built the Montgomery house," Thatcher said. "Or at least started it."

"Oh?"

"He established this Moorish-Mediterranean style. Probably the most famous is Mar-a-Lago, now owned by Donald Trump. It was built by Edward F. Hutton for his wife, Marjorie Merriweather Post, the breakfast cereal heiress. It's a mere seventeen-acre estate with a one hundred-plus-room mansion. It has a nine-hole golf course, a seventy-five-foot-high tower, cottages, citrus groves, greenhouses, and an underground tunnel to the beach. Trump's turned it into a private club. I'll take you there, if you like."

When I didn't respond, he turned to me and asked, "I know you said you didn't come here to party, but it's all right to enjoy yourself while you work, isn't it?"

"Depends," I said.

"On what?"

"How much I enjoy myself and how much I work," I replied, and he laughed.

We pulled up in front of a restaurant called Ta-Boo. The maitre d' recognized Thatcher and greeted him immediately. I looked at the women and men drinking, talking, and laughing at the long bar. Many of the women were attractive and dressed in sexy, expensive-looking outfits.

"And who might this pretty young thing be?" the maitre d' asked Thatcher.

"Be careful, she's doing research on Palm Beach," Thatcher warned him.

He laughed and led us to a table in the gazebo room.

"Anybody who's anybody in this town will be here one night or the other during the week," Thatcher said. "The combined wealth of the people eating and drinking here is probably close to the gross national product of most Third World nations."

I glanced around and mentally agreed.

"Despite the location, the prices aren't outrageous," Thatcher said when the waiter brought us a menu and asked if we wanted a cocktail.

Thatcher looked to me.

"I'm not sure," I said.

He ordered a Cosmopolitan, and I acted as if I knew what it was and ordered the same.

"So," he said, "aside from the geriatric Don Juan at the pool, did you get some rest?"

"Yes, but I'm not here for rest," I said.

"Still disappointed about the Montgomerys?" he asked.

I looked up. "Yes. I can't help wondering about them, how they ended up this way."

He shrugged. "Most of what I know about their past, I've been told, you understand. I was only a little boy when Grace Montgomery returned from what everyone knows was a mental clinic in South Carolina.

"In the beginning, Grace's mother, Jackie Lee, attempted to fool Palm Beach society by putting out the story Grace was suffering from a brain tumor and had to have a delicate operation, but as time passed, the reality overtook the fiction, and Jackie Lee fell off the A-list."

"What does that mean exactly?"

"In Palm Beach, that's akin to having leprosy. She was no longer invited to the important balls, dinners, and parties. She was already involved with Kirby, who everyone believes seduced Grace and made her pregnant, which might have exacerbated her mental condition. When Jackie Lee's fortune was depleted and her reputation was lost, Kirby decided to seek greener pastures."

"When was Linden born?"

"About a year before Grace went to the clinic. Jackie Lee was able to perpetrate her fiction for quite a while, my parents say, because Grace was so withdrawn and such a recluse; none of her contemporaries saw or socialized with her for months and months. She was so rarely seen that she was forgotten, so she could have been pregnant and no one would have known."

"Why did they permit her to have a child?"

"Bunny, my mother, says Grace kept her pregnancy a secret and actually wore girdles. She says it was part of the girl's madness or shame. It's not uncommon for a woman to blame herself for a man's aggression. I have had to talk some of my clients into going after the men in their lives, and justly so."

"What did Jackie Lee do to make it look as if she were pregnant, stuff pillows in her dress?"

"Exactly."

"That's hard to believe."

"Not really. Take it from one who knows," he said. "For the residents, creating fantasies about themselves is a Palm Beach parlor game, and even if you know someone is fabricating, you go along with it. It's almost being considerate to do so."

"What does Linden do?" I asked. "I mean, just paint, or did he go to school for something?"

Thatcher laughed.

"What's so funny? You said he didn't make much money painting, didn't you?"

"You can always tell when someone isn't from Palm Beach. People here don't do anything. They live to spend, not earn. If you don't know that, you're not from Palm Beach."

"But you said the Montgomerys were destitute."

"In Palm Beach terms but not in actuality. They have a handsome income from the rental and some trust and Social Security funds. Linden is just an artist, or at least he believes he is. As I said, occasionally, people buy one of his paintings as a form of amusement. They are all so dark and depressing, but they've become something to stimulate talk at a cocktail party. If you really are interested, I'll take you to the Richard Hanson Gallery on Worth Avenue and you can see a few."

"You said people here live to spend, but you work," I pointed out, and he laughed.

"I like to think of myself as different." He looked up at me. "I hope you do, too."

"I don't know you well enough to decide one way or another," I said.

The waiter brought us our drinks before he could respond.

"Well, then," he said after the waiter left. "Here's to your getting to know me well enough."

He clinked his glass with mine and looked over the rim as he sipped, those eyes of his twinkling with delight.

What are you doing, Willow De Beers? I asked myself. *End this, and get back to your purpose before you . . .*

Before I what?

That wasn't a very difficult question. The answer hung on Thatcher's every smile and rested comfortably in the softness of my heart: *be careful before you fall into something you might not be able—or willing—to escape.*

8

Blowing My Cover

We both ordered a light dinner, and Thatcher chose a bottle of white wine. When he read off the wine list to me, I tried to pretend I was familiar with some of them. Neither my adoptive mother nor Daddy drank much wine at home. My A.M. loved champagne, but she usually had it in the house only when they had a special dinner party.

My limited social experiences would surely unmask me, I thought. He would soon realize I was much younger than I had claimed, certainly no graduate-level student.

"So let's talk a little about you," he said. "Where are you from?"

I hated piling one lie over another and decided I would tell as much of the truth as I could.

"I'm from a little community near Columbia, South Carolina, called Spring City."

"I don't see any engagement ring on your finger. Have you no serious relationship awaiting your return?"

"Not anymore," I replied.

"Ah-ha! Recent breakup, then?"

"Is this heading for the, what did you call it, the *Shiny?*"

He laughed. "Hardly. Have you had many serious relationships?"

"No."

"Too busy, too involved with your work?"

"Something like that," I said. "I didn't go to college to find a husband, and I'm not afraid of being on my own," I said firmly.

"Now that we have that settled," he said, laughing.

"Well, I'm not!" I insisted.

"An independent woman. Good. Have you done much traveling?" he asked.

"No, not really. My mother wasn't fond of traveling, especially with a child, and my father was a workaholic."

"*Wasn't* fond?"

"She was killed in a car accident a little over two years ago."

"Oh. Sorry. What does your father do?"

"He's a doctor," I said.

Thatcher smiled.

"What?" I asked, holding my breath.

"I bet he's into psychiatric medicine, right?"

"What makes you say that?"

"You're interested in the subject. It's common for children to want to do what their parents have done."

"Is your father an attorney?" I countered.

"Hardly," he said. "My grandfather began the Eaton department store chain in New England. My father assumed an executive position the day after he graduated from the University of Pennsylvania with a bachelor of arts degree and practically no business education. His first executive act was to appoint someone who knew what he was doing to be his assistant, and then he got back to the golf course."

"He doesn't have a New England accent," I commented.

"All his life, he went to private schools here and in Europe. Not long after my mother and he were married, my grandfather passed away. My grandmother had died the year before, and Daddy was the sole heir. He sold off a majority interest in the stores, and he and my mother came to Palm Beach for the season and then spent their winters on the Côte d'Azur. My sister and I attended private schools from the moment we could. I grew up thinking parents were people you visited on holidays."

"I had a nanny care for me most of my life," I confessed. His warm tone of revelation encouraged my own. "My mother wasn't really into being a mother, either."

"So, you see, we have a lot in common after all," he declared.

"I often wonder if I'll be that sort of parent." I looked up at him. "I bet you wonder the same thing, and that's why you're not involved with anyone."

"Oh," he said, smiling, "I'm being analyzed. Wonderful. What makes you so sure I'm not involved with anyone?"

"Your parents as much as said so, and you've asked me out to dinner in your hometown where people know you. Am I right?"

His smile seemed to turn more into a mask attempting to hide his true feelings. "It's so much more interesting and exciting for a man and a woman to leave some mystery, some questions between them, don't you think? If we analyze and examine each other too thoroughly, we'll touch old wounds, strip away some scars. Secrets are romantic," he added, returning that twinkle to his eyes.

"Okay," I said, seizing the opportunity. "No more revelations. No more personal questions, then."

"Let's drink to it," he said, pouring the remaining wine into our glasses.

He was a little too agreeable, too quickly, I thought, but I didn't want to look a gift horse in the mouth.

We toasted, his eyes moving from boyish charm to manly interest as they swept over my face and made me aware of my own feelings. The wine was getting to me quickly because of my emotional fatigue, I thought. I was actually a bit frightened of myself, of the warm feelings I felt when I looked at him, of the excitement in my heart and the way that excitement washed down over my breasts and into the small of my stomach.

I'd really believed I was in love with Allan, but maybe it was solely because I convinced myself I had to be. He was perfect and correct and confident, everything I expected a man for me should be, but after only a few hours with Thatcher, I felt something I had not felt before. It was as if his smiles, his eyes, his fingers touching my hand, had awakened some sleeping wildness within me. I could see myself shake out my hair. I could feel my eyes burning with desire. I could taste sex on my lips and feel the blood fill my face with exquisite heat. Did he see this? I wondered and felt myself blush with embarrassment.

"Are you all right?" he asked when I looked down quickly.

"To be honest," I said, "I'm not used to drinking much, even wine at dinner."

"Good. I'll save money."

"Maybe I should go back to the hotel," I suggested.

"Of course not!" he cried. "I promised to show you some of the Palm Beach nightlife. We're going over to the Leopard Lounge at the Chesterfield Hotel. It should be jumping enough by now. And don't worry about drinking. You put ginger ale in a champagne glass like some of the women do at affairs here, and no one will know the difference."

He signaled for the waiter before I could offer any resistance, and soon after, we were pulling up to the Chesterfield on Cocoanut Row. Everyone seemed to know Thatcher there. We couldn't move a foot without someone reaching to shake his hand or a young woman trying to hug him or kiss him on the cheek. The music was loud, everyone trying to talk and laugh over it.

Of course, it was easy to see why the bar was known as the Leopard Lounge. Everything had spots on it: tablecloths, drapes, rugs, wallpaper, chairs, even the vests the waiters wore. Overhead was a painting of red satyrs with voluptuous nude women. I thought I spotted a famous female pop singer sitting at the corner of the bar, and later, I was positive I saw an actor who was in the most recent blockbuster. Money, celebrity, glitter, and excitement flowed in waves through this club, and Thatcher seemed accustomed to it and quite at home.

He pointed out a Saudi billionaire, two best-selling female authors, and a British lord. Everywhere I looked, there were attractive young women dressed in suggestive, abbreviated clothing. People around me seemed to be competing with jewelry and designer garments. When I made a remark about it to Thatcher, he pulled me back so we could talk and look at the crowd.

"I don't want to write your paper for you, but if you observe with any sort of objective eye, you can see that despite their wealth, people here are very insecure."

"How do you mean?" I asked.

He shrugged. "Older women, even the very rich ones, are threatened by the more attractive younger ones capturing their husbands' eyes. Everyone worries about his standing on the social ladder, even to the point of what table they are given at restaurants and certainly where they are seated at events. Disappointment over things like that can lead to deep depression. You could do well starting your career here," he said. "But for now, just enjoy it," he declared, and pulled me out onto the dance floor.

Was I wrong to be having such a good time? When we went to order another drink, I opted for a vodka and tonic instead of the ginger ale. He raised his eyebrows but smiled and ordered it. A little while later, we were dancing again. It did seem as if I were at some great party, even a New Year's celebration.

"Does this go on every night?" I screamed.

"During the season, yes," he shouted back. "But I'm not out every night. You heard my parents. To them, I always have my nose to the grindstone and don't enjoy myself enough."

"That doesn't seem true," I cried.

He drew closer to me. "Enough to them is ninety percent play and ten percent work. Everyone says life's too short and justifies the hedonism and partying with that. You can practically hear it in the music and see it in their faces: life's too short."

"Isn't that true?"

"The more they say it, the shorter it gets," he said, and we both laughed.

For a while, I lost myself in the music. I had another drink and then felt myself sink in the chair. My eyes seemed to have a mind of their own and kept trying to shut.

"I guess I had better get you back to your hotel," he said, gazing at me. "I know that look when I see it. I've seen it enough."

"What look?"

"Trust me," he said, taking my hand. He put down money for the bill, and we made our way out.

When we stepped outside, I felt as if I had just popped out of a womb of madness. The music was still ringing in my ears. The whole world seemed to go topsy-turvy. He helped me into the Rolls, and we flew off. The warm night air flowed around me, through my hair, caressing my face.

"So, what do you think of Palm Beach nightlife so far?"

"I can see why everyone wants to be rich and ignore reality," I declared.

"Do you? Really? After so short a visit, you've made that conclusion?"

"I don't know," I said. "I'm too tired to think."

He laughed and drove on. When we reached the hotel, he insisted on escorting me to my room.

"I don't want any more geriatric Don Juans making passes at you, especially now," he said, "when you're so helpless."

"I am not helpless," I insisted, but nearly tripped over my own two feet.

He held my hand, and we went through the lobby and into the elevator. Moments later, he was standing with me at the door.

"Allow me," he said when I took out my key. He opened my door for me.

We both looked into the room and then at each other. Was he going to suggest he come in? Was I going to let him? My good old inner arguments were starting, a part of me hoping he would, a part of me bawling myself out for having that hope and reminding me why I had come here in the first place.

"You'd better get some sleep," he said, quickly ending the struggle within me. "Me, too. I have a deposition at nine in the morning. It should take only an hour and a half, and then I'll come by and pick you up to take you to my parents' brunch, okay?"

"Yes," I said. "Thank you. I had a good time."

"I'm glad. You're a lot of fun to be with," he added.

It brought a smile to my face, and he filled that smile quickly with a soft but lingering kiss on my lips and then whispered, "Good night."

I wavered in the doorway and watched him turn and go back to the elevator. Then I stepped into my room and closed the door.

I was asleep almost before my head hit the pillow.

And I overslept.

What woke me was Thatcher's call from his car telling me he had finished with his deposition and was on his way to the hotel.

"What?" I cried, looking at the clock. "Oh, no!"

"I woke you?"

"Yes, but I'll be ready," I promised.

I hurried to shower and dress, chastising myself for permitting this to happen. I wanted to go back to Joya del Mar very much, hoping somehow to find a way to see my mother again. I brushed my hair quickly and tied it back as my mother had tied hers the day before. When I gazed at myself in the mirror, I thought anyone could see the resemblances between us. Was it wishful thinking?

I put on a sleeveless light blue sweater and a ball skirt. Just in case it was breezy, I tied a matching cardigan over my shoulders and then slipped into a pair of sandals I had brought along. I hoped I wasn't dressed too casually, but I didn't have much time to think about it and worry over it. Thatcher was already knocking on my door.

"Amazing," he said, smiling.

He wore a blue blazer, a pair of white slacks, and black loafers.

"What?"

"I expected to find you still rushing around, half dressed."

"Sorry to disappoint you," I replied.

"Believe me, Isabel, you're not in the least disappointing," he countered.

He kept his eyes on me as if he were determining the meaning of every aspect of my reaction: the look in my eyes, the movement of my lips, the way my shoulders turned.

"Shouldn't we be going?" I asked to fill the soft silence.

He nodded. I stepped out and closed the door. There was something about the way he looked at me and then looked away that stirred my pulse. He was quiet all the way down and through the lobby, even after we pulled away from the hotel.

"Something wrong?" I finally asked. "I'm not intruding or anything, after all, am I?"

"Oh, no. Far from it. My parents love impressing strangers and love meeting new people. That's the variety now that adds the spice to their lives. Different people are like different flavors of ice cream or different recipes for dinner. They love nothing more than experimenting," he said. "Even here, people grow tired of each other."

"I must say you puzzle me, Thatcher. How can you live and work in a world for which you have so little respect?" I asked.

"Is that really so unusual?" he threw back. "I read somewhere that something like eighty percent of working people hate their jobs and are bored with their social lives." He smiled at me. "You don't have to be rich to be unhappy."

I laughed. "Funny way to put it," I said.

"At least I'm being honest with you, aren't I, *Isabel?*" His voice had taken on a harder, colder tone.

"Yes," I said. "And I do appreciate that."

"Good. So now, let me ask you to reciprocate."

"Pardon me?"

He drove in silence for a while, and then he pulled off to the side of the road at a place where we could see the ocean quite unobstructed.

"I'm pretty friendly with everyone at The Breakers," he began, "as you can imagine. I often have a business lunch there, and I've been to many, many socials there. I've been involved with representing the hotel *and* some of its more affluent guests."

"What are you getting at, Thatcher?"

"I know the people behind the desk well, too, and one of them, a woman, I'll admit, who might have catty motives, asked me about you this morning and how I knew you, et cetera."

"Oh?"

"She didn't refer to you as Isabel Amou. She referred to the name on your credit card instead."

"Oh," I said, feeling my stomach fill with lead. I turned away from him and looked out at the soft, undulating waves. Why hadn't I thought of that?

"Who are you? Why are you here under false pretenses?" he asked. "I'm sorry, but I'm bringing you into my home, exposing my parents to you. I have to know. I don't think you're some sort of spy or some sort of con, but . . . well, you can understand my surprise and curiosity, can't you?"

I nodded.

"Well?"

This was too soon, I thought, too soon for someone other than my real mother to know the whole truth. And shouldn't she be the first to know it, anyway?

"You were right last night when you guessed my father was a psychiatrist," I began. "What you don't know, perhaps, is that he was one of the nation's most prominent."

"Was? He's gone, too?"

I wanted to bite off my own tongue. Truth had a way of rushing from my mouth. Why hadn't I paid closer attention to my adoptive mother and her techniques for bending, twisting, and hiding the truth?

"Yes," I said, "but I was afraid, and Dr. Anderson agreed, that if I presented myself as Willow De Beers, people might not be so forthcoming."

He grimaced. "That's a bit of a stretch, Willow."

"No, it isn't," I insisted. "You wondered why I haven't had many serious relationships with men in my life. Well, most, if not all, of the boys I've dated or known knew who my father was and expected I would be analytical, even critical. They were all terrified of my father. I could count on the fingers of one hand how many actually came to my home and met him, and when they did, they were so nervous they looked guilty of something or guilty of some bad intention."

He stared at me, pondering.

"It was the same at college, even with some of my teachers, especially the sociology professor and the psych professor. It was as if I were the daughter of Jonas Salk or Madame Curie attending medical school. In one of my classes, one of my father's books was required reading."

Thatcher still looked skeptical. I felt I had to keep adding truth to the recipe.

"My father began and ran a famous clinic, the Willows," I said.

Thatcher's eyes widened. "Yes."

"You've heard of it, right?"

"I have, yes."

"Some of the patients in that clinic came from Palm Beach," I added.

His eyes brightened more. "Grace Montgomery."

"Yes," I said. "Grace Montgomery. If Linden knew who I really was . . ."

"He might have undergone a spontaneous combustion, right before our eyes," Thatcher said, nodding. "Did you come here expressly to interview Grace?"

"I had it as an objective, yes," I said. That was certainly true.

"I see. Well, that does change things."

"I didn't like lying to you. I was uncomfortable."

He nodded slowly. "Well, Palm Beach isn't exactly the capital of truth," he said. "People lie to themselves here almost as much as they lie to others."

"It's not so different from other places in that respect, Thatcher."

He turned back to me, his eyes softer, now devoid of distrust and accusation. "Maybe not." He thought a moment. "Okay. I actually like this," he said, starting the car again and putting it into drive. "But when Linden Montgomery finds out who you really are, he's going to be very upset," he warned. "He's paranoid as it is."

I wondered how much of that was prophecy.

The Eatons had two other couples at their brunch: Lord and Lady Thomas, both well into their seventies, and George McCluster and his wife, who was introduced to me as Dolly. Lord Thomas had been a British high court justice. George McCluster was presented as one of the most successful real estate agents in Palm Beach. He looked to be in his early fifties, but his wife's age was difficult to guess because of all the cosmetic surgery she had undergone. To my surprise, she was proud of it.

"My wife's skin has been pulled back so tightly so many times," George remarked in front of her, "that she can't quite close her eyelids, even when she sleeps. Right, Dolly?"

"It's not that bad, and besides, it's a small price to pay. I don't see why anyone should tolerate wrinkles," she preached.

"Not everyone can afford cosmetic surgery," Thatcher said softly, and winked at me.

"Nonsense. It's a matter of priorities. Spend less on other things; save for it. There should be a cosmetic surgery plan similar to the Social Security plan. Money should come out of people's salaries automatically, that's all."

"Great political platform for our next presidential candidate," Asher Eaton cried, drawing the headline in the air before him. "Vote for me, and vote for no wrinkles."

Everyone laughed.

We were sitting on the rear loggia overlooking the pool. The Eatons' chef, Mario, was grilling lobster. A large bowl of Caesar salad had already been prepared, and there were breads and rolls. A separate table with a variety of desserts that Bunny pointed out included truffle demi-glacé and something called Giandika chocolate cake with fresh raspberries, "just like they served at the last event held at the Ritz-Carlton," she concluded.

We were drinking mimosas, which were glasses of orange juice mixed with champagne. After I had been introduced, they all seemed eager to offer their opinions concerning wealth and morality.

"I, for one, think the more money you have, the more opportunity you have to be a good person," Dolly McCluster said. "Look at how much we all give to charity. Could we do that if we weren't well off?"

"There are many who are but are very tight with their pocketbooks, I'm afraid," Lady Thomas said quietly. She spoke so softly it was hard to hear her at times, whereas Dolly McCluster practically bellowed when she talked.

"Having money does eliminate a major motivation for crime," Thatcher's father suggested. He looked at

Thatcher, but Thatcher didn't agree or disagree. "I mean, people don't have to steal if they have money, right?"

"I don't know about that, Asher," Lord Thomas ventured to say. "The wealthy don't steal to eat or to have expensive cars, of course, but some rich people I've known and have had before me as defendants have attempted extortion, fraud, and other things to become more powerful, perhaps."

"What's an unfriendly stock takeover of a company if not a form of stealing?" Lady Thomas said, and most of the others looked at her as if she had blasphemed.

"No, I think that's just good business," George McCluster said. "What do you think, Thatcher?"

"I think . . . I think I'm rather hungry," he said, and everyone laughed.

"Very diplomatic of you," I told him as we went for our food. Two maids, which I thought was overkill considering the small number of guests, stood behind the tables serving us.

"I just didn't want to influence your conclusions," he said, smiling.

At the table, the conversation went from the latest economic news to the latest Palm Beach gossip. The women were very concerned about a fashion outrage at the last charity ball. Someone had come in a pants suit with too much midriff showing.

"A belly button is not exactly appetizing," Dolly said.

"It depends," Asher commented. The women all turned to him. I could see he had Thatcher's impish smile at times, or, rather, Thatcher had inherited his. "On whether it's an innie or an outie."

The men laughed.

Throughout the conversations, I kept catching Thatcher looking at me, studying my reactions. He continually wore a smile of amusement. Since I had told him something of the truth, it was as if we were both conspirators now.

Before we had a chance to get to the desserts, Jennings appeared. "There is a phone call for you, Mr. Eaton," he told Thatcher.

"Oh?"

He excused himself, and, as if he had been the one keeping them from focusing on me, they all turned and began to fire questions about my work, my home and family, and my impressions of Palm Beach so far. I tried to be as diplomatic as Thatcher, who returned to announce he had to leave immediately to go to court.

"What?" his mother cried. "Now? We're having brunch."

"It's a weekday, Mother. You might have noticed people are at work. Something was moved up unexpectedly. It won't be long, but I have to appear."

"Don't you have a lunch hour?" she countered.

"Yes, Mother, but it usually doesn't run more than three," he said, smiling.

"Ridiculous. What about this poor young woman you've brought? Is she to be a slave to your work habits?"

"She can stay, obviously," Thatcher offered as a compromise. "I'll go and come back."

"Good," his mother said. "I would have had our driver take you back to your hotel anyway if he wasn't," she told me. She glared at Thatcher. "How anyone could pass up freshly baked Giandika chocolate cake is a mystery to me."

Thatcher laughed and then pulled me aside to ask if I wanted to stay.

"Yes," I said, my gaze moving off to the beach house.

"I'll return as soon as I can. Sorry about this."

"I'm fine," I said. "I'm enjoying it."

"I knew you would," he said. He kissed me quickly and left.

When I turned to rejoin the brunch party, I saw Thatcher's mother had been watching us. She smiled as she approached me.

"Walk with me for a few minutes," she said. "I do like to walk after I've stuffed myself like that. Besides, the rest of them are in a big argument about how to renovate the yacht club, and that is so boring."

We started down the walkway toward the beach.

"Thatcher obviously is somewhat taken with you," she continued. "Do you know that you are the first young lady he has brought to this house for over two years now?"

I shook my head.

"He didn't tell you about Mai Stone?"

"No. Who is that?"

"I suppose that's good," she said. "I suppose I shouldn't have even mentioned her name."

"But you did," I said quickly.

"He'd be very upset with me if he knew," she replied.

There was a pathway that ran parallel to the beach.

We followed it for a while, she obviously trying to keep her lips clamped shut.

"Oh, you would find out from someone else, anyway," she finally decided. "He and Mai were practically engaged when she and her parents were invited to spend a week on this Greek billionaire's yacht. As it turned out, he had a son who had fancied Mai for some time. The talk was he bought her for his son. The Stones were suddenly buying property on the south end and soon building one of the biggest estates on the island."

"Why would Mai have agreed?"

"She lives like a princess on her own island."

"She couldn't have been very much in love with Thatcher if she let someone sell her into a marriage," I said angrily.

"That's exactly what I told Thatcher, ten thousand times if I told him once, but he refused to accept it. I hated to see him so heartbroken. That's why he became such a work-centered young man. Goodness knows, he doesn't need the money.

"As I said, you're the first young lady he has brought to this house for years. Not that he hasn't been on dates. I know he has, but he hasn't been with the same woman twice, as far as I know."

"I'm sorry," I said. "But, Mrs. Eaton . . ."

"Bunny, please."

"Bunny. I really didn't come here to find romance."

"Why, my dear, that's the best sort of romance there is, the one you never expected," she said. "When I first met Thatcher's father, I thought he was the most spoiled young man in the world. I had no intention of ever becoming his wife, but he was persistent, and he charmed me in so many little ways; I woke up one day and discovered I was in love. What a surprise! That's the best there is."

"I suppose so," I said.

"How long did you plan on staying in Palm Beach?"

"Maybe a week."

"Oh, it's so expensive at The Breakers. If you decide to stay longer, it would cost so much. I have an idea," she added so quickly I knew it wasn't remotely spontaneous. "Why don't you just stay here? We have so much room in the house, and we aren't expecting any guests for another month at least."

"I don't think . . ."

"It would be such fun. We'll invite different people over every other day practically, and you can listen and question them all. It will save you all that footwork. You don't even have to tell them what you're up to. Just let them talk."

"But you don't really know me, Mrs. Eaton."

"Bunny," she corrected.

"Bunny. How can you . . ."

"Oh, I know you. I know you. Look at you. How could it be a mistake? Asher will be so pleased."

I started to shake my head.

"In fact, you should move in tomorrow. Why waste another dollar?"

"I really didn't intend to be here that long. I didn't bring enough clothes and . . ."

"So you'll buy some new clothing. What could you possibly need?"

I started to shake my head again. She seemed so determined. Was she hoping to be like Mai Stone's parents and buy her son a wife?

"It's settled, then," she decided before I could respond.

I was going to refuse more firmly as we turned a corner and looked down the beach. There, set back in the tall grass, was an artist's easel. However, I didn't see anyone anywhere.

"What's that?" I asked Bunny.

"Oh, that must be Linden's."

"But where is he?"

"Who knows? Maybe he's crawling in the sand looking for shells. Don't pay attention to him. C'mon," she said. "We'd better get back."

"I'll be right along," I said, staring at the easel.

"Don't be long," she advised, and started toward the house.

I continued down to the easel and stopped to look at what was on it.

A picture had been sketched in, the painting of it just begun.

It was a picture of someone standing in the entryway of a house. He was looking out at a young woman who resembled me, I thought.

In the ocean seen behind her, a woman was drowning.

It all put a chill in my heart.

"Hey!" I heard.

Linden was coming up over the hill in front of me. I turned, and, with my heart thumping like a flat tire, I ran up the beach to the walkway. I didn't stop running until I reached the loggia where everyone was enjoying the desserts. They looked up surprised.

"Are you all right, dear?" Bunny asked immediately.

"I . . . just need to use the bathroom," I said, and hurried inside, their confused and surprised faces turning to follow me.

In the bathroom, I looked at my face in the mirror.

"Go home, Willow De Beers," I told that face. "You're trying to get back something that never existed and probably never will."

"I can't," I replied. "I've got to try."

"Why?"

Why? I thought.

The first word most babies uttered was *Mama*.

I was almost nineteen years old, and I had yet to say it once.

That's why.

9

A Night for Romance

"**I**'m not sure I'm doing that," I said when Bunny jumped up as soon as Thatcher returned to tell him I was staying at the house.

"Oh, of course you're sure," she declared as though she knew my mind better than I did.

Lord and Lady Thomas and the McClusters had left, and Thatcher's father had gone into his office to phone someone about the golf game he was planning for the following morning. Bunny had been showing me around the house, especially where I would stay.

"Look at the size of these rooms!" she cried. "And how far away the guest suites are from our bedrooms. Why, we won't even realize you're here, and you'll have as much privacy as you wish."

That was not an exaggeration. The rambling structure did seem to go on forever, and the rooms were enormous by any standard. The bedroom she suggested for me was, according to her, designed by Addison Mizner himself.

"He wouldn't do a house unless he could put his stamp inside as well as outside," she said.

The room was easily twenty feet by forty, with its own sitting area, large-screen television, stereo, and secretary desk—hardly what anyone would think of as a guest bedroom. It was done in soft, warm colors: salmon and beige and a pale green she called celadon.

Bunny pointed out a beautiful vase in a sort of turquoise glaze. "That's his signature color, Mizner Blue. "It's as if he left his fingerprints," she declared, and then whispered, "It makes the house more valuable. Someday, we might buy it. We're leasing with an option to buy."

I nodded and continued to look about the room. The ceiling-high windows were draped in salmon silk, and a pair of French doors opened to a balcony that looked out at the sea.

The centerpiece was the oversized bed with an enormous arched engraved headboard. She said the furniture was in the Spanish style Mizner favored. There was a very pretty area rug over the parquet floor and a center chandelier that seemed to fit the motif so well it might have been created before electric lights were invented and used to hold candles first.

The room did have a wonderful view of the beach and, more important to me, a view of the beach house.

I stood out on the balcony and looked down at it. Bunny Eaton saw the direction of my gaze.

"This was once Grace Montgomery's bedroom, you know," she said.

I turned. "Oh?"

"The poor young woman was supposedly seduced in this very room," Bunny added dramatically, and walked to the bed, looking at it as if she could see the actual seduction being replayed on its sheets and pillows. "Here she lay, young and vulnerable and trusting. Kirby Scott was a very handsome man, and charming—the sort who could have his hand down your dress before you even realized he was nearby. How could she resist? She must have felt terribly guilty, felt as though she had stolen her mother's lover from her. That was why she kept it a secret so long, I'm sure.

"I haven't changed a thing, really, not a sheet, not a pillow, not a pillowcase," she said.

From the excitement in her voice and in her eyes, I think she believed that would add an attractive romantic element, like being where your favorite soap opera was shot or something.

On the contrary, it gave me the dreads. My mother's mental problems might have had their origin in this very room.

"Are you sure all that happened here?" I asked, embracing myself and stepping back into the room.

"Oh, yes. The real estate agent who was representing the Montgomerys at the time was absolutely positive. Things like that are part of what they call disclosure. At least, they are here in Palm Beach where everyone wants to know that sort of thing and isn't put off by it."

She studied me a moment and must have seen the revulsion in my face. It was almost as if I could see myself being violated.

"That doesn't bother you, does it? I mean, we could put you in another room just as easily. It's just that I thought this was the nicest and had a wonderful view. It has the best bathroom, too. The most up-to-date: a bidet, a multihead shower, magnifying mirrors, and just look at the work in here," she declared as if she were trying to sell the house to me.

I gazed in at the beige and white tiled wall behind the toilet, the rich sink cabinet, and the large oval mirror above it. The floor looked like chipped turquoise inlay. The shower stall had a marble seat in it.

"Well? Compares with what you have at The Breakers, doesn't it?"

"That isn't a worry of mine, Bunny. As I told you, I'm here to work on my—"

"Oh, please," she said, throwing up her hands and fanning the air between us as if she were waving away smoke, "don't start talking like a Ms. instead of a Miss and drown me in boredom with all that work you want to do."

I started to laugh.

"Come along," she said. "I'll show you our bedroom. We just had it redone by this new interior decorator who is the rage of Palm Beach. Thatcher's room is down there," she said, flipping her hand to my right as we left the bedroom. "He has his own entrance to the house. Sometimes, we don't see him for a week. I swear, I wonder if he is deliberately avoiding us sometimes."

She smiled at me.

"Maybe that will soon change. As long as you're here, at least."

I shook my head and followed after her as she rattled on and on about each and every curtain, artifact, and piece of furniture along the way, not failing to attach the cost of each as well. Just after the tour was completed and we returned to the rear loggia, Thatcher appeared.

"Well," Bunny pounced, "was it worth it for you to rush off to that dreary courthouse and interrupt your parents' wonderful brunch?"

"Yes, Mother," he said. "I settled the case in less than half an hour."

"I'm sure you could have done it over the phone," she insisted, refusing to relent.

He shook his head and laughed.

"What have you been doing since I left?" he asked me with some trepidation in his eyes.

"Gossiping," Bunny answered for me. "And enjoying it," she added firmly.

"I'll bet."

"I'd better return to the hotel. I'm expecting some messages," I said, even though I wasn't.

"Just go back and pack up," Bunny told me. "Why spend another night there?"

"I'll see," I said.

"There's nothing to see about," she wheedled. "You'll be far more comfortable here, and you will be able to accomplish a great deal more in a shorter time."

"Mother, will you let the woman make up her own mind?" Thatcher said.

"I'm just trying to point out the obvious advantages, Thatcher."

"If they're obvious, they don't have to be pointed out," he countered.

She thought for a moment. "Sometimes, we don't see the most obvious things," she replied, sounding as if it were something she had drawn out of her well of memorable sayings.

Thatcher shook his head.

"Here," Bunny said, handing me a pink card with gold trim. "Our phone number. Call me if you need any help with anything, anything at all."

"She's not planning on moving furniture here, Mother."

"Nevertheless, there it is," she said, nodding at the card.

"My mother is just impossible," Thatcher told me as we started for the door.

"Thank you for inviting me, Bunny. Please tell Mr. Eaton I said thank you, too."

"You had better start calling him Asher. If you don't, he'll complain about how old you make him feel," she warned.

I promised I would.

"How old you'll make him feel," Thatcher mimicked as we made our way to his car. "Everyone clings to his or her illusions here as if they were holding on for dear life."

"Present company excluded?" I asked.

He smiled back at me, and we got into the car.

"Why is it I suspect I was the main topic of conversation?" Thatcher asked.

"She worries about you," I told him.

He raised his eyebrows skeptically. "Bunny? Worries? People in Palm Beach don't worry. They just find out what the solution to the problem will cost and then buy it. Didn't you see the sign on entering the island?"

"What sign?"

"There's one that reads, 'Check your worries at the gate. Smile or turn right around and leave.' Do you know there is no cemetery or hospital in Palm Beach? Death and sickness are not tolerated."

We both laughed.

I studied him for a moment. I wanted to return to the house and stay, of course. What a wonderful opportunity it presented to me. I could approach my mother again but in a quieter, softer, gradual manner. However, I didn't want my motives misunderstood. I was certainly not here to play any Palm Beach romance games.

"Do you feel like telling me about Mai Stone?" I asked him.

"I knew it! I knew she brought all that up. Did she tell you her parents sold her to an Arab billionaire for his son?"

"Yes. It's not true?"

"Of course not. Mai was always unpredictable. It was what I liked and didn't like about her," he said.

"How can you be so contradictory about that, especially with someone you supposedly loved?"

He looked at me, those beautiful eyes turning darker as his face became serious.

"There's a little contradiction in every romance, and especially in every marriage. Each person has to give up something he or she wants. That's compromise. For Mai, it would have had to have been sacrificing some of her impetuosity, her unpredictability. She hated being tied down by any set of rules, and she took great pleasure in being outrageous, whether by defying style or etiquette or her lover's wishes."

He laughed.

"She drove around in her new sports car without putting on her license plates for the longest time. She was stopped three times by the Palm Beach police. She kept getting tickets, and I kept settling them. The fourth time, the patrolman was prepared and had a screwdriver. He put them on himself. I loved her for her carefree, wild ways, but I grew annoyed and tired of it as well."

"But you gave her an engagement ring, didn't you?"

"I gave it to her, but she didn't wear it. She took it and promised she would eventually. Sometimes, she put it on before we went out, but before the evening ended, she usually had it off."

"She was teasing you."

"I think she was teasing herself, maybe challenging

herself," he said. "At times, I felt like a bystander, observing, waiting on the sidelines." He looked at me. "Talk about your split personalities. I never knew which Mai Stone I was picking up, and sometimes didn't know until the evening was nearly ended. She made surprise into a career."

"You must have been very much in love with her to put up with all that."

"I thought so, but now I'm not so sure I wasn't simply putting myself through some form of torture."

"Why would you do that?" I asked.

"To cleanse my soul of all my previous romantic sins," he said without a beat of hesitation, his eyes back to twinkling impishly.

"I'll bet," I said. "That's the first thing you said that I believe."

He roared and drove on.

"You should take Bunny up on her offer. There's a computer you can use in my home office. I don't really use it much. The office is adjacent to my bedroom in what I like to call the Far Eastern wing of the estate. Besides it being on the east end, the furniture is all Oriental in style."

"Talk about surprises. The house is full of them," I said.

"What do you mean?"

"Bunny told me Grace Montgomery was seduced in the room I would have."

"That's the legend."

"You don't believe it?"

"I don't know," he said, shaking his head. "Exaggerations are like an indigenous crop here. People harvest and spread them like jam and pass them around . . . like that campfire game, what's it called? You know, where someone begins by whispering a secret, and it gets passed along, exaggerated, changed, until it arrives at the end, almost entirely different from what it was at the beginning."

"I don't know that game," I said.

He raised those skeptical eyebrows again. "Oh? How come?"

"My father taught me how to hold onto the truth," I said softly.

He gazed at me a moment and then looked ahead and said in a soft tone of voice, "Before you leave, please teach me how that's done."

We were both strangely quiet for nearly the remainder of the trip back to The Breakers.

I shouldn't feel so different, so peculiar about myself and my life, I thought. Everyone, no matter how well-to-do, how successful in life, carries the burden of some heavy secret or secrets.

Everyone is a little bit haunted. There are ghosts within us all, truths we keep bouncing away like bubbles we are afraid to let settle inside because we're afraid they will burst and poison us with the reality we can't face or with which we can't live.

I was beginning to understand why the wealthiest people clung to their illusions here. Thatcher wasn't wrong. They used their money to escape from themselves. My mother and my half-brother, Linden, had lost their wealth. They couldn't afford illusions. They could do nothing but look into the mirror and see themselves as they really were, including their pasts, their memories, their pains and defeats.

Maybe I could change that. Maybe, somehow, I could change it for them.

And in doing so, change it for myself.

"What are your plans for the evening?" Thatcher asked as we drove into The Breakers.

"I have no plans," I said.

"There's an exhibition I've been invited to attend . . . some artist who's supposedly doing wonderful things by hand-painting digital images. Would you like to go? It's being held at the gallery that exhibits a few of Linden's paintings."

"Oh?"

"They'll have some wine and cheese, but we can have a nice dinner afterward at a quieter restaurant than where we were last night, a place on the beach where the entertainment will just be the sea and the sky."

"I'd like that," I said.

"The exhibition begins at seven. Why don't I come by then. The gallery is only ten minutes or so away from the hotel."

"Okay," I said as we pulled up to the front and the valet hurried to open my door.

Thatcher reached for me. "Think about staying at the house. Seriously. Look at the gas I'll save."

"Oh?"

"I'm just trying to do my best to conserve energy," he joked.

"Right," I said, and stepped out.

As I walked into the hotel, I thought what I should really do between now and the time he returned was buy myself something nicer to wear, something a little more elegant. *I'm not doing it to develop some romantic fling here in Palm Beach,* I told myself. *I'm doing all this to work myself successfully into my mother's world.*

It's like a disease here, my conscience cried, *a disease that builds your immune system, only it makes you immune to the truth.*

I'm not lying to myself, I thought. *Am I?*

As I hurried toward the boutique, I'm sure I looked like one of Daddy's patients arguing with herself in the corridor of the Willows. I tried on a black sleeveless, fitted dress with a crew neck and a kick pleat. Perfect. To go with it, I bought a pair of high-heeled, open-toe sandals. Then I pondered over some costume jewelry and decided in the end to look simple and classic. Once that was done, I went up to my room to wash my hair. I was feeling drab, and my eyes looked tired. I called room service and had them send up an ice-cold fresh cucumber, something I had often seen my adoptive mother do. I sliced it and put the thin slices over my eyes while I rested.

Was I being too vain?

No matter what I was doing, there was no reason not to look my best, I thought.

How I hated all these contradictory feelings. When would they end? Or do they ever end? Thatcher seemed to be telling me he believed they were a part of life, and especially any relationship. Maybe I was learning more here about myself than I had ever intended.

I was just putting the finishing touches on my hair and makeup when he knocked at my room door.

"Hi," he said, and whistled. "You look great!"

"Thank you."

He was wearing a black silk shirt open at the collar under an aqua-blue blazer. Beneath his cuffed black slacks, I saw he wasn't wearing socks with his soft leather loafers. He looked dapper, relaxed, and elegant all at once.

He gazed past me into my room.

"You don't look as if you've packed your things," he remarked with disappointment.

"I'm still undecided," I said. "I'm not even sure I'm staying in Palm Beach much longer, anyway."

"Oh? Well, let me see what I can do to help you decide to stay," he added with that cute little smirk on his lips. "Madam," he said, offering his arm.

I laughed and joined him. An elderly couple was already at the elevator, the man in a tuxedo and his wife so bedecked in jewelry I wondered how she could move. They glanced at us suspiciously, even a bit disapprovingly, I supposed because of our joviality. Thatcher hoisted his eyebrows and winked at me as we all stepped into the elevator.

"So," he said, "I'd like permission to call you by your real name tonight."

The elderly couple swung their eyes at us so quickly and so simultaneously I almost burst out laughing.

"Is that all right with you?" Thatcher pursued.

"Yes," I said quickly, giving him a hot look of reprimand that only widened his smirk.

The couple exchanged looks and pulled closer to each other and farther away from us. When the doors opened, Thatcher stepped aside to let them go first, and they practically charged out through the lobby.

"That was very sneaky of you," I said.

"I can't help enjoying being a little outrageous, especially in front of obviously snobby people, people who take themselves too seriously."

"Wasn't that your complaint about Mai Stone?" I countered like a courtroom attorney myself.

He wasn't easily thrown off balance. It probably came from all his negotiating and trial experience. Without hesitation, he shook his head.

"Mai enjoyed being outrageous in front of anybody, snobby or not. She was playing on her own stage. Besides," he said, turning at the front entrance, "let's keep to the promise we made to each other last night."

"What?"

"No more historical revelations. No more personal questions, remember? Let's just have a good time in the here and now. The past, like the future, will take care of itself."

Last night, I'd thought I had more reason to want that than he did. Tonight, I wasn't so sure.

The gallery was already quite crowded by the time we arrived. Almost everyone there knew Thatcher. He introduced me as Isabel Amou and simply told people

I was visiting Palm Beach. Very few tried to find out much more about me once they heard I was from South Carolina and not from a particularly wealthy family. Thatcher said I was a former college acquaintance.

"See how easy it is to create fictions here that people will willingly accept?" he whispered.

We wandered through the gallery, sipping wine. After a while, he turned me into a side room to show me Linden's work.

There were only three pictures, each darker and more eerie than the last. In the first, a young man, not unlike Linden, was lying on the beach, turned on his side and leaning on his elbow to talk to someone beside him, only that someone was a skeleton on its back. Everything else in the picture was realistic, almost photorealistic, but in strikingly vibrant colors, the colors you might see in a nightmare.

"He's interesting in a way," Thatcher admitted. "Inserting some horrific or surrealistic element into the realistic setting. Don't you think?"

"Yes," I said, moving to the next, which showed a woman walking along the beach holding the hand of a little boy who was literally sinking into the sand. Though he was half buried, the woman seemed unaware of it. The ocean had a crimson, almost bloody tint beneath a setting sun.

In the third picture, a small gathering of happy-looking young people stood at the shore, some eating, some drinking, all laughing and smiling, while in front of them, an older woman who resembled my mother was caught in a wave, her arms stretched toward them in desperation.

"Not hard to read the meaning of this one, I suppose," Thatcher observed.

"There's a great deal of anger in all these pictures," I said. "It makes you feel sorry for him."

"Pity is not something people here have time or an inclination to express," Thatcher said. "It won't sell the pictures." He took one look at my face and added, "Let's get out of here. I'm sorry I showed you these. I didn't mean to depress you. You're looking too beautiful for that."

I flashed him a smile and turned away so he wouldn't see the sadness in my eyes. Did my mother share this terrible agony? What was their world like, their everyday lives in that beach house? Did I really want to enter it?

It took us nearly twenty minutes to make our way back through the crowd. So many people stopped Thatcher to ask him questions about cases he had completed or was involved with now. Some of the younger women looked for any possible excuse to get him to pause and speak with them. He was polite with everyone but clung tightly to my hand and worked relentlessly to get us through.

When we broke out into the street, he apologized. "I'm sure you would have liked to stay and talk to more people to gather information for your project, but I'm being selfish tonight. I'm not sharing you."

"It's all right," I said. "It wasn't exactly the setting I

wanted. Too many distractions, and I don't think those people would have been forthcoming."

"Then maybe my mother is right: you would do better using Joya del Mar and permitting her to invite people to meet you. There you could ensnare them with your questions and twist the truth out of them."

"Yes," I said, laughing. "Maybe."

We drove out of Palm Beach to a place called Singer Island, where he took me to a restaurant that had a patio facing the ocean, not more than forty feet away. Against the horizon, the stars looked as if they were falling into the sea.

"It is beautiful here," I said. "Thank you for bringing me."

"I knew you would like it. I haven't been here in a long time."

"Why not?"

"Beautiful things aren't enjoyable unless you share them with someone special," he replied. "Don't you agree?"

"I suppose," I said, trying to be cautious. Being with Thatcher in so romantic a setting, I found myself feeling as though I were teetering on the edge of some great precipice. If I let myself go, I would fall deeply into the mystery of the darkness beneath. I was both attracted to it and afraid of it.

His good looks, his charm, and his interesting personality were enticing in and of themselves, but much more so for me sitting in the warm night with a candle flickering on his face and the mesmerizing sound of the ocean softly soothing us beneath a sky so bright with stars it looked like the beginning of all time. I felt I had stepped into a fairy-tale world where magic was as common as daylight, where every word between us seemed like poetry, every sound around us part of the symphony, music composed for us alone, as if the whole world were suddenly devoted to one purpose: ensuring our happiness above and beyond the rest of the world.

"What kind of an answer is 'I suppose,' " Thatcher said, not settling for my caution. *"Beauty without the beloved is like a sword through the heart.* Something Christina Rossetti wrote that I read once and never forgot."

I turned away quickly. Of course, he was right, and of course, this was what my mother and my father must have suffered for so many years after having discovered a great love they were forced to give up. I couldn't help but mourn for them both. My heart ached.

"I'm sorry," Thatcher said, reaching across the table to put his hand over mine. "I didn't mean to be so deep and serious, especially tonight."

"No," I said, shaking my head, unable to stop the tears from clouding my eyes. "It's beautiful, and you're right."

I took a breath to get myself back on track.

"But according to your mother, you haven't been looking all that hard to find someone with whom you could share beauty and happiness."

"There's a lot my mother doesn't know about me," Thatcher said almost angrily. "I bet there was a lot your mother didn't know about you."

"Oh, yes," I said, laughing. "Oh, yes."

"There, you see." He reached for the wine list. "Let's have something special tonight. We've got to celebrate my settling another case favorably, among other things," he said.

"What other things?"

"Our being honest with each other, Willow. I actually like that name a lot. It fits you far better than the pseudonym."

He fixed that winning smile on me, holding me in the candlelike flame in his eyes until I realized it and looked quickly at the menu.

Careful, Willow De Beers, I told myself. *You're leaning too far over that precipice.*

You're going to fall.

After a wonderful dinner and a walk along the beach, we returned to my hotel. The meal, the wine, the soft conversation, holding hands while we walked in bare feet, laughing and teasing each other . . . all of it gave me a pleasant sense of deep calm. He seemed to feel the same way. Neither of us said much during the ride. All that passed between us was an occasional glance and smile. He had kissed me twice on the beach, and the taste lingered on my lips. Caution and conscience flew off like ribbons loosened in my hair and carried into the darkness behind me.

Even after we pulled up to the hotel and he got out and took my hand, we said little. We walked through the lobby, barely noticing anyone or anything else. In the elevator, we stared at the doors impatiently. When they opened, I felt my heart skip beats and then thump with greater anticipation. At my door, he slipped his hand around my waist. I opened the door and had started to flip the light switch when his other hand took mine gently and brought my arm down at my side.

He closed the door, and in the darkness, we kissed again, a long, warm, and wet kiss that made my spine electric, my breasts tingle.

"Willow, Willow," he whispered.

He lifted me into his arms and carried me to the bed. I looked up at him and watched him start to undress. All the while, I didn't move. It seemed almost like watching a scene in a movie, like watching something that was happening to someone else.

Shirtless, he knelt to kiss me and gently lift me so he could unzip my dress. He moved it over my shoulders and down my arms. There was just enough light coming through the windows to electrify his eyes.

"You're so beautiful," he said.

He cupped and kissed each of my breasts. I moaned and let my head go back onto the pillow as his lips traveled down over my stomach. In minutes, he had my dress completely off, and moments later, we were both naked.

I heard him unwrap a contraceptive.

"We're safe," he whispered.

I knew it was important, but it sounded like a commercial. He sensed it could break our mood and was over me with his lips, his hands, as quickly as he could be. How wonderful he smelled. I loved running my hands through his hair and then feeling his firm shoulders and wrapping myself around him.

Our lovemaking began slowly, building and building, lifting me out of my body until I felt my passion crash again and again against him like the waves outside crashing against the shoreline. My cries rose and fell with each undulating rush of pleasure. I wasn't an experienced lover. In fact, Allan was the only other man with whom I had been this intimate, but it seemed to me that Thatcher was unselfish in his loving. He was concerned and determined that I would be as pleased as he was, whereas Allan always made me feel I was there to serve his needs, and if I was lucky enough to enjoy it, all well and good.

Thatcher and I didn't just come to an abrupt end, either, which was something that usually happened between Allan and me. Thatcher's retreat was very slow, loving, full of caresses and kisses, holding onto me as if he didn't want ever to leave me. It was like being placed softly back into yourself rather than experiencing a brusque uncoupling where I was left to break my own fall.

We lay beside each other, catching our breath, not talking, but still holding hands.

Finally, he spoke. "There's definitely something to be said about two people being drawn to each other magically," he said. My silence seemed to frighten him. "Right?" he asked.

"Yes," I said.

I believed it, but I was full of mixed emotions about it, feeling both afraid and guilty.

I could hear Daddy's questions.

Do you like him, Willow?

Yes, Daddy.

Is it more than just a passing fancy?

I think so, Daddy.

Do you feel special with him?

Oh, yes, Daddy.

Does it seem like he feels that way about you?

Yes, yes, it does.

We've got to take risks with people sometimes, Willow. Don't you agree?

I do, Daddy.

Then leave that feeling of guilt outside your door. It has no place here, it seems, right?

Yes, right, Daddy. Yes.

"What?" Thatcher asked.

Had I spoken aloud?

"Nothing," I told him.

He propped himself on his elbow and leaned over me, running his forefinger down my nose to my lips and then between my breasts.

"It sounded like you said yes. I hope it was a critique of our lovemaking," he kidded.

"More than that. It was a critique of the whole night," I said.

He laughed. "So, did I succeed?"

"With what?"

"Getting you to reconsider whether you would leave or not?" he asked.

"Maybe that was why I said yes," I told him, and he smiled and kissed me again.

He didn't leave for another hour. I assured him that as soon as I was up, packed, and checked out, I would drive to Joya del Mar. He had a full day in court, but he promised he would be home in time for dinner.

"Knowing my mother," he said, "I'm sure she'll do something extra special. I'll call her as soon as I can, let her know you are coming first thing in the morning, and ask her to go easy and give you a chance to settle in."

"Okay," I said. Despite the opportunity and my desire to be near him, I was still very nervous. This could lead to even bigger and bigger mistakes, I thought. I promised myself that the moment I saw that happening or the moment I felt uncomfortable, I would leave.

Maybe I would just go home and write a long letter to my mother and leave it at that. Maybe that made a lot more sense, or maybe it was too late to do anything like that. It wouldn't be much longer before I would know.

My intention to sleep late, have breakfast in my room, and then dress and leave calmly was shattered by the ringing of my phone at seven-thirty. It was Aunt Agnes. Hearing her voice was almost more of a shock than the phone ringing itself. It was as if she had somehow broken through my wall, a wall built to keep out reality and responsibility.

"What are you doing there?" she screamed.

It took me a moment to clear my head. I had been in such a comfortable sleep, gliding on a cloud, feeling warm and snug and safe.

"Aunt Agnes?"

"Yes, yes. Whom did you expect? I tried to reach you at your college residence, and then I called the dean's office, and they told me you had taken a leave of absence. It sounds more like a leave of your senses."

"How did you find me?" I asked, annoyed.

"I forced that man at your house to tell me. I practically had to threaten him with police action."

"You had no right to do that, Aunt Agnes."

"I have no right? I have a responsibility to my poor dead brother's memory to look after you, Willow."

Her concern for me was quite out of character. What did she really want?

"What is it? Why are you calling me?"

"The condition of the house, for one."

"What condition?"

"I had people go there to pick up my things, and the report I received was absolutely horrible. Your so-called caretaker is back to his drinking."

"No, he can't be," I said.

"Well, he is. What are you doing down there? And at The Breakers! What is this? Why did you leave college? Why didn't you tell me first, ask my opinion? Well?"

"I have some personal things to sort out, Aunt Agnes. I need to be alone."

"In Palm Beach! And at The Breakers! What sort of alone is that? Are you with someone? Well?"

"I don't want to discuss it over the phone, Aunt

Agnes. It's really not any of your business. Thank you for your concern."

"What? What about the house? He's liable to set it on fire."

"I'll call him. I'm sure whoever told you those things exaggerated. He's probably feeling low about Daddy's death and just needed to be comforted."

"With alcohol? What sort of comfort does that bring?"

"Please, Aunt Agnes. It's very early."

"Early? It's nearly eight. What sort of things are you sorting out down there, Willow? You know, a young woman with your inheritance becomes a target for unscrupulous gigolos, especially in Palm Beach. You're not experienced enough or old enough to handle yourself in those circumstances. Don't you sign any papers, and don't you marry anyone. I should come right down there," she threatened.

So that was it, I thought. She was worried I would give away the family jewels.

"No one is taking advantage of me, Aunt Agnes. That's not why I'm here."

"Well, why are you there? Why can't you tell your aunt?"

"I'm not ready to tell anyone anything. You'll just have to trust me," I said.

"Your father would be very upset with you, Willow."

Was she right? Would Daddy have disapproved of all of this, especially confronting my mother now?

"You had better come to me."

"No, Aunt Agnes. Thank you. Thanks for calling."

"Willow—"

I hung up, and then I took the receiver off the hook.

I'll be gone today, and she won't be able to find me, I thought.

No one will be able to find me until I find myself.

10

Love or Madness?

Now that Aunt Agnes had stirred the cauldron of turmoil inside me like some witch who worked her curses over the telephone, I couldn't remain in bed. I ordered in my breakfast and packed my things. Fuming over her phone call, I decided to call Miles to see how much of what she was saying was purely exaggeration. It rang so long I thought he wasn't going to answer at all or that he might have already been driven out by Aunt Agnes. Finally, he picked up.

"De Beers residence," he said, and cleared his throat. He sounded as if he might have been crying.

"Miles, are you all right?" I asked immediately.

"Willow? Is that you?"

"Yes, Miles."

"Listen to me," he said in a throaty whisper before I

could ask him anything. "I have strange and wondrous news to tell you."

"What?"

"The last few nights, I heard sounds coming from your father's office. At first, I thought it might just be field mice, so I laid some traps. I caught nothing. This morning, I rose before dawn and walked as quietly as I could to the office. You'll never imagine what I found."

"What?" I said, holding my breath. Had someone burglarized my father's office? Had Aunt Agnes, wondering why I had spent so much time there, gone back there to search it?

"Your father's computer was on. It was on and running. There were words on the screen."

"I don't understand, Miles. What are you saying? Someone was searching my father's computer files?"

"No, no, no. No one has come into the house uninvited."

"Then . . . what do you mean?"

"Don't you see, Willow? Your father is completing his unfinished work. All you will have to do when it's completed is print it off and send it to his publisher. He can't rest in peace until that happens. I'm sure of it."

For a long moment, I couldn't speak. I had never heard Miles talk like this.

"Miles, are you positive the computer was on?"

"Oh, yes, yes. I saw the glow coming from the desk and looked very closely."

"Did you shut off the computer, Miles?"

"No, no, I didn't touch a thing. I haven't touched a thing in the office since . . . since your father's passing.

When I went back and looked again, there were additional lines on the screen."

"Miles, be honest with me now. Are you drinking? Aunt Agnes thinks you are."

"Oh, no, no," he said. "I'm fine. All is fine."

"Okay," I said. "I'll call you in a day or so and let you know where you can reach me."

"Wondrous," he said. "Wondrous."

"Miles, someone will be coming to the house from Bell's real estate agency early next week. Let them look around, and they will set up a schedule with you to show interested buyers the property," I told him, remembering arrangements I had begun right before I left for Palm Beach.

"They have already called, Willow. They will be here on Monday. Maybe that's why your father is working so hard and fast," he said, the excitement in his voice rising. "Of course. Now it makes sense. He wants to be sure his work is completed before the estate is sold out from under him."

I didn't know what to say to him over the phone.

"I'll call you" was all I could manage, and then I hung up. Regardless of my feelings toward Aunt Agnes, I couldn't deny having the same sort of anxieties about Miles now. I would have to get back there soon, I thought. His story about my father's computer actually put a chill in me. It was madness with meaning, for I knew my father had left a book unfinished, and I knew how he must have hated that and perhaps even had it as his last thought.

In the meantime, I decided it would be prudent for

me to phone Mr. Bassinger. Luckily, he was in his office. I asked him if he could manage to stop by and check things out. I explained my concern without accusing Miles of drinking, but I did tell him what Miles had said about the computer.

"I understand," Mr. Bassinger said, reading between the lines. "I'll see to it."

"Thank you. When you want to reach me, I'll be at this number," I said, and read the number off Bunny's card.

"I'll call you as soon as I can," he promised.

As soon as I had my breakfast and dressed, I went down and checked out of the hotel. My luggage was loaded into my car, and I was off to Joya del Mar. The shaky timbre of Miles's voice and his story lingered like the insistent aftermath of a particularly vivid nightmare. I couldn't help but imagine the ghost of my father seated in front of his computer. The image remained on the screen of my imagination all the way to my mother's family estate.

Jennings answered the call box in his dry, impatient tone of voice again, shutting me off abruptly and starting the gates the instant he heard my name.

However, he was there waiting for me when I drove up.

"I'll take your bags to your room, miss," he told me.

"Oh, thank you. Where is Mrs. Eaton?"

"She has not yet risen, but Mr. Eaton left me word concerning your arrangements," he said. "Would you like a cold drink on the rear loggia after you are settled in? Iced tea, perhaps?" he asked.

Even if he wasn't the most pleasant person I had met, he was at least efficient and professional, I thought.

"Yes, that would be nice."

"Very good, miss," he said, and I entered the house and went up to what would be my room. I walked out onto the balcony and looked at the ocean. It was a truly magnificent day, the clouds pasted like puffs of smoke against the vibrantly blue sky. I could see a luxury cruise ship gliding along as if the ocean had turned to aqua ice. There were dozens of sailboats and yachts, turning it all into a grand playground for the rich and fortunate.

What was exciting about having the ocean in your backyard was that the scene changed so often. There was always something new to look at, and nature itself was never uninteresting or monotonous. Someday, I thought, I would like to live near the sea.

Jennings put my luggage on luggage stands and then asked me if I would like him to unpack them.

"No, that's fine. I'll do it all later," I said.

"Very good. Your iced tea will be ready in a few minutes," he said, and left.

Now that I was alone in the room that had supposedly been my mother's, the room in which all the terrible things had happened to her, I felt a strange foreboding, as if I were truly trespassing on the forbidden past. Perhaps Daddy in his wisdom had good reason to keep all this from me. Perhaps I was defying fate or challenging it by coming here and trying to unravel the twisted and painful past that had bound my parents and left them locked up in a room filled with ill-fated love and unfulfilled promises. Every kiss, every touch was definitely a promise of sorts. Love, especially a great and all-consuming one, so enriched their lives that they were surely surprised by reality themselves. Even someone as intelligent and perceiving as my father had fallen victim to the longings of his own heart. Otherwise, he would never have begun this journey that led to nowhere except disappointment, defeat, and pain, not only for himself but for my mother, whom I am sure he never meant to harm.

"Go home, Willow," I whispered. "Don't let your head rest on this pillow tonight. Who knows what nightmares are stored within it, what images would haunt your sleep?

"Go home, Willow, go home. You have ghosts enough there to populate your dark world of dreams as it is. You don't have to add the ones who reside here."

Thinking so deeply, I left the room and didn't realize I was on the rear loggia until Jennings cleared his throat behind me and brought my iced tea on a silver tray.

"Thank you, Jennings. When does Mrs. Eaton rise?"

"It varies," he said almost solely out of the right corner of his mouth, "depending on the evening before, which often extends into the day after."

"I see."

"Yes," he said. "If you don't, you soon will," he added without emotion. "Do you require anything else, miss? Some crackers and cheese, perhaps?"

"No, thank you," I said.

"Very good. If you need anything, I'll be close by,"

he said, and retreated into a corridor as if he were a statue that came to life at the sound of his name.

The service people here don't respect the people for whom they work, I thought, *but I doubt that it bothers people like Bunny and Asher Eaton.* It was almost as if they saw themselves as levels and levels above the rest of the world whose criticism and ridicule fell far too short to disturb them, much less do them any harm. This certainly was a unique place, I thought. Maybe my contrived reason for being here, my study, was a good idea after all. I laughed to myself, sipped some iced tea, and sat back to look out at the sea and think.

Less than a minute or so later, I saw Linden emerge from the house carrying his leather case in one hand and his easel over his left shoulder like a lance. He made his way down the beach and disappeared around the bend. My heartbeat quickened with the realization that if I was going to do this, I should do it now, immediately, or else go home.

I rose and walked down the path to the beach and then followed in his footsteps. When I came around the bend, I saw he was just setting up his easel. He didn't see or hear me approaching. Rather than come right on him, I thought I would call out.

"Hi," I said.

He paused and looked at me, with a face not angry this time so much as it was surprised and curious.

"Looks like we'll never be rid of you as long as the Eatons are our tenants." He turned away from me and continued to set up his easel.

"I'm really not the big bad bogeyman," I said. "You've misunderstood my motives and my purpose."

"Right," he muttered. "Of course, it has to be my fault."

"I like your work," I said, ignoring his sarcasm.

He turned back to me, his right eyebrow lifted. "Is that so? And where did you see my work?" he challenged with angry disbelief. "The Eatons don't have anything in the house. One of the first things they asked when they moved in was to have my paintings taken down and out. Bunny, as she likes to be called, said they were too depressing and would upset their guests. The truth is, all of their guests depress and even sicken me," he said.

"Oh," I said.

He tilted his head a bit. "You're now one of their guests?"

"I'm afraid so," I replied. He almost smiled. He nodded and unzipped his case instead.

"I'd be afraid so, too. So," he continued, "where did you see my work—or is that just something you think will win me over?" he stabbed.

"No, it's not. I am not in the habit of saying things I don't mean," I shot back at him, my face filling with crimson indignation.

This time, he did soften his lips into something bordering on a smile.

"Really. We have a sincere person in the world of insincerity, pretension, and cosmetic surgery."

"For your information, I saw three of your paintings at a gallery last night."

"Oh." He turned, his skepticism challenged. "And?"

"I think your work is very interesting, especially the way you put something surreal into the real."

I was so nervous I used Thatcher's words and hoped they were the right ones. I did believe it.

Now both of Linden's eyebrows were up. "Is that so? Have you studied art?"

"In college, yes."

"Who are your favorite artists?" he asked, whipping his question like someone testing and challenging.

"I'm not crazy about abstract art, but I find works like Mondrian's *Broadway Boogie-Woogie* fun. I like Jackson Pollock's *Moon Woman* and actually have a poster of it in my room at home. My father loved Salvador Dali and had a large print of *Three Sphinxes of Bikini* in his office. Something about your work reminds me of Dali. Maybe it's the colors."

He stared, a look of amazement on his face.

"What's the matter?" I asked.

"Nothing," he said quickly.

"You thought I was just humoring you and that I knew absolutely nothing about art, correct?"

"Most people I meet here are empty, mindless. I call them Hollows. They don't even have enough substance to cast shadows," he said bitterly.

"I noticed that."

"Noticed what?" he asked quickly.

"In your paintings, the people, except for the woman and the boy, cast no shadows."

Now, he actually smiled. "You do surprise me, Miss . . . what was your name?"

It was so heavily on the tip of my tongue to tell him the truth that I actually fumbled with it for a moment.

"What did you say?"

"Isabel," I said, remaining the coward.

"Right, yes. Well, Isabel, I will admit I'm a little impressed."

"Thank you. What are you planning on doing today?"

"Don't you remember what Thatcher said?"

I shook my head.

"I set up, and I wait. I cast my line for inspiration, and on a good day, I catch something."

"I hope this will be a good day for you," I said.

He nodded. "How long are you to be a guest of the Eatons?"

"Not that long," I replied. "A few days, maybe a week. Would it disturb you if I just sat here?" I asked.

Without replying, he continued to set up his paints. Then, suddenly, he turned on me, his face back to that look of rage.

"I don't understand what you're doing here. What do you want from us?"

I had seen my father defuse people, as he liked to call it, often enough to know what to do. I shrugged and smiled, looking as calm as I could.

"To be honest, Linden, I don't know myself. I had this idea, and it was approved, and now I'm struggling to make sense out of it."

My honesty took him by surprise. The nearly blue rage in his face began to recede.

"I have this theory that we all have trouble enough dealing with what's real and what isn't in our lives, but people who are insulated more, protected by their wealth and position, might have an even more difficult time discerning what's real and what isn't. Of course, they might not care, anyway."

He stared at me again and then shook his head. "All right," he said. "I'm curious. What have you been told about my mother and me?"

"Oh, not that much, really."

"You weren't told she was raped by her stepfather and as a result had a mental breakdown and was placed in a clinic?" he asked, the bitterness practically dripping from his mouth.

My heart was pounding, but I kept as cool as I could and gazed out at the sea first to find support in the beauty it possessed.

"Yes," I said. "I was told something like that, but that isn't exactly the sort of information I'm here to gather."

"Oh, that's not the sort of information you're here to gather. It's not important, huh?"

"That's not what I'm saying. I'm trying . . ."

"Have you any idea what it's like to have people looking at you, thinking there he is, the child of a rapist? I'll tell you so you don't have to guess or do research. You have a feeling of nonidentity, almost as if you don't exist at all. When I was younger but old enough to understand, I often looked into the mirror, half expecting to see no reflection.

"Of course, my grandmother did the best she could. For most of my life, I lived believing my grandmother was my mother. You've heard that, I'm sure," he said, his eyes steely cold. "We're a favorite coffeetime conversation topic. I bear the Montgomery name, but it's like a gift of charity. I have no blood relationship to it. I might as well think of myself as an adopted child who just happens to be living now with his real mother."

I couldn't respond for a few moments. *How alike we are,* I thought. Most of my life, my adoptive mother had me believe I was the child of a rapist, too. Could I tell him without revealing it all?

"I had no intention of getting into those sorts of things, Linden."

"Well, what sorts of things are you getting into, then?"

"The Montgomerys were very wealthy once, weren't they?"

"So?"

"Well, your mother experienced a life of great wealth and now lives a different life. I simply thought she might be a very good resource. You, too, I suppose," I said. "You and your mother are people who have lived the changes and could make comparisons."

His eyes calmed. I could almost see the waves receding inside them.

"I told you what I think of these wealthy people," he said, tossing a gesture toward the house. "They think of themselves as substantial, important, meaningful because they can buy yachts and estates and have grand parties and wear designer clothing. My mother has more substance in her pinkie finger than most of them have in their whole bodies, in all their bodies together!"

"That's why I'd like to meet her and talk with her," I said quickly.

He studied me a moment. "Who are you?" he asked. "I don't mean your name. I mean, where are you from? Who are your people?"

"I'm from South Carolina. I'm an only child. I've lost both my parents."

"Are you engaged or anything?"

"No," I said. "How about you?"

He threw his head back and laughed madly — so madly and so long I was a bit frightened.

"Me? You have to be kidding, of course. Why, I'm like a leper in this town. A girl here take me seriously? Please. I used to go places, hang out with some friends, but I've become too weird for them — or too bitter," he added more honestly. "I am bitter."

"My nanny used to say that bitterness is like an animal feeding on itself, a buzzard that eats its own heart. *Um corvo que coma seu próprio coração*."

"What?" he asked smiling.

"She was Portuguese. She was really the one who brought me up," I said. The more of the truth I revealed, the better I felt about my white lies and little deceptions.

"Yeah, well, for me, bitterness keeps me alive," he said.

"Sometimes, we are unhappy so much, we think we can't live without it," I said.

"Is that another of your nanny's sayings?"

"Yes, in a way."

He stared again and then nodded as some conclusion came to him. "Okay," he said, "I'll make a deal with you."

"What?"

"I'll talk to you. I'll answer as many questions as I can for you. I'll even let you meet my mother."

"What do I have to do?" I asked, holding my breath.

"Pose."

"Pardon?"

"Pose for me so I can paint you."

"Pose?"

"I don't mean nude," he said, "although I'll admit that from a purely artistic viewpoint, you are beautiful and would make an excellent subject. However, I'd like you more in a flowing long skirt with just a little of your leg showing as you sit on the dune here. I'd like you barefoot, and I'd like your hair down and to have you wear an off-the-shoulder peasant girl's blouse. No jewelry, not even earrings. No makeup, either. Just you sitting here looking out at the ocean is all I want."

"I don't have that sort of clothes with me," I said.

"It's all right. My mother has the clothes. She'll lend them to you, or to us, I should say, and I'm sure they will fit you well enough. Well?" he followed quickly.

"How long do I pose? I mean, hours and hours?" I asked.

He finally laughed warmly, freely, and when he did, his face looked much younger.

"No more than two hours a day for three days. How's that?"

"Okay," I said. "It's a deal."

His eyes brightened, and then he looked out at the

sea. "For now, though, I'd like to be alone." His voice had changed back to the harder, colder, angrier tone. It was as if he had another self, a part of him that came from the dark side and took him over firmly.

"Okay." I stood up. "When can I meet your mother?" I dared to ask, and held my breath.

"Tomorrow, after we have our first session on the beach. I'll be out here by ten, which should give you enough time to rise, have breakfast."

"What about the clothing?"

"It'll be here. You can go over the hill there and change."

"And your mother?"

"You'll come to the house about two-thirty. She and I have a glass of lemonade together and just sit quietly on the patio.

"Don't tell her about our bargain," he added sharply.

"All right."

"I don't want her to think . . . I mean, she might not understand," he said.

"But you're getting her to give me the skirt and blouse," I reminded him.

"I didn't say that. I said she would lend them to us. She just doesn't have to know she is," he added.

I was going to ask why keeping it a secret was so important, but I thought I heard Daddy tell me to stop, to be grateful for what I had achieved, and not to push too hard. Everyone is fragile, he would say.

"Okay. See you later," I said, and walked back toward the house. When I looked at him again, he had gone down to the water. He stood in the incoming tide and stared out as if he saw something. I could see nothing, but then again, I wasn't looking at the world through his eyes.

Just before I turned to go back up the walkway to the house, I heard a vigorous honking of a boat horn and looked out to see someone in a long speedboat waving and bouncing along toward the shoreline. As he drew closer, I realized it was Thatcher. He gestured emphatically for me to go down to the dock which was just below the beach house. Surprised and amused, I hurried back over the beach as he pulled the boat alongside the dock.

"What are you doing?" I called. "I thought you were very busy today."

"I had a postponement at court and then met with the client who owns this boat. I gave him four hours for free in exchange for using the boat. Come on aboard."

"Come aboard? But . . ." I looked back at the house. "I haven't even met with your mother today yet. She doesn't know I am here, and . . ."

"She's probably still in bed. C'mon. I only have four hours."

"But . . ."

He reached up and helped me get into the boat.

"What is this?" I asked, looking over the strangely shaped boat. "It looks like a giant bullet."

Thatcher laughed. "It travels that way. It's a Magnum 80 with a top speed of seventy-four miles an hour. Those are twin eighteen-hundred-horsepower engines. It sleeps ten," he said, then shifted and shot off before I had a chance to say a word. In seconds, we were bouncing over the water so hard I screamed. The spray flew up around me.

"I'm not dressed for this!" I shouted.

"Just hold on."

I can't deny it was very exciting, so much so that it took my breath away.

"The way this boat was customized, it cost about a million, eight hundred thousand," Thatcher explained when he slowed us down. "Not bad, huh?"

"It's like an airplane on water."

"Yes. Here," he said, putting me in charge of the controls. "Take it for a spin."

"Me?"

"Why not? Try it," he urged. I shook my head. "C'mon, Willow, take some chances. Once in a while, it's fun to challenge fate."

The way he looked at me, fixed his eyes intently on my face, made me think he knew everything.

With great hesitation, I changed places and listened to his instructions. Moments later, I could feel the boat humming beneath me, its power and size impressive. It was like riding a whale. I thought being a passenger was exciting, but having some control of it was twice as thrilling.

"You're doing fine," he said. "Give it to her."

I shook my head, but he accelerated, and we shot forward, hitting the waves so hard I thought my heart was going up and down like a yo-yo inside me. After a while, we slowed again and just cruised calmly.

"I know a great spot for lunch," he said, taking over.

I sat back. The fingers of the wind had played havoc with my hair, but I didn't care. The salt spray, sunshine, and warm air were beguiling. I truly felt as if I had stepped onto a magic carpet.

"Do you do this often?" I asked him.

"I used to do a lot of sailing, but lately I haven't been out on the water very much. I can't remember the last time I did something like this on a weekday," he added, his eyes twinkling at me.

"Maybe I'm a bad influence."

"Maybe you're a good influence. You heard Bunny. I work too hard."

"Where's this wonderful place for lunch?" I asked as we continued farther out to sea and the shoreline began to disappear. "Cuba?"

"You'll see," he promised.

After a few more minutes, he cut the engines and dropped anchor.

"I don't understand," I said. "Why have you stopped?"

"We're here," he declared, and held out his arms. "Can you find a prettier, quieter, more private place? This happens to be my favorite spot," he said, and started down the steps. "C'mon, help me bring up lunch."

I followed him to the galley, where there were breads and rolls, meats, cheeses, bottles of wine, and fresh fruit.

"Well?" he said.

"It's a banquet," I declared.

We fixed our sandwiches and platters of fruit, and then he brought up the wine. Sitting at the table with the wide expanse of ocean around us, far enough out so we could no longer see the shore, I did feel we were in a special place. Occasionally, we caught sight of a sailboat, but it was as if there were invisible walls between us and the rest of the world. No one came very close.

He poured the wine, and we toasted.

"A loaf of bread, a jug of wine, and thou beside me," he recited.

"You know how to sweep a girl off her feet," I said.

"Are you off your feet, Willow?" he asked, his face suddenly so serious.

"Well, I can't walk on water," I replied.

He smiled. "Avoiding the answer, huh? You're just as afraid of becoming involved with someone as I am. That's what I like about you," he added before I could offer any denial.

"Why?"

"Too many women around here are too eager. It's not a challenge."

"I don't see myself as a trophy, Thatcher."

"I don't mean you are. I have this old-fashioned idea that anything good, really good, should not be easy to achieve or possess. Too much is taken for granted, especially here," he said. "As you can imagine from the way my parents live, instant gratification is the rule, not the exception. I grew up getting whatever I wanted, whenever I wanted it. So did my sister—she still does, actually."

"Then how did you get this new, wiser perspective on life?" I asked.

He shrugged. "Just lucky, I suppose."

He rose and took off his shirt before he sprawled on the deck, a wide, silly grin on his face. The rocking of the boat, the wine rushing through my blood, and the warm sea air continued to enchant me. I rose to sit beside him. We could hear the terns calling to each other over the water and the low murmur of boat engines in the distance. The clouds were gliding toward the horizon.

"My mother's right. I work too hard," he muttered, and then looked up at me. "Let me know whoever it is who sent you here," he said. "I'd like to thank him or her personally."

During all the time I had been with Allan, I had never felt such need as I did this moment when my eyes locked on Thatcher's. The air between us seemed to crackle with electricity, drawing our lips closer and closer until I was leaning over him and kissing him. He did not embrace me. He made me press myself to him as if he wanted me to commit my body and passion first. I don't know if I could have resisted or should have resisted the clamoring within me, but I didn't. I kissed him again, and he put his arm around my waist and brought me down beside him.

"You know," I said, teasing him with my lips, kissing the tip of his nose, his cheek, and just below his lips, "you're keeping me from my project."

"Really? I thought I *was* your project," he teased back, and then kissed me long and hard. "Did you ever make love on a boat?" he whispered.

"What do you think?"

He laughed and lifted me into his arms. "I don't see

how you can write a paper on Palm Beach society without making love on a boat," he said.

I didn't offer any resistance. Slowly, carefully, he carried me below to the master stateroom. Seconds later, we were naked and in the throes of lovemaking even more passionate than the evening before. Every once in a while, I heard the voice of caution within me, questioning me, demanding to know what I was doing, how I had managed to get so close and involved with another man so quickly. Was it madness or love? Was it out of some desperate need to find someone so I wouldn't be alone? Was I too vulnerable, or had the good fates smiled down on me and brought me some-one very special, someone who would truly love me as much as, if not more than, I would love him?

Afterward, we napped in each other's arms for nearly half an hour. He woke me with a kiss.

"We had better start back," he said. "I don't want to owe my client any more time. He's the sort who will take advantage."

I dressed quickly, and we cruised at a far slower, gentler pace back to the dock at Joya del Mar. When I stepped off the boat, I felt as if I had returned to earth from some fantasy journey.

"I'll be home about six," he said. "Don't let Bunny talk you into doing anything outrageous tonight."

"Okay," I said, laughing.

I watched him speed off, slapping the waves and flying into the distance like some fairy-tale prince re-turning to the pages of a storybook and leaving me wondering if I had dreamed it all.

When I turned to head back to the house, I saw Linden watching me from the front of the beach house. I started to wave to him, when he turned away abruptly and went inside. It was like a cold slap on my face.

This was going to be hard, I thought. This was going to be very hard.

11

The Ladies of Palm Beach

"**D**arling, I'm so happy you made the right decision," Bunny cried as she came down the stairs and saw me in the great room. "Have you had lunch yet?"

"Yes."

It was nearly four o'clock, and she was just thinking of lunch?

"Oh, poo. I'm sorry I wasn't down in time for you. I hate eating alone, don't you?"

I was about to tell her I hadn't eaten alone but thought maybe it was better I didn't. I just thought Thatcher would feel more comfortable if his mother didn't know our comings and goings.

"These days, I'm a golf widow. You know how they call some women football widows during the football season? Well, when Asher gets into his golf game, I had better find things to occupy myself and friends to join me, or I'll be staring at the walls waiting for him to remember he has a wife. At least I'm grateful he's not Michael Strentchild. Do you know Michael Strentchild?"

"No," I said.

"Of course you do. He's the grandson of Strentchild cutlery, the biggest cutlery company in North America. He was divorced recently, a bad divorce, and do you know what he went and did?"

"What?"

"He had his wife's face put on all his golf balls just so he could smack at her. Asher claims he's driving the ball yards farther than ever." She laughed. "Put that story down in your book, if you like."

"I'm not writing a book, Bunny."

"Well, you know what I mean," she said, waving her hand in the air between us as if she could wave away words and thoughts at will. "Did Jennings take good care of you while I was struggling to get out of bed? Are you set up in your room? Do you have everything you need?"

"Yes, I'm fine. Thank you."

"Thatcher called and laid down the law . . . absolutely no guests for dinner tonight. I told him that was wasting your time, that you were here specifically to meet significant people, but he was adamant."

She winked and smiled. "I think he'd like you all to himself. I can't say I blame him. Matter of fact, Asher and I have a dinner party tonight at the Carlsons'. I'll have them here one night. Broderick Carlson's father was the CEO of Packard-Willis, probably the biggest trucking firm in North America. I used to say America, but Dolly told me I'm leaving out Canada, and it wasn't accurate to leave out Canada."

I nodded, trying to look impressed and grateful.

"Look at your face," she suddenly cried. "Have you been lying on the beach? You're absolutely red."

"Oh, am I?"

"Don't you know how dangerous the sun's rays are, especially for a woman? I must get you right to my vanity table and have you put on some special cream designed to counter the ultraviolet damage. Come along," she insisted, taking my hand and marching us both back to the stairway.

"But I'm holding you back from eating your lunch," I said.

"Oh, food. What a nuisance," she declared, and continued to ascend, lecturing about skin and beauty all the way to her room and after. All the while, I kept thinking Linden might not be so wrong in his view of things and people around him. Maybe this is a hollow place.

"Now, just look at my face," Bunny said, sitting herself down in front of the vanity mirror. "If you didn't know I was Thatcher's mother, would you be able to predict my age with any real accuracy? Well?" she said, insisting I respond.

"No," I said. "I mean, I would never guess you are as old as you are."

"Exactly. And it's not because I had a cosmetic procedure two years ago. That was just a little thing I did for my eyes. It's my skin, my complexion, that keeps me looking young. See here," she said, opening a jar of skin cream. "This is a special formula from France. It's made up of herbs, a secret recipe. I don't mind paying five hundred dollars a jar for it. It works!"

"Five hundred dollars?"

"And this," she said, "is a lotion that comes with it. You rub it in every night before you go to sleep."

"How much was that?"

"Five hundred, or six, I don't remember. Age is complexion, but it is also attitude. You've got to think young to be young," she said.

"Yes, my mother had similar ideas," I said.

"She did? There, you see? How old does she look?"

"She died a few years ago in a car accident," I said.

"Oh, dear. How dreadful for you. Anyway," she said, bouncing out of a dark thought as quickly as it had come on, "she was right—and looked young right up to the day she died, I bet. Now, sit right here and put this cream on immediately," she ordered, getting up. "We live in the Sunshine State, but we have to avoid the sun. I have some wonderful hats with wide brims for you to wear."

She opened her closet door, which she had done when she had given me the tour. It was as long and as wide as most people's bedrooms and filled with clothes, shoes, and hats. It had its own sitting area, mirrors, and even a television set.

"Feel free to borrow anything you want, my dear. In fact, I want you to think of this whole house as your home, too, while you're here, okay?"

"Thank you."

"Good. Rub that cream in evenly."

We heard a gentle *ding-dong* and then Jennings's voice. "Madam?"

Bunny went to her intercom and pressed a button. "Yes, Jennings?"

"Your guests have arrived," he said.

"Oh, wonderful. Since Isabel has eaten, I was afraid I'd have to nibble on something alone. Tell them we'll be right there," she said, and turned to me. "I have some people for you to meet. Thatcher said not to invite anyone to dinner, but he didn't say anything about high tea," she declared, and clapped her hands.

"High tea?"

"Well, it isn't exactly high tea the way the English think of it. This is more like the high tea at the Empress Hotel on Vancouver Island or something—finger sandwiches, biscuits. The Carriage sisters and I have our tea times once a week like clockwork. They are great gossips. Somehow, they know where to look to find everyone's dirty laundry. Aren't I clever? You'll love these two women. They are core Palm Beach. Their husbands were big developers here, brothers. Two brothers married two sisters. Isn't that a good story?

"The brothers died two years apart, and I swear, Thelma and Brenda Carriage won't marry again unless they find two brothers who are suitable. Come right down," she concluded breathlessly. "You can get wonderful information from them, I'm sure."

She hurried out of her bedroom, leaving me gaping stupidly after her, wondering if this whole place wasn't a private mental clinic after all.

I looked at myself in the mirror and then rubbed in her cream. Five hundred dollars for a four-ounce jar? Maybe it worked, or maybe it was just snake oil for the rich. Every class of society had its con men. Those who preyed on Palm Beach society were probably just better educated, more sophisticated, and better dressed. It didn't hurt if they came with a French or other European accent, either, I supposed.

Anyway, I had to go downstairs to meet her friends and play the part I had cast myself in for my contrived drama. Soon, I assured my troubled spirit, soon I'd be able to step off the stage and be in the real world, the world of truth. Just for now, just for a little while, I would put on the makeup and the costumes and stand in the lights.

Bunny held her high tea in the sitting room where I had first met her and Thatcher's father, Asher. When I entered, one of the Carriage sisters was standing up, modeling her outfit as if she were on a fashion runway. She had short platinum hair, very curly in front. Her sister, a dark brunette, also had short hair but straighter and styled so severely it looked like a hat. Even though it was difficult to tell which one was older, they both looked as if they were in their early sixties.

"Oh, Isabel, you're just in time to see Brenda's fashion show," Bunny said, laughing.

Both sisters turned to me, Brenda's eyes softer, bluer, Thelma's more gray and steely. I thought Brenda had a softer face altogether, although they both had hard, sharp features, thin noses, tight lips that looked like slashes when pressed together, and taut cheeks wrapped so firmly around their facial bones their skin looked absolutely translucent, tissue-paper thin. Thelma's chin was rounder and her neck a bit longer.

"Thelma, Brenda, this is our houseguest, Isabel Amou."

"How do you do," Thelma said first. She said it with such clipped pronunciation it almost sounded angry. Brenda laughed and shot forward to extend her hand.

"Hello," she said, and returned to their conversation as though my entrance, my very existence, was truly insignificant. "Despite what Thelma thinks, this is the rage," she declared.

"For a teenager, perhaps," Thelma muttered.

"What do you think, Isabel?" Brenda asked, turning back to me.

"It looks comfortable," I said.

She was wearing a long, light, white tunic-style shirt over a pair of black cropped pants and leather flip-flops. I noticed her toenails were painted a bright silver. Both of the Carriage sisters were full-figured women. Thelma was in a more conservative slenderizing sweater and skirt outfit and did look more her age.

"Oh, it is comfortable. It's a chic Maharani, the modern Indian woman look. I don't know why my sister is so critical. If we don't experiment with style occasionally, what will we experiment with? We're past the time when we experimented with sex," she added.

"Brenda!" Thelma said sharply.

"Well, we are, aren't we? Or, at least, I am. I can only speak for myself. I suppose there are women our age still on the hunt, so to speak."

"You know there are," Thelma said. She turned to Bunny. "Just yesterday, I told her what I had heard about Casey Freyman and her gardener. Gardeners, I should say."

Brenda laughed. "Well, more power to her. They say Viagra can help women, too," she said.

"Sit down, you fool. I swear, Bunny, I spend most of my day mending the fences my sister cracks in this town with her foolish gossip and childish behavior."

"That's what an older sister is for," Brenda said, sitting down but petulantly.

"Please, join us, Isabel," Bunny said, gesturing toward the free chair.

I sat.

"What would you like?"

"Oh, I'm not hungry, thank you."

"How about something to drink, a Bloody Mary, perhaps? Brenda is having a Mai Tai."

"No, thank you. I'll just have some iced tea. That is iced tea?" I asked, nodding at the pitcher.

"Oh, yes."

She didn't make any effort to pour it into a glass, so I began to reach for it, and, almost out of thin air, a maid appeared, poured the iced tea for me, and then, as quickly as she had come, stepped out of the room.

"Your house servants seem to come out of the woodwork," I remarked.

Bunny laughed. Thelma raised her eyebrows, and Brenda nodded, smiling.

"That's how they are supposed to appear," Bunny said.

Thelma turned her body completely toward me. "I understand you are here to dissect Palm Beach society," she said. "Put us all under a microscope."

"Not exactly dissect," I said, smiling nervously. "I'm working on a thesis paper."

"About rich people," Bunny added quickly.

"Yes," I admitted.

"I can't think of anything more boring," Thelma said. "The younger generation here is a completely spoiled, self-centered, degenerate bunch, and the older generation is absorbed with the effort to be younger, as you can see from my sister's behavior. Every club will be like the one you've just visited; every affair will be a carbon copy of the affair you've just attended."

"If you dislike it so much, why do you continue to live here?" I asked, actually curious about it.

Her sister laughed.

"Where else would I live?" Thelma snapped back at me. "Most of the rest of America is plagued with crime and filth."

"And if she moved away, whom would I have for my Wednesday teas?" Bunny cried as if it were a real worry.

"You'd find someone else pretty quickly," Thelma told her.

Bunny just laughed and then leaned toward me and admitted she would.

Thelma looked satisfied that she was right. Her eyes fixed on me again. "Where are you from?"

"South Carolina," I said.

"Where?" she pursued.

"A little community outside Columbia called Spring City. And I am a student at the University of North Carolina."

"How did you come to this place?" she followed.

"Thelma, you're behaving like a private detective," Bunny intercepted, seeing the look on my face.

"I . . . a friend of my father's . . . made some introductions for me," I stuttered.

"Oh? And who would that be?"

"Thelma!"

"I'm just trying to make some polite conversation, Bunny," she said, but pulled back to nibble on a finger sandwich.

"Has this modern Indian woman look reached the Carolinas yet?" Brenda asked me.

"I think I've seen women on campus wearing it, yes."

"You see?" Thelma said. "Women on campus. I'm sure there are no students your age, Brenda."

"This is not a style for young women only. Madeline assured me of that," Brenda insisted.

"Madeline would assure you of anything to make a sale," Thelma told her sharply, and then turned back to me. "What business is your family in?"

"My father was a doctor," I said.

"Really. Is he retired?"

"He passed away recently."

"Oh, I'm sorry," Brenda said.

"And your mother?"

"She died a few years ago in a car accident."

"Oh, dear me, dear me," Brenda moaned. "Must you extract all this horrible information from the poor girl, Thelma?"

"Whether I do or not does not affect the reality of it, Brenda. My sister has always resembled an ostrich," she said, "keeping her head in the sand."

"I have not!"

"I suppose you will hear some talk of it if you interview the gossips in this town, but when my sister's husband, Marshall Carriage, died in his sleep, Brenda kept anyone from knowing about it for three days. She didn't even tell me."

Brenda's face looked as if it would crumple into sobs any moment.

"I think she expected a resurrection. It could have been quite a little scandal if that autopsy showed anything but heart failure," she added, stabbing her sister with a look that would have pierced an army tank.

"I have always found that if you ignore unhappiness long enough, it often goes away," Brenda calmly defended herself. "Did you ever notice a dead bird? One day, it's there, and then the next or a week later, it's often gone."

"Something ate it or carried it off," Thelma said in a tone of frustration.

"So what? It was gone, wasn't it?"

"Oh, give me strength," Thelma said. "Do you see this girl ignoring the unpleasantness in her life? I asked her about her parents, and she told me. She didn't manufacture some tale to hide the ugly truth, did she?"

"Oh, this is exactly the sort of thing you wanted to hear, Isabel," Bunny said enthusiastically. "Life in Illusion, the Palm Beach Story," she wrote in the air.

"Really," Thelma said dryly. She fixed her suspicious eyes on me again. "I have heard about people coming around here pretending to be one thing or another when in truth they were spies for some family member who was trying to determine what assets she or he might have been cheated out of through some dishonest settlement."

"She's hardly that," Bunny said, quickly coming to my defense.

"Maybe," Thelma said, nodding. "Affluent people have to be more skeptical, more cautious by necessity. Remember what Willie Sutton replied when he was asked why he robbed banks."

"What did he say?" Bunny asked her.

"He said because that was where the money was. It's the same for us. They come here because this is where the money is, Bunny. Really, you and my sister are two sides of the same coin."

"I hope it's a rare coin," Bunny said, laughing.

"Unfortunately, here it is not." Thelma shifted her eyes at me again.

"I'm just a student, Mrs. Carriage," I told her. "I have no other agenda."

She stared sternly at me, her eyes unrelenting. The silence was heavy.

"I know what," Bunny declared. "I'm going to have a party."

"What? When?" Brenda asked quickly.

"Saturday night. There—it's decided, and Isabel can meet a number of people at once instead of pecking away."

"Maybe a party isn't a place where people really say and think what they believe," I offered gently. Bunny seemed so excited by her own idea, and I hated to throw any cold water on it.

"Perhaps in the rest of America that's so; however, it's certainly not true here," Thelma said. "A few glasses of shampoo, and they'll let down more than their hair."

"I love parties!" Brenda declared, beaming.

"To you, every day is one big party," Thelma said.

"Well, it is for us, isn't it?" she shot back. The truth of the statement was too hard to deny, even for Thelma, who just pressed her lips together to form that slash of purple across her face.

"Perfect, then," Bunny said, clapping her hands together. "Now, let's work up a guest list. We'll keep it small, say one hundred or one hundred twenty-five people."

"That's small?" I asked.

Even Thelma laughed. "This is the party capital of the world," she said. She glanced at Bunny. "I'm not sure you have enough time to do it right."

"We will. We will," Bunny insisted.

"One of the hardest things to do here is make an impression," Thelma explained. "What might seem like an extravaganza to you and your friends back in Spring City is ho-hum here."

"Well, this one won't be. We'll have a tent, of course, and set everything up around the pool. We'll get that company to put a dance floor over it, the way the Cooks did at their affair, remember? I want all the chairs decorated with fresh flowers."

"And lights," Brenda said. "You should string them up everywhere."

"Right, I will. We'll set up four bars, and I'll get Maxim to cater the food. I'll go right there in the morning and plan the menu. Thelma, you and Brenda should come along with me."

"I'll see," Thelma said.

"Have them make things you can't get in any restaurant around here," Brenda said. "I love when people do that."

Bunny nodded. "And for music . . . we'll get that twenty-piece orchestra the Grafters had at their affair."

"You can't book an orchestra on such short notice," Thelma said.

"Asher will double their fees, or else Thatcher will find a way; he always does. And if that doesn't work, we'll get that black singer who's the rage these days, the one who plays piano. I'll fly him in from New York."

"Oh, this is sounding wonderful," Brenda cried. "And just in time, too. We had nothing exciting to do this weekend, did we, Thelma?"

"We have nothing exciting to do any weekend, as far as I'm concerned," she said.

Then she paused, looked at Bunny for a moment and then at me and then back to Bunny.

"What?" Bunny asked, a smile on her lips.

"There's something else going on here, Bunny."

"What?"

"I don't know," she said. "You're a plotter."

Bunny laughed nervously.

"You're part of some conspiracy," she accused, looking at me.

"If I am, I'm not aware of it," I said.

"Maybe," she said with those skeptical eyes hovering on me, making me feel naked for a moment. "And then again, maybe not."

Bunny looked up at me as if Thelma Carriage had pulled a curtain apart. Then she shook off the thought and went back to discussing her gala event.

Maybe it was the pressure I felt myself under at the tea, or maybe it was just the spontaneous sea escapade I had taken with Thatcher earlier, but I was so tired I excused myself to take what I thought would be a short nap. When I awoke, however, night had already fallen, and I was shocked to discover it was a little after nine. The moon was casting a luminous ribbon over the ocean as far as the horizon. It was so full and bright, it swallowed the light of the stars around it.

I wondered where Thatcher was and imagined he had been wondering about me. I went into the bathroom and washed my face in cold water. I felt confused, almost drugged.

The house was very quiet, and at first I thought Thatcher had simply given up and gone out, but when I went down, I saw him sitting on the rear loggia, sipping a cocktail and looking out at the same moonlight that had impressed me the moment I awoke. He wore a short-sleeve white silk mock turtleneck and a pair of black slacks.

For a moment, I stood back and studied the way he gazed pensively at the sea. I used to enjoy watching Daddy when he didn't know I was watching. I knew it wasn't fair and that I would not like people observing me this way, but to me it was the best way to capture honesty: faces without protective expressions, bodies relaxed and unguarded, no pretension, no role playing. Daddy was just a man. Thatcher was just a man, but oh, I thought, what a handsome and intelligent-looking one.

"Hi," I said, coming up beside him.

"Hey." He rose quickly. "How are you? I was worried about you. I looked in on you, saw you were dead to the world, and let you be. Bunny told me you met the Carriage sisters."

"Yes," I said, raising my eyebrows.

"Thelma can be quite trying, and Brenda is so child-like she's full maintenance, as demanding as a five-year-old." He grimaced. "I heard about Bunny's plans for one of her parties. I'm sorry," he said. "I don't think that's the sort of thing you were after."

"That's okay," I said.

He pulled a chair out for me. "Hungry?"

"Just a little," I said.

"I thought we might have a bite out here, some simple Mexican food. I had the staff mix up some margaritas for us." He stirred a pitcher and poured me a glass.

The servants here must have their ears to the wall, I thought, for the maid began to bring out our food almost the moment he filled my glass.

"What sort of Mexican food?"

He uncovered each serving dish. "I ordered up some fajitas, enchiladas, a few burritos."

"This is what you call a bite!" I exclaimed.

Thatcher laughed. "Nothing is small here, especially egos," he said. "Oh, before I forget. There was a phone call for you."

"For me?"

"Yes." He took a slip of paper out of his jacket pocket and handed it to me. It was a message from Mr. Bassinger. It just said everything was fine, but I should call him whenever I had an opportunity to do so.

"I hope there aren't any problems," Thatcher said.

"No. It's just the family attorney. He checked on my property while I was away."

"I see. Must be a family friend, too, for him to take a personal interest."

"Yes."

Thatcher's eyes lingered on me like the eyes of someone searching for hidden truths. I avoided his gaze and considered the food.

"Everything looks and smells so wonderful."

"I'm sure it is. My parents have a great chef."

"They have their own chef?"

"Just for breakfast, lunch, and dinner," he remarked. "The only things my mother has ever cooked up are scandals and little social intrigues."

I laughed. We had a nice dinner and talked quietly. He told me more about his youth, a little more about his sister and her family and about some of his travels. He had been to just about anywhere I would have wanted to go. I had the impression he often had gone with someone, although I didn't think that someone was ever the infamous Mai Stone.

Afterward, we took a walk on the beach, held hands, kissed occasionally, and then, when he saw my eyes were closing, he suggested we go in and get some sleep.

"Too much sun and too many margaritas," I said.

"As long as it isn't too much of me," he teased.

"Hardly," I said. His eyes brightened, and then we walked back to the house. He saw me to my room and left to go to his suite.

I was asleep even before I pulled the blanket toward my chin.

But I woke up abruptly in the middle of the night as if I had a sixth sense that never slept, one that heard and saw and felt things beyond my body. I gazed at the clock and saw it was two o'clock in the morning. Looking out my windows, I saw the moon was long gone, and the stars it had captured in its glow were free to blaze. I rose slowly, almost like a sleepwalker who heard a voice calling to her. I felt myself drawn to the balcony and stepped out into the cooler night air. The sea breeze swirled around me and played with the hem of my nightgown. I took a deep breath and prepared to go back to bed when a light caught the corner of my eye, and I moved to the railing.

At first, I could see only the light. It looked as if it was moving, but what I understood a moment later was that the light came from a lantern someone was holding and swinging gently from right to left. As my eyes grew more accustomed to the darkness, I realized it was my mother standing out on the dock. She was dressed in a sheer white nightgown that seemed to absorb the starlight and glow.

What was she doing?

I studied the inky dark sea before her but saw only the lights of an ocean liner way off, against the horizon.

Whom was she expecting?

How strange it all looked.

Impulsively, I went back inside, slipped into the robe and slippers Bunny had provided for me, and hurried out. There were lights on throughout the house, but it was very quiet, so quiet I could hear the sound of the surf through an open window. I tiptoed down the stairway and through the corridor to the rear loggia.

I could see the lantern still swinging in the darkness below, and I started down the walkway toward the beach house, my heart thumping. Almost halfway there, I stopped. What was I doing? How could I just come upon her in the middle of the night like this? Did she even know I was here? Did Linden tell her? Would

I frighten her so badly she would flee, embarrassed perhaps that I had discovered her out here this late at night? She wouldn't want to see me tomorrow, I thought.

I stood there debating with myself too long. By the time I started toward the dock again, she had turned away and was heading back toward the beach house. I thought about calling out to her, but I didn't. I just walked more slowly. She disappeared around the corner of the house before I arrived.

Now that I was down here in a nightgown, robe, and slippers myself, I felt foolish. I started to return to my bedroom, even though I knew it was going to be very difficult to fall asleep after this. Suddenly, I heard a movement and froze. Gradually, I turned back, studying the darkness, perusing every shadow.

I saw nothing and was about to give up when I heard the sound again and focused my eyes on the dark corner where it seemed a shadow lifted off the walls of the house and took three-dimensional form right before my eyes. Seconds later, Linden walked into the light. The sight of him took my breath away. I gasped and brought my hand to the base of my throat as I stepped back.

"What are you doing there?" I managed to ask in a very deep whisper.

"I was going for a walk," he said quickly. "What are you doing out here this late?"

"I saw . . . I was on my balcony, and I saw your mother out on the dock."

"My mother on the dock? This late at night? That's ridiculous," he said. "You must have been dreaming or imagining it."

He drew closer. He was wearing a light blue jacket, no shirt, a pair of pants, and no shoes.

"No, I'm sure I did."

"You did not see my mother. You did not," he insisted.

"Someone was there," I said. "Waving a lantern."

"A lantern? What is this? Are you manufacturing some story to write about?"

"No, really, I . . ."

"I have seen no one on the dock," he said firmly, "and I've been out here a good twenty minutes. The darkness, the lights, the ocean can play tricks on your eyes. Haven't you heard the stories seafaring men told, how they swore they saw their wives and mothers walking on the water thousands of miles from shore and home?"

He looked out at the sea. "There are just too many reflections, the stars; all of it can tease and tickle your imagination or your wishful thinking, that's all. That's all it was."

I nodded. "Maybe you're right," I said.

"Of course I'm right. I've lived here all my life. I should know." He paused and stared at me. "You should go back to sleep."

"Why are you out so late?" I asked. "It's after two in the morning."

"I have always had insomnia. Even as a child," he added. "I hated nap time because it didn't work for me."

"Don't you get exhausted?"

"You can be what they call overtired and still not fall asleep," he said.

"Maybe you should see a doctor, then."

"Don't you think I have? All they can do is pre-scribe some addictive drug. My mother gives me a cup of hot milk, and that helps, but other than that, it's my particular curse. We all have our private curses to live with, Isabel, don't we?" he asked pointedly. Even in the darkness, I could see how intense his eyes were.

All I could do was nod.

"You should go back to bed," he said. "And don't forget our bargain," he added, then turned and walked back to the house, choosing to stay in the shadows as if he were some nocturnal creature afraid of being seen.

I hurried back inside.

Why did he insist she wasn't out there on that dock? How could he not have seen her?

Was I imagining it after all?

As I feared, I tossed and turned and fretted in and out of nightmares until the first light of morning spread like warm butter over my face and shook my eyelids. I groaned awake and then lay there wondering about all that I had seen and heard just hours ago.

Had I dreamed it?

Or was my mother on that dock with a lantern, and was Linden hovering in the shadows?

Who were they, this mother and son who lived like hermits on this posh estate?

And how much of what and who they were was in me as well? Was my adoptive mother right about me after all, that I would develop some strange mental malady? Would I end up on a beach at night, staring into the darkness? Maybe for my mother there was nothing but darkness, even on the brightest, sunniest days. Was that my destiny as well?

Like a reader terrified by the words on the page, I was afraid to turn it and continue.

But I knew I had no choice. This was my story, too, now. These were my pages to read. I no longer had the luxury of ignorance. I already knew too much, and, like a ravenous glutton, I was eager to keep swallowing whatever new truth I could consume.

12

Linden

I had just started to rise when I heard a gentle knock on my door.

"Yes?"

Thatcher poked in his head and smiled. He was already dressed in a suit and tie and looked chipper and awake.

"I'm sorry," he said. "I would have breakfast with you, but I have to go to Miami today on business. I'll be gone most of the day, but if you're up to it, I'd like to take you to dinner."

"That sounds good to me," I said.

He smiled, looked to his side, and then came into the room to kiss me.

"It's nice to have someone like you here to greet first thing in the morning," he said softly. "It sort of jumpstarts the day." He kissed me again. "Gotta go," he said, and hurried to the door. "Don't let my mother and any of her other friends drive you crazy. Go and do whatever you want, and don't let her talk you into anything," he warned. He waved and closed the door. It opened instantly, and he was there again. "I'll have Jennings call you in a minute to see what you want for breakfast. I suggest you enjoy it on your balcony. Did you know Palm Beach has the best sunrise in America? Its rays are directly on the town: nature's spotlight."

"Oh, really?" I laughed. "You're still playing the role of president of the chamber of commerce."

"Some people here take that stuff about nature and energy very seriously, Willow. They believe in something called *feng shui*. Ever hear of it?"

I shook my head.

"It's an ancient Chinese discipline bringing everyday life into harmony with nature, and that includes interior decorating, how you set up your furniture. Time, space, and action are designed to increase energy, harmony, healing, et cetera, et cetera," he said, waving his hand. "Don't get Bunny started on it. She has redesigned the living room ten times following one guru or another."

Harmony with nature, I thought. It sounded wonderful. Everyone was searching for some comfort, some sense of security, even the wealthiest among us. I guessed in the end, we were all afraid of being alone.

"Anyway," Thatcher said, "enjoy the morning, and pretend I'm with you," he ordered with a smile, and was gone again.

I felt as if my day had been jumpstarted, too. I guess it is possible to be swept off your feet, I thought, and dropped my head back to the pillow. What was happening? I didn't come here for this.

The intercom rang before I could get into an argument with myself again. It was Jennings asking what I wanted for breakfast. I ordered and then rose and went out onto the balcony. It was a glorious morning. I could understand why people might feel they were blessed living here. I gazed at the dock again and revived my memories from the night before. *Perhaps today,* I thought, *perhaps today after I finally speak with my mother for a while, I'll understand what is happening to me.*

I went in and took a quick shower. I was out and in my robe again before the maid brought up my breakfast. Maybe it was the sea air, or maybe it was burning up so much energy tossing and turning in my sleep, but I was ravenously hungry and ate nearly everything on the tray. Then I put on a pair of shorts and a halter top, slipped into my sandals, and headed downstairs to uphold my half of the bargain I had made with Linden.

He was there on the beach, already prepared for work. He glanced at me and looked away. "I didn't think you would show up," he said in that sullen tone.

"Why not? I said I would."

He looked at me again, this time with a somewhat infuriatingly sarcastic smile on his face. "People here promise to do lots of things they never intend to do."

"I'm not from here, remember? Besides, we made a bargain. Does that mean you won't keep your half? You're from here."

He stared at me a moment. I thought he was going to say something very nasty, but suddenly his face brightened, and he laughed. "Okay," he said. He nodded at a large paper bag. "The clothes are in there."

I gazed into the bag, then took it over the little hill to where the day before he had suggested I go to change. Everything fit as if it had always been mine, and I loved the lavender scent. When I returned, he looked at me with appreciation, maybe even more. His eyes moved over me, slowly taking in my face, my throat, my breasts and waist, and then up again slowly until he and I were standing there staring at each other. For a moment, I wondered if he saw something of himself in me, enough to suggest who I might really be. Was that the reason for his close scrutiny?

His expression changed a little, the wall he kept between us crumbling enough for me to see another side of him, a softer side.

"You look just the way I expected you would," he finally said.

"And what was that, exactly?" I asked.

"Like someone fresh, innocent."

"Well, that's me," I said with a grin.

"To my artistic eye, at least," he remarked with a smirk.

"Where do I go?" I asked, not hiding my annoyance. He seemed to have a talent for hitting nerves, like some clumsy dentist.

"Oh. Just sit over here," he said, marking a small rise in the beach, "and gaze out at the ocean."

I sat, and he studied me a moment.

"May I?" he asked, coming over and putting his hands on my shoulders.

"Yes, of course."

He turned me slightly, and then he put his hands under my hair and spread the strands as he wished. He stepped back, contemplated me, and moved to my legs and smoothed out the skirt.

"Are you comfortable enough?" he asked.

"For now. I don't think I can sit here like this and not move for two hours," I warned.

"I'm not expecting you to remain like that for two straight hours. You can take frequent breaks," he said, and hurried back to his easel as if he were afraid I might jump up and run off and he would lose the moment. He worked with frenzied, quick motions, feasting on my image, digesting it and reproducing what he saw inside himself.

"I'm sorry if I frightened you last night," he said, about ten minutes after he had begun.

I started to turn toward him.

"Oh, please, hold the pose for as long as you can."

"Right. I'm sorry you have trouble sleeping. Whenever that happens to me, I hate it. I wake up cranky and angry at myself for worrying too much or eating the wrong things, whatever."

"Yes," he said, "but I suppose people would say I wake up cranky and angry regardless of how I sleep."

"No. Really?" I teased. "I wonder why they would have such a thought."

"Very funny." He relaxed his shoulders. "I am what I am," he said with a shrug.

"Is it like that for you every night?"

"Just about," he said. He paused. "I'd rather you didn't talk about our little encounter. People will only tell you it's a symptom of inherited madness, especially the Eatons."

"If that were true about insomnia, there would be quite a few people suffering from mental illness out there."

"Who says there aren't?" he shot back. "If you get thirsty, I have some cold lemonade in my bag there," he said, nodding toward a white cooler.

"Okay, thank you."

We were both quiet for a while. Out of the corner of my eye, I watched him work. He seemed possessed by it, intense, determined. The effort made the veins in his neck stand out and the veins in his temples as well. He bit down on his lower lip so hard at times I thought he would surely draw blood.

"This is a very beautiful place to work," I said.

"I don't always work here. Sometimes I take my sailboat and go to a bay nearby where I can enjoy even more solitude. I'm often interrupted by the noise from the house or even some of the Eatons' guests wandering over to see what the mad artist is up to."

"You like being alone?" I asked.

He shot me a look as if I had asked the dumbest question.

"Often, I like being alone," I continued, "but I do enjoy being around people, too. Too much introversion isn't good, but not ever wanting or being able to be alone isn't good, either. It is like being afraid of the voices inside you that will become vocal if there is nothing else to distract or diffuse them."

"You sound like a psychology major. Is that what you are?"

"Yes," I said, smiling.

He stopped working. "That's not why you really came here, is it? I mean, if someone set you on us deliberately—"

"Oh, no," I protested. "I'm doing an entirely different project . . . it's for my sociology class."

That wall began to build again as his eyes turned cold and skeptical.

"Besides," I said, "it wouldn't be an honest analysis if I snuck up on someone. It would be the worst sort of betrayal. You have to win trust in order to understand people and their problems and especially if you want to help them."

"How do you know so much about it?" he asked. "You sound like you're more than just a student."

"My father was a psychiatrist," I said.

"Oh." He looked relieved. Was he worried I had been a patient? "Poor you," he added, and returned to his work.

"Why poor me?"

"It's enough to have people analyzing you when you leave home, but to have it day in and day out like my mother had to bear, that has to be difficult."

"It wasn't easy being a teenager," I admitted.

He nodded. "I'll bet it wasn't. It was hell for me," he said.

"Why?"

Again, he gave me a look suggesting I had asked another dumb question. He didn't reply. He worked. I watched a sailboat turning to head back to wherever it had come from. The beehive sound of a motorboat made me think of Thatcher for a moment, and then I saw an airplane dragging a banner advertising a special at some restaurant.

"Take a break," he said after another ten or fifteen minutes, and opened his insulated bag to get the cold lemonade. He poured me a glass.

"Thank you."

He poured himself one and sat near me. "Have you and Thatcher become an item already?"

"What?"

He turned, and for a moment he seemed like a violin strung too tightly, ready to twang at the least careless touch.

"Why is it women have to play it so coy? You know what I mean."

"I don't think it's just women who play it coy," I snapped back at him. I held my breath. Would he go into a tantrum at my stern tone and end it all?

He surprised me with a smile. "You're right. Men can be just as affectedly modest, or phony, I should say—especially Thatcher."

"You don't like him?"

"I don't care about him enough to like or dislike

him. I just know who he is, how he was raised, and what he does for a living."

"Didn't he help you and your mother?"

"Yes, but it wasn't for any altruistic reason. He got his fees and his notoriety being the attorney for the madwoman and her mad artist son, I'm sure."

"He doesn't seem like that sort of a person. He's quite critical of those who are like that around here, in fact. Sometimes he sounds so critical I wonder why he continues to live here."

"Have you asked him?"

"Yes."

"And what did he say, something like 'Where else would I live?' "

"Something like that. What about you? Why do you stay here if you hate it so?"

I thought he would give me that look again, but he didn't. "I stay for my mother," he replied.

"Why does she stay?"

"She stays because she thinks . . ."

"What?" I asked almost breathlessly when he held the rest of his reply inside him.

I do not know what it was that made him decide to tell me. Maybe he felt something that bound us spiritually. Maybe he was suffering so with all his unspoken secrets gnawing away within his heart that he just had to open the doors. Daddy called it mental bleeding and said people in pain had to relieve themselves. He just had to make sure he was there when they did and get them to trust him enough.

"She thinks . . . thinks someone wonderful is coming for her," Linden revealed in a whisper. "Someone who will take her away from all this, erase years and years of pain. She dreams."

I could barely breathe. The breeze lifted my hair and caressed my face. The salt spray felt good on my skin, and the ocean's combing of the beach resembled a lullaby that was there to keep us both calm, meditative, safe.

"That's her new madness," he continued.

"Why do you say that?" I asked. "Why call it madness? Everyone dreams of good things for him- or herself."

He was silent, and then he turned to me. "I lied to you last night. She was out there on the dock. You didn't imagine it, and I go out after her to make sure she doesn't . . ."

"Doesn't what?"

"Do anything more than stand out there waving that lantern."

"Why does she do that?"

"Something in her past, some promise someone made to her, maybe . . . I'm not sure. She won't say."

"I don't understand," I said, shaking my head.

He turned back to me. "She thinks he's coming. She's a little lighthouse guiding him back to her heart. Crazy, right?" He was back to being belligerent. "Good copy for an article or for a study or just for coffeetime gossip?"

"No," I said. "It's not crazy at all."

His eyes widened with surprise. "Why do you say that?"

"It's just a hope, a dream. You don't have to worry that she's going out there to hurt herself," I said. "She's going out there to keep herself alive. That's what hopes and dreams do for us. They help us go on."

He stared more intently at me, and then, as if realizing he was permitting me to enter places inside him that no one was supposed to enter, he looked away quickly.

"That's nice," he said, "but I don't have any hopes and dreams."

"Sure you do," I said. "Otherwise, you wouldn't be an artist."

He gazed at me again, some glint in his eyes brightening like a lamp that had been kept shut up in the attic and was finally taken out and turned on. The fury and the darkness seemed to slide off his face as if he had been wearing a mask of ice that had begun to melt. Beneath it was a young man who could love and dream and work and live. I had a glimpse of him, but only a glimpse.

"Then I had better get back to work," he said, smiling, and jumped to his feet. "You okay with it?"

"I'm fine," I said.

"Good. Thank you."

He returned to his easel, and once again we were two halves of the same precious artistic moment, capturing some truth, doing what he had told Thatcher he did, casting a line for inspiration and finding it, only this time, with me or even . . . because of me.

* * *

We broke at noon. He didn't want me to see his work in progress but promised I could after the next session. I changed out of the clothes, and he headed back to the beach house, telling me to come by at two-thirty to meet his mother as we had planned.

Asher and Bunny were up and having coffee when I entered the house. They were both surprised to see me.

"We thought you had gone off to do some interview," Asher said.

"Where have you been, dear?" Bunny asked.

I told them what I had been doing and my bargain with Linden. Asher seemed amused, but Bunny looked concerned.

"I don't know if she should be spending so much time with them, Asher, and especially with Linden, alone on the beach like that."

"Oh, he's harmless," Asher said.

"I was hoping you would go with me to the meeting of the committee planning the Cancer Ball," Bunny complained. "You would see and meet many wealthy Palm Beach residents. It will be so much more enjoyable, and you can learn so much more than you possibly could from Grace Montgomery and Linden."

"I appreciate that," I said, "but I've already made these arrangements."

"Oh, they won't even remember or care," Bunny insisted, waving her hand in the direction of the beach house as if there were some smoke in the air she could clear away.

"However, I would remember, and I do care," I said.

"Let her carry out her own business in the manner she sees fit, Bunny," Asher gently reprimanded.

"I'm just trying to help her," she protested. "She's a stranger here. She doesn't know these people. She doesn't know whom to see and whom not to bother with, does she?"

"I appreciate that, Bunny. Thank you," I said.

"Then you're coming along?"

"No, I can't," I said.

"I have to get ready to go," she said with a pout. How could a grown woman be so spoiled and childish, and how could she have a son like Thatcher? I wondered. "I'll be leaving in an hour should you change your mind," she told me, and marched out of the room.

Asher shook his head and smiled after her. "Bunny is very used to getting people to do whatever she thinks they should. She's actually like a fragile piece of expensive china that we have to set down gently all the time. It takes so little to shatter her happiness, especially these days," he added.

"Why these days?"

"She's feeling . . . older. We are no longer permitted to acknowledge her birthday, no presents, no special dinners, and especially no parties. Women here lie about their ages more than women in Hollywood. She still refuses to permit Whitney's children to refer to her as Grandmother or even Nana. They have to call her Bunny, just like everyone else," he said with a smile. "Actually, I think they enjoy calling her that. I think to this day, our granddaughter Laurel thinks Bunny is a cartoon character come to life."

"How old is Laurel?"

"Twelve. Our grandson Quentin is fourteen. He's a very serious young man. Bunny has a harder time with him, but they're both beautiful, talented kids. You'll meet them on the weekend at the party," he said.

Jennings appeared. "Lunch, Mr. Eaton," he announced dryly.

"Oh, wonderful," Asher said. "Will you join me for a bite, Isabel?" He stood up and held out his arm. Even at midday, he was wearing a light blue sports jacket, a dark blue cravat, a white shirt, and white pants with a pair of boat shoes.

"Yes, thank you," I said, smiling. I could see from whom Thatcher had inherited his charm.

"So what do you think of all this?" he asked, sweeping his arm over the patio, across the grounds and the private beach, the pool, the buildings and gardens.

"It's very impressive," I said. "It is truly more like a hotel than a home. You have everything here, anything anyone could possibly want."

"Yes," he said, laughing. "I believe it was Ogden Nash who wrote about the rich, *I don't mind their having a lot of money, and I don't care how they employ it. But I do think that they damn well ought to admit they enjoy it.*"

We both laughed. To a certain extent, I liked him for his lack of modesty concerning his wealth. So many people I knew through Daddy and especially through my adoptive mother were secretive about their money. They made excuses for spending and tried to justify every extravagance as if they were worried some envious person would try to take it all away from them or they would be cursed for having so much. That was certainly not the case here. Even in the short time I had been here, I saw that people wore their wealth like badges, outbuilding, outdriving, outdressing each other, and, as Thelma Carriage had said yesterday, even outpartying each other.

"Did you always live like this, Asher?"

"Yes, I suppose so," he said.

As usual, a literal banquet had been prepared for just the two of us: platters of prawns, salads, roast beef, turkey, and poached salmon plus a dessert table. The two maids stood behind the tables looking as if they would soon compete for the opportunity to spoon some creamed onions onto Asher's plate or mine. We just nodded or pointed to something, and they filled our plates and brought them to us after we sat.

"How can you eat like this every day?" I wondered without hiding my astonishment.

"Oh, I don't think we eat like this every day. We have the opportunity to, but we don't," he said nonchalantly. His eyes twinkled a bit. "I suppose my son has been voicing his criticism of our lifestyle. Does he have a laundry list of complaints?"

"Not really," I said, trying to be diplomatic about it. "At least, he hasn't made it a major topic of discussion."

"Oh? I'm sure he will. He takes after my grandfather," Asher confided. "Serious, full of ambition, and very competitive. He hates coming in second and goes into a depression if he loses a case or doesn't settle it to his liking.

"I'll warn you right now," he added, "he doesn't take well to rejection, and if he's set his eyes on you, he'll come at you from now until the end of time."

"You make him sound dangerous," I said, smiling.

He shrugged. "There are all sorts of dangers out there," he replied, gazing at the sea. "Physical ones can sometimes be the least painful or frightening. I'll give you some thoughts to help your study of this world here. The wealthy can buy out of most of the problems that plague ordinary folk. I have never worried about an automobile breaking down, an appliance going bad, an electric or plumbing problem, much less a bill, and Bunny certainly hasn't, either. Everything becomes relative in a sense, however. She might have a fit if the restaurant she goes to with her friends doesn't have the wine she wants or the champagne or the appetizer. She could even get sick over the disappointment.

"If our children have problems, we hire therapists, tutors, specialists, and hardly skip a beat in our daily lives. If our marriages come apart, we hire good lawyers and work out dissolutions and then go off to the Côte d'Azur to recuperate from the tension. Sometimes, we don't even let death disrupt us. The husband of a rather wealthy, well-known woman died last year just at the beginning of what we call the season here. She was so annoyed that she would miss certain events mourning his passing that she put his body on ice and postponed the funeral.

"Most of this is nothing more than amusing to me, but to my son, it's practically criminal. Yet I will tell you," he added, his face suddenly turning very serious, "I don't think he's anywhere nearly as happy as Bunny and I are. He broods too much. He has some demons to get out of his system." He looked toward the beach house.

"Sometimes," he continued, almost in a whisper now, "I think he's more like Linden Montgomery than he knows."

He looked at me—expectantly, I thought.

"I don't know either of them well enough yet to agree or disagree," I said.

He nodded and smiled. "Very good answer."

"It's the truth, Asher."

"I'm sure it is," he said. "Well, I guess I've been a little like Thatcher here. I didn't mean to be so serious. It's your fault," he said, pointing a finger of accusation at me. "You're too serious, Isabel. You're too focused. Where's your hedonism when you need it the most?" He laughed at my expression. "Take advantage of us."

"I already have," I said. "Your hospitality . . ."

"No, no, that's not even a drop in the bucket. Feel free to do anything you want. Bunny would love to take you on a shopping spree for clothes, for example. Just mention it to her."

I couldn't help the way my mouth gaped. How could anyone be so rich or unconcerned about being exploited? Why was that amusing?

"Something tells me you are trying to corrupt me, Asher Eaton," I said, and he burst into a fit of laughter.

"I think that's it," he said, nodding. "You're right. People like you make us too aware of our wastefulness and extravagance. We have to corrupt you in order to feel better about ourselves."

"And maybe that's why you're a little annoyed at Thatcher," I suggested.

"Very good," he said. "You could be a social worker for the rich or a psychologist, I suppose." He gazed at the beach house again. "Maybe that's also why Grace and Linden bother Bunny so much. Grace makes her afraid," he said.

"Of what?" I asked, holding my breath.

"Of losing it all and becoming like that . . . a shadow on the beach, a prisoner of memories. Do you know what is the worst fear and danger to us Palm Beach royals, Isabel?"

"What?"

"Loneliness," he said. He looked at the beach house again. "Loneliness."

I guess I was right about that, I thought. *I guess I have inherited some of Daddy's instinct and perception.* Now the question was what would I do with it?

Asher apologized again for being too serious and then insisted I go look at his game room, where he had a beautiful pool table, a genuine working slot machine, and a set of electric speed cars. He told me he and some of his male friends bet ridiculously high sums of money on the toy car races and swore someone lost fifty thousand dollars one night.

When I looked at the time, I excused myself, thanked him for the lunch, and went up to my room to change and freshen up for what I had come all this way to do: meet and get to know my real mother.

Just as Linden had promised, she and he were sitting on their patio, having coffee and talking quietly. I paused for a moment and watched them before they saw me approaching. My mother was still dressed only in that housecoat I had seen her in when I first set eyes on her. Her hair was tied back, and she wore no makeup. There was, however, a soft, almost meditative peace in her face, just a tiny suggestion of a smile in her lips. She nodded at something Linden had said, and then they were both quiet, both still, gazing out at the sea and looking as if they had fallen back into one of Linden's pictures.

"Hello again," I said, stepping toward them on the walkway. My mother looked surprised, of course, but I thought, or perhaps hoped, she looked pleased, too.

"Hello," Linden said.

At that, I saw the surprise grow brighter in my mother's face. She glanced at him, obviously waiting for him to drive me away. When that didn't happen, she turned back to me.

"Is it always so lovely here?" I asked, edging closer to them.

"No," Linden said sharply. "We have hurricanes and humidity and sand flies. But they're just not permitted on Worth Avenue."

"I suppose there isn't a part of the country that doesn't have something negative about it," I replied, my eyes mostly on my mother, who kept her eyes on me and kept that gentle smile on her lips.

Suddenly, however, some dark thought crossed her

mind, and that smile evaporated. She looked as if she were going to get up and go inside.

"I don't want to intrude on your privacy," I said very quickly. "But I have so short a time to spend here and so few interesting people to speak with about my topic. I've gotten all I think I can get from the Eatons," I added.

Linden looked very pleased with that remark. "I'm not surprised. That well is rather shallow," he said. He looked at his mother and then at me. "All right," he added. "We'll give you a few minutes of our very busy time. What do you want to know?"

My mother looked more frightened now than surprised. My heart began to pound. I certainly didn't want her to see me as any sort of threat.

I smiled and looked at the chair beside her. "May I?" I asked.

"Go on, go on," Linden said impatiently.

I sat. "Is this where you grew up, Mrs. Montgomery? Where you spent your childhood?"

"Of course it is," Linden replied for her.

I acted as if I hadn't heard him and kept my eyes on my mother, my silence indicating I would wait for her to speak even if it meant sitting here until nightfall.

"Part of it," she said softly, "but not in this house."

"She knows that, Mother," Linden said, practically jumping at her.

"I imagine you must have felt like a princess," I said, "living behind castle walls in such luxury."

"More like a prisoner than a princess," Linden responded.

She turned and looked at him hard for a moment and

then turned back to me. "No," she said. "I did feel like a princess once. You're right. I used to pretend it was a castle with a moat and guards on the walls, a place where I was so safe nothing could touch me, not even germs."

Linden blew air between his lips, shook his head, and turned to the sea. "Some castle, some protection," he muttered.

"I wasn't born here," she continued. "I was nearly sixteen when my mother and I came to live here."

"Where did you live before?" I asked as gently as I could. I felt as if I were moving through a mine field, tiptoeing and hoping I wouldn't trigger some explosion. Linden seemed, as usual, to be on the verge of spontaneous combustion, and my mother looked as if she could burst into tears at any moment as well; just one wrong word, one wrong look, would ignite them both.

"We lived in what people here would call a rather modest home in West Palm Beach," she said. "My mother was a very attractive young woman who had come here from Norfolk, Virginia. My father was a naval officer who was killed in a helicopter accident when I was only fifteen."

"How sad," I said.

"He was a very handsome man with a promising career ahead of him. My mother used to call him the admiral because she truly believed he would become one someday. I remember that. It got so she even referred to him that way when she spoke to me. 'The admiral's coming home this weekend,' she would say. I was young enough to believe he had the stripes and the rank, and he would laugh and tell my mother she had better stop calling him that, or I would be telling all my friends at school my father was an admiral in the U.S. Navy. We were very happy then," she said, her smile deepening with her memories.

"How did you come to live here?" I asked. If she only knew I was learning about my own family, I thought.

"My mother was a very independent, strong-minded woman. She wasn't going to waste away as some navy widow, not for a second. One day, she picked us up and moved us to West Palm Beach. She had a background in the service industry."

"A waitress," Linden interjected with a smirk.

"Yes, she was a waitress when she and my father first met, but she was capable of being a manager, as well. She got a job as a waitress in a friend's restaurant, one of the better West Palm Beach restaurants, and there she met Winston Montgomery, who was Linden's grandfather."

"He was never my grandfather," Linden insisted on correcting.

"In name," she said, "but really more because he was very kind to me. Right from the beginning, he treated me as if I were truly his very own. I never felt unwanted or like some second-class citizen, not with Daddy Winston, as I used to call him."

"Daddy Winston," Linden muttered.

"He gave my mother whatever she wanted. He couldn't do enough to make her happy. He built onto the main house for her, but he was somewhat older than she was, and my mother was never fully accepted by Palm Beach society. We were in the social directory because of my stepfather, but . . ."

"The Sears catalogue," Linden inserted.

"The Who's Who," she continued. "My stepfather was rich and powerful enough to keep anyone from blatantly snubbing my mother, but she was snubbed nonetheless."

"She was lucky," Linden said.

"Winston died when I was twenty-one, and my mother took up with someone for a few years."

"She knows about all that," Linden said. "Don't you?"

"Not really," I said. "But I'm not here to dredge up any unpleasant memories for you, Mrs. Montgomery."

"That's nice," Linden said dryly.

She simply held her eyes on me. I felt very self-conscious and looked away quickly. "If you had to list five or six things that you lost when your family lost its wealth and position in Palm Beach, what would be number one in your mind?" I asked her.

Linden looked just as interested in her answer.

She smiled at me and then sat back a moment. "Having no sense of yourself," she replied.

"You mean now, you don't know who you really are?"

"Oh, no," she said. "When we were in all that, when we were part of all that, I never knew who I was, and I don't think my mother did, either. We were defined by what we owned. But those things come and go or fade or go out of style so quickly. No, no," she insisted. "It's only now, only afterward, that I have a sense of myself." She smiled. "It's like being in spotlights or in the headlines. It's glamorous, exciting even, but you never get to look at anything, really look at it, especially yourself.

"My mother used to look in her mirror and wonder what happened to the woman who used to look back. I remember her saying that. I remember it very well because it happened to me, too.

"When the lights went out, we stood in the much dimmer light, but we could see things we had never seen before," she said. "I think we saw the people we had been and lost."

She laughed. "Don't misunderstand me. I'm not against being rich. I've been both rich and poor, and rich is better. I'm just against being so absorbed in the glamour that you forget you're just another member of the human race. Maybe it's easier for that to happen here."

"No cemeteries or hospitals," I murmured, more to myself than to her and Linden, but they heard.

"Yes," my mother said, smiling. "Maybe you understand. I'm sorry. I'm a little tired suddenly." She rose. "It's nice to have met you. I hope you'll come by again," she said.

"I'd like that."

"Me, too," she said. She glanced at Linden.

He had been sitting there as much in awe of his mother as I was, I thought. He blinked his eyes and nodded.

"Yes, yes," he said. "Go rest, Mother."

"Have a good day," she told me.

We watched her go into the house, and then I stood up. I truly felt as if I had crossed a barrier of time. I had cleared away some fog and had a long look at my own past, hidden and buried for so long.

"Well," Linden said.

"Thank you." I started off the patio, but he caught up with me immediately.

"I don't know why she did that," he said.

"What?"

"Told you all those things. She hasn't spoken of those things for years. And that answer she gave you . . . surely, it was something she has been thinking about a long time, but she never said it to me."

"I'm very grateful."

"No," he said. "I'm not trying to get you to appreciate it. I'm telling you I appreciate it." He smiled. "There's something about you, Isabel. Something special. I think that was what made me want to paint you."

I started to shake my head.

"No," he said, taking my hand and looking at me so intently my heart began to skip beats. "I want this to be the greatest painting I have ever done. It will be. Will you go sailing with me tomorrow to my private bay?"

"But you've already begun on the beach here," I said, not wishing to upset him.

"That doesn't matter. The painting isn't there. It's here." He pointed to his temple. "I do my best work at the bay. It's only about half an hour at the most. I'm a good sailor, better than Thatcher, believe me," he said.

"That's not my concern."

"What is, then?" he practically demanded.

I thought a moment. "Nothing. Okay, I'd like to see your bay."

"Great," he said, smiling. "No one, no one, has gotten my mother to talk like that," he repeated, and started back toward the patio. "I'll see you in the morning."

Spirited, he rushed into the house and left me standing there.

Why was it I felt as if I were standing in quicksand?

13

The Party

It was six-fifteen, and I was getting ready to go out to dinner with Thatcher. He had called and left word with Jennings that he would pick me up at seven-thirty.

Mr. Bassinger had called as well. Fearing something had happened to the house or Miles, I phoned him back as soon as Jennings gave me the message.

"Is there anything wrong, Mr. Bassinger?" I asked as soon as he said hello.

"Your aunt Agnes has been calling me and saying things that were very disturbing."

"Like what?"

"She is convinced you're at the mercy of some fortune hunter down there, Willow, someone who is taking advantage of your vulnerability. She actually threatened to hire a private detective to locate you and follow you around. I can't say she won't do it," he warned.

"If she does, I'll never speak with her again."

I was almost ashamed to ask him about Miles's fantastic tale, but I did. "You did check on my father's office when you were in the house, didn't you, Mr. Bassinger?"

"Oh, yes. Nothing was turned on and running, and Miles said nothing to me about any computers. It was probably all a dream that he has already forgotten. I did speak with him in detail and outlined how your father provided for his needs. He'll be fine once the house is sold."

"I'm glad," I said, relieved.

"You are all right, are you not, Willow? I would hate for your aunt to have even an inkling of truth."

"Don't worry. She couldn't be more wrong about me and what I'm doing."

"It has to do with the papers I gave you, doesn't it?" he asked.

"Yes."

"I don't know what was in them, of course, but I feel confident telling you that there is nothing your father would want less than being the cause of any further unhappiness for you, Willow."

"I know. Thank you," I said.

It was, of course, my biggest and deepest worry: would I cause my mother more unhappiness, and would I do the same to myself?

The knock at my door startled me.

"Come in," I called, and Thatcher appeared. He

looked concerned, upset, his eyebrows turned in on each other like those of a man with a very bad headache.

"I thought we weren't going until seven-thirty," I told him. I was in my robe, and I had yet to fix my hair.

"No, we're not late or anything. I just . . . Bunny got hold of me while I was driving back from Miami."

"Oh?"

"She told me what you were doing with Linden Montgomery."

"I see."

"You're posing for him?"

"Yes. It's nothing, really. Not nude," I added quickly, thinking that was his concern.

"I'm glad of that, but regardless, I don't think you should get too involved with that guy, Willow. He's far too unstable. I mean, you've seen his work and how he behaves."

"I understand. Don't worry," I said.

"But I will worry. I feel partly responsible, introducing you to him and all," he insisted.

"I think I will know when to back away from him, Thatcher. It's all right," I said a little more firmly.

He shook his head. "Okay," he said, "but don't say I didn't warn you when he becomes even more bizarre."

"Right," I said.

He nodded but stood there staring at me.

"I'll be fine, Thatcher. Really, I will," I said, smiling to reassure him.

"Okay. I'll go shower and change for dinner." He

started to turn and stopped. "Actually, from the way she spoke, I think my mother was really more upset that you chose to be with Linden over being with her at her charity ball meeting. She insists you missed a great opportunity. I told her not to worry, I'd make up for it tonight."

"What do you mean? Why tonight?"

"Before the day ended, I received an invite to the party on Hope Farris's yacht. Hope is the seventy-year-old heiress to the Farris fur empire. She's been married five times, and I had the honor of doing the prenuptial agreement for the last one. The marriage lasted fourteen months. She's celebrating another successful divorce tonight," he said. "She was recently quoted in the newspaper as saying, 'For someone like me to be married and to escape with only the loss of a used Rolls-Royce is a fortunate accomplishment.' The reason I remember," he said with a wide, silly grin of pride, "is that it is all the result of my work."

"Celebrating a divorce? Why get married if you've failed four previous times?"

"Another Palm Beach game," he said. "What of it? We'll have fun."

"But a yacht party? I don't know as I have anything to wear for that."

"With a black dress and a rope of pearls, you can go anywhere according to Franklin Noyce, the resident fashion guru of the month, and I know you have the black dress."

"But not the pearls."

"Bunny has enough to string between here and

Europe. She'll provide them," he said. "I'll let her know. Hey, don't look so worried. You're going to have a good time and meet enough of the A-list to get all the information you need to complete your work."

"Okay," I said.

Maybe in a day or two, I'll be able to tell him the truth and end this fictitious story, I hoped. Would he be angry or happy after that? Surely, he would understand. If he really cared for me, that is.

He left, and I returned to working on my face and hair. It wasn't twenty minutes before Bunny burst into my room with ropes of pearls dangling around her neck.

"It's the Fashion Firewoman!" she cried. "Here to put out the burning of beauty."

I couldn't help but laugh.

"It's not funny. I'm serious. Put on your dress," she ordered, "and we'll see what works the best."

"I'm really not into jewelry," I said as I slipped into my new black dress.

"Of course you are. Every woman is into jewelry, either in her fantasies because she can't afford it or in real life because she can. We've been created to wear the world's gems. What's a diamond without a setting to be worn on a woman's finger or in her earlobe or around her neck? Just some glittering raw stone greedy men will kill each other to possess. Precious stones are not meant to be in safety deposit boxes. They are meant to adorn our bodies, and that's that," she said as if she had the power to pronounce the final word on any subject and end any argument.

I sighed and shook my head. She stood back and studied me a moment. "If you're going to wear your hair up like that, you need matching earrings," she decided. "I have the perfect pair for this necklace." She lifted it off the pile around her neck. "It's from the Etoile collection. Cultured pearls. Do you know anything about pearls, dear?"

"My mother had yards of them, but I never paid much attention to what she wore," I said honestly.

"What a pity. I made sure my daughter had a proper education when it came to precious stones. Who wants to be made the fool and ooh and aah over imitation jewelry? There are plenty of sorry young women in this town who thought the ring they were given was a flawless diamond only to find out from a jeweler that it was either a VS1 or a WS2. When it comes to diamonds especially, you have to pay attention to the four C's, my dear."

"The four C's?"

"Clarity, color, cut, and carat. Don't be impressed by the women you see here wearing big diamond rings. Why, some of them don't even know they're wearing cubic zirconia, imitation diamonds. My eyes are trained well enough to tell.

"Anyway, this necklace is sixteen inches long with a cultured Tahitian pearl clasp. The diamonds are set in platinum—and look at their clarity."

"It sounds expensive," I said.

"Expensive?" She considered it. "I think it was fourteen thousand."

"Bunny, you're not serious. You want me to borrow a fourteen-thousand-dollar necklace?"

"And the earrings. I think they were six or seven."

"I would be too nervous," I said, backing away from her and her pearls.

"Oh, please," she said, her face pained. "It's all insured."

"But fourteen thousand."

She grimaced. "The only other one I would suggest," she said, lifting it off her neck, "is this, also cultured pearls. . . ." She paused. "Do you know the difference between natural and cultured pearls?"

"No," I said, "but something tells me I will soon."

"You should know," she chastised with her eyes as well as her tongue. "Natural pearls are born quite by chance when the oyster can't get rid of some particle inside and coats it with layer upon layer of a smooth, hard substance called nacre. It takes years to make this tiny bead into a wonderful, lustrous pearl. To create a cultured pearl, the oyster's shell is opened with surgical precision, and the irritant, usually a mother-of-pearl bead, is placed inside, which causes the oyster to produce the nacre. These happen to be Japanese Akoya."

"And how much was that?"

"This?" She stared at it a moment. "I think . . . yes, Asher got it at Tiffany's. He paid something like ten or eleven thousand."

"Don't you have any costume jewelry?" I asked.

"For what purpose? I don't understand these women who own beautiful things but get copies made to wear out in public. Why own the original? Stop worrying. You're not exactly going to walk on the streets of some city ghetto. You'll be quite safe, and the other women will envy you.

"I think I'd rather have a woman's envy than a man's love," she said with a laugh.

Two days ago, that remark might have shocked me, but at the moment, it seemed a perfectly natural thing for Bunny Eaton to tell me.

In the end, I took the second choice, and she sent down the matching earrings. At precisely seven-thirty, Thatcher came by.

He wore a stylish tuxedo and looked positively debonair. He paused in the doorway and gazed in at me. He was silent so long I thought he was trying to decide how to get out of taking me. Maybe he thought I looked too plain to be at a party with these wealthy Palm Beach women.

"Well?" I finally said.

"My God, Willow, you're absolutely beautiful."

He said it with such depth of sincerity and appreciation it took my breath away. For a moment, I couldn't speak, and I felt as light as air. I glanced at the floor to see if my feet had left it and if I was floating.

"It's your mother's pearls," I said, and he laughed.

"Hardly. This is one of those occasions when the woman bedecks the jewels and not vice versa."

"Thatcher Eaton, where do you come up with these great lines?" I teased.

He stopped smiling. "From my heart, Willow, from my heart," he said.

The teasing grin flew off my face, and he kissed me softly.

"Come on, let's blaze a trail through Palm Beach society," he urged.

How could I not feel on top of the world here? I was with a very handsome, very successful man. I was wearing expensive jewelry. We were getting into a Rolls-Royce Corniche convertible and going to a yacht party on a wonderful warm night in Palm Beach. I was doing all this, me, Willow De Beers; not a pauper but, until a few days ago, just another college student expecting to attend the weekend beer bash at Allan's fraternity. I truly felt like a princess.

"I'm a little nervous about this, Thatcher. I've never been to a yacht party," I admitted.

"A party is a party. There's just more of everything here: more servants, perhaps, and more glitz. The Germans drink beer at their parties. The French drink wine at theirs. People in Palm Beach drink champagne, that's all. A student of human behavior such as you should understand that," he added with a wink.

He could make all this seem as common and ordinary as he wanted, I thought, but the moment we drove up to the dock and heard the music and saw the lights, the women glittering like diamond statues, the parade of servants with silver trays, and the recognizable celebrity faces here and there, I threw his attitude out the window. My legs actually trembled as we walked up the gangplank to the deck, where a very pretty hostess stood ready to greet us and all the other arriving guests. She handed us glasses of champagne.

"Good evening. Welcome," she said, and we stepped onto the deck.

A six-piece combo was playing. I saw tables of roasts, lobster, platters of shrimp, freshly roasted turkeys, Cornish hens, pheasant under glass, almost anything anyone could think to have at a party, with bowls and bowls of salads, a fresh vegetable bar that looked as if it had been lifted from a farmer's market and brought here, and a table just for breads and rolls.

"Let's find Hope Farris and then get something to eat," Thatcher said. "I'm starving."

We were practically elbow to elbow with people. The yacht was the biggest I had ever seen, but, according to Thatcher, apparently everyone Hope invited had decided to attend.

"She's probably disappointed."

"Disappointed? Why?"

"Everyone overbooks his or her parties. The worst thing is to throw a party and not have it well attended. It could take you down ten points on the A-list meter. My parents invited two hundred for the weekend."

"Two hundred! Your mother told me a hundred, a hundred and twenty-five," I said.

"That's what she expects on such short notice, but you never know."

We paused, and he smiled at someone, waved to another.

"Good mix. I see dozens of trust-fund babies, some nouveau riche like Thomas Carter over there, owner of UX.com, and a number of the old ruling class. That's

Mildred Callwell, one of the grande dames of Palm Beach society—her husband owns Perk-Up Coffee. And that elderly lady in the wheelchair back there wearing the diamond tiara and clinging to the butterfly Judith Leiber purse like it contains her emergency heart medicine is Countess Von De Myer. She does have a legitimate title and actually lives in a castle in Belgium.

"You see those two men," he said, nodding at two very elegant-looking gentlemen, identically slim, with identically tan, almost identical black mustaches and styled hair. They were standing back, smoking long, thin cigarillos, and smiling slyly at the beautiful young women who walked by them.

"Yes."

"They're what are known as walkers. They haven't got anything, even though they look rich and success-ful. In return for free meals and entertainment, they es-cort wealthy women to events like this. Some pretend to hold titles like duke or baron this or that, but every-one knows they are full of what makes the grass grow greener."

"If everyone knows they're phony, why would any well-to-do woman want to be seen with them?"

"You need to have *someone* on your arm, and it's nice to have someone who makes a good appearance. The party givers want there to be more men to ask the unescorted women to dance, make conversation, that sort of thing. It's like those men who are hired by cruises to dance with women.

"Besides, there's always the possibility some people don't know they are all show and no substance," he said. "Illusion and reality, huh? Your topic, right?"

"Right," I said nervously. He was always reminding me about my supposed purpose for being there. "Oh, I see the Carriage sisters." I groaned.

"We'll try to steer clear of them, although that might be difficult on a yacht. Where is Hope?" he asked, stretching his neck to look between and above people.

"You don't see her?"

"Not yet. You know," he said, "I've heard of people throwing these parties and not showing up until nearly the end of the evening."

"Why?"

"Some hate them but do them because if they don't, they'll lose their place on the totem pole."

"Is position, rank in society, so important?"

"I think that's what makes everyone here fear death so much more. There's a good chance it's not important in the afterlife," he said with a grin.

"Thatcher! I thought you weren't coming," we heard someone cry above the din. A tall, dark-haired woman with a svelte figure wearing a red silk column gown with an attached chiffon scarf stepped forward through the crowd and held out her hand, the fingers of which were so full of diamond rings I thought she would have trouble opening them. Her eyes were a beautiful jade color, but that looked to be the only natural thing left untouched on her cosmetically altered face with skin tucked tightly under her ears, nose surgically shaved, lips puffed with collagen. Only the small gathering of wrinkles at the base of her throat gave away her true age.

"Hope, how could I not?" he replied.

She laughed and leaned forward to give him a double air kiss, one next to each cheek.

"I'd like you to meet Isabel Amou," he said. "She is visiting from South Carolina."

"Oh, yes," she said, giving me her hand. "I've already heard all about you."

"The Carriage sisters?" Thatcher asked.

"Better than the CIA," Hope said. "Call me this week. I have something I need done with my property in Puerto Rico," she told him. "Please," she said to me, "enjoy. I have two of Tania Morgan's kinetic works of party art starboard behind the dessert bar. It seemed appropriate," she added with a laugh. "For some reason, my male guests appreciate the work more. Oh, there's Donald," she cried, and moved away.

"What is she talking about, kinetic works of party art?" I asked.

Thatcher raised his eyes and led me through the crowd toward the dessert bar, where we could see a thick gathering of people. When we came around, I saw two nude women completely coated with what looked like liquid silver, seated back to back, legs crossed, arms at their sides. Neither moved a muscle. Their eyelids must have been glued open. They looked like statues, human bookends. From what we heard around us, it seemed every ten minutes, they rose and switched sides, and that was what made them kinetic art.

"It's like the changing of the guard at Buckingham

Palace," a tall, thin gentleman with balding gray hair said. He had lips that looked as if they were made of rubber. "You don't want to miss it."

"I think we'd rather get something to eat," Thatcher quipped, and directed me toward the buffet.

We had just sat at a table when two older couples approached us.

"Don't get up," the shorter of the two men said as Thatcher began to rise. "Thatcher, you remember Mitch Rosewater and his wife, Brownie, don't you?"

"Yes, yes, of course," Thatcher said, rising nevertheless to shake the taller man's hand and greet his wife. "We met at the Pullmans' party, right?"

"Yes. Rather sedate party compared to this, what?" he said. He was obviously English.

"I'd like you all to meet Isabel Amou, just visiting from South Carolina," Thatcher said. The line was already so connected to my name I thought I'd have to include it whenever I signed anything. "Isabel, may I present Tom and Melinda Dancer. Tom is, you should pardon the expression, also an attorney," Thatcher said with a wide grin.

"Merely a paper pusher compared to Thatcher here," Tom Dancer said, extending his hand to me. His wife was studying me so hard I thought I had some of the pâté on the end of my nose.

"You're actually staying with Asher and Bunny Eaton at Joya del Mar, aren't you?" she asked.

"Yes," I said. "What happened? Did it get into the newspapers or something?"

Everyone laughed.

"No one burps in this town without the rest of us hearing it," Tom said.

"Have you met Grace Nutcase and that son of hers yet?" Melinda asked me. "Really, Thatcher," she continued, not really waiting for my response, "I don't know why your parents don't just buy the property out from under them and get them off the grounds. With a loony like Linden wandering about, I wouldn't feel safe. And who knows what Grace might do one of these days. She could set fire to the place or something."

"Oh, don't exaggerate, Melinda," Tom Dancer said. "I'm sure it's not quite that bad. Is it, Thatcher?"

"No," he said. "They stay to themselves most of the time." He glanced at me. "As long as they remain that way, there is no problem."

"I would still have trouble sleeping at night," Melinda insisted.

"She's not a dangerous woman," I said sharply. "Far from it."

"Oh, then you have met her?" She pounced.

"Yes."

"Well, don't just sit there. Tell us about her. No one has seen her for years. What does she look like? Is it true she walks around barefoot in ripped old garments and has lost her teeth and has sand flies in her hair?"

"Absolutely not," I said firmly. "She is, in fact, one of the most attractive women I've seen here. A naturally beautiful woman, with no need for cosmetic surgery or makeup," I said pointedly. It wasn't hard to see that both she and Brownie had contributed considerably to some cosmetic surgeon's pension plan.

"Really?" She and Brownie Rosewater exchanged expressions of some disappointment. "And does she speak intelligibly or babble mad things?"

"She spoke to me, and she was very informative and pleasant to be with," I said a bit more calmly, realizing my face had turned crimson.

"Really," she said again, her skepticism and bitterness drooling at the corners of her mouth.

"Yes, really. I have yet to have a conversation with anyone here in Palm Beach that was as pleasant. You're missing a lot by not inviting her to your events," I added.

The women looked at each other and then laughed.

"I guess you have a lot to teach this young lady about Palm Beach, Thatcher," Melinda said.

He shifted his eyes to me and then looked at her. "She's learning. I've been here all my life, and I'm still learning," he added, and they all laughed.

"Hey, enjoy," Tom Dancer said. "I'll call you this week on that matter of the Crosby Mall."

"Right. Nice meeting you," Thatcher said to the Rosewaters.

The moment they stepped away, they all burst into hysterical laughter at something Melinda had said.

"People here are very cruel to each other, aren't they?" I asked Thatcher.

"Maybe; maybe not any more than they are anywhere else. At least they don't go around shooting each other."

"Not with guns, but they do a pretty good job with words," I said.

"You came to the Montgomerys' defense rather vehemently for someone who has just met them, Willow. That surprised me almost as much as it did them. You're sure you're not getting too involved with Linden?" he asked again.

I pushed my plate away and looked out at the crowd of mega-millionaires, their jewelry competing, their designer clothes flashing before me. If they could walk about with price tags dangling, they would, I thought.

The sound of applause by the dessert bar indicated the liquid silver women had changed position again. The band got louder. Laughter whipped through the air around us. I felt my head spinning.

"What's wrong?" Thatcher asked.

"I don't know. I'm suddenly not very hungry. Maybe having so much to choose from overwhelms me. I'm beginning to believe there is such a thing as being too rich."

"Not here," he said. "The relative security, the enormous wealth, the magnificent weather, this city with streets that glitter and stores that look like they have a branch in heaven itself, create this sense of being above the world, Willow. It's not an altogether unpleasant high."

"It's just as addicting as any terrible drug."

"Is it so bad to be addicted to nice things?"

"You confuse me, Thatcher. Sometimes you're so negative about this world, and yet . . ."

"Yet I'm in it? I participate?"

"Yes, exactly."

He nodded. "Walt Whitman wrote, *Do I contradict myself? Very well then I contradict myself. I am large. I contain multitudes*. We're all complicated. You're full of contradictions, too, Willow. And secrets," he added. "Right?"

I looked away.

"Just be careful," he said. "Secrets have a way of twisting themselves around your heart like a python and choking the joy out of you."

He started to eat again. The music grew louder. I nibbled on my food without any enthusiasm.

"You want to go?" he said suddenly.

"Where?"

"Let's just walk on Worth Avenue or something."

"You want to be here, Thatcher. There are people you want to see and talk to, I know."

"I'm fine with it," he said. "Let's go. We can get ice cream sundaes or something."

"We're going to go walking in the streets dressed like this and stop at an ice cream parlor?"

"Here it's no big deal. We won't even attract a second look."

"What about Hope Farris? Won't she be insulted if you and I run out this early?"

"She won't even know we've left," he said, rising. "Come on," he urged.

I smiled and got up. We made our way back through the boisterous crowd and hurried down the gangplank to his car. Shortly after, we were cruising down Worth

Avenue. *Maybe Thatcher's right,* I thought. *Maybe we are all full of contradictions, and maybe there's nothing strange about being complicated to each other and even to ourselves. It's even good. Who wants to be predictable?*

Yes, that's the thing about most of the people I've met so far, I thought. *They're all so predictable.*

No wonder Thatcher was in love with Mai Stone, and no wonder he was heartbroken, no matter how he tried to hide it.

Once we were away from the rich and the famous, Thatcher seemed more relaxed and himself. We parked and then walked the street holding hands, stopping at store windows. He pointed out what he called the doggie bar, a halfmoon-shaped tiled trough with a silver spigot that provided fresh water for the expensive dogs whose owners bought them Chanel collars and Gucci dog beds. He showed me one in a window. It sold for fifteen hundred dollars.

"Most people don't treat their children as well," I said.

"To these people, the dogs are their children. Don't knock the pet industry, either. It's big everywhere, not just here," Thatcher said, once again offering some defense to what I believed was indefensible.

Eventually, we stopped at an ice cream parlor on Peruvian Avenue, and no matter what Thatcher had told me, I still thought people looked at us oddly, sitting there and ordering sundaes in our formal evening wear. However, somehow, I enjoyed this far more than

I enjoyed or would have enjoyed anything at the yacht party. I told Thatcher so.

"Maybe you're just anti–rich people," he said.

"I'm neither poor nor angry at rich people," I told him. "I'm not on any social crusade here."

"No, I don't imagine you are," he said. He stared at me a moment and then smiled and said, "When are you going to tell me why you are really here, Willow?"

I nearly choked on my last spoonful. "What do you mean?"

"I think you know what I mean, but that's all right. Whatever the reason, I'm grateful it brought you here," he said quickly.

I felt like bursting out with the truth, but the waitress appeared and asked us if we wanted anything else. We said no, and he paid the check.

Neither of us spoke as we walked back to the car.

When he got in, he started to laugh.

"What?"

"I can just imagine Bunny if I tell her what we really did tonight and where her pearls were seen," he said.

I laughed, too. It felt so good.

Of course, his parents weren't home when we arrived. They had gone to an event of their own.

"Tired?" he asked.

"No."

"You haven't been to my suite of rooms yet, have you?"

"Inviting me up to see your etchings?"

"I assure you," he said, "I have no kinetic art waiting. You're the only kinetic art I'm interested in."

"Is that so?"

"Yes," he said. "It's so."

We ascended the stairs holding hands and went down the corridor to his room, where our lovemaking started slowly, almost indecisively, as if neither he nor I were sure what we wanted. He kissed me on the cheek while I looked at his art and his collection of Bosson heads from England. He caressed my neck, then rested his hands on my shoulders. I pressed my cheek to his right hand and then moved away to gaze at the framed photographs on his desk.

"Is this Mai Stone?" I asked, lifting a picture of him on a sailboat with a beautiful, tall brunette, both of them in shorts and sailor's caps.

"Yes," he said. "Early vintage, not long after we met. If I only knew then what I know now," he added, mostly for my benefit, I thought.

"She's very pretty; beautiful in fact."

"And no one exemplifies the adage 'Beauty is only skin deep' more than she does."

He was determined to reduce her as a threat to me.

"If you have so many unpleasant thoughts about her, why do you still have this picture out on your desk?" I asked.

He shrugged and smiled. "It's a good picture of me, don't you think?"

"Right," I said, putting it back.

He spun me around roughly and held my shoulders firmly as he looked into my face.

"Look, Willow, I'm not going to lie to you and tell you that you are the first woman I've ever been with or cared for, and I would tend to doubt I was the first man you have ever been intimate with or cared for, but if we hold our pasts over our heads like sins, we'll never see who we are now. The truth is, I was capable of having feeling for someone else, but I have more feeling for you. Is that so terrible?"

"No," I said softly.

He smiled. "Then let's throw the baggage of bad memories overboard and sail on together with lighter hearts," he said, and kissed me.

The kiss was long, hard, and almost desperate. I wanted to hold back, to put on some brakes and slow our momentum toward each other. I was too involved in what I had come to do here now. But Thatcher was a man for whom the word *no* didn't exist or, if it reared its ugly head, only made him try harder. I was swept under the tide of his passion. I couldn't help but want to ride the waves of his love.

It carried us both to his bed, where we were soon entwined, naked, holding onto each other as tightly as two people being carried off in a hurricane. Afterward, like two exhausted swimmers who had reached the safety of the shore, we lay quietly beside each other. He fell asleep, and then I rose, got dressed quietly, and returned to my room.

Suddenly, I felt guilty, and not because I had made love to him again. It was more of a self-chastisement over losing direction, purpose. It was the wrong time to fall in love. I was like a teenage girl passing notes in class to the boy on whom she had developed this great crush when the teacher notices and gets angry that she wasn't paying attention to the lesson . . . only I was the teacher.

Nothing could have brought it home to me more than what I saw after I got undressed for bed and went to the balcony door to close the curtain.

There she was again.

My mother.

On the dock, swinging her lantern in the night.

Looking for the dream she had been promised.

14

Painted into a Corner

Thatcher left a message for me in the morning that he had to go to a negotiation at an office in Jupiter Beach and would call me later in the day. Just like yesterday, after I had breakfast and came downstairs, I found the house empty and quiet. Bunny and Asher had apparently had another one of their late nights. How people could spend so much of their lives going from one party or recreational activity to another without ever doing very much that was substantial was a mystery to me. Weren't they ever tired of seeing the same people, saying the same things, eating the same food? I bet neither Asher nor Bunny had ever gone into the kitchen and made a peanut butter and jelly sandwich. With service people everywhere, servants coming out of the woodwork, and business managers handling every single financial concern, what did they do for themselves beside seek ways to be entertained? It was not hard to see why one of the most feared things here was boredom.

Still, I knew lots of people who would say, "Give me the chance to be frivolous. I'll risk fighting boredom as the biggest challenge of my life any day." Who knows, I wondered, maybe they were right and I was wrong. Maybe the rest of us were like the mythical Sisyphus, pushing boulders up a steep hill only to have them roll back down whenever we got too close to the top. We were cursed with endless ambition. The only ambition Bunny and Asher seemed to have was finding a new caterer for their upcoming weekend extravaganza.

I was nervous this morning. I hadn't told Thatcher that I had agreed to go sailing with Linden to his private bay. I was sure he would have been upset enough not only to insist I didn't go but to speak to Linden as well, and that would only have made things terrible just when I was succeeding in entering our mother's world. I really had no choice if I wanted to continue to win his trust.

He hadn't forgotten. He was waiting for me, and not in a pair of old jeans and a well-worn sweatshirt; he was actually wearing what looked like a relatively new sailing outfit, including a cap. I sensed that this wasn't something he did often. His smile of anticipation set off the wind chimes in my head, little alarms of panic.

"Everything we need is already in the sailboat," he called as I started toward him. "And what a beautiful day. Perfect sailing wind. I brought along lunch, too. I thought you might enjoy doing something different," he said, nodding toward the house and adding, "different from that. It's just something simple," he said when I didn't react. "Good bread, cheeses, some wine. If you don't want to, it's all right," he followed, practically leaping on my small hesitation. "I just thought you might like it."

"No, no, it's fine, Linden. I just didn't want to dominate your day."

"Dominate my day?" He laughed. "I don't think of days anymore, or weeks or months. Time just seems to run together for me. My mother usually has to remind me what day it is, sometimes even what month."

We stopped on the dock.

"Well, here she is. My yacht," he said. "It's nothing at all like the speedboat Thatcher was driving. This is just a twelve-foot, gaff-rigged wooden sailboat. All that's left of the Montgomery navy, I'm afraid."

It didn't look all that much bigger than a rowboat to me.

"Is it safe to go out far with it?" I asked.

"The Vikings crossed the Atlantic in a boat not much more than twice the size of this. I'm a good sailor," he added. "Better than Thatcher. I grew up here on this beach, on this ocean, while he was enjoying the high life, but if you don't feel as safe with me as you felt with him, that's fine. Forget it," he said abruptly.

He was so explosive, like a decanter of nitroglycerin just waiting to be nudged off the table so it could hit the floor and blow up everything around it. One wrong word, one wrong expression, even a sigh in the wrong place, could send him pounding away, his head down, his arms flying up like some hermit charmed out of his cave rushing back to the safety of his silent darkness.

"No, no," I said quickly. "I have no doubt you're a wonderful sailor. I was just curious. I don't know anything about sailing."

"If you don't know anything about sailing, then how do you know I'm wonderful at it?" he asked.

I shook my head and smiled at him.

"What?"

"Let's just say I'm psychic and leave it alone, Linden."

Even he had to smile at that. "Okay, okay," he said. "Let's go, then."

I looked at the beach house. "Your mother knows I'm going along with you, doesn't she?"

He gazed at the house, his eyes darkening a bit and his forehead going into thoughtful folds.

"Yes," he said. "Let's go," he repeated more sharply.

He stepped into the boat and held his hand out to guide me.

"You can sit right there," he said, nodding. "This is a simple, one-man operation. You can just enjoy the trip."

"What did she say?"

"Who?"

"Your mother. I suppose you told her everything, then, my posing for the picture as well, right?"

He was quiet as he untied the boat and then pushed off and hoisted the sail.

My question hung in the air like a fallen leaf caught in the wind.

"I didn't tell her about the painting, no," he finally replied. "She really took to you yesterday, I thought."

"What do you mean, you thought? Did she or didn't she?"

"I asked her about you right after you had spoken with her."

"And?"

"She smiled in a way I haven't seen her smile in a long time and said, 'She's very nice.' She even asked about you."

"She did? Like what?"

"How long you were staying with the Eatons. I told her I didn't know for sure. Then . . ."

"Then what?"

He sat at the rudder. "Then I mentioned I was taking you sailing today, and she became upset."

"Really? Why was she upset?"

"I don't know. I asked her if there was anything wrong, and she just shook her head and went to her room. She didn't talk about it anymore, so I didn't. I think she's just worried I'll get involved with someone and leave her," he offered. "I wouldn't," he added quickly. "I mean, I'd get involved with someone, but I wouldn't leave her.

"Here we go," he cried as the wind filled the sail.

Of course, it wasn't anywhere as fast as it was with Thatcher on the speedboat, but being this close to the water, getting the spray in my face, feeling the wind, and bouncing on the waves, it was just as exciting, if not more so.

Linden did look at home on the sea. His whole demeanor changed. His face filled with a glow, and his eyes picked up the blue of the water and the sky. He no longer looked as fragile and no longer looked depressed or forlorn. He was energized and alive, and that change had a good effect on me.

I never realized how beautiful it was to sail, to feel the water beneath us, the wind in my hair, the breeze caressing my face. I couldn't help but squeal with delight when he made a turn so sharply that the boat seemed ready to tip and just hung in the air for a few seconds before righting itself and bouncing on.

He laughed at my reactions.

"Give me a sailboat any day," he shouted, "over a multimillion-dollar motorized yacht. This way, you're part of the process. You're connected. Understand?"

"Yes," I said.

He smiled. "I thought you would. I knew you would."

He looked so pleased, as much with himself as with me, and I wondered when he had last felt this way. It wasn't a bad thing I was doing, being with him, giving him some companionship, helping him enjoy things he should have no problem enjoying every day, was it? I wasn't wrong. *Silence,* I told the chimes in my head. *Stop the alarms. I'll be fine. We'll be fine. There's nothing wrong with this, no danger.*

I sat back and laughed. "Look," I cried, pointing to a pair of male waterskiers. They waved at us and turned to send the spray in our direction.

"A couple of showoffs," Linden shouted in their direction, even though there was no way they could possibly hear him.

We saw speedboats and dozens of other sailboats. He pointed out a luxury liner.

"Probably going to the Fort Lauderdale pier," he said, raising his voice again. The wind played havoc with our voices, but settling back, feeling myself being swept along, I didn't want to hear anything but the wind and the boat on the water and the cry of terns. He pointed vigorously at a small inlet as he turned the sailboat in its direction. It was caught between two well-combed beaches but hidden by rocks and the way it was carved deeply out of the shoreline.

"Linden Beach," he called, and laughed.

Minutes later, we were at the shore. He hopped out, beached the boat, and reached up to take me at the waist. I had my shoes off and expected to wade in, but he showed remarkable strength in those lean arms and carried me to dry land instead, his lips practically grazing my cheek.

"Isn't it beautiful here?"

"Yes," I said.

"We'll set up by those rocks there," he indicated, and returned to the boat to get his things.

"Need any help?"

"No, I'm fine. Relax. Just enjoy it."

I liked the feel of the cool water and sand on my

feet. Some curious terns swooped down to get a better look at us and then veered away, sounding as if they were laughing. I placed my sandals on the rocks and watched him set up his easel and then go back to the boat for the rest of his things. He handed me the paper bag holding the clothes I had worn for posing the day before.

We both instantly realized there wasn't any place for me to have privacy, not for some distance.

"Oh. Well, I'll keep my back to you," he said. "As far as those people go," he said, gesturing toward the other boats in the sea, "they're too far away to make head or tail of it. Is that all right?"

"Yes," I said.

I unbuttoned my blouse and slipped it off. He knelt and leaned over his paints and brushes while I continued to change into the skirt and peasant blouse.

"Ready," I said, and he turned, smiled, and explained where he wanted me to sit.

"How can you paint me in two different places?" I asked.

"The background isn't important. You're what's important," he replied.

I took the same position and gazed around the cove. It did look untouched. But how could it remain undisturbed in the midst of one of the world's most developed water playgrounds?

"How come this place is undiscovered?" I asked.

"It's not exactly undiscovered. It was just left undeveloped by the original owner of the estate inland from here. I'm sure it won't be like this too much longer. I heard he's died and the family is dividing the spoils. Won't surprise me to see a hotel built over there soon. Ready?"

"Ready? I don't have much to do."

"Sure you do. Look out at the sea and hold that beautiful pose," he said. "In other words, relax and be yourself."

I waited until he had been working for a good fifteen or so minutes before speaking.

"What makes you so positive your mother was upset about your taking me sailing, Linden?"

"I know when my mother is upset about something. We've been so close, half the time I can tell her moods even before she can. Stop worrying about it. She'll be fine when she sees I'm coming back and not sailing off into the sunset with the first beautiful young woman who talks to me," he added.

"How does she spend most of her day?"

"She reads, watches a little television, very little, and takes care of me and the house. It's plenty. I never heard her say she was bored."

"She never goes anywhere?"

"Nope."

"Not even to a movie or a restaurant?"

He paused.

"I'm sorry," I said quickly. "I don't mean to break your concentration."

"It's all right. No, my mother is quite introverted, as, I suppose, am I. It doesn't mean we're mentally ill," he added pointedly. "I do what shopping we need to have done. We're fine."

"She doesn't have any old friends who call or come around?"

He laughed. "Old friends? Hardly. She was persona non grata even before she had her problems. You can imagine how it was when she returned." He thought a moment. "There was someone who came around once."

"Who?"

"Someone from the place she had been at when she needed treatment," he said, and started working again.

"You mean, like her doctor?" I held my breath. Had my father paid her a visit after all?

"No, not her doctor. Doctors don't take that much interest in you once you're no longer their responsibility and they can no longer earn money from your troubles," he said bitterly.

"Then who? Was it another patient from the clinic?"

"Might have been, yes. My mother didn't want to tell me much about her, but I remember it wasn't a very pleasant visit. When she left, my mother went into a rather deep depression. It lasted days, matter of fact. So maybe she was better off not renewing old friendships, huh?"

"Could it have been a nurse from the clinic?"

He shrugged.

"Maybe. I don't know. I thought it might have been some kind of follow-up visit, but my mother insisted it wasn't, and I never saw the woman come around again. I knew she wasn't from Palm Beach, that was for sure. I remember she had an unusual name . . . Nadine. I don't hear that name often. Do you?"

"No."

Nadine Gordon, I thought. The nurse who suspected, the one Dr. Price thought had a crush on my father. She had come here, but why?

"Look at that," he said, pointing to the sky. A plane was spewing some advertisement by writing it in dry ice or something across the magnificent blue. "Pollution, even up there. I'm surprised the kings and queens of Palm Beach don't complain. It's crass commercialization of their air space. I guess everything's for sale; everything has a price."

He returned to his painting as if it were a true avenue of escape from the reality around him he despised so much. I watched him lose himself in his work again, his face tightening with the intensity of his efforts. I said nothing more, afraid to break his concentration. Nearly twenty minutes later, he seemed to realize he had been in his own world and came up out of it like something rising from the sea before us, exploding out of the water. He looked surprised at his own accomplishments.

"Wow. You've been a great model." He studied his work in progress and nodded. "Yes, you have," he said, and turned back to me. "You know how you realize you have a great model?"

"How?"

"It's when you get so lost in the moment, in the artistic inspiration, that you don't even realize the model is there. I know that sounds silly or contradictory, but it's as if I see beyond you, within you, into your very heart and soul, and for that period of time, everything else ceases to exist for me. It just flows from you to me or through me to the canvas. Understand?"

"I think so, yes," I said. "It sounds very exciting, at least for you."

"It has been. Thank you." He put his brush down and came beside me, folding his legs and sitting. Then he took a deep breath, enjoying the air. I laughed at his exuberance, and he smiled at me.

"This is the sort of day that happens so rarely in a lifetime, a day filled with so much special feeling, you can't ever forget it or duplicate it. Every moment doesn't have to be similar to the one before it, but it often seems like that, doesn't it? At least, it does for me. It's only when I work or get the opportunity to meet someone like you and get you into my work that I rise above the mediocrity.

"Gosh, listen to me mouthing off like this," he said, catching his breath and realizing how much he had said. "I'm sorry."

"No, it's nice. It's like being invited into a special place, an artist's world, seeing and feeling everything the way he does, at least for a moment or two. Thank you for sharing it," I said.

He stared at me. "You're remarkable," he said. "It's as if you came out of one of my dreams, my fantasies—just appeared, sort of like a kindred spirit. You feel that, too, don't you?"

I was at a loss for words, for a way to slip out of this far too emotional moment, but he mistook my silence for agreement and brought his lips toward mine.

As if the air between us was filled with shocking

electricity, I pulled back and away from him abruptly. He was caught, committed, exposed, his desire naked, and that filled his face with blood so fast I thought the top of his head would explode. It instantly retreated, forming deep white patches of anger and disappointment at the corners of his lips.

"Am I that distasteful?" he asked, infuriated.

"No, no," I said. "I was just taken by such surprise."

"Right. I forgot. You're becoming Thatcher Eaton's latest amusement, off-limits to the likes of someone like me." He pushed himself to his feet.

"No, Linden. I'm no one's amusement."

"Oh, no, you're in control of everything. Just like all the others he's paraded through that house and taken to his bedroom." He paused and looked down at me. "You have been to his bedroom already, haven't you?"

"That's not really something I'd like to discuss, Linden."

"Of course not," he said, darkening his eyes, eyes that seemed to know all the wicked and tricky ways of the world.

Should I tell him the truth right here and now? I wondered. *Should I explain why we can't become lovers?* Was it right to tell him that before I had spoken with my mother? Maybe she didn't want him to know—or anyone to know, for that matter. What should I do?

I felt so desperate and so foolish. Why didn't I see this coming? Why did I think I could prevent it?

He stood there, with his hands on his hips, staring at the sea, the anger rising in his face like mercury in a thermometer.

"Linden, please . . ."

"It's all right," he said. "I've lost the moment. It happens."

He started to put his things away.

"But what are you doing? We still have lots of time, don't we?"

"Artists are finicky people," he muttered. "We do illogical, inexplicable things. Don't blame yourself. It's not the first time this has happened, believe me."

"Can't we just continue so you can get your work done?"

"I can't work when I get like this. I'm sorry. I have it all in here, anyway," he said, pointing to his temple. "I took the picture, and I can replay it whenever I need to. Don't worry about it. You fulfilled your part of the bargain."

He started to pack up. He moved with such abrupt, almost violent actions I was afraid to try to stop him. He loaded the boat.

"Linden . . ."

"Please change," he said, turning his back to me. "I need to go back."

"I didn't mean to hurt your feelings, honest I didn't."

"Right."

"I can explain. Maybe not right at this moment, but I can and I will someday. I promise," I said, "and you'll understand."

"Change," he repeated, not looking at me.

I did so quickly and handed him the clothing. He shoved it back into the bag and threw it into the boat.

"Let's go," he said.

He practically lunged at me and lifted me again, but he kept his face turned away until he had lowered me into the boat. Then he pushed off and got into it.

"It seems a pity to waste the day, Linden," I said softly.

"What of it? I've wasted many," he said, and turned us away from his private little paradise.

I looked back and watched us move farther and farther from it until we made a turn and it disappeared altogether, just like so many precious moments in both our lives.

It was as if the winds of fury had gathered. We made it back to the dock in what seemed to me to be half the time it had taken to get to the bay. He tied up the boat and reached in to help me step out.

"Will you want me to pose for you again tomorrow?" I asked softly.

"No, that's fine," he said. "Don't waste any more time with me." His whole body was now heavy with self-pity. I wanted so much to put my hand on his shoulder to reassure him, to promise him again that soon, very soon, he would understand, but I didn't dare touch him. He kept his back to me, and his shoulders were hoisted like the shoulders of a hawk, protective, aggressive, ready to pounce on some prey.

As I started off the dock and toward the main house, I saw my mother staring at me from the loggia of the beach house. She and I gazed at each other for a long moment, and then she turned and went inside. I made up my mind I would see her before this day was over, and I would tell her who I was. Somehow, however, I had a deep feeling inside me that she knew. Was it possible for a mother to pick out her child from everyone else in the world, even though she had never set eyes on her since her birth? Was there a magical connection that couldn't be broken or hidden?

I would soon find out, I thought, and that both excited and frightened me.

"Well, where were you?" I heard as I trudged up toward the rear loggia.

Bunny and Asher were sitting at a table having some breakfast.

"You didn't just come in from sailing with Linden, did you?" Bunny asked.

"As a matter of fact, yes, I did," I said. "It was quite enjoyable. He's a good sailor."

They both looked a bit stunned and exchanged concerned glances.

"How can you get so chummy with Linden Montgomery, of all people?" Bunny practically demanded. Did she believe I was getting romantically involved with him, after she had laid a trap for Thatcher and me?

"He's really desperate for company," I explained. "I think his angry demeanor is all a façade. If people would simply be kind to him . . ."

"How can anyone be kind to him? He won't respond to a simple hello or look at anyone who speaks to him. Believe me, I've had a number of my friends meet him down at the beach, and he growls at them. They all think he's absolutely mad, and when you put his artwork together with his behavior, you can come to no other conclusion. I hope you will listen to my advice and stop getting involved with him.

"Surely, he cannot be of any value when it comes to your work," she concluded.

"On the contrary," I said. "He and his mother have been the most informative and valuable interviews I've had to date."

She practically gasped and then turned her head sharply to Asher, who smiled at me.

"I know what she's doing, Bunny. She's getting a variety of views and perspectives. It's very important to her project, I'm sure. A good interviewer has to win the trust of the person he or she is interviewing, right?"

"Exactly," I said.

That seemed to bring some relief to Bunny, who relaxed her shoulders and dropped her hand from the base of her throat.

"What about a cup of coffee or perhaps a mimosa?" Asher asked.

"Surely, the sea air has stirred your appetite a little," Bunny insisted.

"I would love a cup of coffee," I said, and sat at the table. The maid emerged from where she was standing just inside the French doors and poured me a cup.

"Everything we hoped for my party tomorrow night has come to pass," Bunny said. "I have well over a hundred confirmed guests and more calling in every hour. I have the orchestra I wanted, and when you see the menu, you will be as excited as I am. There are some surprises, too, some very important Palm Beach people and some singers and movie stars among the guests."

"Everyone loves a good party," Asher added, smiling.

"Don't you ever get tired of all this entertaining, attending events?" I asked.

"Why, of course not," Bunny said. "It's the season. Don't you know what that means? People from all over the world have come here to gather at these events, renew old acquaintances, share new discoveries. It's the most exciting time of the year for us. We would never think of missing anything, would we, Asher?"

"Gloria Van De Mere had herself brought in an ambulance to the fundraiser for battered women last week," he said by way of replying. "She had just come out of the hospital after a gall bladder operation. She went from the ambulance to a wheelchair to the ball, accompanied by her nurse."

"Gloria Van De Mere's father created the Chump Charlie Hot Dog chain," Bunny tacked on. "They are neck and neck with Holy Dog for the majority share of that fast-food market."

"Absolutely brilliant people working for them," Asher said.

I listened to them go on and on about their guests for the party, rattling off the names of businesses, chain stores, clothing designers, drug company heirs, CEOs of major corporations, a veritable Who's Who of wealth and power in America.

"All on our little doorstep," Bunny said proudly. "And all for you, dear," she pointed out. "Asher, Thatcher, and I will introduce you to everyone and anyone you wish to meet."

"I'm exhausted just thinking about it," I said. I was serious, but that made them laugh.

Afterward, I went to my room to change, and Thatcher called to tell me he was sorry but he would be tied up with meetings all the way through dinner. I told him I was fine and not to be concerned.

"What have you been doing with yourself?" he asked suspiciously.

"Enjoying the day," I said. "But organizing the information I have already gathered as well."

"Good. I'd hate to be responsible for your failing your course," he quipped. However, there was some concern in his tone. I had the feeling he had already spoken with Bunny, who was giving him a minute-by-minute report on my comings and goings. Maybe it wasn't a good idea to stay here after all.

At precisely two-thirty, I made my way toward the beach house, hoping that my mother was sitting outside and having her tea again with Linden. When I turned the corner, however, I saw no one was there. Disappointed, I walked out toward the beach and stood looking at the ocean, wondering if I should just go knock on the door and ask to speak with her.

"Isabel Amou," I heard, and turned to see her standing behind me. She was wearing a light white shawl over her shoulders and a sleeveless white dress. She was barefoot, and her hair was down.

"Hello," I said.

She studied me a moment and then smiled softly and folded her arms under her breasts.

"Walk with me," she said, starting off to her left.

I caught up quickly, my heart thumping so hard I thought I would fold up on the beach like some limp chiffon scarf.

"How is your father?" she asked after we had walked in silence for nearly a minute.

I stopped. She stopped and turned to me.

"You know who I am?"

"Of course," she said. "First, I could see him in you the moment I set eyes on you, and second . . ."

"What?"

"Your name." She laughed softly. "A long time ago, I heard of a nanny named Isabella whose charge had nicknamed her Amou."

I remembered her letter to Daddy. Subconsciously, perhaps, I had used the name hoping to give myself away.

"Yes, he told you that."

"It wasn't a very subtle clue."

"Did he keep in touch with you much?"

"I have some letters," she said, smiling softly—at the memory of each and every word on the stationery, I was sure. "It was more difficult for me to write to him, but I did what I could. Did he send you to me?"

"Not directly, no, but I think he wanted me to meet you someday," I said.

"Wanted?"

Every muscle in her body, every tiny muscle in her face, froze in anticipation. The tears in my eyes were answer enough.

"When?" she asked, holding her breath.

"Last week," I said.

She looked out at the sea so quickly it was as if she expected something out there to confirm my words.

"How?"

"An unexpected heart attack," I said, my throat closing, my words cracking.

She lowered her head, turned, and continued to walk. I followed alongside her. Neither of us spoke for a while.

"Once, a long time ago, we played a game of fantasy," she said. " 'One day,' he told me, 'I will no longer be able to control myself. I will no longer care about the consequences, and I will come to you.' I knew he was wishing more than promising, but I joined him.

" 'And I'll be waiting for you,' I said. 'I'll never stop waiting for you. I'll expect you to come at night.'

" 'I'll come by boat. You'll see the light of it in the darkness growing brighter, larger, as I draw closer.'

" 'And I'll be on the dock, waving a lantern to guide you,' I told him.

"Silly, I suppose, especially for us, especially for people who knew how dangerous fantasy could become, but it was our little extravagance, our flirtation with the forbidden, forbidden happiness."

She paused and turned to me with a hard, serious look on her face. "You must never think badly of him for what happened between us at the clinic. For us, it was no longer a clinic. I was no longer a patient, and he was no longer a doctor."

"I know," I said. "I read his diary."

"His diary?" She smiled. "Your father kept a diary?"

"Yes. It was almost a bigger surprise than what was in it," I said.

"Someday, maybe, you will give it to me to read."

I didn't say yes. I wasn't sure what to do. Was it something my father had wanted her to read? Did he know for certain that I would seek her out? She seemed to understand my indecisiveness and kept walking, silent, the tears now streaming down her cheeks. I looked back at the beach house.

"Did you say anything to Linden today? After we returned from the sailing?" I asked.

She shook her head, stopped, and tried to swallow down her grief. "I must tell him, I know," she said. "He will not understand. He has suffered so much because of me already. I hate to add another lump of pain to the burden he carries." She sighed deeply, so deeply I thought her heart had cracked. "But I know I must. I know," she said. Then she turned to me and smiled. "You are as beautiful as he described. He did a wonderful job with you, he and that nanny of yours. I know how unpleasant your adoptive mother was. I know that from between the lines of what he wrote.

"He didn't want me to feel any guilt, and so he made it sound much better than it was for you, I'm sure."

"She was truly more of a mother to me, my Amou."

"I'm glad of that." She paused and shook her head. "It was painful for him, watching you grow up."

"Why?"

"He wrote how much you reminded him of me and how he felt he had to keep his deep love for you in control so your adoptive mother would never suspect you were really his daughter. He hated being so formal with you at times."

"And I hated it, too, but recently we grew closer to each other."

"I am glad of that."

"I'd like to spend more time with you, too, get to know you and let you get to know me," I said, "the way a mother and a daughter should know each other."

"Yes, I'd like that. You're not in college?"

"I took a leave of absence after I was given Daddy's diary and learned about you."

"What do these people, the Eatons, think? Have you told them the truth about why you are here?"

"Oh, no, never. They think I'm on some sort of study project, as you were first told. No one but me and Dr. Price knows the truth about us."

"Yes, and someone else," she said.

"Nadine Gordon?"

"Yes," she said with surprise. "Who told you about her? Was she in your father's diary, too?"

"No. Dr. Price told me of her. But today Linden told me she had come to see you some time ago. Why?"

"She hoped to blackmail me. She was a despicable person, jealous, cruel to the patients, and especially to me."

"What did you do?"

"I threw her out."

"I would have thought she would have tried to blackmail my father, not you."

"That was the irony of it all. She truly did love your father and couldn't get herself to be cruel to him. Whereas she would enjoy being cruel to me. For all I know, however, she might have extracted something from him."

"I don't know," I said, shaking my head.

"It doesn't matter very much now," she said. She looked at the sea again. "None of it matters, except how it affects Linden and you."

"I'd like to be his friend, his sister, if I can, if he'll let me," I said.

She looked at me intently for a few moments and then glanced back at the beach house.

"I should have told him long ago. It would have been so much easier for all of us. Secrets have a way of growing into little cancers, eating your heart and your soul."

I nodded, biting down on my lower lip, trying to squeeze back the tears that were burning beneath my lids. Surely, Daddy had suffered secrets like this as well, and for so long and so privately.

She smiled at me and stroked my hair. "Just looking at you brings back so many wonderful memories of your father. Willow. What a wonderful name to have given you. No one knew how special it was but your father and me. It made him so happy. I see his smile in your smile, the same light in your eyes. I am truly glad you have come back to me," she said. "Even after all this time."

"But I've brought you bad news. I was afraid I would bring you pain, and I have."

"Yes, but it's over. The bad news is over," she said. It sounded so much like a prayer.

I smiled back at her.

Behind us, a tern cried mournfully as if it had overheard her words and knew that fate hadn't quite satisfied its hunger for tears. Not yet.

15

The Waters Rise

My mother repeated her promise to tell Linden everything that evening. If it went well, she would bring us together tomorrow, she told me. I warned her about the Eatons' big affair. She had already gotten word of it through some of the servants, who sympathized more with her and cared more for her than they did for Bunny and Asher.

I would have thought the Eatons would stay home and rest for their big extravaganza, but Bunny had Jennings inform me that they were going to another dinner party and would not be available to have dinner with me. I was to request anything I desired, however.

"Anything you want," he said. "The chef is standing by."

Jennings stood there, waiting as if I were on death row, ordering my last meal before my execution.

"I'm not terribly hungry, Jennings. Just some cheese, crackers, and fresh fruit with some coffee will be fine. I'll take it in my room," I told him.

"Very good, miss," he said with a small bow. He retreated, and I sat on my balcony and gazed down at the beach house, wondering what was happening, where and when my mother was beginning her disclosures to Linden, and how he was reacting. It kept me on pins and needles, and when the phone rang, I practically leaped out of my clothes.

It was Thatcher again. "Just checking on you to see what you're doing. Are you going into town, meeting anyone?"

"No. I'm just having something light here in my room, on the balcony, actually."

"I'll stop by to see you as soon as I get home," he promised.

"That's fine," I said. "Don't worry about me."

"My parents wanted to take you along with them to their dinner party, but I wouldn't let them," he revealed. "I don't want to share you. You're liable to meet some prince of industry and drop me like yesterday's news."

"You're prince of industry enough for any girl," I replied, and he laughed.

"I've got to get back to the table. We're fighting over a mere five million dollars."

"Chump change," I quipped.

"Now you sound like a Palm Beach girl," he teased. "See you soon. I really don't think it will be all that much longer, and I'm only a few driving minutes away now."

"If you hurry and settle, you can share my cheese and crackers."

"Um. That's the best reason to settle that I've heard all day."

We both laughed before we said goodbye.

Fooling around with him over the phone buoyed my spirits some and put my nerves in the closet for a while. Then Jennings brought my light dinner, and I sat on the balcony nibbling on crackers and cheese and pieces of fruit. Funny, I thought, but I'd either been too busy or too preoccupied to think about my college friends. It also surprised me how quickly I had relegated Allan to a back shelf in my emotional memory. Maybe that was because whenever I did think about him and recalled the way he had reacted to my troubles and problems, I grew angry and disappointed.

When I was little, Daddy used to say you have to toss your bad memories and dreams into a dark hole and bury them. First, visualize the hole, and then enjoy dropping them in, one by one. Sometimes, that really did work.

I wanted it to work tonight. It was a good night to try. The darkness seemed to creep up on the world this evening, coming in from the sea and the distant horizon like some blanket being unfurled until it reached our shore and rose up and over the house. A heavily cloudy sky made the stars play peekaboo, twinkling between the shoulders of the billowing marshmallow whiteness and then disappearing in a wall of bluish gray that ominously waved the finger of some coastal storm. I saw the breakers were higher, whiter. If the ocean could growl, it would right now, I thought.

However, it didn't rain. It turned out to be an idle threat, the clouds finally coming apart, shredding into long slivers of paper-thin fog being chased back toward the horizon by winds from the west. The sky cleared considerably. The victorious constellations brightened with pride and turned the heavens into a dazzling display of jewelry once again. I felt mesmerized by the majesty and had almost fallen asleep staring up at the sky when suddenly the loud clap of a door being slammed below jerked me back to a fully awake state of mind.

I leaned over the balcony and looked down at the beach house. Moments later, Linden appeared, walking quickly toward the beach, his arms flailing about as if he were having a vehement argument with himself. Even from this distance, I could see his hair was wild. Under the glow of the stars, his head looked on fire, in fact. He paused, gazed up at the house and at me, I thought, and then charged forward, disappearing around the bend.

What had happened? How did she tell him? What had she said about me?

I looked back at the beach house, but my mother wasn't coming out after him. Concerned now, I hurried out and down the stairs to the rear loggia. I looked for signs of Linden and saw none. I was worried for him. I remembered how shocked and disturbed I was reading my father's story, but for Linden to hear it from his mother now, so many years later, must have been twice as traumatic. He had to understand that he wasn't alone, that I shared his astonishment, I thought, and started after him.

I trudged along the beach until I was well beyond

the property, but I didn't see him. I called out for him
and listened, but he didn't respond. On my way back to
the house, I paused where he and I had first begun the
painting and saw something piled on the sand.
Approaching, I discovered it was his clothing. I spun
about and searched the sea. Finally, I spotted his head
just above the water, bobbing with the waves. I ran
down to the shoreline and called out to him. Either he
couldn't hear me, or he wouldn't.

I saw his head disappear, and my heart just about
dropped into my stomach.

"Linden!"

I turned toward the house. There was no one else
outside. I spun around like a madwoman, screaming
for someone, anyone. In the inky darkness, there were
only the shadowy shapes of some bushes and trees.
What was the point of my shouting? Looking out
again, I saw his head emerge and then go under once
more. Now in a true panic, I stripped off my clothing
as quickly as I could and waded into the sea.

We had a pool at home, and I was a fairly good
swimmer, but it was one thing to swim in a pool of
calm water and another to swim against the powerful
ocean, especially the way it was tonight. It wasn't long
before I was breathing hard, from both the effort and
my fear. I swallowed water, spit and choked and fought
to keep myself moving toward him, or at least where I
had last seen his head. For a few moments, I could not
see him at all, and when I turned about in the water, I
realized I had swum out quite far.

I shouted and shouted for him. The sea made me

bob and struggle, but I kept it up as long as I could until I actually felt the cold pang of fear travel up my spine along with my desperate attempts to catch my breath. In a purely defensive mode now, I started back toward the shore. A wave lifted me and brought me down so hard I thought I had all the breath knocked out of me. It was as if a strong hand were holding me under, too.

I cried out in desperation and started to panic, flailing about wildly to keep myself afloat. Suddenly, I felt something wrap itself around my waist and pull me forward. Shocked and terrified, I started to battle against it, only to realize it was Linden, holding me up.

"What are you doing?" he screamed. "Stop it! Swim slowly, calm down."

He kept his arm around me until I started my stroke again, and together we drew closer to the beach until, finally, I could stand. I coughed and spit out the saltwater and then, finally, catching my breath, turned to him. In the starlight, we were both naked, glimmering.

"What were you doing?" he asked me.

"I thought you . . . were drowning," I said.

"That's right. I was drowning," he replied, "but the ocean refused to accept it."

He trudged back to the shore and fell onto the sand. I walked out as quickly as I could and started for my clothing.

"You were going to save me?" he asked, the laugh in his voice. "You, by yourself?"

"Yes," I said. "I was."

"Another one who hopes to save the world?" he

asked with cynicism dripping from his lips. "You see how hard it was for you to fight against the waves out there," he said. "Get used to it, Willow. I know now that's your real name, Willow. Well, Willow, there's a tide of fate sweeping over both of us. You have as much chance of stopping it as you do turning that sea around."

"I don't believe that," I said.

"Yeah, well, from what I hear from my mother . . . our mother, I should say, you haven't been aware of it very long. You haven't lived under the curse long enough to know it's there along with fate itself, playing with us, amusing itself, tinkering with our hearts and minds, fooling with our emotions, sometimes even permitting us to taste a little happiness so that when it pulls it away from us, we can fully understand just how much we have lost and how terrible is our particular destiny.

"Welcome to the family," he said, then spun around and walked toward his clothes.

"I don't believe any of that, Linden," I called to him across our patch of darkness. "And I know you don't, either."

He laughed, madly.

"Together," I continued as I struggled to get on my clothes, "we can make sense out of this. We can restore understanding and love and hope to our mother and to ourselves."

"Please," he said. "You don't know what you're talking about. Don't make me feel any sicker than I do, if that's possible. If there is one thing that can do it, though," he said, approaching me, "it's false hopes and stupid cotton-candy dreams. Just listen to the ocean," he said. "Come out here at night and listen to it whenever you get so you believe you can change anything, and you'll hear the same song men and women have heard since time began, the same roar of laughter. That's the voice of fate. Shouting back at it is like shouting directly into a wall."

"No," I said.

He seized my shoulders and spun me around to face him. I pressed the blouse I was holding against my naked breasts. He stared at me a moment and then turned me again so I would face in the direction of the house. I could see the lights in the upstairs hallway.

"A long time ago, our mother was raped in that very house; not seduced, raped. And I was born of that. I'm tainted with it, spoiled, understand? I have his blood in me. Years later, our mother, as you know, was raped again, when she was just as vulnerable, and you were born of that."

"No," I said, shaking my head. "That's not true. That's not how it was."

"And you were born," he repeated. "So you see, we're really very much alike, aren't we? Maybe we should forget we're half-brother and half-sister, huh? Maybe we should give into the stream of lust that has produced us."

"No," I said as he pulled my arms apart so that my blouse came away from my naked bosom. He stared down at me.

"Maybe we should confirm it all right on this beach," he spat.

My heart was pounding so hard that I didn't have

the strength to pull my arms from his hands. But suddenly, he released me, and I hurried to put on my blouse.

"What difference would it make?" he muttered. "What difference does any of it make, anyway?"

He started off. I slipped on my sandals and hurried after him.

"Linden, wait. That's not what happened at my father's clinic. That's not the truth."

He walked faster, practically running from me. As he charged down the beach, I slowed up. He went back toward the beach house, and I emerged from the shadows into the lights of the estate. My clothes were wet from my soaked body, my blouse clinging around my breasts like tissue paper and just as translucent. I looked after him a moment and then turned toward the house—and stopped sharply.

Standing there, his eyes wide with shock, was Thatcher.

"What did you both do, fall out of a boat?" he asked facetiously.

"No."

"I didn't think so. I hope you had a good time, at least," he said, and turned away to start back to the house.

"Thatcher, wait!" I cried.

He stopped and spun around. "Funny," he said. "I thought you would be the one in for a surprise or two here, and what do you know, I'm the one who gets all the surprises. Doesn't seem quite fair, does it?"

"You don't understand," I said. "I didn't come here for the reasons I gave you. I'm not doing any study of the Palm Beach society."

He shook his head, smiling. "I really didn't think you were, Willow. Is that your real name, or is that another surprise?" He looked toward the beach house. "What, do you know something I don't know about Linden Montgomery's net worth? Or do you just favor the sad, wacky type? Is the sex better with someone like that? A bit kinky? What?" he practically screamed, his eyes wide, his lips stretched with his anger and fury. "Or are you the kind who doesn't tell? I've met one or two of those. I thought I'd met every sort, actually, but that was before I met you."

Tears were streaming down my face so fast I thought I was in a downpour. My throat closed up.

"What bothers me the most," he continued, "was how sincere and honest I was with you. I feel like a fool, but that's the way you women like us, at a disadvantage, isn't it?"

I shook my head. "Thatcher . . ."

"Don't bother," he said, holding his hand up like a king making a royal declaration that couldn't be changed or delayed. "I wouldn't believe anything you told me now, anyway."

He turned again and walked faster toward the house. Before I took another step, he was inside, the door closing behind him.

What a mess of everything I have made, I thought. Linden was more depressed and hurt than ever. My mother was shut up in the darkness of her own disappointments knowing now that my father would never come for her. And I had driven Thatcher back into the very pool of cynicism he had stepped out of when we met and made love and had begun to believe in something greater than ourselves.

I should just go home, I thought. I should just return to the life I had before and pretend Daddy's diary never existed or that it was someone else's work of fiction. In a way Allan might have been the smartest one of all. Maybe his advice was the advice I should have taken. Now, it was too late even for that.

It's best just to go, I thought. *It's best just to leave. I'll write my mother a letter and explain afterward.*

I went into the house and up to my room, where I changed out of the wet clothing. Then I began to pack my things. *If I can't get a flight out, I'll check into one of those airport hotels,* I thought. I didn't even want to bother calling. I would just drive to the airport and take my chances.

I sat at the desk and wrote a quick thank-you note to Thatcher's parents, asking them to forgive me for my abrupt departure and adding simply that it couldn't be avoided. I was sure their party would be a big success anyway and told them so. When I was ready, I called for Jennings. He looked surprised at the sight of my suitcase, but he didn't ask any questions.

"Please see that Mr. and Mrs. Eaton get this note, Jennings," I told him, and handed it to him.

"Very good, miss. Would you like me to take your suitcase down to your car?"

"It's not necessary, Jennings. I can manage," I said.

"I'll take them down to the foyer, then," he insisted.

I supposed that somewhere in the rules that governed the behavior of house servants here, it would be a loss of face for him not to take my suitcases down. I nodded, and he left. After wiping the remnants of my tears away, I followed. When I reached the bottom of the stairway, I made a turn to the rear loggia. I wanted one more look at the beach house. I stood out there, debating whether or not to try to say goodbye. I thought it would be just too complicated and maybe even more painful to face my mother at the moment. A letter would have to suffice, I decided finally, and turned to leave.

Thatcher was sitting quietly in the oversized armchair. He had come down and had been watching me all the while.

"Where are you going?" he asked.

"Home."

"Where is home? You can tell me the truth now."

"It's where I said it was, South Carolina. Most of what I told you was true, Thatcher."

"Uh-huh."

"That's right," I said, turning sharply at him. "Uh-huh. I'm sorry you have shut me out so firmly, convincing yourself that I'm deceitful and false and conniving, but you don't know anything," I told him.

He held his skeptical smile. "And your father and mother are really deceased?" he continued as if I were on a witness stand and he was being the clever trial attorney.

"That's correct."

"And your father was a doctor, a psychiatrist?"

"Yes."

"Who happened to have been Grace Montgomery's doctor? You said she was sent to his clinic."

"That's all true, Thatcher, yes."

He smiled coldly. "How convenient for you. What did you do, get hold of her records or something?"

"In a way," I said, "but that wasn't what brought me here. I'm no fortune hunter. I'm not here to play what you called the Palm Beach game. I couldn't care less about all that, if you want to know. I'm not as wealthy as most of the people in your parents' world, but I'm far from poor. I don't have yachts and thousands of dollars' worth of jewelry, but I have more than enough to keep me from selling myself into an affair so I can become a citizen of this artificial world."

I laughed. "You know something, Thatcher? Now that I have been here and have seen some of it, I just might propose the study paper to my psychology teacher next semester and maybe come back and really do it."

I started to cross the room.

"All right," he said, his fingers pressed together into a cathedral. "I'll bite. Your father was Grace Montgomery's doctor, and she was in his clinic. Why would that bring you here to involve yourself with Linden?"

I stopped and looked at him. There was still anger and cynicism in his face, but there was pain, too. His eyes saw only betrayal.

"I didn't come here to get involved with Linden, at least not the way you are suggesting."

"What other way, then?"

"I came here, Thatcher, to meet and get to know my real mother."

His eyebrows lifted. "I don't understand. Your real mother?"

"After my father died, I was given a diary he had written and had kept with his close personal friend and attorney with the instructions to give it to me only after his passing. I read the pages and learned that he and Grace Montgomery had become lovers at his clinic."

"What are you saying? Your father had an affair with his patient, and she became pregnant with you? Grace Montgomery?"

"Yes," I said. "But if you read the diary, and if you speak with Grace, you understand it wasn't what it sounds like. It wasn't a doctor taking advantage of a vulnerable patient. She remained in the clinic long after she could have gone home because she was truly in love with him, and he with her."

"You're telling me, then, that Linden Montgomery is your . . . your half-brother?"

"Exactly. Tonight, our mother told him the truth, and when he heard it, he was so depressed about his life that he thought about drowning himself. I saw him out there, and I went in to save him, only it turned out he had to save me."

"Why would it depress him so to have you as a half-sister?" Thatcher asked, and quickly thought of the answer to his own question. I just stood there looking at him. "Oh," he said. "I get it. You're the prettiest, nicest young woman who has given him the time of day in years." He looked down at the floor.

"I've just hurt everyone by coming here," I said. "Wiser people told me to leave it be, but I couldn't. Anyway, that is what I was trying to tell you out there when you saw us returning from the beach. I'm sorry I hurt you. Goodbye," I said, and started out.

"Wait a minute. Does Grace know you're leaving?"

"No. I thought I would write to her in a day or so."

"That doesn't sound fair. You come in here like something blown in from the sea and then fly away?"

I felt my face crumpling, my lips trembling so hard they were knocking against my teeth. "I can't stand any more . . . sadness, any more . . . *dor no coração, peso na alma.*"

"What?" he said, squinting and scrunching his nose.

A laugh and a smile broke through my veil of misery. "Pain in the heart, weight on my soul. Something my nanny Amou used to say."

"Portuguese?"

"Yes."

He stood and walked toward me slowly. "I went up to my room very angry, as you know. I paced about, raging at myself, at you, at my parents, anyone, anything, and then I stopped and reviewed it and reviewed it and told myself there has to be some other explanation for all this. I just won't accept what it all looks like on the surface. So I came down here to speak to you."

He smiled. "I'm glad I did. You're not going anywhere, Willow, especially now that I know your interest in Linden Montgomery is purely sisterly."

I started to shake my head.

"You came here for a purpose, and you shouldn't

leave until you've completed that purpose. You can't just come into your mother's life for a day, say hello and then goodbye, have a good life, nice to have met you. Whatever trauma your arrival has caused will be gone, wiped out by the love you've brought as well. I'm sure once he settles down, Linden will realize how lucky he is to have someone like you as a sister."

"You really think so?"

"Yes, but I'm also really being selfish. I'm not ready to say goodbye to you. I don't think I will ever be."

He stepped up to me and wiped the tears off my cheeks with his handkerchief, and then he kissed each cheek and held me for a long moment.

"Only one thing," he whispered.

"What?"

"Let's not tell my parents any of this just yet, especially right before their party, okay?"

"Why not?" I asked, pulling back, a flutter of alarmed butterflies tickling under my breast like little warnings.

"Trust me. The less they know, the better we'll be. They have lived lives with no pain, no worries, no conflicts so long, they crack over a corky-tasting wine. The last thing my mother could handle is being the target of any gossip. Imagine what the Carriage sisters will do with this," he added, smiling.

"I'm tired of hiding the truth, Thatcher, and I don't care a damn about the Carriage sisters."

"After the party, there will be plenty of time for the truth. Hey," he said, "here, as you know, the truth is often something with a bitter taste. People can take it in small doses only and never all at once. Illusions and deceptions are so much more digestible."

He went for my suitcases. "Well?" he asked, turning.

The two voices within me began debating again, the one urging me to stay, the other urging me to flee.

"You can always leave," he continued, seeing my indecision. "That's easy. It's not always as easy to return."

It stopped the debate. I nodded and turned slowly to go back up the stairway, hoping I had not made a more serious error of judgment.

Thatcher and I spent the night together, lying side by side in my bedroom this time. He asked me so many questions. It was as if my telling him the truth had opened the door to his caring more and wanting to know more. I described what my early life had been like, told him about Amou in more detail and especially about my adoptive mother and how severe she could be. He wanted to know a lot more about my father, and he was intrigued with the story of him and my mother.

"It does sound like they were truly in love and," he added, "later in a great deal of pain. I think it helps me understand Grace more, why she is the way she is, why she has been so introverted. I've always liked her and hated the ridicule and the cruel things people say about her. It's why I wanted to help her with her legal problems, why I was proud of myself for being able to do that.

"I even tried being a friend to Linden at different times. I'm really the one who engineered his exhibits in the galleries here. He doesn't know that. If he did, he wouldn't have let the paintings be hung and sold. He doesn't want anyone's help, especially anyone from Palm Beach.

"Once, I even tried to go sailing with him. He came close to agreeing. I talked about the boat and asked his opinions and invited him aboard. It was almost as if he was fighting with someone inside him, some other Linden, who unfortunately won out."

"I do that, too," I said.

"What?"

"Argue within myself, two voices."

"Uh-oh, is this a family thing?" he asked semi-seriously.

"Maybe, but probably not. You don't talk to yourself, argue with yourself?"

"We're all a bit schizophrenic, is that it?"

"Yes," I said.

"Well, I don't believe that," he said. "Yes, I do. No, I don't. Yes, I do."

I slapped him on the arm. "Stop teasing me, Thatcher Eaton."

He laughed and reached out to pull my lips to his. We kissed, and then, when I leaned back, I saw he still had his eyes closed and wore a smirk of satisfaction.

"What are you thinking, Thatcher Eaton?"

"I'm thinking how miserable I would have felt if someone had told me you were my sister," he said. "I might have rejected the truth and risked incest."

"You're such an idiot," I said, and kissed him again.

We made love, and this time, we stayed with each other until the morning light came bursting through the

windows, exploding on the walls like the opening of a
dark curtain and the beginning of a new performance. I
could almost hear the applause greeting us. How I
hoped it wasn't premature.

We had breakfast together downstairs on the rear
loggia, and then he went off to finish some work he
had left at his office, and I prepared to spend the day
talking with my mother and Linden. Thatcher's parents were still asleep, but before I walked to the beach
house, the people setting up for the extravaganza arrived and began to put up the tent, the tables, the flowers, and the strings of lights. Before long, I counted
well over two dozen people working. How the Eatons
could sleep through all this was beyond me. Jennings,
however, seemed well in control; clearly, he had super-
vised a number of events such as this.

I found my mother sitting by herself, drinking coffee and looking out at the sea. She smiled when she
saw me, but she didn't hold the smile long. Her face
was quickly filled with concern and worry.

"Good morning," I said. I looked about. "Where's
Linden, not yet up?"

"Oh, no, he was up very early this morning, almost
at the crack of dawn. He took his sailboat and went to
wherever he goes to work in private."

"That beach he calls Linden Beach," I said, and sat
down.

"Would you like some coffee?"

"No, thank you. Did he tell you he and I met last
night after you had revealed the past to him?"

"No."

I hesitated. Should I tell her he acted suicidal?

"I saw him walking on the beach and joined him."

"He was very unhappy about it all. He took it badly. He made me feel I had betrayed him by not confiding in him long before this. I should have, of course. It wasn't right to keep such a thing a secret for so long."

"You never knew I would come."

"No, but it was still part of my past and, therefore, part of his."

"There are things a mother can rightly keep from her children, things that are hers and hers alone because she is a woman, too," I offered.

She liked that. "Only two women would understand, however," she said, smiling like a coconspirator.

"Why shouldn't the same be true for men, for a father? Just because you are both parents doesn't mean you don't have private lives, fantasies, dreams that are your own."

"It's too raw right now for him," she said, nodding at the water. "He's too emotional to be rational about it. Your father used to say sometimes you just have to put your emotions in a room by themselves and deal with your problems thoughtfully, intelligently. Later, you can swing by and pick them up and let them know your decisions."

She laughed. "He made it all sound so simple. After a while, I began to believe it was. Part of the illusionary world he and I created for each other while I was there, I suppose.

"But let's not talk about me anymore, not until you've exhausted yourself talking about yourself. I want to know everything, when you had your first loose tooth, your first boo-boo, your first crush on a boy, the first time you put on lipstick, everything."

"Where should I start?"

"At the beginning, your earliest memories. Don't leave out a detail. Everything is important," she said, and sat back expectantly.

I laughed. "I'll keep you here forever."

"I hope so," she said. She leaned forward to touch my cheek and stared at me. "I hope so."

When I left her hours later, Linden still had not returned.

"He often stays out the whole day," she explained to ward off my concern. "He'll avoid this place as much as he can now that he knows the Eatons are having one of their affairs."

"I'll come by later to see him," I promised.

"Good. Perhaps if the three of us sit quietly and talk . . ." Her voice trailed off like a dream that wouldn't be tied down.

"Yes," I said, and went to the main house, where Bunny was flying about, dictating orders to servants, tossing commands like rice on a wedding party. She was intent on rearranging the furniture, carrying on about the change of energy her *feng shui* decorator had predicted. She told me Asher was in the game room watching a basketball game on television "as if there was nothing in the world to do."

From what I could see, there wasn't, at least for him. Her army of servants had everything well under control. All she could do was look for things to make herself appear busy. From the way the servants reacted to her exclamations, I could see they knew how to humor her, hiding their smiles behind their hands and behind her back.

Suddenly, she realized I was there and spun on me. "What are you wearing tonight? Not that same black dress?"

"It's the only formal thing I have, Bunny."

"Oh, dear, dear, I should have asked you earlier and taken you to Monique's for something just out of Paris. At least wear my best pearls. You don't have to worry about them. You're only going to be on the grounds."

"Okay," I said, relenting more to escape than anything.

She didn't forget. Ten minutes later, a maid delivered them to my room.

While I rested for the party, I called home. The phone rang and rang, but Miles didn't answer. I hated bothering Mr. Bassinger. I should have gone home by now and checked everything for myself. Perhaps Miles had just left to do some shopping, or perhaps he was sleeping. I made a mental note to call again in an hour or so.

I didn't, however. I became too engrossed in my preparations for the party, and then Thatcher came by to see how I was doing, and soon after that, he and I descended and began to meet people who were arriving in their limousines and Rolls-Royces and Mercedes. The music had started. The servants were circulating with trays of champagne and hors d'oeuvres. Women in very

expensive-looking designer gowns and dazzling jewelry were everywhere. These people all acted as if they
hadn't seen each other for years, when I knew from
what I overheard that many had seen each other at least
twice this week alone.

Finally, I met Thatcher's sister, Whitney, and her
husband, Hans, who looked every bit of twenty years
older than she was. He was stout and bald with just a
trim patch of pale yellow hair along his freckled skull.
Whitney was taller than Hans, even an inch or so taller
than Thatcher, with a longer, leaner face. Her thin lips
pursed together into a fine line when she wasn't talking or eating or smiling what I thought was a forced
smile. Her eyes were darker, more critical and unfor-
giving, albeit nicely shaped. Her posture was stiff, and
as she perused the guests, her head moved almost as if
it were totally independent of the rest of her body.
How did someone so stern-looking come from two
such fluffy parents?

"My mother has told me a great deal about you,"
she said when she took my hand. Hers felt cold, but
she held mine as firmly as would a man. "Most of it
ridiculous, I'm sure," she added.

"Well, I don't know what she told you, but I'll try to
live up to the good things," I said, and Thatcher
laughed. She raised her eyebrows at him and then
looked at me with more curiosity.

I thought Hans was polite and nice enough, but he
was quickly distracted by the food and some friends he
recognized. Standing behind them during the introductions were their two children, Thatcher's niece Laurel

and nephew Quentin. They were like two well-trained puppies. Fortunately, while Quentin was nearly a clone of Hans, Laurel looked as if she had inherited the softer features of Thatcher and Whitney's side of the family. As I would expect, they looked as if they had been forced to come and were bored the moment they stepped into the house. It was painfully obvious to them that they were the only teenagers attending.

I was introduced to so many people so quickly my head began to spin. Asher seemed as eager to bring me around as did Thatcher or Bunny, stealing me away to hold onto his arm as if he had discovered me. They made me feel a bit like Audrey Hepburn in *My Fair Lady,* the poor girl who was changed into a sophisticated princess. Bunny even embarrassed me a bit by announcing that I was wearing her pearls. Out of the corner of my eye, I saw Whitney shaking her head in disapproval and whispering into some woman's ear, turning her expression into a mirror of her own critical one. It was as if her words were eardrops that could make all the women at the party of one face.

Thatcher finally rescued me and took me out onto the dance floor they had created over the pool. Under the streaming lights and the blazing stars, with the twenty-six-piece orchestra seemingly playing for us and us alone, I felt swept up in his arms. When I looked about, I saw that most eyes were on us, Whitney's the most envious of all, perhaps. Asher and Bunny were standing by, looking like the duke and duchess who had found and even created the proper woman for their prince. Eventually, other people joined us, and I didn't feel as self-conscious about every step and turn we made.

The food was as extravagant as could be: fresh lobster and prawns, prime rib and filets with sauces that came directly off menus from France's best restaurants, vegetables so dressed and seasoned I didn't recognize carrots and peas, and tables of fish dishes from Dover salmon to octopus. The Viennese dessert table seemed a mile long, with pastries and cakes that reeked of calories.

"You can gain weight just looking at it," I told Thatcher.

He looked so handsome, happy, and light-hearted. I didn't think it was possible to give him a better gift than the gift of truth I had given him earlier. He as much as said so when he leaned over to whisper, "Willow, you are the first girl I have been with who makes me feel safe and with whom I don't have to put on airs or be defensive. Thanks for trusting me."

His words lifted me. We stole a quick kiss and then danced again. I didn't think I would enjoy such an opulent, ostentatious party, but I wished it would never end, that Thatcher and I would somehow get stuck in time, that the earth itself would stop spinning, and we would be like the figures on John Keats's famous urn, whose beauty would never fade, whose love would never wilt. I'd willingly surrender forever to this wonderful night, I thought.

But nights do end, and stars do sink into the light of day.

When Thatcher and I twirled to the corner of the

dance floor, I was able to see beyond the stream of lights and the party. I could see the dock.

My mother was standing there, holding her lantern.

My heart skipped a beat, and I squeezed Thatcher's arm so tightly he paused.

"What is it?"

"Something's wrong," I said. "Grace." I nodded toward the dock, and he looked at me with concern.

Quietly, we slipped away and hurried down to her.

"Grace," he called as we hurried onto the dock. "What's wrong?"

"Linden," she said, turning to me, her eyes blood-red with worry.

She didn't have to say it.

I said it for her.

"He hasn't come back."

16

The Search

"**W**hat are you talking about, Thatcher?" Bunny Eaton cried. "We can't call the Coast Guard here now! I have a party going on. Do you realize who is here?"

He had pulled his mother and father into the study to tell them what was happening.

"He's out there somewhere, maybe injured," Thatcher said calmly.

Asher shook his head and stared at the floor.

"Of course he's not," Bunny insisted. "It's just like him to disappear like this. You know he's not mentally well. We'll be the laughingstock of the town if we react. You just don't interrupt a party for something like that. It will remind all these people who the land-lords are and what an embarrassment they are."

"A man's life could be in danger, Bunny," I said, fighting to control myself. "Grace is sick with worry."

"Well, what of it? She's probably sick with worry every day, having a son like that. Asher, will you say something!" she screamed at Thatcher's father.

He looked up at Thatcher. "Gone all day, you say?"

"From sunrise, according to Grace."

"Oh, I'm sure that's some idiotic exaggeration. She probably doesn't know what time of day it is," Bunny muttered.

"That's not true," I snapped back at her.

She looked up at me, her eyes blazing with fury. "Can you tell me what has happened here that you are such a cheerleader for those two loonies?"

Thatcher and I exchanged a look that she plucked like a butterfly out of the air.

"What is it? Well?" she demanded of him. "What's going on, Thatcher?"

He glanced at me again and then turned to her. "It's nothing but concern for someone's life, Mother."

She folded her arms across her chest and fumed.

"I think Thatcher will have to make the call, Bunny," Asher said.

"Let Grace Montgomery make the call herself. At least we can blame that on her when the boats and the spotlights and the alarms and bedlam begin," she said.

"I don't understand how you can be so cruel, Bunny," I couldn't help but say. "This is a mother who is concerned for her son, whose child might be in some terrible danger."

"Oh, you just met the woman. You don't know them the way we know them," she replied.

"Yes, I do." I was so sick of the pretending.

"How? How could you possibly know anything significant about them?"

"I do."

She started to grimace at me disdainfully, as if to say, "You don't know what you're talking about," when I blurted it out.

"I'll tell you how. Grace Montgomery just happens to be my real mother."

If a bomb had gone off in the room, it wouldn't have had a greater effect on her. Her eyes seemed to explode in her head. Her face flushed. Her hands fluttered up toward her throat like birds with injured wings, and she stepped backward as though she had just been struck in the face. She gasped and turned to Asher, who was looking at me with almost as much surprise.

"Grace Montgomery is your mother?" he asked, to confirm what his ears had heard.

"Yes. It's the real reason I came to Palm Beach. I just learned about it recently, and I wanted to meet her and get to know her."

"Oh, my God!" Bunny cried, looking up at the ceiling, her eyelids fluttering as if she were on the verge of losing consciousness. "All this happening on the night of our party!"

"Mother, take it easy. Sit, and I'll get you some water." Thatcher eased her into a chair. Asher went to the door and called to a maid to get a pitcher of cold water and some glasses quickly. Bunny's head slumped a bit, and then she raised it and shook her head at me.

"How could she possibly be your mother?"

"My father and she were lovers," I said calmly. "How else?"

She continued to shake her head but turned to Asher. "I don't understand. What is she saying?"

"My father was the chief psychiatrist at the clinic she went to. It was there they fell in love," I told her.

"The doctor had a love affair with her?" She shifted her eyes to Thatcher quickly. "Did you know all this time?"

He shook his head. "No. Actually," he said, looking at me, "not until today."

"Today? Oh dear, dear, dear . . . today . . ."

"Thatcher, we have to call the Coast Guard," I said. "Are you going to do it, or should I?"

"Go down to your so-called mother's home and do it," Bunny snapped at me. "Deceiving us like this, pretending to be someone you're not, enjoying our hospitality . . . making me have this party to introduce you to . . . to . . . my God," she said, pressing her hands to the base of her throat again. "The former governor of the U.S. Virgin Islands is out there!"

"Take it easy, Mother," Thatcher urged.

The maid arrived with the tray of water and glasses. Thatcher poured a glass for Bunny. She drank it and sat back, her eyes closed.

"I'm going down to the beach house to call, Thatcher," I told him, and started away.

"I'll be right there," he said.

"I think I'm having heart failure," Bunny cried, and squeezed his arm. "Can you imagine the scandal? Her father was that woman's doctor. Get Whitney in here,

Asher. Quickly. She'll know better how I should handle this. Hurry!" she ordered as he followed me out.

"I'm sorry," Asher said as we split to take two different paths. "It's just too much of a shock and at the wrong time."

"I don't think there would have been a right time for her, do you?"

He didn't reply. I hurried down to the beach house to make the call.

Nearly half an hour later, the Coast Guard cutter arrived at the dock, and Grace and I went out to speak with them. I could see that their arrival had indeed caused some commotion and interest at the party. The orchestra even paused. All the while I was waiting with my mother, I had expected Thatcher to come join us, but he still hadn't, even with the arrival of the Coast Guard.

Grace explained as much as she could to the captain, and I did my best to describe where I thought Linden's beach was. He promised they would do a vigorous search and call for a helicopter immediately. Ten minutes later, the sight of the helicopter combing the beach with its powerful beam brought the party to a standstill.

As if any sort of trouble, tension, possible serious injury, and even death were like a giant hand snapping its fingers to break the spell they were all caught in, the mega-millionaires, chiefs of industry, politicians, and television and movie stars began to flee the scene.

"It's like the sinking of the *Titanic*," I muttered. "All of them fleeing to save their reputations from drowning."

My mother smiled and then looked out toward the boat lights again. She and I were now glued to our seats on the front loggia, waiting to hear the phone ring, waiting to see some sign of a returning sailboat or Coast Guard cutter.

Finally, I saw Thatcher coming our way.

"Sorry," he said as he approached us. "We had to get Dr. Anderson to prescribe a sedative for my mother. She just isn't capable of dealing with any sort of crisis, no matter how large or small."

"I never saw anyone as spoiled as that," I said. "She can't think of anyone but herself. You've all made her that way, Thatcher."

"Probably," he admitted, then slanted a look at my mother. "But you know, we all have to live with what we've created."

"Not always," I said. "Sometimes, we can change things."

He nodded, but not with any real agreement, and looked out at the sea.

"Any word at all?" he asked.

"Not yet," my mother said. "How could they not have found him or what happened to him by now? He couldn't have gone that far in such a small boat."

"He's been gone all day, Grace," Thatcher said softly. "He could have gone pretty far."

"I need something to drink, something cold," she said. "Anyone else?"

"No, thank you," Thatcher said. I shook my head and watched her go inside.

"She's the one who is supposed to be unbalanced,

and she's the one we tell the cold, hard truth. Doesn't that strike you as a bit odd, Thatcher? A bit unfair, how the rich and the privileged are so protected?"

"I'm not making any excuses for my parents, Willow. They are what they are. None of it matters at the moment."

I agreed with that. "What do you really think happened to him?"

"He might have gone too far out, or he might have gone ashore someplace, hidden the boat, and traipsed off somewhere. He's capable of something like that. Who knows? A search at night isn't easy."

"I feel so responsible," I moaned, and swayed back and forth, embracing myself.

"Nonsense," Thatcher said, coming to my side. "You can't blame yourself for his erratic behavior. You didn't come here to hurt him, or anyone else for that matter."

"It doesn't matter what your intentions were if the results are the same," I said.

"Of course it does. You can't say something like that to an attorney," he joked. "Intent is nine-tenths of the settlement."

"Right," I said. I looked back at the front of the beach house. "I'm staying with her now, Thatcher."

He nodded. "Okay."

"I'll go back for my things in a while."

"No one's throwing you out, Willow."

I raised my eyebrows. "I don't think I'm up to brunch with your parents tomorrow."

"After a day or so, they'll put this all behind them, and . . ."

"But I can't. Let's just leave it be," I said. "Until this ends, let's just leave it be."

"Sure," he said, pulling back. "Whatever you think best, Willow."

We were both silent, staring out at the water and the beam from the helicopter. Suddenly, it pulled back and away, the beam shutting off. Minutes later, we heard the phone ringing inside the beach house. My heart paused and then pounded. Thatcher and I looked at each other and waited, neither speaking, holding our breath.

My mother emerged. "It was the Coast Guard," she said, pressing her hand against her heart. "They found him some distance from that beach. The boat was caught up in some vegetation and rocks."

"How is he?" I asked.

"They said he suffered some sort of accident, a blow to his head. He was conscious but very confused. They really couldn't tell much more about his condition. The cutter is taking him to the pier in Fort Lauderdale, where an ambulance will bring him to the hospital."

"Let's go," Thatcher said quickly. "I'll take you both."

I reached for my mother's hand, and we followed Thatcher out to his car.

"What could have happened?" I asked as we drove away.

"Lots of things," Thatcher said. "Tossed by a wave, he lost his footing and fell against the side of the boat. A gust of wind caught him unaware, and the boom struck him. When you're out in nature, a man alone is always in danger," Thatcher added.

"Linden has always been alone," my mother murmured. "In nature or otherwise."

I pressed my hand to hers, and we rode on in silence.

The ambulance had already brought him to the emergency room, and the doctors were attending him by the time we arrived. We waited anxiously until the ER doctor came to see us.

"I am his mother," my mother said quickly, and he turned directly to her. "How is he?"

"His head wound required nearly fifty stitches. He has suffered a skull fracture and a concussion. Prelim.nary tests indicate the presence of a subdural hematoma."

"What does that mean?" my mother asked.

"The head injury causes blood to collect between the inner and outer membranes of the brain. This, in turn, creates pressure which we have to relieve."

"How?"

"A surgical procedure, I'm afraid," he said. "I have sent for Dr. Parker Thornberg, a very highly respected neurological surgeon."

"Yes," Thatcher said, "I've heard of him."

The doctor turned to him and smiled. "He'll be here very soon to confirm the diagnosis," he said.

"Can I see my son?" my mother asked.

"You can, but I have to tell you he has some amnesia at the moment, which is not unusual or uncharacteristic of the condition. It's rarely lasting. Its longevity is directly related to the severity of the injury, and once we get him on the mend—"

"He doesn't know who he is?"

"He's very confused."

"Maybe when he sees her, he'll remember and realize what's happened to him," Thatcher suggested.

"Maybe," the doctor said, but the way he smiled and glanced at him told me probably not.

She started away with him, paused, and looked at me.

"For now, I think it's best I go myself."

"Of course," I said, and sat down, my eyes dropping to my fingers twisting and turning on themselves nervously in my lap.

"Don't you even think of blaming yourself for any of this, Willow. I told you he's always been impulsive, stubborn, and high-strung. You heard Grace in the car. Linden has always been a loner. Who knows how he tore up the waves out there, having himself a tantrum."

"I just wish that when I packed my bag to come here, I had brought along happiness and hope, not more trouble and sadness," I said.

"Your coming should have been a wonderful thing—is a wonderful thing. Anyone who takes it otherwise has no one to blame but him- or herself," Thatcher assured me.

I leaned back. Suddenly, I was feeling so tired, the fatigue going to the very bottom of my soul. I thought I could sleep forever, put my head on a pillow and, like Rip Van Winkle, not wake up for years and years. Maybe I would be better off. How I wished I was a little girl again and Amou was at my side, a willing pillow against whom I could rest my head and dry my tears to the sounds of her soft voice, her singing, her reassurances and promises.

I missed her so.

I closed my eyes and actually did drift off. When I opened my eyes again, Thatcher was standing in the doorway, speaking to a tall, thin, distinguished-looking man in a dark blue suit. They shook hands, and Thatcher turned to me. I sat up quickly and ground the sleep out of my eyes.

"Who was that?"

"Dr. Thornberg. They are going to operate on Linden as soon as possible. He thinks he can relieve the pressure easily enough and get him on the mend physically but warned about the potential for what they call post-traumatic stress disorder," he said, lowering his voice.

"What's that, exactly?"

"When someone experiences a life-threatening event, he or she can have some psychological problems afterward, Willow. I've done some malpractice cases, so I had to prepare some research that touched on this. I'm no expert, and I'm just giving you the doctor's standard warning. Complicating matters," he added, gazing down the hallway to be sure my mother wasn't nearby, "are Linden's personality and psychological problems before he was even injured. They could be inflamed, exaggerated."

He paused and took a breath. "But what's the point of drawing up horror scenarios? Let's just wait and see and deal with it later."

"My poor mother," I said.

Thatcher put his arm around me and gave me a squeeze.

We returned to our seats to wait for her. About half an hour later, she came back to tell us basically what we already knew: they were preparing Linden for surgery. We moved to another waiting area, and Thatcher went to get us some coffee. The doctors warned us it could be hours.

I sat beside my mother and tried to comfort her.

"I handled this very badly," she moaned. "I should have realized that someday it would all come home. Let this be a lesson to you, Willow. Secrets don't stay buried. They might hibernate like bears, but when their time comes, they'll appear again, and all you have done is delay the inevitable. A pain held off just builds and builds until it comes charging back at you, more furiously than before."

"It's wrong to blame yourself," I told her.

"Whom should I blame, you? For wanting to meet and know your real mother? Or your father, for loving me so? Maybe Linden is right to think fate toys with us sometimes," she said dejectedly. "Poor Linden, lost in a maze now, twirling about. Inside himself, he must be so terrified, so alone."

Tears streamed down her cheeks.

"He'll be fine. You'll see. He'll be fine. We'll work it all out," I assured her.

She smiled at me. "You don't know how much you looked like your father just then. It threw me back years."

"I'm glad," I said. "I often think of him being with me, especially when I need him the most."

She stroked my hair and smiled through her tears.

Thatcher appeared with our coffee, and we settled down for the wait.

Hours later, as predicted, Dr. Thornberg appeared.

"The operation went well," he said.

"Will there be any aftereffects?" my mother asked quickly.

The doctor and Thatcher exchanged glances.

"We'll see," Dr. Thornberg said noncommittally.

My mother nodded slowly. "Yes," she whispered. "We'll see."

They let her see Linden, even though he was still under sedation. I stood in the doorway and watched her kiss him and whisper in his ear, and then I put my arm around her shoulders, and we left the hospital.

It was already morning. The sun was pressing back the blanket of darkness, and the stars were beginning their daily retreat. The estate was strangely still, the party decorations, the lights, the tables and chairs and dance floor not yet removed, streamers and deflated balloons drifting in the morning breeze.

"We all need some sleep," Thatcher said. He smiled at me. "I feel like my parents must feel coming home from one of their very late affairs. We'll all get up together, I'm sure."

"I'll just run up and get my things," I told him. "I won't leave her alone now."

He nodded. "I'll be by later. Call me if you need anything, Grace," he told her.

She thanked him, and he and I went up to the main house.

"I'm sorry about my mother, the things she said before," he told me.

"That's the least of my worries now, Thatcher."

"Right," he said.

I went for my things, and we parted.

When I returned to the beach house, my mother showed me what she considered the most comfortable guest room, and then we kissed and hugged, and she went to her own bedroom. I thought I would drop into a dead sleep the moment my head hit the pillow, but I lay there with my eyes open, wondering how all this had happened so quickly and what I was to do next. A voice within urged me to rest and let the events to come show their faces in due time.

You can't deal with any of it now, anyway, Willow, I heard a voice that sounded so much like my father's tell me. *Put your thoughts on pause control.*

Don't worry.

Everything fortunate and unfortunate will be there to greet you when you awaken.

You can count on that.

I felt the presence of someone and opened my eyes. My mother was standing in the doorway, her hands clasped against her breasts. She was already dressed.

"What is it?" I asked, sitting up quickly.

"I woke up. I thought I heard Linden calling for me, so I phoned the hospital, and they told me he was awake, but he was still very disoriented and confused. He must be very frightened. I have to go to him," she said.

"I'll be up and ready in ten minutes."

"I could just call for a taxi. You've hardly had any sleep," she said.

Indeed, only four hours had gone by.

"I'm fine. I couldn't sleep, anyway."

"I'll make some coffee so we can have that, at least," she said, and went off while I threw cold water on my face, ran a brush through my hair, and put on my clothes.

She had the coffee waiting for me.

"I just made us some toast," she said. "I thought we should have something in our stomachs."

I nibbled on a piece with some jelly and swallowed some coffee. A few minutes later, she and I got into my car and drove out of the estate.

Linden was still critical, of course, and they wanted only one of us to go in. I sat and waited, getting myself some more coffee from the coffee machine. She was in the intensive care unit only a little more than twenty minutes before she emerged looking very distraught.

"How is he?" I asked immediately.

She shook her head. "He didn't seem to recognize me. There was nothing in his eyes to indicate he had. One of the nurses said he mumbled something very strange."

"What?"

"He wanted to know why there were so many skeletons walking about, including her. It's as if he thinks he's in one of his own paintings or something."

"Don't think anything terrible about this, Mother. He's just out of surgery. Wait until you get a chance to speak with the doctor."

She nodded, suddenly looking terribly exhausted and weak.

"We should go home, and you should try to get some real rest."

"I'll rest here," she said. "You go back."

"No, I won't leave you like this."

She smiled. "We're still practically strangers to each other, Willow, and yet you've already been kinder to me than people I've known my whole life."

"Get used to it," I said, and she widened her smile to a small laugh.

I did talk her into going to the hospital cafeteria for some hot food, which restored both of us somewhat. When we returned to the ICU, the doctor was there. He stepped out to speak with us.

"It's too early to tell the extent of it," he began, "but your son will be experiencing some posttraumatic stress in reaction to his accident. I'm not going to stand here and give you a laundry list of everything that *might* occur. Suffice it to say," he added with a tone of supreme authority, "that there will be *some* effects, and he will probably need some therapy. In the final analysis, it might be nothing much, really."

"Or it might," my mother said.

"Or it might be more extensive, yes. Let's get him functioning again and take it all a step at a time, Mrs. Montgomery."

He glanced at me.

"I'm his sister," I said.

"Well, that's nice. He has support. He's going to be fine eventually. That's the important thing."

He smiled quickly and started away.

"Thank you, Doctor," I called after him. He just lifted his hand and continued.

"I don't know if I could ever be someone who treats

people's troubles as day-to-day work," my mother muttered. "I told that to your father once, too."

"What did he say?"

"The secret is not treating it like day-to-day work. The secret is treating every cure as if it was a miracle in which you were lucky enough to have played a role. There aren't many like him, though," she added with a deep sigh.

She went back in to spend time with Linden, and I collapsed on the settee in the waiting room, closing my eyes and getting myself some rest. I woke up when I felt someone nudging me and looked up to see Thatcher standing there.

"I thought you two might be here, after I saw your car was gone. How is he?"

I told him what the doctor had said.

"At least he's being honest. The rest, as Shakespeare says, is in the womb of time."

"Aren't we all?" I muttered. I was tired and cranky and disgusted with everything. I had a sudden urge to go home. I longed to be in my own home, walking my own grounds, feeling closer to my father.

I suddenly remembered that I had called and Miles had not answered.

"I've got to make a phone call," I told Thatcher, and he handed me his cell phone.

"I'll get myself some coffee," he said.

I called and waited as it rang and rang and rang. Now I was convinced something was not right, so I sifted hurriedly through my purse until I found Mr. Bassinger's phone number. Thatcher returned while I was calling Bassinger's office. His secretary put me right through.

"Willow, I've been waiting to hear from you," he said immediately.

"Did you call me?"

"Yesterday, midafternoon. Didn't you get the message?"

"No," I said, looking up at Thatcher. "What's happening, Mr. Bassinger?"

"I'm afraid it's not good news. Miles is gone."

"Gone? You mean he left the property?"

"No. He's passed away, Willow. Apparently, your aunt Agnes had someone look in on the house regularly. Fortunately, I should say. He wasn't dead long, not quite a day. I got there just after the police and the ambulance had arrived. He was found in your father's office, clutching a pile of blank paper, his eyes open wide like someone who's died of shock. It was confirmed as heart failure. Ironic how they both went the same way, but in Miles's case, it isn't so hard to understand, considering his life and all he's gone through, that is.

"I have people in the house, cleaning it up. There were prospective buyers set to visit it yesterday, but we had to put that off, and now we have to disclose Miles's death. Where are you? What are your plans?"

"I'm staying someplace else for now," I told him, and gave him my mother's phone number. "I'm not sure how long, but I'll call you very soon. What about Miles's funeral?"

"Your father had all those things prearranged. We'll do it day after tomorrow. I expect they'll release the body today. Sorry about all this happening, all this bad news on top of bad news."

You have no idea, I thought.

"My father's death broke his heart. My father was his only friend. I should have realized," I said.

"You can't save the world, Willow. You have an obligation now to take good care of yourself and fulfill your and your father's dreams. Stay in touch, and call me if you need anything, anything at all," he said.

I thanked him and ended the call.

Thatcher took one look at my face and knew it wasn't good.

"What?" he asked, and I told him about Miles.

"Why did he die clutching blank paper?" he wondered.

"I think he saw something on it that no one else could see. That doesn't mean it wasn't there," I added.

"Huh? I don't understand."

"Me, neither," I said, and rose to greet my mother.

"He's resting comfortably, but he is still disoriented. Nothing he says at the moment makes much sense, I'm afraid. It's going to be a long journey back," she added with a deep sigh.

"Then you had better take good care of yourself, Grace," Thatcher said. "You'd better get some real rest and be strong."

"Yes. Yes, that's sensible advice." She looked at me. "For you, too."

"I have to leave for a while, Mother," I said. "I have to go home." I had already told her about Miles and described how close he and my father had been.

"Miles?"

I nodded. "He's passed away."

"Oh, I'm sorry. You have too much to carry on those young, fragile shoulders, Willow. You go home and straighten out your legal matters and everything. You should return to college, too. I'm sure your father would not approve of your throwing it all aside," she said.

"I'm not, but . . ."

"I'm not going anywhere, and from the looks of things, neither is Linden. It would only make me feel more miserable to know you were sacrificing so much because of me."

"I'm not doing anything I don't want to do," I said.

She smiled. "I know, but that doesn't mean it's good for you or right. Pretend your father is sitting there listening to us," she said, nodding at an empty chair. "What do you think he would tell you to do? Listen to that voice," she advised softly, "that voice inside you."

I took a deep breath and looked at Thatcher. He stared at me a moment, and then he looked away.

"Take me home," my mother said. "I do need some more sleep."

"Okay."

"I just have to check on some things at my office," Thatcher said quickly. "I'll come by as soon as I can."

His cell phone rang. "I'll see you later," he promised as he answered the call.

I threaded my arm through my mother's, and we leaned on each other as we walked to the elevator.

"You haven't known Thatcher very long," she said.

"No, I haven't."

"He's a very bright man and, I always thought, a very nice man, despite the world he comes from and lives in, but we're sometimes too weak to do battle against all that, and it changes us."

"I know."

She smiled. "I think you're a very smart young lady. I see the way he looks at you and the way you look at him. Sometimes, it doesn't have to take that long to know there's magic there.

"But," she said, looking off into her own world of memories, "often magic isn't enough. Just remember that, and you'll be fine."

Would I? I wondered.

Would I really?

17

Coming Home

After realizing that there wasn't much more I could do here at the moment, I called and made reservations for my flight home. I wouldn't let Miles be buried with no one there to mourn his passing. My mother arranged for transportation to and from the hospital for herself and assured me she would be fine.

"You would be surprised at how many people here do look in on me from day to day," she said.

"I don't think I would be so surprised."

She laughed and then grew serious. "Strange how people have to hide their good deeds, their sincerity. They're afraid the Eatons might fire them if they found out how they took care of my immediate grounds or shopped for me along with shopping for them. I would hate anyone suffering because of me," she added, "but I can't talk them out of helping me."

"That's good."

Before my early evening flight, she and I had a light dinner. We ate on the patio and talked and talked. I continued to describe my early years and the house and the property back in South Carolina.

"Your father loved it," she said. "It sounded beautiful to me then, like some forbidden paradise."

"I know. I have mixed feelings about selling. It's too much for me alone, and it's full of memories, but I almost feel like I'm betraying him by selling."

"No. I'm sure he would want you to be comfortable and live your own life. Like you said, it won't be the same to you with him gone, and now Miles gone, too. Cut yourself loose, Willow. Let go." She looked out over the beach and the grounds. "That was something I regret I was never able to do. If I had, maybe it would have all turned out very differently.

"I hate regrets, don't you? Regrets haunt. Do all that you can to avoid them, even if it means making little mistakes, losing a little money or some time. Satisfy yourself that you tried this or that. Explore, and never be afraid. It's so hard to be timid in this world, especially here; but I suspect it's not much different anywhere else.

"Unfortunately, aggressive, self-centered, obnoxious people get their way too often. Don't be afraid to put them in their place," she said, looking toward the main house. "They'll turn you into another one of their possessions if you don't stand up to them right from the start."

"That will never happen to me," I vowed.

She smiled. "I believe you."

I kept waiting for Thatcher to show, but he didn't,

nor did he call. Finally, I thought I had better call him
and let him know my flight arrangements immediately.
His phone service patched me through.

"I got tied up in one of those endless meetings," he
explained. "Something I thought was settled was not.
I'll get there as soon as I can."

I told him my flight time.

"Oh, really? Well, you'll be back," he said lightly—
was it to ease his disappointment or something else?

"I'll be back to see my mother, yes," I said pointedly.

"Good. I've got to return to the meeting. Have a
great trip," he said.

The conversation left me a little cold, but I didn't let
my mother see.

Next, I called Mr. Bassinger and told him of my
plans. He said he would be at the airport to pick me up
and drive me home.

"Oh, you don't have to go to any trouble," I told him.

"No, no. On the way, I'll review some of the legal
matters I've completed," he said.

I thanked him, and then, on my way out to say
goodbye to my mother, I paused and glanced into the
room that Linden had been using as a studio. There
was a black sheet over the easel, and I was very curious about whether or not it covered the painting he had
been doing of me. I felt a bit guilty sneaking about and
looking at the picture without his approval, but I was
leaving now, and I couldn't help myself.

I went into the room and lifted the sheet away. For a
moment, I just stared. It didn't look like me at all. It
looked like my mother. It was as if he had known the

truth all along, had seen it with his artistic eye, as if when he worked, he had a prophetic vision.

I covered it quickly and hurried out.

"Well, I'd better be off," I told my mother. "I've got to return the rental car and all."

"Call me."

"Every day."

"If I'm not here, I'll be at the hospital until he's released."

"Please take care of yourself," I told her.

"You do the same," she said.

We hugged and held onto each other as if we were never going to see each other again. Neither she nor I wanted to be the first to let go, but she finally let go and kissed my cheek. She smiled and went back inside quickly.

With tears streaming down my face, I carried my suitcase up toward my car. Halfway there, I heard Bunny call to me. She came down from the rear loggia, a glass of "shampoo" in her hand.

"Leaving us?" she asked, her voice back to sounding childishly joyful.

"Yes, for a while. I have things to take care of back in South Carolina."

"It's probably much better for you back there, anyway," she said. "Everyone knows the story by now. I had to tell them why my party was ruined, didn't I?" she followed, defending herself. "Anyway, what's done is done. Leaving is smart. You'll only be tainted by your family's history here, and a young woman like you doesn't need all those disadvantages and burdens."

"Thanks for the silly advice," I told her.

She pulled up as if I had snapped a whip beside her.

"If you think that's silly advice, you're not half as intelligent as I thought you were. Let me give you some advice that's definitely not silly," she continued rapidly. "Don't think that Thatcher will be here waiting for you, feeling sorry for you or otherwise. I would never permit him to throw his life away, his wonderful reputation and his career, by marrying a Montgomery woman."

"I am not a Montgomery woman," I said, closing on her, my spine a steel rod. "My name is Willow De Beers, and my father was one of the nation's most prominent psychiatrists. What happened to my mother was tragic, but that doesn't make her in any way inferior to you or anyone in your family, Bunny.

"And as for Thatcher, if he doesn't have a mind of his own when it comes to his own life and who he wants to be with and love, I wouldn't want him calling me, anyway. I certainly wouldn't chase after him."

"That's ridiculous. Why any woman would give her—"

"I'm not any woman, Bunny, at least any woman around here," I said firmly as I pulled up my shoulders. "Have a good night, or should I say good party?"

I turned sharply and walked on, my heart pounding. I hoped I could live up to all I had told her.

Don't you believe you can? I heard my father ask.

Yes, I said.

Then you can. Challenge every doubt about yourself as soon as it rears its ugly head.

I got into the car and drove away without looking

back, even when I reached the gate and waited for it to open. I wanted only to look forward now.

The flight was delayed at takeoff but afterward was quick and uneventful. Mr. Bassinger was there at the arrival gate to greet me. He took my bags, and we went directly to his car. I could tell immediately that he had something to reveal.

"You didn't just come here to pick me up, Mr. Bassinger. What's wrong?"

"I didn't want you to be surprised," he began, "but your aunt Agnes is at the house. She knew about Miles, of course, and she had her attorney call me. There's no legal grounds for her to have a say in anything, but that doesn't mean she can't cause a commotion. She's been digging around, trying to find out why you went to Palm Beach and what you are doing there," he continued. "I'm not asking you to give me details, but I don't want her challenging every action we take with your estate."

"I'd like to tell you what I was doing, Mr. Bassinger. I think my father intended for me to do that after I opened the envelope and read his papers."

"If you feel it has nothing to do with any of this, I don't have to know," he said.

"It's fine. You were his trusted friend, and that makes you mine, too."

"I appreciate that, Willow," he replied, and I told him everything.

"I knew your father didn't have a happy marriage," Mr. Bassinger said after listening. "I'm not passing judgment on anyone. None of that changes anything here, Willow. Don't let your aunt convince you otherwise," he advised.

Before we arrived home, he gave me all the details about Miles's funeral and told me he would be by in the morning to pick me up and take me to the funeral parlor. It seemed so odd to arrive at the house and not find Miles waiting for me at the door to greet me and carry in my bags. There were lights on throughout, but there was still a sense of desertion, emptiness, as if the heart of it were gone and it was only a shell now. Mr. Bassinger helped me carry my bags to the door.

"I'll be fine now," I told him. "Don't worry. Thank you for everything."

He smiled and said good night.

I opened the door with my key and entered. "Aunt Agnes?" I called.

A moment later, she appeared at the top of the stairway.

"Well," she said, "it's about time you came home."

She was wearing a hair net and a robe. Her face was covered in some rejuvenation cream, which made her look ghoulish under the overhead chandeliers.

"I had people here all day today cleaning," she continued as she descended. "You have no idea what a mess things were, what that deranged man had done."

"What had he done?"

"What had he done? There was food left everywhere, even on trays up in your father's bedroom, as if he had brought it to someone. We're lucky we don't have rats here. Your father's office was a shambles, books and papers strewn about, and the kitchen . . . the kitchen had dishes piled sky high, bits and pieces of food all over the floor, things rotting on the stove. I practically had to have the house fumigated. The pest control left only a few hours ago. When I arrived here, I found windows open and doors open. Any sort of creature could have come inside, including snakes!

"What do you suppose would have happened if a prospective buyer had been brought here this morning?" she cried, throwing up her arms. "How could you have left him alone here? What were you doing down in Palm Beach? Why is it such a big secret? Why did you leave college?" She fired her questions in shotgun fashion in the hopes of getting me to answer anything.

"Well? Why are you standing there looking at me as if *I* am the crazy person?" she demanded when I continued to stare at her in silence.

I realized now that the Eatons knew who I really was and why I had gone to Palm Beach, it wouldn't be long before it was public information. Who knew how fast it would spread? It might even be a front-page story in their precious social newspaper by now. There was no point in my keeping any of it to myself anymore, and I actually felt that it would bring me some relief to open the doors of the vaults of secrets. With almost sadistic pleasure, I smiled at my aunt.

"You and I have to talk, Aunt Agnes. We might as well do it right away and get it all over with. I'm actually happy you decided to put your nose in my business this time."

"I guess you are," she said, still quite swollen with pride in all she had managed since she had arrived. "Maybe now you'll pay more heed to my advice."

"Maybe. I have a lot of advice to get," I said cryptically. "Why don't we go into the sitting room right now and talk?"

She looked at me suspiciously.

"You're not going to tell me you went ahead and married someone in Palm Beach, are you?"

"No. Absolutely not. Nor am I engaged."

"Good," she said. "Very well, let's talk. I hope to have things well in control here in a day or so and then return home. We have Margaret Selby's wedding hovering over us, and goodness knows how much I have had to carry on my shoulders. Young people today are far too flighty to do things correctly. When I was her age, I was already married and managing a home and a husband. There wasn't time to be flighty," she continued as she sat in what had been Daddy's chair. She looked so small in it, like a child trying to be an adult. It brought a wide grin to my face.

"What are you laughing about?"

"Nothing," I said. I took off my jacket and sat on the couch.

"Well?" she asked when I let a long pause fall between us. "I would like to get to bed soon. I'm exhausted from all that I had to do and exhausted just thinking about what is left to do."

"As you know," I began, "and know well and never failed to remind me of, either through innuendos or direct remarks, I am an adopted child. My mother was a patient at Daddy's clinic."

"Of course, I know all that. Do you think your father would have kept such information from me? I was his only sibling, his trusted sister. He told me more than he told your mother. What of it?"

"Adoptive mother," I corrected.

"Whatever. What's the point of plowing up the same dirt again and again?"

"No point, except it's not the same dirt, as you say, Aunt Agnes. It's new dirt."

"What are you talking about, Willow De Beers?"

I smiled. "You don't know how much you sounded like my adoptive mother just then, reminding me of my given name as if it were branded on my forehead so I couldn't see it unless I looked in the mirror."

"Well, she had some good qualities. Despite her poor family losing its inheritance, she had breeding. I would have made more of an effort to prevent the marriage otherwise. And what of it? Reminding you that you were given a cherished, well-respected old family name is not a fault. You were very fortunate my brother had so much charity in his heart."

"Oh, you think it was simply his charity, then?"

"Of course it was simply that," she said, straightening out her robe. She looked as if she were sitting on needles the way she shifted in the chair nervously. "I have to get upstairs and wipe off this cream. It's set long enough. Please, move to the point," she demanded.

"Well, I'm happy to tell you that it was far more

than simple charity for my father to bring me here to live. As it turns out, I wasn't given the name De Beers as a benevolent gift. I wasn't given anything. I was a De Beers at birth," I concluded.

She simply stared at me. Her eyelids fluttered a bit, and then she pursed her lips and tightened her cheeks until they dipped like saucers. It was as if the air within were being drawn down her body.

"What is that remark supposed to mean?" she said in a hoarse whisper.

"It means that my father, your brother, was really my father and not just in name," I said.

She seemed to shrink before inflating again. Even under the cream, I could see the crimson tint coming into her cheeks.

"Are you sitting there and saying that my brother impregnated one of his own patients?"

"It was a great deal more than just that, Aunt Agnes. They were truly in love, and, in fact, she remained at the clinic longer than she had to. When she gave birth, he brought me home. My adoptive mother never knew the truth."

"What truth? Some scandal story a mentally ill person spread and that you have taken up as gospel?" She leaped to her feet. "If you should so much as whisper such a ridiculous tale in anyone's ear, why, I'll—"

"Aunt Agnes," I said calmly, "this wasn't a story told by a patient. This is a story Daddy told me."

"That's a lie, a bald-faced lie you are spreading yourself to . . . to . . . give yourself more standing in the community or maybe to justify your inheriting all this!" she screamed. "My brother never said such a thing to you, and you know it."

"No, he didn't say it," I replied.

She relaxed her shoulders and sat again. "Exactly."

"He wrote it," I said.

"What?"

"He put it in the form of a letter and a diary that he had left with Mr. Bassinger to give to me in the event of his death, which Mr. Bassinger did. I tracked down my real mother and discovered she lives in Palm Beach, and that was why I went there," I added. "She told me more about Daddy and her, and I told her as much as I could about my life. We've grown very close in a very short time."

She stared at me, as if she had been turned to stone. "Your father wrote a diary . . . Mr. Bassinger knows all about this?"

"He does now. He never looked in the sealed envelope, but since people in Palm Beach all know and might even be spreading it over the civilized world like hot butter over bread by now, I thought it was prudent to tell him, and now, of course, I think you should know as well. Isn't it wonderful? I'm really related to you by blood, and to your family, your whole family, cousins, everyone!" I cried with deliberately exaggerated happiness.

Her mouth seemed to come unhinged in the corners. Her lip drooped.

"I don't . . ." She pressed her hand to her heart. "I think I'm getting sick," she said.

"Oh, would you like a glass of water, something

stronger, perhaps?" I asked with such over-the-top concern I thought she would see through it for sure, but she was too involved in her own worry and shock.

"What? Oh, yes, a glass of water. Yes," she said, and sat back so hard it looked as if she had lost complete control of her body.

I went to the kitchen and poured some water into a glass. When I returned, she was still sitting and staring blankly at the wall.

"Here you go," I said.

She looked at me and then at the water.

"Thank you," she said, taking it and drinking. "How could Claude have done such a thing?"

"I think it was wonderful, actually. He was truly in love, and so was she."

"In love . . . how do you fall in love with a mentally ill woman?"

"Well, you have what I would call an uneducated view of mental illness, Aunt Agnes. Most people suffer some neurosis or another. My mother had good reason to become depressed to the point where she needed professional help. What of it? Mental illness is illness. We don't look down on people who need heart bypasses or their gall bladders removed, do we? You're sick, you get professional attention, that's all."

"It's far from the same thing."

"Only to the uneducated."

"Stop saying that. I had a fine education. I attended charm school, too. Oh dear, oh dear," she said, shaking her head, "all this just at the wrong time. A big story in Palm Beach, you say?"

"Could be."

"Well, who is this woman? Is she in a hospital there?"

"There are no hospitals in Palm Beach, Aunt Agnes, nor are there cemeteries. The rich and the famous don't want to be reminded that there is such a thing as illness and death. They keep it hidden backstage."

"Well, nearby, then," she snapped at me. My calmness and my good mood were driving her mad.

"No. She lives on her family's multimillion-dollar estate with her son."

"She has a son, too? Don't tell me . . ."

"No, Daddy was not his father."

"Thank goodness for little things," she muttered. "How many children did this woman have and how many men?"

"Just two," I said. "And the first was not by mutual consent."

"Not what?"

"She was raped by her stepfather," I said bluntly.

"My God! Does the scandal ever stop? We won't be able to show our faces anywhere."

"We'll be just fine," I said. "So, I think I'll settle in, take a hot shower, and maybe make myself something to eat. Are you going with me to Miles's funeral tomorrow?"

"Miles's funeral? Of course not. I'll finish up here and . . . go home," she said, still confused and spinning.

"That might be best, Aunt Agnes."

"Yes," she said, nodding. "Yes."

I walked out and paused in the doorway to look

back at her. She hadn't moved. She continued to stare at the wall, clutching the glass of water so hard and tightly in her hand that the veins were embossed right down to her wrist.

I picked up my bags and went upstairs to my room.

Before I went to sleep, I reached my mother on the phone, and she told me Linden's physical condition was improving, but he was still "like someone caught in a fog."

"They have recommended a therapist, and he's coming to see him in the morning," she told me.

"That will be good. I'm sure he or she will be able to help him, Mother."

"I hope so. It's heartbreaking to see him like this."

"He'll improve," I promised. I paused, wondering if I should ask. She seemed capable of reading my mind through the phone line, however.

"Has Thatcher called you?" she asked.

"No, not yet. Have you seen him?"

"When I returned from the hospital, I saw his automobile was here, but I haven't spoken with him. It looks like they're having some sort of a dinner party, too. There are about a half dozen cars," she said. "How are you doing?"

"I'll be all right," I said. "I think I had better stay here and tend to my problems and decisions."

"Absolutely, Willow. And please, return to college. Don't put your life on hold because of me. I couldn't stand knowing I was responsible for anything like that," she pleaded.

"I'll see. Don't worry."

"I'll put it all in a hole and cover it," she told me, repeating the advice my father had given her. I smiled, and we said goodbye.

I wandered through my house, looking into rooms and remembering so much, seeing Amou, my father, even my adoptive mother, as they had all looked to me when I was very young and not yet aware of all the dark and troubling things waiting for me outside these doors. I ended up sitting in my father's office. The books and papers had been shoveled around, presumably in Aunt Agnes's attempt to get things looking organized after whatever delusions Miles had suffered in here.

Poor Miles, I thought.

I sat thinking of him until the miniature grandfather clock bonged midnight. I realized that Thatcher had still not called. I fought back thinking about it and, finally exhausted, went up to bed and fell asleep almost immediately, only to be awakened in the morning by the sound of vacuum cleaners and voices below and outside. I looked out and caught sight of Aunt Agnes throwing orders at people as if she were a slave owner overseeing a plantation. She had window washers doing every pane in the house, the landscape people cutting and trimming, even people painting and touching up railings and shutters.

I put on my robe and went down to get some breakfast. While I sipped my coffee in the breakfast nook, she came marching in, screaming at the army of maids, demanding they get under the furniture and polish every piece until they could see their faces reflected in it.

"Don't you think you're overdoing it a bit, Aunt Agnes?" I asked dryly.

"Overdoing it? I had nightmares last night imagining what my father would have felt like to come home to find this place in the condition it was in. This is prime property and must not be undersold.

"I didn't get a chance to tell you last night because we were so involved in the family scandal, but the real estate agents called again and want to bring a prospective buyer here tomorrow. They can't hold the people off any longer, or they will lose the sale."

"Why are you so worried about it, Aunt Agnes? It's mine to give away," I said bluntly.

"Why? Do you think I could sleep nights knowing my father's property was stolen by some smart buyer who took advantage of what's been happening here? It's still the De Beers family estate, isn't it? How you waste the money afterward is not the point. It's a matter of family pride. It doesn't surprise me that you would find such a thing curious. These are old-fashioned ethics. You young people today don't put any value on things that are lasting and true and filled with heritage. Everything is disposable to you."

"That's not true," I said. "At least, it's not true for me. I can't speak for other young people," I added, my meaning sharply clear.

She grunted. "Yes, well, years from now, you'll send me a thank-you note, I'm sure," she concluded, satisfied with herself. She went off to continue supervising, and I went upstairs to prepare myself for Miles's funeral.

Mr. Bassinger was right on time. The first thing he

asked was how things had gone between my aunt and me. I described the conversation, especially her reactions. There was a constant small smile on his lips.

"Well, I can't say she isn't doing the right thing sprucing up the place, Willow. This is a very desirable property. I can't see her getting anything from it now, but should something dreadful happen to you, God forbid, I can easily envision her and her clan scratching and clawing their way into it all. It wouldn't be the first family I've seen think about such things and do all they could to ensure their legal rights to inheritances. Greed changes the faces of many relatives when it comes to that."

"I will be healthy and live a long life just to prevent it," I promised him, and he laughed.

"I hope so."

We were the only ones at the funeral parlor's chapel. The minister recited appropriate psalms and spoke about the burdens we all carry through this short life which was often more of a test than a smooth ride. He knew from the things Mr. Bassinger had told him that Miles was devoted to my father, and he praised him for that loyalty and love. I felt as though I were crying for my father as well as myself when the tears began to streak down my cheeks.

We followed the hearse to the cemetery where my father had purchased a plot just for Miles, not far from his own. Afterward, I stopped by his grave to say a prayer and tell him what I had done and how grateful I was that he had left his diary for me so I could have a real mother after all.

It all left me so weak and tired. When I returned

home, I ignored the workers and went up to my room to lie down. I slept well into the afternoon. I had little appetite, but I did go down and make myself some toast and tea. By dinnertime, all the workers were gone, and Aunt Agnes appeared, dressed, her bags left at the front door.

"I've done all I can here," she said. "I have to go home. I've asked the real estate agents to inform me of the offers so I can have my lawyers give you the best advice."

"I have my own advisor and lawyer, Aunt Agnes. Don't trouble yourself," I said.

"I don't consider it trouble to look after my family's property," she threw back at me. "What are your plans now?"

"I'm not sure," I said.

Thatcher had still not called, and I was considering returning to college.

"Should the property sell quickly, I will have to see about the furnishings, unless, of course, they are bought along with the house. I want my father's things kept somewhere safe until I have a home of my own."

"You can ship anything to me," she said. "I have room and can keep it for you."

"Thank you," I said. In my mind, I thought if I did, I'd probably not see any of it again.

"I would strongly suggest you call me to discuss any and all decisions from this day forward. Despite finding your so-called real mother, you are still an inexperienced person when it comes to worldly matters."

"I'll muddle through," I said.

She pursed those thin lips into a line of disgust and snapped her head back.

"I should hope you won't have to muddle," she said. "Please don't feel obligated to attend Margaret Selby's wedding," she added. Her voice was hard, her smile faint and sardonic. I had been waiting for something like that. She was terrified I would bring my scandal along and disrupt the festivities.

"I don't view it as an obligation, Aunt Agnes."

"Nevertheless, we—I—realize all the pressure on you now, and certainly Margaret Selby would understand."

"Oh, I imagine she would, once you explain it all to her, Aunt Agnes," I said with a smile to match the cold one she had put on for me.

"Yes. Well, as I said, call me." She paused as she started to turn away and looked back at me again. "What have you done with that diary you claim my brother wrote?"

"It's not a claim; it's a fact," I said.

"Yes, well, where is this document?"

"It's safe with me."

"Who else has read it?"

"No one."

"Well perhaps, if you dispose of it . . ."

"I'd rather burn the Bible," I said, and she widened her eyes.

"I'm merely trying to help you avoid any more gossip and scandal."

"It's too late," I said. "Get used to it."

She shook her head and then fired her words like bullets. "You're very smug and flippant about all this now, Willow, but in time you'll regret that," she warned. She said it with such authority and certainty I did take a breath. "You have no idea how cruel and vicious people can be when they have an opportunity to destroy someone they envy, believe me. Many people are jealous of me and our family. Don't expect kindness and understanding. It's not as glamorous or as romantic as it seems to you at the moment. It's simply good gossip to mine and to mold into mud. You're a well-to-do young woman, and you will, I hope, pursue a career. None of this will be an advantage when it comes time for you to present yourself in the professional and business world."

She came back toward me, lifting her long, bony finger like a pointer and waving it. "You can mock me now and belittle my advice all you want, but in time, you'll come to see things my way, and you'll regret your behavior."

She paused and gathered her shoulders back, then took a deep breath, narrowed her eyes, and continued. "It is the unfortunate burden of mature and experienced people to try to guide the young and then to have to stand by and watch them make foolish errors out of stubbornness or a mistaken value placed on independence. You can spend your life mulling over your regrets, or you can listen and do the right thing and find some contentment.

"Maybe that's not exactly how my brother would speak to you, but I feel in my heart that is what he would mean."

"I'll make my own decisions, Aunt Agnes," I insisted.

Her eyes turned to dark river stones. "Do as you wish," she concluded, throwing up her hand. She turned and marched out of my house.

I heard the door slam behind her, and I was left with the echo of that ringing in my ears and the echo of her warnings and threats lingering in the air.

Now, finally alone, I could sit back and cry. All the people I had loved and who had loved me were gone or far away. My newly discovered mother was overburdened with her sad memories and troubles. Thatcher was now like one of those festive party balloons broken free, drifting in the wind, drifting away.

There was nothing left to do but pack up the memorabilia I cherished in this house and set it aside. The day was fast approaching when I would leave here for good, cast myself out into the same sea as Linden had. I had no idea where the wind would take me, how it would fill my sails, but maybe, like him, I had little choice but to have faith in something bigger than myself: fate or destiny or some good angel who would smile down on me and not let me drift too far or too dangerously close to the rocks.

Suddenly, it began to rain. It grew quickly into a cloud burst, making the house feel damp and chilly as well as dark. The drops tapped on the windows as if nature demanded my attention, reminding me that the world could be cold and cruel and my aunt Agnes's words were not just the warnings of a bitter woman.

Then I heard my father's miniature grandfather

clock bong, its sound traveling freely through the empty house, informing me that time was now the magic carpet taking me along, bringing me closer and closer to the answers for the questions.

Who am I?

What will become of me?

Epilogue

The couple who came to look at the property made an offer the day afterward. We began a negotiation, and for that and what followed, I relied heavily on Mr. Bassinger's advice. Two days later, the couple agreed to our counteroffer, and the property was sold. It was to be a fast escrow. It would close in thirty days, and so I had to use that time to decide what I would keep and what I would put in storage. The couple came back to look over the furnishings and decided in the end to take almost everything except Daddy's office furnishings. The wife wanted to brighten it up with much lighter woods. That was fine to me. I envisioned putting it all in my own home someday.

I spent my time going through the attic, marking things I would consign to thrift shops and things I

VIRGINIA ANDREWS

wanted to be placed in storage. I packed Daddy's books and many of my own things in cartons.

I called my mother every day over the next ten days. Linden was finally well enough to be taken home, but he was still in a dysfunctional state of mind, suffering continuous memory loss, especially about what had happened to him. He had no memory of going out in his sailboat and could tell no one what had been the cause of his accident. The doctors told my mother it was not unusual for someone who experienced terrifying trauma to persist in avoiding thinking about it.

"He's very irritable and seems incapable of concentrating on anything. I tried to get him to return to his painting, but all he does is stare at his easel and his paints and pencils. Most of the day is spent sitting and staring at the ocean. He's lost weight, of course."

"Does he remember me or mention me at all?" I asked.

"No," she said. "I'm sorry."

"He's not the only one who's apparently forgotten me," I complained.

She was silent a moment. "I think Bunny Eaton is working hard on Thatcher, trying to get him involved with this woman or that. I've seen three dinner parties and one afternoon event since you've left, and at each, I've seen young women," she told me.

"Yes, well, good luck to them all."

"I did see Thatcher one day. He came over and asked about Linden, but he was there to talk about something else, really."

"Oh?"

"The Eatons have decided to make an offer on the property and exercise their option. I guess they want to get rid of us enough to buy us out," she said.

"What are you going to do?"

"It's a lot of money. Linden and I could live well someplace else. I am a little worried about how he'll react to that, however, and asked Thatcher to hold off until Linden is stronger and less likely to be negatively affected. The doctors agree," she said.

"What did Thatcher say?"

"He said fine, but I don't think the Eatons will be very patient. Their lease is up in three months, and they either have to buy or extend it."

"You don't have to sell, do you?"

"If I sell, it has to be at the price agreed to, but I don't have to sell. Only I can't keep up the mortgage and the upkeep of the property without their rent or someone's renting it. I'll lose it all in a foreclosure, and they'll get it, anyway. I feel I haven't much choice."

I thought for a moment. "Is Thatcher the only attorney you have had?"

"No. There's an older man, Mr. Kasten. He's practically retired, though."

"Do you have any idea about the cost of upkeep?"

"You mean for the whole estate?"

"Yes."

"No, not really. I have an accountant, Leo Ross. I usually just sign what he tells me to sign."

"I want my lawyer to call him and your lawyer and discuss your situation with them. Is that all right?"

"Why?"

"I have an idea," I said. "Let me see about it first. Just let them both know a Mr. Bassinger will be calling them right away, okay?"

"I don't know. I don't like the sound of this," she said. "I don't want you doing anything that isn't good for you, too, Willow."

"I won't. That's why I have my own attorney. Okay?"

She was silent a moment and then, with some reluctance, agreed.

The moment we ended our conversation, I phoned Mr. Bassinger and told him what I was thinking.

"I'll look into it right away," he promised. "But I'll warn you now, Willow, if this is an impulsive, illogical thing, I'll tell you and strongly advise you against it, even though it is your real mother with whom we're involving you."

"That's what I want you to do," I said.

"Okay," he said.

Two days later, he called for me to come to his office.

"I haven't seen the property, of course," he began, "so I have to rely on what I'm being told about it and on what some friends of mine in Palm Beach have told me as well. From what they all say, these people who have an option to buy it at a set price would, it appears, be practically stealing it."

"That's what I suspected," I said.

"On the other hand, your mother couldn't put it up for sale without their having the opportunity to buy it at that price first. It's in their agreement, understand?"

"So her only option is to keep possession until the present rental agreement and option to buy run out?"

"Yes," he said, smiling. "You're more of a businessperson than your father was, I think."

"Daddy hated to be bothered with such mundane matters as taxes and mortgages and stocks and bonds, I know. He had no patience for it."

"Well, fortunately for him, and for you, he had very good advisors, an excellent business manager and stockbroker, and now, with the sale of your property . . . well . . ."

"Yes?" I said anxiously.

"If you're put on the deed—in other words, if you get a percentage of the asset—it could, with the way the real estate market is exploding down there, be a very good investment. You could carry the costs of the property and still be comfortable, as long as you don't get caught up in the Palm Beach lifestyle and spend beyond your means," he warned.

"There's no danger of that," I assured him.

He laughed. "Never say never is my motto, but okay, you understand what I'm saying."

"Yes."

"Is this really what you want to do, Willow? Do you believe it would be the best thing for your mother and your stepbrother and you?"

"I do, and I think—no, I know for certain—Daddy would want me to do this, Mr. Bassinger."

"Possibly. He was a great deal more romantic than he let on," he said. He thought a moment. "Okay, let me explore it all. I'll get back to you in a day or two, and you can make a final decision then."

"Thank you."

"These people . . ." He looked at his papers. "The Eatons . . . they're not going to be very fond of you, Willow."

"They'll get over it," I said. "They'll pour themselves some champagne, arrange for a party, and spend away their unhappiness. Sadness, disappointment, and defeat are not permitted there, and anyone caught frowning is immediately arrested by the Fun Police."

He laughed. "Why is it I feel you're doing this with an impish grin on your face, Willow?"

"I can't imagine," I said.

He laughed, and I left his office, feeling excited and optimistic. I couldn't wait to get home and call my mother to tell her what I wanted to do.

"And your lawyer thought this was prudent?" she asked.

"More than prudent, a good business decision."

"Is this what you really want, Willow? Because if I thought for one moment that you were doing this out of some sort of pity, or some sort of imagined obligation to your father or to me, I would be very upset."

"It's what I really want," I said definitively. "If it's all right with you, of course."

"How could something as wonderful as this not be all right with me?"

"And with Linden?"

"He's not yet ready to consider such questions, I'm afraid," she said sadly.

"He will be. I'll be there to help and to bring him back. I know I can do some good."

Every medical student, every psychology student,

begins to think he or she can practice, diagnose, and
prescribe before he or she is truly prepared to do so, I
thought the moment after I uttered those words. It un-
derlines the truth behind the old saying that a little
knowledge is a dangerous thing. I knew I shouldn't be
making such promises and claims, but I couldn't help it.

"Oh, I believe in you, Willow. Very well," she said
after a moment of thought. "Have your attorney do
what has to be done and call my accountant. Maybe together we can do battle against all the forces that
would destroy us."

"Yes," I said, smiling, "we can and we will."

I was very excited after speaking with her and immediately called Mr. Bassinger, asking him to get
things arranged as quickly as possible.

In the days that followed, I completed the packing
and storing of valued family possessions and Daddy's
office furnishings. Aunt Agnes called very soon after
she had been informed of the sale. I hadn't called her,
but she had her spies.

"Why didn't you phone me immediately?" she demanded the moment I said hello.

"Aunt Agnes?" I asked, pretending not to recognize
her voice.

"Yes, yes. Well?"

"Call you about what?" I asked, expressing innocence and ignorance.

"The estate! How could you not realize what I was
asking about?"

"I've had so much on my mind these past days,
Aunt Agnes. Please forgive me. And, oh, please tell

Margaret Selby that I will not be able to attend her wedding after all. I have to return to Palm Beach for some important business matters."

"What business matters?"

"Oh, just some investments, nothing glamorous," I said.

"Investments? In what?"

"Why, property, of course. Real estate is the best sort of investment these days, Aunt Agnes. I'm surprised you don't know that."

"I know it. What sort of real estate, commercial?"

"No. Please, don't bother yourself so with all this. You have so much going on back there with the wedding and all. I'll be fine. I have Mr. Bassinger helping me, of course."

She was silent a moment, digesting it all quickly. "Why would you return to that place, considering the information everyone there has about you and your . . . real mother?" she asked.

"Daddy taught me never to run and hide but to face my problems head on and never be intimidated by them. Good advice, don't you think?"

"No," she snapped. "I would prefer living where people didn't resent me or mock me."

"There is probably no place in the world where that doesn't happen, Aunt Agnes," I said. I meant to her, of course, but she missed the point and rattled on and on about how I should put such an idea to bed and come live with her. She made the argument that using my inheritance, she and I could fix up her property and make it very comfortable. In time, she would introduce me to fine young men of some social standing, and I, like Margaret Selby, would marry. The very idea of such a thing nearly made me sick.

I thanked her but tried to make my *no* as definite as I could. She refused to accept it as such and ended by predicting that I would realize she was right and turn to her one day.

"I'll be here for you, waiting," she promised. "Out of respect for my poor dead brother."

"That's very kind of you, Aunt Agnes. Have a wonderful wedding party," I added, and hung up, feeling as if I had just cut the last cord tying me to my old life.

It was time to start anew.

However, I didn't want to give up on my career and education, so next I looked into what educational institutions were available. I located Florida Atlantic University in Jupiter, which was about a forty-minute drive from Palm Beach. I called and learned they had the program I wanted to pursue. I next asked that my transcripts be sent from the University of North Carolina and made arrangements to matriculate the next semester.

Feeling I had taken a good hold of my life and the future for my mother, Linden, and myself, I completed the rest of my arrangements. I decided to keep my father's old Mercedes. He had always maintained it well. It looked practically brand new. Right after the escrow closed, I packed the car with as much as I could and had the rest of my things sent to my mother's home — my home, now.

"I'm coming!" I cried into the phone. "I'll be leaving for Palm Beach in the morning."

"I can't deny I'm very excited about it, Willow. I did sit with Linden today and explain it to him, and his eyes did seem to widen and brighten with interest."

"Oh, good."

"Then he returned to his depressed state, the light dimming again."

"We'll get it burning brightly. I won't stop trying until we do."

"I know," she said. "I'm grateful." Then she paused and said, "Thatcher called this morning. He had heard from my accountant, and he was quite shocked. 'I can't guarantee you that my parents will remain your tenants,' he said, and I said I was not expecting them to remain and, in fact, would like not to go on renting the property."

"What did he say?"

"He thought I had taken leave of my senses, of course, and tried to convince me that I was making a very big mistake. Then . . ."

"What?" I could sense her hesitation. "He didn't threaten you?"

"Oh, no. He was very soft-spoken and concerned. I meant to say he asked about you."

"He did?" My heart began to pound, even though I didn't want to feel that I would go running back to him the moment he showed me the slightest interest. "What did you tell him?"

"I asked him why he didn't just call you directly, and he said he was planning to, but he wanted to give you a chance to settle down. I know he thinks you're not coming back here, at least for a while. He did sound very sad about it. In the end, he muttered that he was going to call you soon."

"Won't he be surprised," I thought aloud.

"Yes, I imagine he will be quite surprised," my mother said.

"I'll see you very soon," I told her.

"Have a safe trip," she said.

I had thought a great deal about Thatcher during the time I had been home. Every time the phone rang, I had expected it to be him, making some excuse for why he hadn't called earlier, blaming his work or whatever. I was even prepared to be understanding and hide my disappointment. After all, I was sure his parents, and especially his mother, had put all sorts of pressure on him. But it was never him calling.

Up until my final night in the house, I was hoping he would call as he had told my mother, but the phone didn't ring at all after Mr. Bassinger called to tell me everything had been done, my accounts set up, my investment made, my inclusion on the property deed now just a matter of time.

The last, most difficult thing for me was to look into my father's empty office, the furniture all taken and put in storage, the shelves bare. It was truly as though it made his death final, a period placed at the end of a sentence, a door shutting, a light going out. Everything that had been him, that had kept his memory vivid in my mind and in my senses, was gone from this room, the room in which he had done so much of his thinking, his dreaming, and surely his regretting.

"Goodbye, Daddy," I whispered. "I hope what I'm

doing would have pleased you, will please you. It's too painful for me to be here without you. I'm going to be with the one living person who remembers the sound of your voice, your laughter, as vividly as I do and cherishes those memories as much. We have you to share and to bring us closer together. Thank you for that."

I didn't think I would sleep, but I did. It wasn't to relieve fatigue; it was to find escape, to stop my mind from thinking and worrying and mourning. I was up almost with the sun itself. When I walked out of the house for the last time, I took a deep breath and looked over the grounds. So much of what I was, what I had become, was created here. The halls still echoed with Amou's voice. I could even hear my own little footsteps on the stairway. It was time to shut the door on all that, I thought.

I hurried to my car, started the engine, looked back at the front door only once, and imagined they were all there waving goodbye to me: Miles, Amou, and, of course, Daddy. They were all smiling proudly, urging me on, and telling me not to be afraid, to believe in myself.

I couldn't help but look ahead with trepidation, however. There were so many questions looming out there, waiting to be answered.

What would life really be like for my mother and me? Had I made a terrible error using my fortune to keep us in Palm Beach?

Would Linden ever accept me as his sister, and would I bring him hope and help him regain his confidence and his life?

Would Thatcher be amazed and overjoyed at the sight of me and the realization of what I had done?

Everyone out there suffers from loneliness in one way or another, I thought. All the rich and the famous weren't really very different from everyone else. They were just as frightened as my mother and Linden and I were. They could surround themselves with glitter and with lots of chatter, but in the end, it was only the music of the heart that brought any real comfort, and that music couldn't be bought at any price.

That music was the only true gift we could bestow on each other, the gift that would end the fear of being alone.

There was a line I remembered from my father's diary when he was trying to express how much he really did love my mother, when he was trying to explain why he was so positive it was love, grand and beautiful.

All I know, he wrote, *is I couldn't be happy, ever be happy, if she is not, and I know she feels the same way about me.*

That was the gift of love, the music of the heart we could give each other that would keep us from being alone.

Daddy spent so much of his life searching for it, and then he had to lose it.

I pledged to myself that if I ever found it as he had, I would never lose it.

Do you think you can find it? I could hear him ask.

Yes, I have to think that I can, Daddy.

Then you will, he told me.

I could hear him say it over and over as I drove on.

Then you will.

POCKET BOOKS
PROUDLY PRESENTS

WICKED FOREST

VIRGINIA ANDREWS®

Turn the page for a preview of
Wicked Forest. . . .

ow that I was here, that I had made the firm decision to be in-
olved with my real mother's life and family, I felt like some-
ne who had gotten off a roller coaster. I was a bit shaky
gaining my footing, but finally time had slowed down for
e. I could take a deep breath and let my memories, especially
y most recent, the ones that had been stringing along behind
e like so many ribbons in the wind, catch up and be stored in
e safest places in my brain. They were no longer to be ig-
ored, but I could draw upon them for lessons and wisdom to
ide me through the days ahead.

Right before I had left for my second year of college,
addy and I had a wonderful hour or so together after dinner
the rear patio of our South Carolina house. Quiet moments
gether like that were as rare as shooting stars. I hadn't the
urage to ask for them. Puppies unabashedly snuggle at the
et of their loving masters, hoping to be stroked. I envied
em their obvious play for love. Growing up in a home in
ich my adoptive mother always made me feel as if I were an
invited guest made me timid and withdrawn.

I feel certain now that Daddy would have told me all of the truth in a face-to-face meeting eventually and not left it for me to read as part of some postmortem. In a real sense, he had to reinvent himself for me first, change from one sort of a man to another, from a guardian to a father, from someone merely full of concern and responsibility to someone full of love. He was in the process of doing just that before he died. Perhaps he waited too long, but none of us ever really believes in the end of ourselves. We always feel there will be one more turn to make, one more mile to go, one more minute to enjoy, and the opportunity to do what must be done will not be lost.

"I'm so glad you're enjoying college, Willow," Daddy began that warm spring evening that now came up out of my pool of memories vividly. I recalled how the stars burned like the tips of candle flames growing stronger with every passing minute.

"I am, Daddy. I love all my classes and enjoy my teachers. In fact, some of my new friends think I'm too serious about my work."

He laughed, and then he turned to me, his face as serious as it had ever been.

"If we don't love what we do," he told me, "then we don't love who we are, and the worst fate of all is not liking yourself, Willow. You hate the sound of your own voice. You even come to hate your own shadow. How can you ever hope to make anyone else happy if you can't make yourself happy?

"It seems like such a simple truth, but it remains buried beneath so many lies and delusions for most people. I know now that won't happen to you," he said assuredly.

Walking on the beach after breakfast this morning, I recalled that whole conversation and those words of Daddy's. They helped me to understand Linden. He was out there wandering, trying to find a way to escape from himself. Suicide was one avenue to take, and he had tried that, but

ere had to be something better. I was determined to help
m find it.

Laughter coming from the rear loggia of the main house
lled my attention from the ocean and my own heavy
oughts. I had just come up the small rise in the beach and I
as nearly directly behind the loggia. To my surprise, Bunny
d Asher Eaton, who usually partied into the wee hours, were
  and having breakfast with the Carriage sisters, the first two
iends of Bunny Eaton's I had met.

I knew they couldn't help but notice me. However, neither
unny nor Asher said a word.

Even from this distance, I could see the displeasure in
unny's face at the sight of me, probably recalling our nasty
nfrontation just before I left for South Carolina. She turned
ck to her guests quickly and released another peal of exag-
rated laughter as if I were some sort of clown who had wan-
red too far from the circus.

Suddenly Thatcher appeared, obviously dressed for work.
r a moment we gazed at each other. My heart began to
und so hard and fast, I had to take a deep breath. He didn't
ll out and he didn't set out to greet me. As if it had a mind of
 own, my hand wanted to lift and wave, but I kept it down
d chastised my heart for its weakness.

Thatcher said something to the group and then went into
e house.

I lowered my head and continued to walk the beach, then
used and looked out at the sailboats in the distance. The
arm but strong easterly breeze paraded a line of puffy, milk-
hite clouds toward the horizon, and a passenger jet lifted off
e runway at the West Palm Beach airport. I watched it climb,
rning toward the clouds.

"You look like you wish you were on that." I spun around
 see Thatcher coming down a pathway between a row of
shes.

He had obviously gone out of the main house and then to

the left to follow an approach to the beach. I quickly realize
that what he was doing was sneaking around to meet me. The
heat of indignation built quickly in my face.

"What is it, Thatcher?" I asked. "Are you afraid you'll get
spanking if you're caught speaking to me now?"

He had been heading toward me quickly to embrace me, bu
stopped and forced a smile and a laugh.

"I should have known that there isn't any way to deceive th
daughter of a famous psychiatrist," he said. He took the nex
few steps toward me cautiously.

I looked down at his polished new shoes picking up some we
sand. The breeze lifted his hair. There was no doubt Thatche
Eaton was a handsome man. He was broad shouldered and nar
row waisted enough to give the impression he was taller, bigge
than he really was, and his air of confidence, bordering on arro
gance at times, made him appear stronger yet.

It was easy to want to fall in love with such a man, t
surrender to his charm and cast myself with abandon int
his waiting arms. But I didn't laugh at his silly quip. I wa
sure that the expression on my face told him I wouldn
tolerate any featherbrained excuses to justify his failure t
call me after I had left for South Carolina. I certainly wasn
going to ignore the way he was behaving now and fee
sorry for his having to soothe and protect his spoiled mother.

"Look, Willow, there is no question about the right and th
wrong here. Of course my parents are snobs. I never pretende
they weren't, did I?"

"No, you didn't, but you left out your own snobber
Thatcher. I was very disappointed in your failure to call me
You knew I wasn't going home to do enjoyable things, and yo
knew how terrible things were for my mother, Linden and m
back here. It broke my heart to have to leave her, even for
short while, but I'm beginning to wonder if you are capable o
understanding how quickly such love and concern can develo
and flourish when it's honest and true."

"Listen, listen," he said, pleading. "I really was getting ready to contact you. In the meantime, I was working behind the scenes to be sure Linden had the best medical attention possible if he needed anything, and to be sure your mother was all right."

"Why behind the scenes?" I fired back. "You're a grown man, a successful attorney. You led me to believe you had just as little respect for the pompous asses down here as I did."

"That's true. It's still true, but—"

"But what?"

"Look," he said, stepping closer, "you have to compromise a little to succeed in this world. Those who insist on standing on high principles and won't compromise are just as snobby."

"What?" I smiled incredulously.

"That's right. There's another sort of arrogance, an arrogance of being right, of being perfect, of intolerance. Rich people can be pitied, too. For their failings, their insecurities, their imperfections," he added quickly before I could laugh.

I wasn't going to. The truth was, I did pity people like his parents far more than I hated them, much less envied them.

"So how does any of that justify your sneaking around your own property even to speak to me?" I threw back at him.

He sighed and shook his head.

"Look, it might not be obvious to you, but I do have a rather fragile family, especially when you consider my sister and her situation. My parents put on a good facade, but my father especially is carrying a great burden on his shoulders."

"What burden, the supply of champagne?"

"Ridicule if you want, but you're not the only one with problems. My sister's marriage is on the rocks. Her husband isn't as successful as he makes out to be. There's a lot you don't know, Willow. I saw no reason to add my dark shadows to your own. And then, all of this, these revelations about you and Grace . . .

all of it coming at us so fast and so furiously . . . it takes time to adjust, to accept, to understand," he continued.

I stared at him. How reasonable he sounded, how perfectly, damnably reasonable.

"I keep forgetting what a good trial attorney you are, Thatcher Steven Eaton."

I took a deep breath and looked away. Was he right about the way he had behaved? I wanted him to be right. Did that make me weak? Was I willing to delude myself, accept lies so I could be happy, just like so many people here?

Thatcher stepped closer, practically touching me. I turned away from him, actually afraid of looking into those beautiful eyes and weakening.

"You've got to believe I suffered, knowing that you were alone out there, dealing with all your problems without me at your side," he said in a soft, low voice.

I spun on him.

"Then why didn't you just call—just call me once!"

"I thought you would be on your way back sooner," he said. "Especially with Linden still in the hospital and all."

"That's such a lot of hooey, Thatcher," I snapped back at him.

He stared at me.

"You're just fishing for excuses to rationalize your inaction. Your objections are too flimsy, counselor. They're over-ruled."

He nodded, and then he pressed his lips together and took on a different look, a darker look.

"You're right," he said. "There's more."

"What more?" I asked, taken aback by his abrupt surrender.

"Something else happened very soon after you had left."

"What?" I repeated with more force.

He looked away, and his expression when he did so made my heart skip a beat. What else could have happened that was more difficult to accept than all that had happened to me and to Linden and my mother?

"My sister realized how serious I was getting about you," he began.

"So?"

He glanced toward the house as if he was afraid we would be heard and took a few steps farther down the beach so our voices would definitely not carry back there. I walked a little behind him, now almost as nervous as I was angry.

"Normally, her opinions wouldn't matter," he said. "We're as different as a brother and a sister can be, but . . ."

He turned to me quickly.

"But what?"

"I was hoping not to have to tell you any of this yet, or at least until I investigated it all for myself and either confirmed or denied it," he said. "My sister is not above doing something like this to get me to do what she wants."

"Like what?"

He took a deep breath, bit down on his lip and then brushed back his hair.

"You know, of course, who Kirby Scott was," he began.

"Yes. My mother's stepfather, the one who seduced her," I said. "I know about all that."

After a moment more of hesitation, Thatcher said, "Your mother wasn't the only one he seduced."

"What is that supposed to mean? Who else did he seduce, and what does it have to do with us, Thatcher? You're not making any sense and frankly—"

"My mother," Thatcher blurted.

I stared at him. Was this a dream? He was telling me his mother was seduced? And by the same man who had started this whole mess?

"What?" I asked. Surely the devil wind had been playing with our words, twisting and turning them to suit its impish pleasure.

"Let's continue to walk a bit," he suggested as if he had to continue to put distance between us, the house, and his parents with every small revelation.

"Thatcher . . ."

He put up his hand.

"Let me explain. After you had those nasty words with my mother, she had one of her more serious breakdowns. She goes into a deep depression, won't get out of bed, won't eat, sobs uncontrollably. . . . My father calls me whenever that happens and we get her over to what's best described as a spa, where she is given exaggerated tender loving care . . . mud baths, facials, massages, you name it."

"How fortunate for her that it takes so little to restore her happiness," I said dryly.

He didn't respond to my sarcasm.

"One night after she returned, I visited her in her bedroom. She was better, but I could see she was still very distracted. I asked her what it was that was bothering her so much. I suspected it had to do with you and me, of course, but I was prepared to discuss it reasonably. I was planning, in fact, to call you that night, explain what was going on, and find out how you were doing and when you were returning.

"My mother took the wind out of my sails. She started with her concerns that you were the daughter of Grace Montgomery, that your half brother was Linden, that all of the dark mental problems could be passed on to our children . . . on and on like that. I didn't agree, and I talked about your father and did about as good a job on her as I had ever done. In fact, I could see from her face that I was crushing her arguments like bugs on the loggia.

"Finally, she sat back on her fluffy pillow, looked up at me, and told me what Whitney had wanted her to tell. It was like I was a priest in a confessional, Willow. I was stunned. My own mother was admitting to adultery and to me!

"The upshot of it was that Linden was my half brother, too.

She was telling me that there would be an even greater chance of our having a disturbed child. Not only was your mother passing on mental problems to you, but my father, as evidenced by Linden, could have passed his abhorrent behavior on to me. That was her great fear now. Understand?"

I started to shake my head, to shake the words back out of my ears.

"Even if such a story were true, Thatcher, it wouldn't affect us. We still don't have any blood relationship," I pointed out. "My mother's illness wasn't genetic. She was abused! There's no evidence that a mental problem caused by environmental conditions will be passed on."

"I know, but all of it is a scandal nevertheless, and it would create all sorts of complications. I might just have to kiss my legal career down here goodbye if such a story ever got out."

"What of it? You can have a legal career anywhere you want, Thatcher," I countered.

"So you would marry me and leave your mother and Linden the next day?"

I started to reply and stopped.

"You see what I mean, Willow? It's not a black-and-white issue and not something we can decide instantly."

"Your mother would reveal all this, tell the world about her disgrace?" I asked, incredulous. "Just to prevent you from being with me?"

"Maybe my mother wouldn't do it, but I wouldn't put it past Whitney."

"Maybe it's not true. Maybe it's a fabrication just to keep us apart. Maybe . . ."

"Yes," he said. "Maybe so. I need time to confirm all this for myself. In the meantime, I am asking you to be understanding and patient with me. For everyone's sake, not just mine or yours," he added. "Why risk the unnecessary critical attention and gossip? Some of us aren't strong enough to endure any more of that sort of thing."

I knew he meant my mother and Linden. He was right. What they certainly didn't need at the moment was more scandalous baggage placed on their shoulders. What's more, how would Linden react to such news? He despised Thatcher. How would he like to learn Thatcher and he were related, were brothers!

"This isn't fair," I muttered. "None of this is fair, especially if it's true. Why do we have to suffer for their actions?"

"The sins of the parents are visited on the heads of their children," Thatcher said.

Now he was the one gazing at a commercial jet plane lifting toward the horizon and another world, somewhere far enough away from all our pasts.

"Wish you were on that?" I countered.

He smiled. "Very often, yes, but," he said, drawing closer, "only if you were sitting beside me."

"Maybe we'd all be better off if we didn't have the ability to dream," I said.

"Then where would you psychiatrists be?" Thatcher kidded.

I laughed, and he reached out to take my shoulders firmly. For a moment we looked into each other's eyes.

"No matter what the truth is or what obstacles are placed in our way, we'll be together eventually, Willow. I swear," he said, with such confidence and determination, he took my breath away. . . .

**POCKET
BOOKS**

The Rain Series
VIRGINIA ANDREWS®
RAIN
Book 1

Life isn't getting any easier for Rain Arnold. The ghettos
of Washington D.C. are a daily reminder that she must
struggle to hold on to her dreams. Unlike her tearaway
sister, she has battled against the odds to do well at
school and to be a good daughter. But Rain can't
suppress the feeling that she has never really belonged,
that she is a stranger in her own world.

Her instincts are confirmed when she overhears a
revelation from the past. A long-buried secret is about to
change her life beyond recognition. Suddenly everything
Rain has ever known is left behind, and Rain is sent to
live with the wealthy Hudson family. Just as she never
felt a part of the troubled world she was raised in, Rain is
also out of place in the luxury and privilege that now
surrounds her. Will Rain ever be able to fulfil her hopes
and ambitions – and find a place to call home?

0 671 02964 9

£6.99

POCKET
BOOKS

The Rain Series
VIRGINIA ANDREWS®
LIGHTNING STRIKES
Book 2

Torn from the embrace of her poor but loving family,
Rain Arnold now lives surrounded by opulent riches but
feels more like an outsider than ever before. Enrolled in
one of England's most prestigious drama schools, she is
sent to London to live with her great-aunt Lenora.
Treated little better than a servant, nevertheless Rain is
happy; she has new friends, and a new determination to
succeed in her chosen career.

But soon Rain realises that something is dreadfully
wrong. She hears footsteps at night, and the high-pitched
laughter of a little girl. She sees strange lights in rooms
that are supposed to be closed off. Behind the icy sheen
of wealth and privilege lies something unspeakable.
Something that could turn Rain's most precious dreams
into an inescapable nightmare . . .

0 7434 0914 0

£6.99

The Rain Series
VIRGINIA ANDREWS®
EYE OF THE STORM
Book 3

After a successful first year in one of London's finest
drama schools, Rain returns to America to cope with the
death of Grandmother Hudson, the only family member
who truly loved Rain for who she was. Now Rain finds
herself the controlling heir in her grandmother's will,
inheriting the vast millions of the Hudson wealth. Rain
can hardly believe it. Is this a gift or a test?

All she knows is that she is alone to face the rest of the
Hudson family. They will not allow Rain to inherit the
fortune that is their birthright. They will do whatever it
takes to remove this parasitic young woman from their
lives. Rain knows how to fight. And she is not afraid to
try. But the battle for her grandmother's estate is only the
beginning. Rain will soon face a tragedy of her own – a
devastating blow to her dreams that will leave her
shattered. And finally, Rain will have to come to terms
with her own fears to discover the person she truly wants
to be.

0 7434 0914 0

£6.99

**POCKET
BOOKS**

The Rain Series
VIRGINIA ANDREWS®
THE END OF THE
RAINBOW
Book 4

Rain's precious daughter, Summer, is about to turn
sixteen. Like all girls her age, Summer dreams of
growing up and making her own life, of falling in love
and finding her soulmate.

But a devastating tragedy will force Summer to stare into
the cold eyes of adulthood long before she is ready. A
tragedy that will force her to flee the only place she has
ever called home.

All her life, Summer has lived on the Virginia estate
where the Hudson family's secrets have lurked among
the shadows for generations. Now it is time for Summer
to discover secrets of her own. Some she will keep. Some
she will share. And some will haunt her for the rest of
her life . . .

0 7434 0914 0

£6.99

**POCKET
BOOKS**

This book and other **Virginia Andrews** titles are available from your book shop or
can be ordered direct from the publisher.

☐ 0 7434 6832 5	**Ruby**	£6.99
☐ 0 7434 6831 7	**Pearl In The Mist**	£6.99
☐ 0 7434 6830 9	**All That Glitters**	£6.99
☐ 0 7434 6828 7	**Hidden Jewel**	£6.99
☐ 0 7434 6829 5	**Tarnished Gold**	£6.99
☐ 0 7434 4026 9	**Dawn**	£6.99
☐ 0 7434 4027 7	**Secrets of the Morning**	£6.99
☐ 0 7434 4025 0	**Twilight's Child**	£6.99
☐ 0 7434 4023 4	**Midnight Whispers**	£6.99
☐ 0 7434 4024 2	**Darkest Hour**	£6.99
☐ 0 671 02964 9	**Rain**	£5.99
☐ 0 7434 0914 0	**Lightning Strikes**	£6.99
☐ 0 7434 0915 9	**Eye of the Storm**	£6.99
☐ 0 7434 0916 7	**End of the Rainbow**	£6.99
☐ 0 7434 4034 X	**Wildflowers**	£6.99
☐ 0 7434 0444 0	**Into The Garden**	£6.99

Please send cheque or postal order for the value of the book, free postage
and packing within the UK; OVERSEAS including Republic of Ireland £1
per book.

OR: Please debit this amount from my:

VISA/ACCESS/MASTERCARD ....

CARD NO ....

EXPIRY DATE ....

AMOUNT £ ....

NAME ....

ADDRESS ....

....

SIGNATURE..

www.simonsays.co.uk

Send orders to: SIMON & SCHUSTER CASH SALES
PO Box 29, Douglas, Isle of Man, IM99 1BQ
Tel: 01624 83600, Fax 01624 670923
www.bookpost.co.uk
Please allow 14 days for delivery.
Prices and availability subject to change without notice.